P9-DXF-796

A CONJURING
OF LIGHT

TOR BOOKS BY V. E. SCHWAB

Vicious
A Darker Shade of Magic
A Gathering of Shadows
A Conjuring of Light

A
CONJURING
OF
LIGHT

V. E. SCHWAB

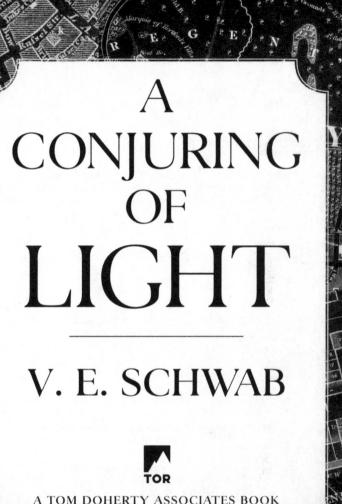

TOR

A TOM DOHERTY ASSOCIATES BOOK
NEW YORK

A CONJURING OF LIGHT

Copyright © 2017 by Victoria Schwab

A Tor Book
Published by Tom Doherty Associates
175 Fifth Avenue
New York, NY 10010

www.tor-forge.com

Tor® is a registered trademark of Macmillan Publishing Group, LLC.

The Library of Congress Cataloging-in-Publication Data
is available upon request.

ISBN 978-0-7653-8746-2 (hardcover)
ISBN 978-0-7653-9415-6 (signed edition)
ISBN 978-0-7653-8748-6 (e-book)

Our books may be purchased in bulk for promotional, educational, or business use.
Please contact your local bookseller or the Macmillan Corporate and Premium
Sales Department at 1-800-221-7945, extension 5442, or by e-mail at
MacmillanSpecialMarkets@macmillan.com.

First Edition: February 2017

Printed in the United States of America

0 9 8 7 6 5 4 3 2 1

For the ones who've found their way home

Pure magic has no self. It simply is, *a force of nature, the blood of our world, the marrow of our bones. We give it shape, but we must never give it soul.*

—MASTER TIEREN,
head priest of the London Sanctuary

ONE

WORLD IN RUIN

I

Delilah Bard—always a thief, recently a magician, and one day, hope-fully, a pirate—was running as fast as she could.

Hold on, Kell, she thought as she sprinted through the streets of Red London, still clutching the shard of stone that had once been part of Astrid Dane's mouth. A token stolen in another life, when magic and the idea of multiple worlds were new to her. When she had only just discovered that people could be possessed, or bound like rope, or turned to stone.

Fireworks thundered in the distance, met by cheers and chants and music, all the sounds of a city celebrating the end of the *Essen Tasch,* the tournament of magic. A city oblivious to the horror happening at its heart. And back at the palace, the prince of Arnes—Rhy—was dying, which meant that somewhere, a world away, so was Kell.

Kell. The name rang through her with all the force of an order, a plea.

Lila reached the road she was looking for and staggered to a stop, knife already out, blade pressing to the flesh of her hand. Her heart pounded as she turned her back on the chaos and pressed her bleed-ing palm—and the stone still curled within it—to the nearest wall.

Twice before Lila had made this journey, but always as a passenger.

Always using Kell's magic.

Never her own.

And never alone.

But there was no time to think, no time to be afraid, and certainly no time to wait.

Chest heaving and pulse high, Lila swallowed and said the words, as boldly as she could. Words that belonged only on the lips of a blood magician. An *Antari*. Like Holland. Like Kell.

"*As Travars.*"

The magic sang up her arm, and through her chest, and then the city lurched around her, gravity twisting as the world gave way.

Lila thought it would be easy or, at least, *simple*.

Something you either survived, or did not.

She was wrong.

II

A world away, Holland was drowning.

He fought to the surface of his own mind, only to be forced back down into the dark water by a will as strong as iron. He fought, and clawed, and gasped for air, strength leaching out with every violent thrash, every desperate struggle. It was worse than dying, because dying gave way to death, and this did not.

There was no light. No air. No strength. It had all been taken, severed, leaving only darkness and, somewhere beyond the crush, a voice shouting his name.

Kell's voice—

Too far away.

Holland's grip faltered, slipped, and he was sinking again.

All he had ever wanted was to bring the magic back—to see his world spared from its slow, inexorable death—a death caused first by the fear of another London, and then by the fear of his own.

All Holland wanted was to see his world restored.

Revived.

He knew the legends—the dreams—of a magician powerful enough to do it. Strong enough to breathe air back into its starved lungs, to quicken its dying heart.

For as long as Holland could remember, that was all he'd wanted.

And for as long as Holland could remember, he had wanted the magician to be *him.*

Even before the darkness bloomed across his eye, branding him with the mark of power, he'd wanted it to be him. He'd stood on the banks of the Sijlt as a child, skating stones across the frozen surface, imagining that he would be the one to crack the ice. Stood in the Silver Wood as a grown man, praying for the strength to protect his home. He'd never wanted to be *king,* though in the stories the magician always was. He didn't want to rule the world. He only wanted to save it.

Athos Dane had called this arrogance, that first night, when Holland was dragged, bleeding and half conscious, into the new king's chambers. Arrogance and pride, he'd chided, as he carved his curse into Holland's skin.

Things to be broken.

And Athos had. He'd broken Holland one bone, one day, one order at a time. Until all Holland wanted, more than the ability to save his world, more than the strength to bring the magic back, more than *anything,* was for it to end.

It was cowardice, he knew, but cowardice came so much easier than hope.

And in that moment by the bridge, when Holland lowered his guard and let the spoiled princeling Kell drive the metal bar through his chest, the first thing he felt—the first and last and *only* thing he felt—was relief.

That it was finally over.

Only it wasn't.

It is a hard thing, to kill an *Antari.*

When Holland woke, lying in a dead garden, in a dead city, in a dead world, the first thing he felt then was pain. The second thing was freedom. Athos Dane's hold was gone, and Holland was alive—broken, but alive.

And stranded.

Trapped in a wounded body in a world with no door at the mercy of another king. But this time, he had a *choice.*

A chance to set things right.

He'd stood, half dead, before the onyx throne, and spoken to the king carved in stone, and traded freedom for a chance to save his London, to see it bloom again. Holland made the deal, paid with his own body and soul. And with the shadow king's power, he had finally brought the magic back, seen his world bloom into color, his people's hope revived, his city restored.

He'd done everything he could, given up everything he had, to keep it safe.

But it still was not enough.

Not for the shadow king, who always wanted more, who grew stronger every day and craved chaos, magic in its truest form, power without control.

Holland was losing hold of the monster in his skin.

And so he'd done the only thing he could.

He'd offered Osaron another vessel.

"*Very well . . .* " said the king, the demon, the god. *"But if they cannot be persuaded, I will keep your body as my own."*

And Holland agreed—how could he not?

Anything for London.

And Kell—spoiled, childish, headstrong Kell, broken and powerless and snared by that damned collar—had still refused.

Of course he had refused.

Of course—

The shadow king had smiled then, with Holland's own mouth, and he had fought, with everything he could summon, but a deal was a deal and the deal was done and he felt Osaron surge up—that single, violent motion—and Holland was shoved down, into the dark depths of his own mind, forced under by the current of the shadow king's will.

Helpless, trapped within a body, within a deal, unable to do anything but watch, and feel, and drown.

"Holland!"

Kell's voice cracked as he strained his broken body against the frame, the way *Holland* had once, when Athos Dane first bound him. Broke him. The cage leached away most of Kell's power; the collar around his throat cut off the rest. There was a terror in Kell's eyes, a desperation that surprised him.

"Holland, you bastard, fight back!"

He tried, but his body was no longer his, and his mind, his tired mind, was sinking down, down—

Give in, said the shadow king.

"Show me you're not weak!" Kell's voice pushed through. "Prove you're not still a slave to someone else's will!"

You cannot fight me.

"Did you really come all the way back to lose like this?"

I've already won.

"Holland!"

Holland hated Kell, and in that moment, the hatred was almost enough to drive him up, but even if he wanted to rise to the other *Antari*'s bait, Osaron was unyielding.

Holland heard his own voice, then, but of course it wasn't his. A twisted imitation by the monster wearing his skin. In Holland's hand, a crimson coin, a token to another London, Kell's London, and Kell was swearing and throwing himself against his bonds until his chest heaved and his wrists were bloody.

Useless.

It was all useless.

Once again he was a prisoner in his own body. Kell's voice echoed through the dark.

You've just traded one master for another.

They were moving now, Osaron guiding Holland's body. The door closed behind them, but Kell's screams still hurled themselves against the wood, shattering into broken syllables and strangled cries.

Ojka stood in the hall, sharpening her knives. She looked up, revealing the crescent scar on one cheek, and her two-toned eyes, one yellow, the other black. An *Antari* forged by their hands—by their mercy.

"Your Majesty," she said, straightening.

Holland tried to rise up, tried to force his voice across their— *his*—lips, but when speech came, the words were Osaron's.

"Guard the door. Let no one pass."

A flicker of a smile across the red slash of Ojka's mouth. "As you wish."

The palace passed in a blur, and then they were outside, passing the statues of the Dane twins at the base of the stairs, moving swiftly beneath a bruised sky through a garden now flanked by trees instead of bodies.

What would become of it, without Osaron, without *him*? Would the city continue to flourish? Or would it collapse, like a body stripped of life?

Please, he begged silently. *This world needs me.*

"*There is no point,*" said Osaron aloud, and Holland felt sick to be the thought in their head instead of the word. "*It is already dead,*" continued the king. "*We will start over. We will find a world worthy of our strength.*"

They reached the garden wall and Osaron drew a dagger from the sheath at their waist. The bite of steel on flesh was nothing, as if Holland had been cut off from his very senses, buried too deep to feel anything but Osaron's grip. But as the shadow king's fingers streaked through the blood and lifted Kell's coin to the wall, Holland struggled up one last time.

He couldn't win back his body—not yet—not all of it—but perhaps he didn't need everything.

One hand. Five fingers.

He threw every ounce of strength, every shred of will, into that one limb, and halfway to the wall, it stopped, hovering in the air.

Blood trickled down his wrist. Holland knew the words to break a body, to turn it to ice, or ash, or stone.

All he had to do was guide his hand to his own chest.

All he had to do was shape the magic—

Holland could feel the annoyance ripple through Osaron. Annoyance, but not rage, as if this last stand, this great protest, was nothing but an itch.

How tedious.

Holland kept fighting, even managed to guide his hand an inch, two.

Let go, Holland, warned the creature in his head.

Holland forced the last of his will into his hand, dragging it another inch.

Osaron sighed.

It did not have to be this way.

Osaron's will hit him like a wall. His body didn't move, but his mind slammed backward, pinned beneath a crushing pain. Not the pain he'd felt a hundred times, the kind he'd learned to exist beyond, outside, the kind he might escape. This pain was rooted in his very core. It lit him up, sudden and bright, every nerve burning with such searing heat that he screamed and screamed and screamed inside his head, until the darkness finally—mercifully—closed over him, forcing him under and down.

And this time, Holland didn't try to surface.

This time, he let himself drown.

III

Kell kept throwing himself against the metal cage long after the door slammed shut and the bolt slid home. His voice still echoed against the pale stone walls. He had screamed himself hoarse. But still, no one came. Fear pounded through him, but what scared Kell most was the loosening in his chest—the unhinging of a vital link, the spreading sense of loss.

He could hardly feel his brother's pulse.

Could hardly feel anything but the pain in his wrists and a horrible numbing cold. He twisted against the metal frame, fighting the restraints, but they held fast. Spell work was scrawled down the sides of the contraption, and despite the quantity of Kell's blood smeared on the steel, there was the collar circling his throat, cutting off everything he needed. Everything he had. Everything he *was*. The collar cast a shadow over his mind, an icy film over his thoughts, cold dread and sorrow and, through it all, an absence of hope. Of strength. *Give up,* it whispered through his blood. *You have nothing. You are nothing. Powerless.*

He'd never been powerless.

He didn't know how to be powerless.

Panic rose in place of magic.

He had to get out.

Out of this cage.

Out of this collar.

Out of this world.

Rhy had carved a word into his own skin to bring Kell home, and he'd turned around and left again. Abandoned the prince, the crown, the city. Followed a woman in white through a door in the world because she told him he was needed, told him he could help, told him it was his fault, that he had to make it right.

Kell's heart faltered in his chest.

No—not *his* heart. Rhy's. A life bound to his with magic he no longer *had*. The panic flared again, a breath of heat against the numbing cold, and Kell clung to it, pushing back against the collar's hollow dread. He straightened in the frame, clenched his teeth and *pulled* against his cuffs until he felt the crack of bone inside his wrist, the tear of flesh. Blood fell in thick red drops to the stone floor, vibrant but useless. He bit back a scream as metal dragged over—and into—skin. Pain knifed up his arm, but he kept pulling, metal scraping muscle and then bone before his right hand finally came free.

Kell slumped back with a gasp and tried to wrap his bloody, limp fingers around the collar, but the moment they touched the metal, a horrible pins-and-needles cold seared up his arm, swam in his head.

"*As Steno,*" he pleaded. *Break.*

Nothing happened.

No power rose to meet the word.

Kell let out a sob and sagged against the frame. The room tilted and tunneled, and he felt his mind sliding toward darkness, but he forced his body to stay upright, forced himself to swallow the bile rising in his throat. He curled his skinned and splintered hand around his still-trapped arm, and began to pull.

It was minutes—but it felt like hours, years—before Kell finally tore himself free.

He stumbled forward out of the frame, and swayed on his feet. The metal cuffs had cut deep into his wrists—too deep—and the pale stone beneath his feet was slick with red.

Is this yours? whispered a voice.

A memory of Rhy's young face twisted in horror at the sight of Kell's ruined forearms, the blood streaked across the prince's chest. *Is this all yours?*

Now the collar dripped red as Kell frantically pulled on the metal.

His fingers ached with cold as he found the clasp and clawed at it, but still it held. His focus blurred. He slipped in his own blood and went down, catching himself with broken hands. Kell cried out, curling in on himself even as he screamed at his body to rise.

He had to get up.

He had to get back to Red London.

He had to stop Holland—stop *Osaron*.

He had to save Rhy.

He had to, he had to, he had to—but in that moment, all Kell could do was lie on the cold marble, warmth spreading in a thin red pool around him.

IV

The prince collapsed back against the bed, soaked through with sweat, choking on the metal taste of blood. Voices rose and fell around him, the room a blur of shadows, shards of light. A scream tore through his head, but his own jaw locked in pain. Pain that was and wasn't his.

Kell.

Rhy doubled over, coughing up blood and bile.

He tried to rise—he had to get up, had to find his brother—but hands surged from the darkness, fought him, held him down against silk sheets, fingers digging into shoulders and wrists and knees, and the pain was there again, vicious and jagged, peeling back flesh, dragging its nails over bone. Rhy tried to remember. Kell—arrested. His cell—empty. Searching the sun-dappled orchard. Calling his brother's name. Then, out of nowhere, pain, sliding between his ribs, just as it had that night, a horrible, severing thing, and he couldn't breathe.

He couldn't—

"Don't let go," said a voice.

"Stay with me."

"Stay . . ."

Rhy learned early the difference between want and need.

Being the son and heir—the only heir—of the Maresh family, the light of Arnes, the future of the empire, meant that he had never (as a nursery minder once informed him, before being removed from the royal service) experienced true *need*. Clothes, horses, instruments, fineries—all he had to do was ask for a thing, and it was given.

And yet, the young prince *wanted*—deeply—a thing that could not be fetched. He wanted what coursed in the blood of so many low-born boys and girls. What came so easily to his father, to his mother, to Kell.

Rhy wanted *magic*.

Wanted it with a fire that rivaled any need.

His royal father had a gift for metals, and his mother an easy touch with water, but magic wasn't like black hair or brown eyes or elevated birth—it didn't follow the rules of lineage, wasn't passed down from parent to child. It chose its own course.

And already at the age of nine, it was beginning to look as though magic hadn't chosen him at all.

But Rhy Maresh refused to believe that he'd been passed over entirely; it *had* to be there, somewhere within him, that flame of power waiting for a well-timed breath, a poker's nudge. After all, he was a prince. And if magic would not come to him, he'd go to *it*.

It was that logic that had brought him here, to the stone floor of the Sanctuary's drafty old library, shivering as the cold leached through the embroidered silk of his pant legs (designed for the palace, where it was always warm).

Whenever Rhy complained about the chill in the Sanctuary, old Tieren would crinkle his brow.

Magic makes its own warmth, he'd say, which was well and good if you were a magician, but then, Rhy wasn't.

Not yet.

This time he hadn't complained. Hadn't even told the head priest he was here.

The young prince crouched in an alcove at the back of the library, hidden behind a statue and a long wooden table, and spread the stolen parchment on the floor.

Rhy had been born with light fingers—but of course, being royal, he almost never had to use them. People were always willing to offer things freely, indeed leaping at the ready to deliver, from a cloak on a chilly day to a frosted cake from the kitchens.

But Rhy hadn't asked for the scroll; he'd lifted it from Tieren's desk, one of a dozen tied with the thin white ribbon that marked a priest's spell. None of them were all that fancy or elaborate, much to Rhy's chagrin. Instead they focused on utility.

Spells to keep the food from spoiling.

Spells to protect the orchard trees from frost.

Spells to keep a fire burning without oil.

And Rhy would try every single one until he found a spell that he could do. A spell that would speak to the magic surely sleeping in his veins. A spell that could *wake it up.*

A breeze whipped through the Sanctuary as he dug a handful of red *lin* from his pocket and weighted the parchment to the floor. On its surface, in the head priest's steady hand, was a map—not like the one in his father's war room that showed the whole kingdom. No, this was a map of a spell, a diagram of magic.

Across the top of the scroll were three words in the common tongue.

Is Anos Vol, read Rhy.

The Eternal Flame.

Beneath those words was a pair of concentric circles, linked by delicate lines and dotted with small symbols, the condensed shorthand favored by the spell-makers of London. Rhy squinted, trying to make sense of the scrawl. He had a knack for languages, picking up the airy cadence of the Faroan tongue, the choppy waves made by each Veskan syllable, the hills and valleys of Arnes's own border dialects—but the words on the parchment seemed to shift and blur before his eyes, sliding in and out of focus.

He chewed his lip (it was a bad habit, one his mother was always warning him to break because it wasn't *princely*), then planted his hands on either side of the paper, fingertips brushing the outer circle, and began the spell.

He focused his eyes on the center of the page as he read, sounding out each word, the fragments clumsy and broken on his tongue.

His pulse rose in his ears, the beat at odds with the natural rhythm of the magic. But Rhy held the spell together, pinned it down with sheer force of will, and as he neared the end a tingling of heat started in his hands; he could feel it trickling through his palms, into his fingers, brushing the circle's edge, and then . . .

Nothing.

No spark.

No flame.

He said the spell once, twice, three more times, but the heat in his hands was already fading, dissolving into an ordinary prickle of numbness. Dejected, he let the words trail off, taking the last of his focus with them.

The prince sagged back onto the cold stones. "*Sanct,*" he muttered, even though he knew it was bad form to swear, and worse to do it *here.*

"What are you doing?"

Rhy looked up and saw his brother standing at the mouth of the alcove, a red cloak around his narrow shoulders. Even at ten and three quarters, Kell's face had the set of a serious man, down to the furrow between his brows. Kell's red hair glinted even in the grey morning light, and his eyes—one blue, the other black as night—made people look down, away. Rhy didn't understand why, but he always made a point of looking his brother in the face, to show Kell it didn't matter. Eyes were eyes.

Kell wasn't *really* his brother, of course. Even a passing look would mark them as different. Kell was a mixture, like different kinds of clay twined together; he had the fair skin of a Veskan, the lanky body of a Faroan, and the copper hair found only on the northern edge of Arnes. And then, of course, there were his eyes. One natural, if not particularly Arnesian, and the other *Antari,* marked by magic itself as *aven.* Blessed.

Rhy, on the other hand, with his warm brown skin, his black hair and amber eyes, was all London, all Maresh, all royal.

Kell took in the prince's high color, and then the parchment spread out before him. He knelt across from Rhy, the fabric of his cloak pooling on the stones around him. "Where did you get this?" he asked, a prickle of displeasure in his voice.

"From Tieren," said Rhy. His brother shot him a skeptical look, and Rhy amended, "From Tieren's study."

Kell skimmed the spell and frowned. "An eternal flame?"

Rhy absently plucked one of the *lin* from the floor and shrugged. "First thing I grabbed." He tried to sound as if he didn't care about the stupid spell, but his throat was tight, his eyes burning. "Doesn't matter," he said, skipping the coin across the ground as if it were a pebble on water. "I can't make it work."

Kell shifted his weight, lips moving silently as he read over the priest's scrawl. He held his hands above the paper, palms cupped as if cradling a flame that wasn't even there yet, and began to recite the spell. When Rhy had tried, the words had fallen out like rocks, but on Kell's lips, they were poetry, smooth and sibilant.

The air around them warmed instantly, steam rising from the penned lines on the scroll before the ink drew in and up into a bead of oil, and lit.

The flame hovered in the air between Kell's hands, brilliant and white.

He made it look so easy, and Rhy felt a flash of anger toward his brother, hot as a spark—but just as brief.

It wasn't Kell's fault Rhy couldn't do magic. Rhy started to rise when Kell caught his cuff. He guided Rhy's hands to either side of the spell, pulling the prince into the fold of his magic. Warmth tickled Rhy's palms, and he was torn between delight at the power and knowledge that it wasn't his.

"It isn't right," he murmured. "I'm the crown prince, the heir of Maxim Maresh. I should be able to light a blasted candle."

Kell chewed his lip—Mother never chided *him* for the habit—and then said, "There are different kinds of power."

"I would rather have magic than a crown," sulked Rhy.

Kell studied the small white flame between them. "A crown is a sort of magic, if you think about it. A magician rules an element. A king rules an empire."

"Only if the king is strong enough."

Kell looked up, then. "You're going to be a good king, if you don't get yourself killed first."

Rhy blew out a breath, shuddering the flame. "How do you know?"

At that, Kell smiled. It was a rare thing, and Rhy wanted to hold fast to it—he was the only one who could make his brother smile, and he wore it like a badge—but then Kell said, "Magic," and Rhy wanted to slug him instead.

"You're an arse," he muttered, trying to pull away, but his brother's fingers tightened.

"Don't let go."

"Get off," said Rhy, first playfully, but then, as the fire grew brighter and hotter between his palms, he repeated in earnest, "Stop. You're hurting me."

Heat licked his fingers, a white-hot pain lancing through his hands and up his arms.

"Stop," he pleaded. "Kell, *stop*." But when Rhy looked up from the glowing fire to his brother's face, it wasn't a face at all. Nothing but a pool of darkness. Rhy gasped, tried to scramble away, but his brother was no longer flesh and blood but stone, hands carved into cuffs around Rhy's wrists.

This wasn't right, he thought, it had to be a dream—a nightmare—but the heat of the fire and the crushing pressure on his wrists were both so real, worsening with every heartbeat, every breath.

The flame between them went long and thin, sharpening into a blade of light, its tip pointed first at the ceiling, and then, slowly, horribly, at Rhy. He fought, and screamed, but it did nothing to stop the knife as it blazed and buried itself in his chest.

Pain.

Make it stop.

It carved its way across his ribs, lit his bones, tore through his heart. Rhy tried to scream, and retched smoke. His chest was a ragged wound of light.

Kell's voice came, not from the statue, but from somewhere else. Somewhere far away and fading. *Don't let go.*

But it hurt. It hurt so much.

Stop.

Rhy was burning from the inside out.

Please.

Dying.

Stay.

Again.

For a moment, the black gave way to streaks of color, a ceiling of billowing fabric, a familiar face hovering at the edge of his tear-blurred sight, stormy eyes wide with worry.

"Luc?" rasped Rhy.

"I'm here," answered Alucard. "I'm here. Stay with me."

He tried to speak, but his heart slammed against his ribs as if trying to break through.

It redoubled, then faltered.

"Have they found Kell?" said a voice.

"Get away from me," ordered another.

"Everyone *out.*"

Rhy's vision blurred.

The room wavered, the voices dulled, the pain giving way to something worse, the white-hot agony of the invisible knife dissolving into cold as his body fought and failed and fought and failed and failed and—

No, he pleaded, but he could feel the threads breaking one by one inside him until there was nothing left to hold him up.

Until Alucard's face vanished, and the room fell away.

Until the darkness wrapped its heavy arms around Rhy, and buried him.

V

Alucard Emery wasn't used to feeling powerless.

Mere hours earlier, he'd won the *Essen Tasch* and been named the strongest magician in the three empires. But now, sitting by Rhy's bed, he had no idea what to do. How to help. How to save him.

The magician watched as the prince curled in on himself, deathly pale against the tangled sheets, watched as Rhy cried out in pain, attacked by something even Alucard couldn't see, couldn't fight. And he would have—would have gone to the end of the world to keep Rhy safe. But whatever was killing him, it wasn't here.

"What is *happening*?" he'd asked a dozen times. "What can I *do*?"

But no one answered, so he was left piecing together the queen's pleas and the king's orders, Lila's urgent words and the echoes of the royal guards' searching voices, all of them calling for Kell.

Alucard sat forward, clutching the prince's hand, and watched the threads of magic around Rhy's body fray, threatening to snap.

Others looked at the world and saw light and shadow and color, but Alucard Emery had always been able to see more. Had always been able to see the warp and weft of power, the pattern of magic. Not just the aura of a spell, the residue of an enchantment, but the tint of true magic circling a person, pulsing through their veins. Everyone could see the Isle's red light, but Alucard saw the entire world in streaks of vivid color. Natural wells of magic glowed crimson. Elemental magicians were cloaked in green and blue. Curses stained purple. Strong spells burned gold. And *Antari*? They alone shone with a dark but iridescent light—not one color, but every color folded together, natural and unnatural, shimmering threads that wrapped like silk around them, dancing over their skin.

Alucard now watched those same threads fray and break around the prince's coiled form.

It wasn't right—Rhy's own meager magic had always been a dark green (he'd told the prince once, only to watch his features crinkle in distaste—Rhy had never liked the color).

But the moment he'd set eyes on Rhy again, after three years away, Alucard had known the prince was different. *Changed*. It wasn't the set of his jaw, the breadth of his shoulders, or the new shadows beneath his eyes. It was the magic bound to him. Power lived and breathed, was meant to move in the current of a person's life. But this new magic around Rhy lay still, threads wrapped tight as rope around the prince's body.

And each and every one of them shone like oil on water. Molten color and light.

That night, in Rhy's chamber, when Alucard slid the tunic aside to kiss the prince's shoulder, he'd seen the place where the silvery threads knitted into Rhy's skin, woven straight into the scarred circles over his heart. He didn't have to ask who'd made the spell—only one *Antari* came to mind—but Alucard couldn't see *how* Kell had done it. Normally he could pick apart a piece of magic by looking at its threads, but the strands of the spell had no beginning, no end. The threads of Kell's magic plunged into Rhy's heart, and were lost—no, not lost, *buried*—the spellwork stiff, unshakeable.

And now, somehow, it was crumbling.

The threads snapped one by one under an invisible strain, every broken cord eliciting a sob, a shuddering breath from the half-conscious prince. Every fraying tether—

That's what it was, he realized. Not just a spell, but a kind of *link*. To Kell.

He didn't know *why* the prince's life was bound to the *Antari*'s. Didn't want to imagine—though he now saw the scar between Rhy's trembling ribs, as wide as a dagger's edge, and the understanding reached him anyway, and he felt sick and helpless—but the link was breaking, and Alucard did the only thing he could.

He held the prince's hand, and tried to pour his own power into the fraying threads, as if the storm-blue light of his magic could fuse with Kell's iridescence instead of wicking uselessly away. He prayed to every power in the world, to every saint and every priest and every blessed figure—the ones he believed in and the ones he didn't—for strength. And when they didn't answer, he spoke to Rhy instead. He didn't tell him to hold on, didn't tell him to be strong.

Instead, he spoke of the past. *Their* past.

"Do you remember, the night before I left?" He fought to keep the fear from his voice. "You never answered my question."

Alucard closed his eyes, in part so he could picture the memory, and in part because he couldn't bear to watch the prince in so much pain.

It had been summer, and they'd been lying in bed, bodies tangled and warm. He'd drawn a hand along Rhy's perfect skin, and when the prince had preened, he'd said, "One day you will be old and wrinkled, and I will still love you."

"I'll never be old," said the prince with the certainty mustered only by the young and healthy and terribly naive.

"So you plan to die young, then?" he'd teased, and Rhy had given an elegant shrug.

"Or live forever."

"Oh, really?"

The prince had swept a dark curl from his eyes. "Dying is so mundane."

"And how, exactly," said Alucard, propping himself on one elbow, "do you plan to live forever?"

Rhy had pulled him down, then, and ended their conversation with a kiss.

Now he shuddered on the bed, a sob escaping through clenched teeth. His black curls were matted to his face. The queen called for a cloth, called for the head priest, called for Kell. Alucard clutched his lover's hand.

"I'm sorry I left. I'm sorry. But I'm here now, so you can't die," he said, his voice finally breaking. "Don't you see how rude that would be, when I've come so far?"

The prince's hand tightened as his body seized.

Rhy's chest hitched up and down in a last, violent shudder.

And then he stilled.

And for a moment, Alucard was relieved, because Rhy was finally resting, finally asleep. For a moment, everything was all right. For a moment—

Then it shattered.

Someone was screaming.

The priests were pushing forward.

The guards were pulling him back.

Alucard stared down at the prince.

He didn't understand.

He *couldn't* understand.

And then Rhy's hand slipped from his, and fell back to the bed.

Lifeless.

The last silver threads were losing their hold, sliding off his skin like sheets in summer.

And then *he* was screaming.

Alucard didn't remember anything after that.

VI

For a single horrifying moment, Lila ceased to exist.

She felt herself unravel, breaking apart into a million threads, each one stretching, fraying, threatening to snap as she stepped out of the world, out of life—and into nothing. And then, just as suddenly, she was staggering forward onto her hands and knees in the street.

She let out a short, involuntary cry as she landed, limbs shaking, head ringing like a bell.

The ground beneath her palms—and there *was* ground, so that at least was a good sign—was rough and cold. The air was quiet. No fireworks. No music. Lila dragged herself back to her feet, blood dripping from her fingers, her nose. She wiped it away, red dots speckling the stone as she drew her knife and shifted her stance, putting her back to the icy wall. She remembered the last time she'd been here, in this London, the hungry eyes of men and women starved for power.

A splash of color caught her eye, and she looked up.

The sky overhead was streaked with sunset—pink and purple and burnished gold. Only, White London didn't *have* color, not like this, and for a terrible second, she thought she'd crossed into yet *another* city, another world, had trapped herself even farther from home—wherever that was now.

But no, Lila recognized the road beneath her boots, the castle rising to gothic points against the setting sun. It was the same city, and yet entirely changed. It had only been four months since she'd set foot here, four months since she and Kell had faced the Dane twins. Then it had been a world of ice and ash and cold white stone. And now . . .

now a man walked past her on the street, and he was *smiling*. Not the rictus grin of the starving, but the private smile of the content, the blessed.

This was wrong.

Four months, and in that time she'd learned to sense magic, its presence if not its intent. She couldn't *see* it, not the way Alucard did, but with every breath she took, she tasted power on the air as if it were sugar, sweet and strong enough that it was cloying. The night air shimmered with it.

What the hell was going on?

And where was Kell?

Lila knew where *she* was, or at least where she'd chosen to pass through, and so she followed the high wall around a corner to the castle gates. They stood open, winter ivy winding through the iron. Lila dragged to a stop a second time. The stone forest—once a garden filled with bodies—was gone, replaced by an actual stretch of trees, and by guards in polished armor flanking the castle steps, all of them alert.

Kell had to be inside. A tether ran between them, thin as thread, but strangely strong, and Lila didn't know if it was made by their magic or something else, but it drew her toward the castle like a weight. She tried not to think about what it meant, how much farther she would have to go, how many people she'd have to fight, to find him.

Wasn't there a locator spell?

Lila wracked her mind for the words. *As Travars* had carried her between worlds, and *As Tascen,* that was the way to move between different places in the *same* world, but what if she wanted to find a person, not a place?

She cursed herself for not knowing, never asking. Kell had told her once, of finding Rhy after he'd been taken as a boy. What had he used? She dragged her memory—something Rhy had made. A wooden horse? Another image sprang to mind, of the kerchief—her kerchief—clenched in Kell's hand when he first found her at the Stone's Throw. But Lila didn't have anything of his. No tokens. No trinkets.

Panic welled, and she fought it down.

So she didn't have a charm to guide her. People were more than what they owned, and surely objects weren't the only things that held a mark. They were made of pieces, words . . . memories.

And Lila had those.

She pressed her still-bloody hand to the castle gate, the cold iron biting at the shallow wound as she squeezed her eyes shut, and summoned Kell. First with the memory of the night they'd met, in the alley when she'd robbed him, and then later, when he'd walked through her wall. A stranger tied to her bed, the taste of magic, the promise of freedom, the fear of being left behind. Hand in hand through one world, and then another, pressed together as they hid from Holland, faced down sly Fletcher, fought the not-Rhy. The horror at the palace and the battle in White London, Kell's blood-streaked body wrapped around hers in the rubble of the stone forest. The broken pieces of their lives cast apart. And then, returned. A game played behind masks. A new embrace. His hand burning on her waist as they danced, his mouth burning against hers as they kissed, bodies clashing like swords on the palace balcony. The terrifying heat, and then, too soon, the cold. Her collapse in the arena. His anger hurled like a weapon before he turned away. Before she let him go.

But she was here to take him back.

Lila steeled herself again, jaw clenched against the expectation of the pain to come.

She held the memories in her mind, pressed them to the wall as if they were a token, and said the words.

"As Tascen Kell."

Against her hand, the gate shuddered and the world fell away as Lila staggered through, out of the street and into the pale polished chamber of a castle hallway.

Torches burned in sconces along the walls, footsteps sounded in the distance, and Lila allowed herself the briefest moment of satisfaction, maybe even relief, before realizing Kell wasn't here. Her head was pounding, a curse halfway to her lips when, beyond a door to her left, she heard a muffled scream.

Lila's blood went cold.

Kell. She reached for the door's handle, but as her fingers closed around it, she caught the low whistle of metal singing through air. She cut to the side as a knife buried itself in the wood where Lila had been a moment before. A black cord drew a path from the hilt back through the air, and she turned, following the line to a woman in a pale cloak. A scar traced the other woman's cheekbone, but that was the only ordinary thing about her. Darkness filled one eye and spilled over like wax, running down her cheek and up her temple, tracing the line of her jaw and vanishing into hair so red—redder than Kell's coat, redder even than the river in Arnes—it seemed to singe the air. A color too bright for this world. Or, at least, too bright for the world it had been. But Lila felt the wrongness here, and it was more than vivid colors and ruined eyes.

This woman reminded her not of Kell, or even of Holland, but of the stolen black stone from months ago. That strange pull, a heavy beat.

With a flick of the wrist, a second knife appeared in the stranger's left hand, hilt tethered to the cord's other end. A swift tug, and the first knife freed itself from the wood and went flying back into the fingers of her right. Graceful as a bird gliding into formation.

Lila was almost impressed. "Who are you supposed to be?" she asked.

"I am the messenger," said the woman, even though Lila knew a trained killer when she saw one. "And you?"

Lila drew two of her own knives. "I am the thief."

"You cannot go in."

Lila put her back to the door, Kell's power like a dying pulse against her spine. *Hold on,* she thought desperately and then aloud, "Try and stop me."

"What is your name?" asked the woman.

"What's it to you?"

She smiled, then, a murderous grin. "My king will want to know who I've—"

But Lila didn't wait for her to finish.

Her first knife flew through the air, and as the woman's hand moved to deflect it, Lila struck with the second. She was halfway to meeting flesh when the corded blade came at her and she had to dodge, diving out of the way. She spun, ready to slash again, only to find herself parrying another scorpion strike. The cord between the knives was elastic, and the woman wielded the blades the way Jinnar did wind, Alucard water, or Kisimyr earth, the weapons wrapped in will so that when they flew, they had both the force of momentum and the elegance of magic.

And on top of it all, the woman moved with a disturbing grace, the fluid gestures of a dancer.

A dancer with two very sharp blades.

Lila ducked, the first blade biting through the air beside her face. Several strands of dark hair floated to the floor. The weapons blurred with speed, drawing her attention in different directions. It was all Lila could do to dodge the glinting bits of silver.

She'd been in her fair share of knife fights. Had started most of them herself. She knew the trick was to find the guard and get behind it, to force a moment of defense, an opening for attack, but this wasn't hand-to-hand combat.

How was she supposed to fight a woman whose knives didn't even stay in her hands?

The answer, of course, was simple: the same way she fought anyone else.

Quick and dirty.

After all, the point wasn't to look good. It was to stay alive.

The woman's blades lashed out like vipers, striking forward with sudden, terrifying speed. But there was a weakness: they couldn't change course. Once a blade flew, it flew straight. And that was why a knife in the hand was better than one thrown.

Lila feinted right, and when the first blade came, she darted the other way. The second followed, charting another path, and Lila dodged again, carving a third line while the blades were both trapped in their routes.

"Got you," she snarled, lunging for the woman.

And then, to her horror, the blades *changed course*. They veered midair, and plunged, Lila taking frantic flight as both weapons buried themselves in the floor where she'd been crouched a second earlier.

Of course. A metal worker.

Blood ran down Lila's arm and dripped from her fingers. She'd been fast, but not quite fast enough.

Another flick of a wrist, and the knives flew back into the other woman's hands. "Names are important," she said, twirling the cord. "Mine is Ojka, and I have orders to keep you out."

Beyond the doors, Kell let out a scream of frustration, a sob of pain.

"My name is Lila Bard," she answered, drawing her favorite knife, "and I don't give a damn."

Ojka smiled, and attacked.

When the next strike came, Lila aimed not at flesh, or blade, but the cord between. Her knife's edge came down on the stretched fabric and bit in—

But Ojka was too fast. The metal barely grazed the cord before it snapped back toward the fighter's fingers.

"*No,*" growled Lila, catching the material with her bare hand. Surprise flashed across Ojka's face, and Lila let out a small, triumphant sound, right before pain lanced up her leg as a *third* blade—short and viciously sharp—buried itself in her calf.

Lila gasped, staggered.

Blood speckled the pale floor as Lila pulled the knife free and straightened.

Beyond that door, Kell screamed.

Beyond this world, Rhy died.

Lila didn't have time for this.

She dragged her knives together and they sparked, caught fire. The air seared around her, and this time when Ojka threw her blade, the burning edges of Lila's own met the length of cord, and the fire caught. It wicked along the tether, and Ojka hissed as she pulled herself back. Halfway to her hand, the cord snapped, and the knife faltered, missing its return to her fingers. A dancer, off cue. The assassin's face burned with anger as she closed the distance to her opponent, now armed with only a single blade.

Despite that, Ojka still moved with the terrifying grace of a predator, and Lila was so focused on the knife in the woman's hand that she forgot the room was filled with other weapons for a magician to use.

Lila dodged a flash of metal and tried to leap back, but a low stool caught her behind the knees and she stumbled, balance lost. The fire in her hands went out, and the red-haired woman was on her before she hit the floor, blade already arcing down toward her chest.

Lila's arms came up to block the knife as it slashed down, their hilts crashing together in the air above her face. A wicked smile flashed across Ojka's lips as the weapon in her hand suddenly extended, metal thinning into a spike of steel that drove toward Lila's eyes—

Her head snapped sideways as metal struck glass and the sound of a sharp crack reverberated through her skull. The knife, having skidded off her false eye, made a deep scratch across the marble floor. A droplet of blood ran down her cheek where the blade had sliced skin, a single crimson tear.

Lila blinked, dismayed.

The bitch had tried to drive a knife through her eye.

Fortunately, she'd picked the wrong one.

Ojka stared down, caught in an instant of confusion.

And an instant was all Lila needed.

Her own knife, still raised, now slashed sideways, drawing a crimson smile across the woman's throat.

Ojka's mouth opened and closed in a mimicry of the parted skin at her neck as blood spilled down her front. She fell to the floor beside Lila, fingers wrapped around the wound, but it was wide and deep— a killing blow.

The woman twitched and stilled, and Lila shuffled backward out of the spreading pool of blood, pain still singing through her wounded calf, her ringing head.

She got to her feet, cupping one hand against her shattered eye.

Her lost second blade jutted from a sconce, and she pried it free, trailing a line of blood in her wake as she stumbled over to the door. It had gone quiet beyond. She tried the handle, but found it locked.

There was probably a spell, but Lila didn't know it, and she was too tired to summon air or wood or anything else, so instead she simply summoned the last of her strength and kicked the door in.

VII

Kell stared up at the ceiling, the world so far above, and getting farther with every breath.

And then he heard a voice—*Lila's* voice—and it was like a hook, wrenching him back to the surface.

He gasped and tried to sit up. Failed. Tried again. Pain shuddered through him as he got to one knee. Somewhere far away, he heard the crack of a boot on wood. A lock breaking. He made it to his feet as the door swung open, and there she was, a shadow traced in light, and then his vision slid away and she became a blur, rushing toward him.

Kell managed a halting step forward before his boots slipped in the pool of blood, and shock and pain plunged him briefly into black. He felt his legs buckling, then warm arms snaking around his waist as he fell.

"I've got you," said Lila, sinking with him to the floor. His head slumped against her shoulder, and he whispered hoarsely into her coat, trying to form the words. When she didn't seem to understand, he dragged his bloody, broken hands and numbed fingers once more around the collar at his throat.

"Take it . . . off," choked Kell.

Lila's gaze—was there something wrong with her eyes?—flicked over the metal for an instant before she wrapped both hands around the collar's edge. She hissed when her fingers met the metal, but didn't let go, grimacing as she cast her hands around until she found the clasp at the base of Kell's neck. It came free, and she hurled the collar across the room.

Air rushed back into Kell's lungs, heat pouring though his veins. For an instant, every nerve in his body sang, first with pain and then power as the magic returned in an electric surge. He gasped and doubled over, chest heaving and tears running down his face as the world around him pulsed and rippled and threatened to catch fire. Even Lila must have felt it, leaping back out of the way as Kell's power surfaced, settled, every stolen drop reclaimed.

But something was still missing.

No, thought Kell. *Please, no.* The echo. The second pulse. He looked down at his ruined hands, wrists still dripping blood and magic, and none of it mattered. He tore at his chest, tunic ripping over the seal, which was still there, but beneath the scars and the spellwork, only one heart beat. Only one—

"Rhy—" he said, the word a sob. A plea. "I can't . . . he's . . ."

Lila grabbed him by the shoulders. "Look at me," she said. "Your brother was still alive when I left. Have a little faith." Her words were hollow, and his own fear ricocheted inside them, filling the space. "Besides," she added, "you can't help him from here."

She looked around the room at the metal frame, cuffs slick with red, at the table beside it, littered with tools, at the metal collar lying on the floor before her attention returned to him. There *was* something wrong with her eyes—one was its usual brown, but the other was full of cracks.

"Your eye—" he started, but Lila waved her hand.

"Not now." She rose. "Come on, we have to go."

But Kell knew he was in no shape to go anywhere. His hands were broken and bruised, blood still running in ropes from his wrists. His head spun every time he moved, and when she tried to help him up, he only made it halfway to his feet before his body swayed and buckled again. He let out a strangled gasp of frustration.

"This isn't a good look on you," she said, pressing her fingers to a gash above her ankle. "Hold still, I'm going to patch you up."

Kell's eyes widened. "Wait," he said, twitching back from her touch.

Lila's mouth quirked. "Don't you trust me?"

"No."

"Too bad," she said, pressing her bloody hand against his shoulder. "What's the word, Kell?"

The room rocked as he shook his head. "Lila, I don't—"

"What's the fucking word?"

He swallowed and answered shakily. *"Hasari. As Hasari."*

"All right," she said, tightening her grip. "Ready?" And then, before he could answer, she cast the spell. *"As Hasari."*

Nothing happened.

Kell's eyes fluttered in relief, exhaustion, pain.

Lila frowned. "Did I do it ri—"

Light exploded between them, the force of the magic hurling them in opposite directions, like shrapnel from a blast.

Kell's back hit the floor, and Lila's thudded against the nearest wall.

He lay there, gasping, so dazed that for a second he couldn't tell if it had actually worked. But then he flexed his fingers and felt the wreckage of his hands and wrists knitting back together, skin smooth and warm beneath the trails of blood, felt the air move freely in his lungs, the emptiness filled, the broken made whole. When he sat up, the room didn't spin. His pulse pounded in his ears, but his blood was back inside his veins.

Lila was slumped at the base of the wall, rubbing the back of her head with a low groan.

"Fucking magic," she muttered as he knelt beside her. At the sight of him intact, she flashed a triumphant smirk.

"Told you it would wor—"

Kell cut her off, taking her face in his stained hands and kissing her once, deeply, desperately. A kiss laced with blood and panic, pain and fear and relief. He didn't ask her how she'd found him. Didn't berate her for doing it, only said, "You are *mad*."

She managed a small, exhausted smile. "You're welcome."

He helped her to her feet and retrieved his coat, which sat crumpled on the table where Holland—Osaron—had dropped it.

Again Lila scanned the room. "What happened, Kell? Who did this to you?"

"Holland."

He saw the name land like a fist, imagined the images filling her mind, the same ones that had filled his when he found himself face-to-face with the new White London king and saw not a stranger at all, but a familiar foe. The *Antari* with the two-toned eyes, one emerald, the other black. The magician bound to serve the Dane twins. The one he'd slain and pushed into the abyss between worlds.

But Kell knew that Lila had another image in her mind: of the man who'd killed Barron and thrown the bloodstained watch at her feet as a taunt.

"Holland's dead," she said icily.

Kell shook his head. "No. He survived. He came back. He's—"

Shouts sounded beyond the door.

Footsteps pounding on stone.

"Dammit," snarled Lila, gaze flicking to the hall. "We really have to go."

Kell spun toward the door, but she was a step ahead, a Red London *lin* in one bloody hand as she reached for his and brought her other down on the table.

"*As*—" she started.

Kell's eyes went wide. "Wait, you can't just—"

"—*Travars*."

The guards burst in as the room dissolved, the floor gave way, and they were falling.

Down through one London and into another.

Kell braced himself, but the ground never caught them. It wasn't there. The castle became the night, the walls and floor replaced by nothing but cold air, the red light of the river and the bustling streets and the steepled roofs reaching for them as they fell.

There were rules when it came to making doors.

The first—and, in Kell's opinion, *most* important—was that you could either move between two places in the same world, or two worlds in the same place.

The same *exact* place.

Which was why it was so important to make sure that your feet were on the ground, and not on, say, the floor of a castle chamber two stories up, because chances were there would be no castle floor a world away.

Kell had tried to tell Lila this, but it was too late. The blood was already on her hand, the token already in her palm, and before he could get the words out, before he could say more than "don't," they were falling.

They plunged down through the floor, through the world, and through several feet of winter night, before hitting the slanted roof of a building. The tiles were half frozen, and they skidded down another few feet before finally catching themselves against the drain. Or rather—Kell caught himself. The metal beneath Lila's boots buckled sharply, and she would have tumbled over the side if he hadn't grabbed her wrist and hauled her back up onto the shingles beside him.

For a long moment, neither spoke, only lay back against the angled roof, huffing unsteady plumes of breath into the night.

"In the future," said Kell finally, "do make sure you're standing *on the street.*"

Lila exhaled a shaky cloud. "Noted."

The cold roof burned against his flushed skin, but Kell didn't move, not right away. He couldn't—couldn't think, couldn't feel, couldn't bring himself to do anything but look up and focus on the stars. Delicate dots of light against a blue-black sky—*his* sky—lined with clouds, their edges tinged red from the river, everything so normal, untouched, oblivious, and suddenly he wanted to scream because even though Lila had healed his body, he still felt broken and terrified and hollow and all he wanted to do was close his eyes and sink again, to find that dark and silent place beneath the surface of the world, the place where Rhy—Rhy—Rhy—

He forced himself to sit up.

He had to find Osaron.

"Kell," started Lila, but he was already pushing himself forward off the roof, dropping to the street below. He could have summoned the wind to ease the fall, but he didn't, barely felt the pain lancing up his shins when he landed on the stones. A moment later he heard the soft whoosh of a second body, and Lila landed in a crouch beside him.

"Kell," she said again, but he was already crossing to the nearest wall, digging his knife from his coat pocket and carving a fresh line in his newly healed skin.

"Dammit, Kell—" She caught his sleeve, and there he was again, staring into those brown eyes—one whole, the other shattered. How could he have known? How could he have *not*?

"What do you mean, *Holland's back*?"

"He—" Something splintered inside him, and Kell was back in the courtyard with the red-haired woman—*Ojka*—following her through a door in the world, into a London that made no sense, a London that should have been broken but wasn't, a London with too much color— and there stood the new king, young and healthy, but unmistakable. Holland. Then, before Kell could process the *Antari*'s presence—the horrible cold of the spelled collar, the stunning pain of being torn away from himself, away from everything, the metal cage cutting into his wrists. And the look on Holland's face as it became someone else's, the jagged sound of Kell's own voice pleading as the second heart failed within his chest and the demon turned away and—

Kell recoiled suddenly. He was back in the street, blood dripping from his fingers, and Lila was inches from his face, and he couldn't tell if she'd kissed him or struck him, only knew his head was ringing and something deep inside him was screaming still.

"It's him," he said, hoarsely, "but it's not. It's—" He shook his head. "I don't know, Lila. Somehow Holland made it to Black London, and something got inside. It's like Vitari but worse. And it's . . . *wearing* him."

"So the real Holland is dead?" asked Lila as he drew a sigil on the stones.

"No," said Kell, taking her hand. "He's still in there somewhere. And now they're here."

Kell pressed his bloody palm flat to the wall, and this time when he said the spells, the magic rose effortlessly, mercifully, to his touch.

VIII

Emira refused to leave Rhy's side.

Not when his screams gave way to hitching sobs.

Not when his fevered skin went pale, his features slack.

Not when his breathing stopped and his pulse failed.

Not when the room went still, and not when it exploded into chaos, and the furniture shook, and the windows cracked, and the guards had to force Alucard Emery from the bed, and Maxim and Tieren tried to draw her hands away from his body, because they didn't understand.

A queen could leave her throne.

But a mother *never* leaves her son.

"Kell will not let him die," she said in the quiet.

"Kell will not let him die," she said in the noise.

"Kell will not let him die," she said, over and over to herself when they stopped listening.

The room was a storm, but she sat perfectly still beside her son.

Emira Maresh, who saw the cracks in beautiful things, and moved through life afraid of making more. Emira Nasaro, who hadn't wanted to be queen, hadn't wanted to be responsible for legions of people, their sorrows, their follies. Who'd never wanted to bring a child into this dangerous world, who now refused to believe that her strong and beautiful boy . . . her heart . . .

"He is dead," said the priest.

No.

"He is dead," said the king.

No.

"He is dead," said every voice but hers, because they didn't understand that if Rhy was dead, then so was Kell, and that wouldn't happen, that *couldn't* happen.

And yet.

Her son wasn't moving. Wasn't breathing. His skin, so newly cool, had taken on a horrible grey pallor, his body skeletal and sunken, as if he'd been gone for weeks, months, instead of minutes. His shirt lay open, revealing the seal against his chest, the ribs so wrongly visible beneath his once-brown skin.

Her eyes blurred with tears, but she wouldn't let them fall, because crying would mean grieving and she wouldn't grieve her son because he *was not dead*.

"Emira," pleaded the king as she bowed her head over Rhy's too-still chest.

"Please," she whispered, and the word wasn't for fate, or magic, the saints or the priests or the Isle. It was for Kell. "Please."

When she dragged her eyes up, she could *almost* see a glint of silver in the air—a thread of light—but with every passing second, the body on the bed bore less resemblance to her son.

Her fingers moved to brush the hair from Rhy's eyes, and she fought back a shudder at the brittle locks, the papery skin. He was falling apart before her eyes, the silence punctuated only by the dry crack of settling bones, the sound like embers in a dying fire.

"Emira."

"Please."

"Your Majesty."

"Please."

"My queen."

"Please."

She began to hum—not a song, or a prayer, but a spell, one she learned when she was just a girl. A spell she'd sung to Rhy a hundred times when he was young. A spell for sleep. For gentle dreams.

For release.

She was nearly to the end when the prince gasped.

IX

One moment Alucard was being dragged from the prince's room, and the next he was forgotten. He didn't notice the sudden absence of weight on his arms. Didn't notice anything but the glitter of luminescent threads and the sound of Rhy's breath.

The prince's gasp was soft, almost inaudible, but it rippled through the room, picked up by every body, every voice as the queen and the king and the guards inhaled in shock, in wonder, in relief.

Alucard braced himself in the doorway, his legs threatening to give.

He'd *seen* Rhy die.

Seen the last threads vanish into the prince's chest, seen the prince go still, seen the impossible, immediate decay.

But now, as he watched, it was undone.

Before his eyes, the spell returned, a flame coaxed suddenly back from embers. No, from ash. The threads surged up like water over a broken levy before wrapping fierce, protective arms around Rhy's body, and he breathed a second time, and a third, and between every inhale and exhale, the prince's corpse returned to life.

Flesh grew taut over bone. Color flooded into hollow cheeks. As quickly as the prince had decayed, he now revived, all signs of pain and strain smoothed into a mask of calm. His black hair settled on his brow in perfect curls. His chest rose and fell with the gentle rhythm of deep sleep.

And as Rhy calmly slept, the room around him was plunged into a new kind of chaos. Alucard staggered forward. Voices spoke over one another, layered into meaningless sound. Some shouted and others whispered words of prayer, blessings for what they'd just seen, or protection from it.

Alucard was halfway to Rhy's side when King Maxim's voice cut through the noise.

"No one is to speak of this," he said, his voice unsteady as he drew himself to full height. "The winner's ball has started, and it must finish."

"But, sir," started a guard as Alucard reached Rhy's bed.

"The prince has been ill," the king cut in. "Nothing more." His gaze landed hard on each of them. "There are too many allies in the palace tonight, too many potential enemies."

Alucard did not care about the ball or the tournament or the people beyond this room. He only wanted to touch the prince's hand. To feel the warmth of his skin and assure his own shaking fingers, his own aching heart, that it was not some horrible trick.

The room emptied around him, the king first, and then the guards and priests, until only the queen and Alucard stood, silently, staring at the prince's sleeping form.

Alucard reached out, then, his hand closing over Rhy's, and as he felt the pulse flutter in the prince's wrist, he didn't dwell on the impossibility of what he'd seen, didn't wonder at what forbidden magic could be strong enough to bind life to the dead.

All that mattered—all that would *ever* matter—was this.

Rhy was alive.

X

Kell staggered out of the street and into his palace chamber, caught by the sudden light, the warmth, the impossible normalcy. As if a life hadn't shattered, a world hadn't broken. Gossamer billowed from the ceiling and a massive, curtained bed stood on a dais on one wall, the furniture dark wood, trimmed in gold, and overhead, he could hear the sounds of the winner's ball on the roof.

How could it still be happening?

How could they not *know*?

Of *course* the king would have the winner's ball go on as planned, Kell thought bitterly. Hide his own son's situation from the prying eyes of Vesk and Faro.

"What do you mean Holland's here?" demanded Lila. "Here as in London, or here as in *here*?" She trailed in his wake, but Kell was already to his chamber doors and through. Rhy's room stood at the end of the hall, rosewood-and-gold doors shut fast.

The space between their rooms was littered with men and women, guards and *vestra* and priests. They turned sharply at the sight of Kell, bare-chested beneath his coat, hair plastered and skin streaked with blood. In their eyes he read the shock and horror, surprise and fear.

They moved, some toward him and others away, but all in his path, and Kell summoned a gust of wind, forcing them aside as he surged through the mass to the prince's doors.

He didn't want to go in.

He *had* to go in.

The screaming in his head was worsening with every step as Kell threw open the doors and skidded into the room, breathless.

The first thing he saw was the queen's face, blanched with grief.

The second was his brother's body, stretched out on the bed.

The third, and last, was the slow rise and fall of Rhy's chest.

At that small, blessed movement, Kell's own chest lurched.

The storm in his head, held so brittly at bay, now broke, the sudden violent flush of fear and grief and relief and hope giving way to jarring calm.

His body folded with relief; Rhy was alive. Kell simply hadn't felt the faint return of Rhy's heart through the raging and erratic pulse of his own. Even now, it was too soft to sense. But Rhy was alive. He was alive. He was *alive.*

Kell sank to his knees, but before they hit the floor, she was there—not Lila this time, but the queen. She didn't stop him from falling, but sank gently with him. Her fingers clutched at his front, tightened in the folds of his coat, and Kell braced himself for the words, the blow. He had left. He had failed her son. He had nearly lost Rhy—again.

Instead, Emira Maresh bent her head against his bare and blood-stained chest, and cried.

Kell knelt there, frozen, before lifting his tired arms and wrapping them gingerly around the queen.

"I prayed," she whispered, over and over and over as he helped her to her feet.

The king was there, then, in the doorway, breathless, as if he'd run the length of the palace, Tieren at his side. Maxim stormed forward, and again Kell braced himself for the attack, but the king said nothing, only folded Kell and Emira both into a silent hug.

It was not a gentle thing, that embrace. The king held on to Kell as if he were the only stone structure in a violent storm. Held so hard it hurt, but Kell didn't pull away.

When at last Maxim withdrew, taking Emira with him, Kell went to his brother's bed. To Rhy. Brought a hand to the prince's chest just to feel the beat. And there it was, steady, impossible, and as his own heart finally began to slow, he felt Rhy's again behind his ribs, nestled against his, an echo, still distant but growing nearer with every beat.

Kell's brother did not look like a man close to death.

The color was high in Rhy's cheeks, the hair curling against his brow a glossy black, rich, at odds with the mussed cushions and wrinkled sheets that spoke of suffering, of struggle. Kell ducked his head and pressed his lips to Rhy's brow, willing him to wake and make some tease about damsels in distress, or spells and magic kisses. But the prince didn't stir. His eyelids didn't flutter. His pulse didn't lift.

Kell squeezed his brother's shoulder gently, but still the prince didn't wake, and he would have shaken Rhy if Tieren hadn't touched Kell's wrist, guided his hand away.

"Be patient," said the *Aven Essen,* gently.

Kell swallowed and turned back toward the room, suddenly aware of how quiet it was, despite the presence of the king and queen, the growing audience of priests and guards, including Tieren and Hastra, the latter now in common clothes. Lila hung back in the doorway, pale with exhaustion and relief. And in the corner stood Alucard Emery, whose reddened eyes had turned storm-dark irises to sunset blue.

Kell couldn't bear to ask what had happened, what they'd seen. The whole room wore the pall of the haunted, the too-still features of the shocked. It was so quiet Kell could hear the music of the damned winner's ball still trilling on overhead.

So quiet he could—finally—hear Rhy's breathing, soft and steady.

And Kell so badly wished they could stay in this moment, wished he could lie down beside the prince and sleep and avoid the explanations, the accusations of failure and betrayal. But he could see the questions in their eyes as they looked from Lila to him, taking in his sudden return, his bloody state.

Kell swallowed and began to speak.

XI

The boundary between the worlds gave way like silk beneath a sharpened blade.

Osaron met no resistance, nothing but shadow and a step, a moment of nothing—that narrow gap between the end of one world and the beginning of the next—before Holland's boot—*his* boot—found solid ground again.

The way between his London and Holland's had been hard, the spells old but strong, the gates rusted shut. But like old metal, there were weaknesses, cracks, and in those years of questing from his throne, Osaron had found them.

That doorway had resisted, but this one gave.

Gave onto something marvelous.

The castle was gone, the cold less brittle, and everywhere he looked was the pulse of magic. It trailed in lines before his eyes, rising off the world like steam.

So much power.

So much *potential*.

Osaron stood in the middle of the street and smiled.

This was a world worth shaping.

A world that worshipped magic.

And it would worship *him*.

Music drifted on the breeze, as faint as far-off chimes, and all around was light and life. Even the darkest shadows here were shallow pools compared to his world, to Holland's. The air was rich with the scent of flowers and winter wine, the hum of energy, the heady pulse of power.

The coin hung from Osaron's fingers, and he tossed it away, drawn toward the blooming light at the center of the city. With every step he felt himself grow stronger, magic flooding his lungs, his blood. A river glowed red in the distance, its pulse so strong, so vital, while Holland's voice was a fading heartbeat in his head.

"*As Anasae,*" it whispered over and over, trying to dispel Osaron as if he were a common curse.

Holland, he chided, *I am not a piece of spellwork to be undone.*

A scrying board hung nearby, and as his fingers brushed it, they snagged the threads of magic and the spellwork shuddered and transformed, the words shifting into the *Antari* mark for darkness. For shadow. For *him*.

As Osaron passed lantern after lantern, the fires flared, shattering glass and spilling into night while the street beneath his boots turned smooth and black, darkness spreading like ice. Spells unraveled all around him, elements morphed from one into another as the spectrum tilted, fire into air, air into water, water into earth, earth into stone, stone into magic magic *magic*—

A shout went up behind him, and the clatter of hooves as a carriage reared. The man clutching the reins spat at him in a language he'd never heard, but words were threaded together just like spells, and the letters unraveled and rewove in Osaron's head, taking on a shape he knew.

"Get out of the way, you fool!"

Osaron narrowed his eyes, reaching for the horse's reins.

"*I'm not a fool,*" he said. "*I am a god.*"

His grip tightened on the leather straps.

"*And gods should be worshipped.*"

Shadow spread up the reins as fast as light. It closed over the driver's hands, and the man gasped as Osaron's magic slid under skin and into vein, wrapped around muscle and bone and heart.

The driver didn't fight the magic, or if he did, it was a battle quickly lost. He half leaped, half fell from the carriage seat to kneel at the shadow king's feet, and when he looked up, Osaron saw the smoky echo of his own true form twining in the man's eyes.

Osaron considered him; the threads of power running beneath his own command were dull, weak.

So, he thought, *this is a strong world, but not all are strong within it.*

He would find a use for the weak. Or weed them out. They were kindling, dry but thin, quick to burn, but not enough to keep him burning long.

"*Stand,*" he commanded, and when the man clambered to his feet, Osaron reached out and wrapped his fingers loosely around the driver's throat, curious what would happen if he poured more of himself into such a modest shell. Wondering how much it could hold.

His fingers tightened, and the veins beneath them bulged, turning black and fracturing across the man's skin. Hundreds of tiny fissures shone as the man began to *burn* with magic, his mouth open in a silent, euphoric scream. His skin peeled away, and his body flickered ember red and then black before he finally *crumbled.*

Osaron's hand fell away, ash trailing through the night air.

He was so caught up in the moment that he *almost* didn't notice Holland trying once again to surface, to claw his way through the gap in his attention.

Osaron closed his eyes, turning his focus inward.

You're becoming unpleasant.

He wrapped the threads of Holland's mind around his fingers and pulled until, deep in his head, the *Antari* let out a guttural scream. Until the resistance—*and the noise*—finally crumbled like the driver in the road, like every mortal thing that tried to stand in the way of a god.

In the ensuing quiet, Osaron turned his attention back to the beauty of his new kingdom. The streets, alive with people. The sky, alive with stars. The palace, alive with light—Osaron marveled at this last, for it was not a squat stone castle like in Holland's world, but an arcing structure of glass and gold that seemed to pierce the sky, a place truly fit for a king.

The rest of the world seemed to blur around the dazzling point of that palace as he made his way through the streets. The river came into view, a pulsing red, and the air caught in his chest.

Beautiful. Wasted.

We could be so much more.

A market burned in shades of crimson and gold along the riverbank, and ahead, the palace stairs were strewn with bouquets of frost-laced flowers. As his boots hit the first step, a row of flowers lost their icy sheen and blossomed back into vivid color.

Too long, he'd been holding back.

Too long.

With every step, the color spread; the flowers grew wild, blossoms bursting and stems shining with thorns, all of it spilling down the stairs in carpets of green and gold, white and red.

And all of it thrived—*he* thrived—in this strange, rich world, so ripe and ready for taking.

Oh, he would do such wondrous things.

In his wake, the flowers changed again, and again, and again, petals turning now to ice, now to stone. A riot of color, a chaos of form, until finally, overcome by their euphoric transformation, they went black and smooth as glass.

Osaron reached the top of the stairs, and came face-to-face with a huddle of men waiting for him before the doors. They were speaking to him, and for a moment he simply stood and let the words spill tangled into the air, nothing but inelegant sounds cluttering his perfect night. Then he sighed and gave them shape.

"I said *stop*," one of the guards was warning.

"Don't come any closer," ordered a second as he drew a sword, its edge glinting with spellwork. To weaken magic. Osaron almost smiled, though the gesture still felt stiff on Holland's face.

There was only one word for *stop* in his tongue—*anasae*—and even that meant only to unravel, undo. One word for ending magic, but so many to make it *grow, spread, change.*

Osaron lifted one hand, a casual gesture, power spiraling down around his fingers toward these men in their thin metal shells, where it—

An explosion tore through the sky above.

Osaron craned his neck and saw, over the crown of the palace, a sphere of colored light. And then another, and another, in bursts of red and gold. Cheers reached him on the wind, and he felt the resonant beat of bodies overhead.

Life.

Power.

"Stop," said the men in their clumsy tongue.

But Osaron was just getting started.

The air swirled around his feet, and he rose up into the night.

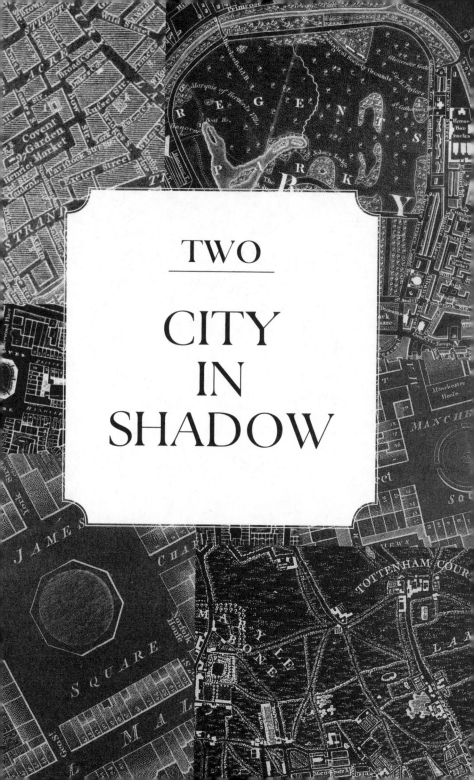

TWO

CITY IN SHADOW

I

Kisimyr Vasrin was a little drunk.

Not unpleasantly so, just enough to dull the edges of the winner's ball, smooth the faces on the roof, and blur the mindless chatter into something more enjoyable. She could still hold her own in a fight—that was how she judged it, not by how many glasses she'd gone through, but how quickly she could turn the contents of her glass into a weapon. She tipped the goblet, poured the wine straight out, and watched it freeze into a knife before it landed in her other hand.

There, she thought, leaning back against the cushions. *Still good.*

"You're sulking," said Losen from somewhere behind the couch.

"Nonsense," she drawled. "I'm celebrating." She tipped her head back to look at her protégé and added dryly, "Can't you tell?"

The young man chuckled, eyes alight. "Suit yourself, *mas arna.*"

Arna. Saints, when had she gotten old enough to be called a mistress? She wasn't even thirty. Losen swept away to dance with a pretty young noble, and Kisimyr drained her glass and settled back to watch, gold tassels jingling in her ropes of hair.

The rooftop was a pretty enough place for a party—pillars rising into pointed crowns against the night sky, spheres of hearth fire warming the late winter air, and marble floors so white they shone like moonlit clouds—but Kisimyr had always preferred the arena. At least in a fight, she knew how to act, knew the point of the exercise. Here in society, she was meant to smile and bow and, even worse, *mingle.* Kisimyr hated mingling. She wasn't *vestra,* or *ostra,* just old-fashioned

London stock, flesh and blood and a good turn of magic. A good turn honed into something more.

All around her, the other magicians drank and danced, their masks mounted like brooches on their shoulders or worn like hoods thrown back atop their hair. The faceless ones registered as ornament, while the more featured cast unnerving expressions on the backs of heads and cloaks. Her own feline mask sat beside her on the couch, dented and singed from so many rounds in the ring.

Kisimyr wasn't in the mood for a party. She knew how to feign grace, but inside she was still seething from the final match. It had been close—there was that much.

But of all the people to lose to, it had to be that obnoxious prettyboy noble, Alucard Emery.

Where was the bastard, anyway? No sign of him. Or the king and queen, for that matter. Or the prince. Or his brother. Strange. The Veskan prince and princess were here, roaming as if in search of prey, while the Faroan regent held his own small court against a pillar, but the Arnesian royal family was nowhere to be seen.

Her skin prickled in warning, the way it did the instant before a challenger made their move in the ring. Something was off.

Wasn't it?

Saints, she couldn't tell.

A servant in red and gold swept past, and she plucked a fresh drink from the tray, spiced wine that tickled her nose and warmed her fingers before it touched her tongue.

Ten more minutes, she told herself, and she could go.

She was, after all, a victor, even if she hadn't won this year.

"Mistress Kisimyr?"

She looked up at the young *vestra,* beautiful and tan, eyelids painted gold to match his sash. She cast a look around for Losen, and sure enough found her protégé watching, looking smug as a young cat offering up a mouse. "I'm Viken Rosec—" started the noble.

"And I'm not in the mood to dance," she cut in.

"Perhaps, then," he said coyly, "I could keep your company here."

He didn't wait for permission—she could feel the sofa dip beside her—but Kisimyr's attention had already drifted past him, to the figure standing at the roof's edge. One minute that stretch was empty, dark, and then the next, as a last firework lit the sky, he was there. From here, the man was nothing but a silhouette against the darker night, but the way he looked around—as if taking in the rooftop for the first time—set her on edge. He wasn't a noble or a tournament magician, and he didn't belong to any of the entourages she'd seen throughout the *Essen Tasch*.

Curiosity piqued, she rose from the couch, leaving her mask on the cushions beside Viken as the stranger stepped forward between two pillars, revealing skin as fair as a Veskan's, but hair blacker than her own. A midnight blue half cloak spilled over his shoulders, and on his head, where a magician's mask might be, was a silver crown.

A royal?

But she'd never seen him before. Never caught this particular scent of power, either. Magic rippled off him with every step, woodsmoke and ash and fresh-turned earth, at odds with the flowered notes that filled the roof around them.

Kisimyr wasn't the only one to notice.

One by one the faces at the ball turned toward the corner.

The stranger's own head was bowed slightly, as if considering the marble floor beneath his polished black boots. He passed a table on which someone had left a helmet, and drew a finger almost absently along the metal jaw. As he did, it crumbled to ash—no, not ash, but sand, a thousand glittering specks of glass.

A cold breeze brushed them away.

Kisimyr's heart quickened.

Without thinking, her own feet carried her forward, matching him step for step as he crossed the roof until they both stood at opposite edges of the broad polished circle used for dancing.

The music stopped abruptly, broke off into half-formed chords and then silence as the strange figure strode into the center of the floor.

"*Good evening,*" said the stranger.

As he spoke, he raised his head, black hair shifting to reveal two all-black eyes, shadows twisting in their depths.

Those close enough to meet his gaze tensed and recoiled. Those farther afield must have felt the ripple of unease, because they too began to edge away.

The Faroans watched, gems dancing in their darkened faces as they tried to understand if this was some kind of show. The Veskans stood stock still, waiting for the stranger to draw a weapon. But the Arnesians roiled. Two guards peeled away to send word through the palace below.

Kisimyr held her ground.

"*I hope I haven't interrupted,*" he continued, his voice becoming two—one soft, the other resonant, one scattered on the air like that pile of sand, the other crystal clear inside her head.

His black eyes tracked over the roof. "*Where is your king?*"

The question rang through Kisimyr's skull, and when she tried to force his presence back, the stranger's attention flicked toward her, landing like a stone.

"*Strong,*" he mused. "*Everything here is strong.*"

"Who are you?" demanded Kisimyr, her own voice sounding thin by comparison.

The man seemed to consider this a moment and then said, "*Your new king.*"

That sent a ripple through the crowd.

Kisimyr stretched out one arm, and the nearest pitcher of wine emptied, its contents sailing toward her fingers and hardening into an icy spear.

"Is that a threat?" she said, trying to focus on the man's hands instead of those eerie black eyes, that resonant voice. "I am a high magician of Arnes. A victor of the *Essen Tasch*. I bear the favored sigil of the House of Maresh. And I will not let you harm my king."

The stranger cocked his head, amused. "*You are strong, mage,*" he said, spreading his arms as if to welcome her embrace. His smile widened. "*But you are not strong enough to stop me.*"

Kisimyr spun her spear once, almost idly, and then lunged.

She made it two steps before the marble floor splashed beneath her feet, stone one instant and water the next, and then, before she could reach him, stone again. Kisimyr gasped, her body shuddering to a halt as the rock hardened around her ankles.

Losen was starting toward her, but she held a hand up without taking her gaze off the stranger.

It wasn't possible.

The man hadn't even moved. Hadn't touched the stone, or said anything to change its shape. He'd simply willed it, out of one form, and into another, as if it were nothing.

"*It* is *nothing*," he said, words filling the air and slinking through her head. *"My will is magic. And magic is my will."*

The stone began to climb her shins as he continued forward, crossing to her in long, slow strides.

Behind him, Jinnar and Brost moved to attack. They made it to the edge of the circle before he sent them back with a flick of his wrist, their bodies crashing hard into pillars. Neither rose.

Kisimyr growled and summoned the other facet of her power. The marble rumbled at her feet. It cracked, and split, and still the stranger came toward her. By the time she staggered free, he was there, close enough to kiss. She didn't even feel his fingers until they were already circling her wrist. She looked down, shocked by the touch, at once feather-light and solid as stone.

"*Strong*," he mused again. *"But are you strong enough to hold me?"*

Something passed between them, skin to skin, and then deeper, spreading up her arm and through her blood, strange and wonderful, like light, like honey in her veins, sweet and warm and—

No.

She pushed back, trying to force the magic away, but his fingers only tightened, and suddenly the pleasant heat became a burn, the light became a fire. Her bones went hot, her skin cracked, every inch of her ablaze, and Kisimyr began to scream.

II

Kell told them everything.

Or, at least, everything they needed to know. He didn't say that he'd gone with Ojka *willingly,* still fuming from his imprisonment and his fight with the king. He didn't say that he'd condemned the prince's life and his own rather than agreeing to the creature's terms. And he didn't say that, at some point, he'd given up. But he did tell the king and queen of Lila, and how she'd saved his life—and Rhy's—and brought him home. He told them of Holland's survival, and Osaron's power, of the cursed metal collar, and the Red London token in the demon's hand.

"Where is this monster now?" demanded the king.

Kell sagged. "I don't know." He needed to say more, to warn them of Osaron's strength, but all he could manage was, "I promise, Your Majesty, I will find him." His anger didn't rage—he was too tired for that—but it burned coldly in his veins.

"And I will kill him."

"You will stay here," said the king, gesturing to the prince's bed. "At least until Rhy wakes."

Kell started to protest, but Tieren's hand settled again on his shoulder, and he felt himself sway beneath the priest's influence. He sank into a chair beside his brother's bed as the king left to summon his guards.

Beyond the windows, the fireworks had begun, showering the sky in red and gold.

Hastra, who hadn't taken his eyes from the sleeping prince, stood against the wall nearby, whispering softly. His brown curls were touched with gold in the lamplight, and he was turning something over and over in his fingers. A coin. And at first Kell thought the words were some spell for calm, remembering that Hastra had once been destined for the Sanctuary, but soon the words registered as simple Arnesian. It was a prayer, of sorts, but he was asking for, of all things, forgiveness.

"What's wrong?" asked Kell.

Hastra reddened. "It's my fault she found you," whispered his former guard. "My fault she took you."

She. Hastra meant *Ojka.*

Kell rubbed his eyes. "It's not," he said, but the youth just shook his head stubbornly, and Kell couldn't bear the guilt in his eyes, too close a mirror of his own. He glanced instead at Tieren, who now stood with Lila, her chin in his hand as he tilted her head to see the damage to her eye, not even the hint of surprise in his own.

Alucard Emery still lurked, half in shadow, in the corner beyond the royal bed, his gaze leveled not on Kell or the rest of the room, but on Rhy's chest as it rose and fell. Kell knew of the captain's gift, his ability to see the threads of magic. Now Alucard stood, perfectly still, only his eyes following some invisible specter as it wove around the prince.

"Give him time," murmured the captain, answering a question Kell hadn't yet asked. Kell took a breath, hoping to say something civil, but Alucard's attention flicked suddenly to the balcony doors.

"What is it?" asked Kell as the man pushed off the wall, peering out into the red-tinged night.

"I thought I saw something."

Kell tensed. "Saw what?"

Alucard didn't answer. He brushed his hand along the glass, clearing the steam. After a moment, he shook his head. "Must have been a trick of the—"

He was cut off by a scream.

Not in the room, not in the palace at all, but overhead.

On the roof. The winner's ball.

Kell was on his feet before he knew if he could stand. Lila, always the faster, had her knife out, even though no one had seen to her wounds.

"Osaron?" she demanded as Kell surged toward the door.

Alucard was on his heels, but Kell spun, and forced him back with a single, vicious shove. "No. Not you."

"You can't expect me to stay—"

"I expect you to watch over the prince."

"I thought that was your job," snarled Alucard.

The blow landed, but Kell still barred the captain's path. "If you go upstairs, you will die."

"And you won't?" he challenged.

Behind Kell's eyes, the image flared, of the darkness swarming in Holland's eyes. The hum of power. The horror of a curse noose-tight around his neck. Kell swallowed. "If I *don't* go, *everyone* will die."

He looked to the queen, who opened her mouth and closed it several times as if searching for an order, a protest, but in the end, she said only, "Go."

Lila hadn't waited around for permission.

She was halfway up the stairs when he caught her, and he wouldn't have if not for her injured leg.

"How did he get up there?" muttered Kell.

"How did he get out of Black London?" countered Lila. "How did he cut off your power? How did he—"

"Fine," growled Kell. "Point taken."

They shoved past the mounting guards, launching themselves up flight after flight.

"Just so we're clear," said Lila. "I don't care if Holland's still in there. If I get a chance, I'm not sparing him."

Kell swallowed. "Agreed."

When they reached the rooftop doors, Lila grabbed his collar, hauling his face toward hers. Her eyes bore into his, one smooth, the other fractured into shadow and light. Beyond the doors, the scream had stopped.

"Are you strong enough to win?" she asked.

Was he? This wasn't a tournament magician. Wasn't even a sliver of magic like Vitari. Osaron had destroyed an entire world. Changed another on a whim.

"I don't know," he said honestly.

Lila flashed a glimmer of a smile, sharp as glass.

"Good," she answered, pushing open the door. "Only fools are certain."

Kell didn't know what he expected to find on the roof.

Blood. Bodies. A sick version of the stone forest that had once stretched at the feet of White London's castle, with its petrified corpses.

What he saw instead was a crowd caught between confusion and terror, and at its center, the shadow king. Kell felt the blood drain from his face, replaced by cold hatred for the figure in the middle of the roof—the monster wearing Holland's skin—as he turned in a slow circle, considering his audience. Surrounded by the most powerful magicians in the world, and not a hint of fear in those black eyes. Only amusement, and the sharp edge of want threaded through it. Standing there, in the center of the marble circle, Osaron seemed the center of the world. Unmovable. Invincible.

The scene shifted, and Kell saw Kisimyr Vasrin lying on the ground at Osaron's feet. At least—what was left of her. One of the strongest magicians in Arnes, reduced to a scorched black corpse, the metal rings in her hair now melted down to dots of molten light.

"Anyone else?" asked Osaron in that sick distortion of Holland's voice, silky and wrong and somehow everywhere at once.

The Veskan royals crouched behind their sorcerers, a pair of frightened children cowering in silver and green. Lord Sol-in-Ar, even for his lack of magic, did not retreat, though his Faroan entourage could be seen urging him behind a pillar. At the marble platform's edge, the rest of the magicians gathered, their elements summoned—flame swirled around fingers, shards of ice held like knives—but no one struck. They were tournament fighters, used to parading around a ring, where the greatest thing at risk was pride.

What had Holland said to Kell, so many months ago?

Do you know what makes you weak?

You've never had to be strong.

You've certainly never had to fight for your life.

Now Kell saw that flaw in these men and women, their unmasked faces pale with fear.

Lila touched his arm, a knife ready in her other hand. Neither spoke, but neither needed to. In palace balls and tournament games they were mismatched, awkward, but they understood each other here and now, surrounded by danger and death.

Kell nodded, and without a word, Lila slipped thief-smooth into the shadows around the roof's edge.

"*No one?*" goaded the shadow king.

He brought a boot to rest on Kisimyr's remains, and they gave way like ash beneath his step. "*For all your strength, you surrender so easily.*"

Kell took a single breath and forced himself forward, out of the shelter at the circle's edge, and into the light. When Osaron saw him, he actually smiled.

"*Kell,*" said the monster. "*Your resilience surprises me. Have you come to kneel before me? Have you come to beg?*"

"I've come to fight."

Osaron tipped his head. "*The last time we met, I left you screaming.*"

Kell's limbs shook, not with fear but anger. "The last time we met, I was in chains." The air around him sang with power. "Now I'm free."

Osaron's smile widened. "*But I have seen your heart, and it is bound.*"

Kell's hands curled into fists. The marble beneath his feet trembled and began to splinter. Osaron flicked his wrist, and the night came crashing down on Kell. It crushed the air from his lungs, forcing him toward his knees. It took all his strength to stay upright under the weight, and after a horrible second he realized it wasn't the air straining against him—Osaron's will pressed against his very bones. Kell was *Antari*. No one had ever managed to will his body against him. Now his joints ground together, his limbs threatening to crack.

"*I will see you kneel before your king.*"

"No."

Kell tried again to summon the marble floor, and the stone trembled as will clashed against will. He kept his feet, but realized by the almost bored expression on the other *Antari*'s face that the shadow king was toying with him.

"Holland," Kell snarled, trying to subdue the horror. "If you are in there, fight. Please—fight."

A sour look crossed Osaron's face, and then something crashed behind Kell, armor against wood as more guards barreled onto the roof, Maxim at their center.

The king's voice boomed through the night. "How dare you set foot in my palace?"

Osaron's attention flicked to the king, and Kell gasped, suddenly free from the weight of the creature's will. He staggered a step, already freeing his knife and drawing blood, red drops falling to the pale stone.

"How dare you claim to be king?"

"I have more claim than you."

Another twitch of those long fingers, and the king's crown sailed from his head—or it would have if Maxim hadn't snatched it from the air with terrifying speed. The king's eyes glowed, as if molten, as he crushed the crown between his hands, and drew it out into a blade. A single, fluid gesture that spoke of days long past, when Maxim Maresh had been the Steel Prince instead of the Golden King.

"Surrender, demon," he ordered, "or be slain."

At his back, the royal guards raised their swords, spellwork scrawled along the edges. The sight of the king and his guards seemed to shake the other magicians from their stupor. Some began to retreat, ushering their own royals off the roof or simply fleeing, while a few were bold enough to advance. But Kell knew they were no match. Not the guards, not the magicians, not even the king.

But the king's appearance had bought Kell something.

An advantage.

With Osaron's attention still on Maxim, Kell sank into a crouch. His blood had spread in brittle fractures across the stone floor, thin lines of red that reached and wrapped around the monster's boot.

"As Anasae," he ordered. *Dispel.* The words had been enough, once,

to purge Vitari from the world. Now, they did nothing. Osaron shot him a pitying glance, shadows twisting in his pitch black eyes.

Kell didn't retreat. He forced his hands flat. *"As Steno,"* he ordered, and the marble floor shattered into a hundred shards that rose and hurled themselves at the shadow king. The first one found home, burying itself in Osaron's leg, and Kell's hopes rose before he realized his mistake.

He hadn't gone for the kill.

That first stone blade was the only one to land. With nothing but a look, the rest of the shards faltered, slowed, stopped. Kell pushed with all his force, but his own body was one thing to will, and a hundred makeshift blades another, and Osaron quickly won, turning the stone fragments outward like the spokes on a wheel, the dazzling edges of a sun.

Osaron's hands drifted lazily up, and the shards trembled, like arrows on taut strings, but before he could unleash them on the guards and the king and the magicians on the roof, something passed through him.

A flinch. A shudder.

The shadows in his eyes went green.

Somewhere deep inside his body, Holland was fighting back.

The fragments of stone tumbled to the ground as Osaron stood frozen, all his attention focused inward.

Maxim saw the chance, and signaled.

The royal guards struck, a dozen men falling on one distracted god.

And for an instant, Kell thought it would be enough.

For an instant—

But then Osaron looked up, flashing black eyes and a defiant smile. And let them come.

"Wait!" shouted Kell, but it was too late.

The instant before the guards fell on the shadow king, the monster abandoned its shell. Darkness poured from Holland's stolen body, as thick and black as smoke.

The *Antari* collapsed, and the shadow that was Osaron moved, serpentine, across the roof. Hunting for another form.

Kell spun, looking for Lila, but couldn't see her through the crowd, the smoke.

And then, suddenly, the darkness turned on *him*.

No, thought Kell, who had already refused the monster once. He couldn't fathom another collar. The cold horror of a heartbeat stopping in his chest.

The darkness surged toward him, and Kell took an involuntary step back, bracing himself for an assault that never came. The shadow brushed his blood-streaked fingers, and pulled back, not so much repelled as considering.

The darkness *laughed*—a sickly sound—and began to draw itself together, to coalesce into a column, and then into a man. Not flesh and blood, but layered shadow, so dense it looked like fluid stone, some edges sharp and others blurred. A crown sat atop the figure's head, a dozen spires thrust upward like horns, their points faded into smoke.

The shadow king, in his true form.

Osaron drew in a breath, and the molten darkness at his center flared like embers, heat rippling the air around him. And yet he seemed solid as stone. As Osaron considered his hands, the fingers tapering less to fingertips than points, his mouth stretched into a cruel smile.

"It has been a long time since I was strong enough to hold my own shape."

His hand shot toward Kell's throat, but was stopped short as steel came singing through the air. Lila's knife caught Osaron in the side of the head, but the blade didn't lodge; it passed straight through.

So he wasn't real, wasn't *corporeal*. Not yet.

Osaron spared a glance at Lila, who was already drawing another blade. She slammed to a stop under his gaze, her body clearly straining against his hold, and Kell stole his chance once more, pressing his bloodstained palm to the creature's chest. But the shape turned to smoke around Kell's fingers, recoiling from his magic, and Osaron twisted back, annoyance etched across his stone features. Freed once more, Lila reached him, a guard's short sword in one hand, and swung the weapon in a vicious arc, carving down and across and through his body, shoulder to hip.

Osaron parted around the blade, and then he simply *dissolved*.

There one moment, and gone the next.

Kell and Lila stared at each other, breathless, stunned.

The guards were hauling an unconscious Holland roughly to his feet, his head lolling as, all around the roof, the men and woman stood as if under a spell, though it might have simply been shock, horror, confusion.

Kell met King Maxim's eyes across the roof.

"You have so much to learn."

He spun toward the sound, and found Osaron re-formed and standing, not in the broken center of the roof, but atop the railing at its edge, as if the spine of metal were solid ground. His cloak billowed in the breeze. A specter of a man. A shadow of a monster.

"You do not slay a god," he said. *"You worship him."*

His black eyes danced with dark delight.

"Do not worry. I will teach you how. And in time . . ."

Osaron spread his arms.

"I will make this world worthy of me."

Kell realized too late what was about to happen.

He started running just as Osaron tipped backward off the railing, and fell.

Kell sprinted, and got there just in time to see the shadow king hit the water of the Isle far below. His body struck without a splash, and as it broke the surface and sank, it began to plume like spilled ink through the current. Lila pressed against him, straining to see. Shouts were going up over the roof, but the two of them stood and watched in silent horror as the plume of darkness grew, and grew, and grew, spreading until the red of the river turned black.

III

Alucard paced the prince's room, waiting for news.

He hadn't heard anything since that single scream, the first shouts of guards in the hall, the steps above.

Rhy's lush curtains and canopies, his plush carpets and pillows, all created a horrible insulation, blocking out the world beyond and shrouding the room in an oppressive silence.

They were alone, the captain and the sleeping prince.

The king was gone. The priests were gone. Even the queen was gone. One by one they'd peeled away, each casting a glance at Alucard that said, *Sit, stay.* As if he would have left. He would have gladly abandoned the maddening quiet and the smothering questions, of course, but not Rhy.

The queen had been the last to leave. For several seconds she'd stood between the bed and the doors, as if physically torn.

"Your Majesty," he'd said. "I will keep him safe."

Her face had changed, then, the regal mask slipping to reveal a frightened mother. "If only you could."

"Can *you*?" he'd asked, and her wide brown eyes had gone to Rhy, lingering there for a long moment before at last she'd turned and fled.

Something drew his attention to the balcony. Not movement exactly, but a change in the light. When he approached the glass doors, he saw shadow spilling down the side of the palace like a train, a tail, a curtain of glossy black that shimmered, solid, smoke, solid, as it ran from the riverbank below all the way to the roof.

It had to be magic, but it had no color, no light. If it followed the warp and weft of power, he could not see the threads.

Kell had told them about Osaron, the poisonous magic from another London. But how could a magician do *this*? How could anyone?

"It's a demon," Kell had said. "A piece of living, breathing magic."

"A piece of magic that thinks itself a man?" asked the king.

"No," he'd answered. "A piece of magic that thinks itself a *god*."

Now, staring out at the column of shadow, Alucard understood—this *thing* wasn't obeying the lines of power at all. It was stitching them from nothing.

He couldn't look away.

The floor seemed to tilt, and Alucard felt like he was tipping forward toward the glass doors and the curtain of black beyond. If he could get closer, maybe he could see the threads. . . .

The captain lifted his hands to the balcony doors, about to push them open, when the prince shifted in his sleep. A soft groan beyond him, the subtle hitch of breath, and that was all it took to make Alucard turn back, the darkness beyond the glass momentarily forgotten as he crossed to the bed.

"Rhy," he whispered. "Can you hear me?"

A crinkle between the prince's brows. A ghost of strain along his jaw. Small signs, but Alucard clung to them, and brushed the dark curls from Rhy's brow, trying to brush away the image of the prince desiccating atop the royal sheets.

"Please wake up."

His touch trailed down the prince's sleeve, coming to rest on his hand.

Alucard had always loved Rhy's hands, smooth palms and long fingers, meant for touching, for talking, for music.

He didn't know if Rhy played anymore, but he had once, and when he did, he played the way he spoke a language. Fluently.

A ghost of memory behind his eyes. Nails dancing over skin.

"Play me something," Alucard had said, and Rhy had smiled his dazzling smile, the candlelight turning his amber eyes to gold as his fingers drifted, chords flitting over shoulder, ribs, waist.

"I'd rather play you."

Alucard threaded his fingers through the prince's, now, relieved to find them warm, relieved again when Rhy's hand tightened, ever so slightly, on his own. Carefully, Alucard climbed into the bed. Cautiously, he stretched himself beside the sleeping prince.

Beyond the glass, the darkness began to splinter, spread, but Alucard's eyes were on Rhy's chest as it rose and fell, a hundred silver threads knitting slowly, slowly back together.

IV

At last, Osaron was *free*.

There had been an instant on the roof—the space between a breath in and a breath out—when it felt as if the pieces of himself might scatter in the wind without flesh and bone to hold them in. But he did *not* scatter. Did not dissolve. Did not cease to be.

He'd grown strong over the months in that other world.

Stronger over the minutes in this one.

And he was free.

A thing so strange, so long forgotten, he hardly knew it.

How long had he sat on that throne at the center of a sleeping city, watching the pulse of his world go still, watching until even the snow stopped falling and hung suspended in the air and there was nothing left to do but sleep and wait and wait and wait and wait . . .

To be free.

And now.

Osaron smiled, and the river shimmered. He laughed, and the air shook. He flexed, and the world shuddered.

It welcomed him, this world.

It *wanted* change.

It knew, in its marrow, in its bones, that it could be *more*.

It whispered to him, *Make, make, make.*

This world burned with promise, the way his own had burned so long ago, before it went to ash. But he had been a young god then, too eager to give, to be loved.

He knew better now.

Humans did not make good rulers. They were children, servants, subjects, pets, food, fodder. They had a place, just as he had a place, and he would be the god they needed, and they would love him for it. He would show them how.

He would feed them power. Just enough to keep them bound. A taste of what could be. What *they* could be. And as he wove around them, through them, he would draw a measure of their strength, their magic, their potential, and it would feed him, stoke him, and they would give it freely, because he was theirs, and they were his, and together they would make something extraordinary.

I am mercy, he whispered in their ears.

I am power.

I am king.

I am god.

Kneel.

And all over the city—his new city—they *were* kneeling.

It was a natural thing, to kneel, a matter of gravity, of letting your weight carry you down. Most of them *wanted* to do it; he could feel their submission.

And those who didn't, those who refused—

Well, there was no place for them in Osaron's kingdom.

No place for them at all.

V

"Two cheers to the wind . . ."

"And three to the women . . ."

"And four to the splendid sea."

The last word trailed off, dissolving into the coarser sounds of glasses knocking against tables, ale splashing onto floor.

"Is that really how it goes?" asked Vasry, tipping his head back against the booth. "I thought it was *wine,* not *wind.*"

"Wouldn't be a sea shanty without the wind," said Tav.

"Wouldn't be a shanty without the wine," countered Vasry, slurring his words. Lenos didn't know if it was for effect or because the sailor—the entire crew for that matter—was soused.

The entire crew, that was, except for Lenos. He'd never been big on the stuff (didn't like the way it muddled everything and left him feeling ill for days), but nobody seemed to notice whether or not he actually drank, so long as he had a glass in his hand for toasting. And he always did. Lenos had a glass when the crew toasted their captain, Alucard Emery, the victor of the *Essen Tasch,* and had it still when they kept on toasting him every half hour or so, until they lost track.

Now that the tournament was done, most of the pennants sat soaking up ale on tabletops, and the silver-and-blue flame on Alucard's banner was looking muddier by the round.

Their illustrious captain was long gone, probably toasting himself up at the winner's ball. If Lenos strained, he could hear the occasional echo of fireworks over the rattle of the crowd in the Wandering Road.

There'd be a proper parade in the morning, and a final wave of celebration (and half of London still in their cups), but tonight, the palace was for the champions, the taverns for the rest.

"Any sign of Bard?" asked Tav.

Lenos looked around, scanning the crowded inn. He hadn't seen her, not since the first round of drinks. The crew teased him for the way he was around her, mistaking his skittishness for shyness, attraction, even fear—and maybe it was fear, at least a little, but if so, it was the smart kind. Lenos feared Lila the way a rabbit feared a hound. The way a mortal feared lightning after a storm.

A shiver ran through him, sudden and cold.

He'd always been sensitive to the balance of things. Could have been a priest, if he'd had a bit more magic. He knew when things were right—that wonderful feeling like warm sun on a cool day— and he knew when they were *aven*—like Lila, with her strange past and stranger power—and he knew when they were wrong.

And right now, something was wrong.

Lenos took a sip of ale to steady his nerves—his reflection a frowning amber smudge on its surface—and got to his feet. The *Spire*'s first mate caught his eye, and rose as well. (Stross knew about his *moments,* and unlike the rest of the crew, who called him odd, superstitious, Stross seemed to believe him. Or, at least, not disbelieve him outright.)

Lenos moved through the room in a kind of daze, caught up in the strange spell of the feeling, the cord of wrongness like a rope tugging him along. He was halfway to the door when the first shout came from the tavern window.

"There's something in the river!"

"Yeah," Tav called back, "big floating arenas. Been there all week."

But Lenos was still moving toward the tavern's entrance. He pushed open the door, unmoved by the sudden cut of cold wind.

The streets were emptier than usual, the first heads just poking out to see.

Lenos walked, Stross on his heels, until he rounded the corner and saw the edge of the night market, its crowd shifting to the riverbanks, tilting toward the red water like loose cargo on a ship.

His heart thudded in his chest as he pushed forward, his slim body slipping through where Stross's broad form lodged and stuck. There, ahead, the crimson glow of the Isle, and—

Lenos stopped.

Something was spreading along the river's surface, like an oil slick, blotting out the light, replacing it with something black, and glistening, and wrong. The darkness slipped onto the bank, sloshing up against the dead winter grass, the stone walk, leaving an iridescent streak with every lapping wave.

The sight tugged at Lenos's limbs, that same downward pull, easy as gravity, and when he felt himself stepping forward, he tore his gaze away, forced himself to stop.

To his right, a man stumbled forward to the river's edge. Lenos tried to catch his sleeve, but the man was already past him, with a woman following close behind. All around, the crowd was torn between staggering back and jostling forward, and Lenos, unable to move *away,* could only fight to hold his ground.

"Stop!" called a guard as the man who'd swept past Lenos sank to one knee and reached out, as if to touch the river's surface. Instead, the river touched *him,* stretched out a hand made of blackish water and wrapped its fingers around the man's arm, and pulled him in. Screams went up, swallowing the splash, the instant of struggle before the man went under.

The crowd recoiled as the oily sheen began to smooth, went silent as it waited for the man—or his body—to surface.

"Stand aside!" demanded another guard, forcing his way forward. He was almost to the bank when the man reappeared. The guard stumbled back in shock as the man came up, not gasping for air, or struggling against the river's hold, but calm and slow, as if rising from a bath. Gasps and murmurs as the man climbed out of the river and onto the bank, oblivious to the waterlogged clothes weighing him down. Dripping from his skin, the water looked clean, clear, but when it pooled on the stones, it glistened and moved.

Stross's hand was on Lenos's shoulder, straining, but he couldn't take his eyes from the man on the bank. There was something wrong with him. Something very wrong. Shadows swirled in his eyes, coiling like wisps of smoke, and his veins stood out against his tan skin, darkening to threads of black. But it was the rictus smile more than anything that made Lenos shiver.

The man spread his arms, streaming water, and announced boldly, "The king has come."

He threw his head back and began to laugh as the darkness climbed the banks around him, tendrils of black fog that reached like fingers, clawing their way forward into the street. The crowd was thrown into panic, the ones close enough to see now scrambling to get away, only to be penned in by those behind. Lenos turned, looking for Stross, but the man was nowhere to be seen. Down the bank, another scream. Somewhere in the distance, an echo of the man's words, now on a woman's lips, now a child's.

"The king has come."

"The king has come."

"The king has come," said an old man, eyes shining, "and he is *glorious*."

Lenos tried to get away, but the street was a roiling mass of bodies, crowded in by the shadow's reach. Most fought to get free, but dotting the crowd were those who couldn't tear their eyes from the black river. Those who stood, stiff as stone, transfixed by the glistening waves, the gravity of the spell pulling them down.

Lenos felt his own gaze drawn back into the murk and madness, stammered a prayer to the nameless saints even as his long limbs took a single step forward.

And then another.

His boots sank into the loamy soil of the riverbank, his thoughts quieting, vision narrowing to that mesmerizing dark. At the edge of his mind, he heard the rumble of hooves, like thunder, and then a voice, cutting through the chaos like a knife.

"Get back!" it shouted, and Lenos blinked, stumbling away from the reaching river right before a royal horse could crush him underfoot.

The massive steed reared up, but it was the figures mounted on top that held Lenos's attention now.

The *Antari* prince sat astride the horse, disheveled, his crimson coat open to reveal bare skin, a streak of blood, a detailed scar. And behind the black-eyed prince, clinging to him for dear life, was Lila Bard.

"Fucking beast," she muttered, nearly falling as she tried to free herself from the saddle. Kell Maresh—*Aven Vares*—hopped easily down, coat billowing around him, one hand resting on Bard's shoulder, and Lenos couldn't tell if the man was seeking balance or offering it. Bard's eyes scanned the crowd—one of them was decidedly *wrong,* a starburst of glassy light—before landing on Lenos. She managed a quick, pained smile before someone screamed.

Nearby a woman collapsed, a tendril of shadow wrapping itself around her leg. She clawed at it, but her fingers went straight through. Lila spun toward her, but the *Antari* prince got there first. He tried to force the fog back with a gust of wind, and when that didn't work, he produced a blade and carved a fresh line across his palm.

He knelt, hand hovering over the shadows that ran between the river and the woman's skin.

"*As Anasae,*" he ordered, but the substance only parted around the blood. The air itself seemed to vibrate with laughter as the shadows seeped into the woman's leg, staining skin before sinking into vein.

The *Antari* swore, and the woman shuddered, clutching at his sliced hand in fear. Blood streaked her fingers and, as Lenos watched, the shadows suddenly let go, recoiled from their host.

Kell Maresh was staring down at the place where his hand met hers.

"Lila!" he called, but she'd already seen, already had her own knife out. Blood welled across her skin as she shot toward a man on the bank, grabbing him a breath before the shadows could. Again, they recoiled.

The *Antari* and—no, the two *Antari,* thought Lenos, for that was what Bard was, that was what she had to be—began to grab everyone in reach, brushing stained fingers over hands and cheeks. But the blood did nothing to those already poisoned—they only snarled, and wiped it away, as if it were filth—and for every one they marked, two more fell before they could.

The royal *Antari* spun, breathless, taking in the scope, the scale. Instead of running from body to body, he held up his hands, palms a span apart. His lips moved and his blood pooled in the air, gathering itself into a ball. It reminded Lenos of the Isle itself, its red glow, an artery of magic, pulsing and vibrant.

With a single surging motion, the sphere rose above the panicked crowds and—

That was all Lenos saw before the shadows came for *him*.

Fingers of night snaked toward him, serpent fast. There was nowhere to go—the *Antari* was still casting his spell, and Lila was too far away—so Lenos held his breath and began to pray, the way he'd learned back in Olnis, when the storms got rough. He closed his eyes and prayed for calm as the shadows broke against him. For balance as they washed—hot and cold at once—over his skin. For stillness as they murmured soft as shoretide in his head.

Let me in, let me in, let me—

A drop of rain landed on his hand, another on his cheek, and then the shadows were retreating, taking their whispers with them. Lenos blinked, let out a shaky breath, and saw that the rain was red. All around him, dew-fine drops dotted faces, and shoulders, settled in mist along coats and gloves and boots.

Not rain, he realized.

Blood.

The shadows in the street dissolved beneath the crimson mist, and Lenos looked at the *Antari* prince in time to see the man sway from the effort. He'd carved a slice of safety, but it wasn't enough. Already the dark magic was shifting focus, form, dividing from a fist into an open hand, fingers of shadow surging inland.

"*Sanct,*" cursed the prince as hooves pounded down the street. A wave of royal guards reached the river and dismounted, and Bard moved quick as light between the armored men, brushing bloodied fingertips against the metal of their suits.

"Round up the poisoned," ordered Kell Maresh, already moving toward his horse.

The afflicted souls didn't flee, didn't attack, simply stood there, grinning and saying things about a shadow king who whispered in their ears, who told them of the world as it could be, would be, who played their souls like music and showed them the true power of a king.

The *Antari* prince swung up onto his mount.

"Keep everyone away from the banks," he called. Lila Bard hoisted herself up beside him with a grimace, arms wrapped tight around his waist, and Lenos was left standing there, dazed, as the prince kicked the horse into motion and the two vanished into the streets of London.

VI

They had to split up.

Kell didn't want to, that much was obvious, but the city was too big, the fog too fast.

He took the horse, because she refused it—plenty of other ways to die tonight.

"Lila," he'd said, and she'd expected him to chastise her, to order her back to the palace, but he'd only caught her by the arm and said, "Be careful." Tipped his forehead against hers and added, almost too low to be heard, "Please."

She'd seen so many versions of him in the past few hours. The broken boy. The grieving brother. The determined prince. This Kell was none of those and all of them, and when he kissed her, she tasted pain and fear and desperate hope. And then he was gone, a streak of pale skin against the night as he rode for the night market.

Lila took off on foot, heading for the nearest cluster of people.

The night should have been cold enough to keep them inside, but the last day of the tournament meant the last night of celebration, and the entire city had been in the taverns, ushering out the *Essen Tasch* in style. Crowds were spilling out into streets, some drawn by the chaos at the river's edge, and others still oblivious, drinking and humming and stumbling over their own feet.

They didn't notice the lack of red light at the city's heart, or the spreading fog, not until it was nearly upon them. Lila dragged the knife down her arm as she raced between them, pain lost beneath panic as blood pooled in her palm and she flicked her wrist, pricks of red lancing like needles through the air, marking skin. Revelers stiffened, shocked and searching for the source of the assault, but Lila didn't linger.

"Get inside," she called, racing past. "Lock the doors."

But the poisoned night didn't care about locked doors and shuttered windows, and soon Lila found herself pounding on houses, trying to beat the darkness in. A distant scream as someone fought back. A laugh as someone fell.

Her mind raced, even as her head spun.

Her Arnesian wasn't good enough, and the more blood she lost, the worse it got, until her speech dissolved from, "There's a monster in the city, moving in the fog, let me help. . . ." to simply, "Stay."

Most stared at her, wide-eyed, though she didn't know if it was the blood or the shattered eye or the sweat streaming down her face. She didn't care. She kept going. It was a lost cause, all of it, an impossible task when the shadows moved twice as fast as she could, and part of her wanted to give up, to pull back, to save what strength she had—only a fool fought when they *knew* they couldn't win—but somewhere out there, Kell was still trying, and she wouldn't give up until he did, so she forced herself on.

She rounded the corner and saw a woman lying in the road, pale dress pooling on the cold stones as she curled in on herself and clutched her head, fighting whatever monstrous force had clawed inside. Lila ran, hand outstretched, and was nearly to her when the woman went suddenly still. The fight went out of her limbs, and her breath clouded in the air above her face as she stretched out lazily against the cold stones, oblivious to the biting cold, and smiled.

"I can hear his voice," she said, full of rapture. "I can see his beauty." She turned her head toward Lila. Shadows slid through her eyes like a cloud over a field. "Let me show you."

Without warning, the woman sprang, lunging for Lila, fingers wrapping around her throat, and for an instant, she felt the press of searing heat and burning cold as Osaron's black magic tried to get in.

Tried—and failed.

The woman recoiled violently as if scorched, and Lila struck her hard across the face.

The woman crumpled to the ground, unconscious. It was a good sign. If she'd truly been possessed, a blade wouldn't have stopped her, let alone a fist.

Lila straightened, aware of the magic as it swept and curled around her. She couldn't shake the feeling that the darkness had eyes, and it was watching.

Intently.

"Come out, come out," she called softly, twirling her knife. The shadows wavered. "What's the matter, Osaron? Feeling shy? A little bare without a body?" She turned in a slow circle. "I'm the one who killed Ojka. I'm the one who stole Kell back." She spun the blade between her fingers, exuding a calm she didn't feel as the darkness shuddered around her and began to pull itself together, thickening into a column before it grew limbs, a face, a pair of eyes as black as ice at night and—

Somewhere nearby, a horse whinnied.

A shout went up—not the strangled cry of those fighting the spelled fog, but the simple, guttural sound of frustration. A voice she knew too well.

The shadows collapsed as Lila cut through them, racing toward the sound.

Toward Kell.

She found his horse first. Abandoned and galloping down the street toward her, a shallow slice along one flank.

"Dammit," she swore, trying to decide whether to bar the horse's path or dive out of the way. In the end she dove, letting the beast barrel past, then sprinted in the direction it had come. She followed the scent of his magic—rose and soil and leaves—and found Kell on the ground, surrounded, not by Osaron's fog, but by men, three of them with weapons dangling from their hands. A knife. An iron bar. A plank of wood.

Kell was on his feet at least, gripping one shoulder, his face ghostly pale. He didn't look like he had the blood left to stand, let alone strike back at the attackers. It wasn't until she got closer that she recognized one of the men as Tav, her shipmate from the *Night Spire,* and another as the man who'd played Kamerov at the Banner Night before the tournament. A third was dressed in the cloak and arms of a royal guard, his half sword held at the ready.

"Listen to me," Kell was saying. "You are stronger than this. You can fight back."

The men's faces contorted in glee, surprise, confusion. They spoke in their own voices, not the echoing two-speak Osaron had used on the roof, and yet there was a lilting cadence to their words, a singsong quality that chilled her.

"The king wants you."

"The king will have you."

"Come with us."

"Come and kneel."

"Come and beg."

Kell stiffened, jaw set. "You tell your king he will not take this city. You tell him—"

The man with the scrap of wood struck out, swinging at Kell's stomach. He caught the beam, wood lighting and burning to ash in his hands. The circle collapsed, Tav raising the iron bar, the guard stepping forward, but Lila was already kneeling, palms pressed to the cold ground. She remembered the words Kell had used. Summoned what was left of her strength.

"*As Isera,*" she said. *Freeze.*

Ice shot from beneath her hands, gliding along the ground and up men's bodies in a breath.

Lila didn't have Kell's control, couldn't tell the ice where to go, but he saw it coming and leaped back out of the spell's path, and when the frozen edge met his boots, it melted, leaving him untouched. The other men stood, encased in ice, the shadows still swimming in their eyes.

Lila straightened, and the night tilted dangerously beneath her feet, the spell stealing the last power from her veins.

Somewhere, another scream, and Kell took a step toward it, one knee nearly giving way before he caught himself against the wall.

"Enough," said Lila. "You can barely stand."

"Then you can heal me."

"With *what*?" she rasped, gesturing to her bruised and battered form. "We can't keep this up. We could both bleed ourselves dry and still not mark a fraction of this city." She let out an exhausted, humorless laugh. "You know I'm all for steep odds, but it's too much. Too many."

It was a lost cause, and if he couldn't see it—but he did, of course. She saw in his eyes, the set of his jaw, the lines in his face, that he knew it too. Knew it, and couldn't let it be. Couldn't surrender. Couldn't retreat.

"Kell," she said, gently.

"This is my city," he said, shaking visibly. "My home. If I can't protect it . . ."

Lila's fingers inched toward a loose rock in the street. She wouldn't let him kill himself, not like this. Not after everything. If he wouldn't listen to reason—

Hooves sounded against stone, and a moment later four horses rounded the bend, mounted by royal guards.

"Master Kell!" called the one at the front.

Lila recognized the man as one of the guards assigned to Kell. He was older, and he shot a look at Lila, and then, obviously not knowing how to address her, pretended she wasn't there. "The priests have warded the palace, and you are to return at once. King's orders."

Kell looked like he was about to curse the king. Instead he shook his head. "Not yet. We're marking the citizens wherever we can, but we haven't found a way to contain the shadows, or shield the city against—"

"It's too late," cut in the guard.

"What do you mean?" demanded Kell.

"Sir," said another voice, and the man at the back took off his helmet. Lila knew him. Hastra. The younger of Kell's guard. When he spoke, his voice was gentle, but his face was tight. "It's over, sir," he said. "The city has fallen."

VII

The city has fallen.

Hastra's words followed Kell through the streets, up the palace steps, through the halls. They couldn't be right.

Couldn't be true.

How could a city fall when so many were still fighting?

Kell burst into the Grand Hall.

The ballroom glittered, ornate, extravagant, but the mood had altered entirely. The magicians and nobles from the rooftop gala now huddled in the center of the room. The queen and her entourage carried bowls of water and pouches of sand to the priests drawing amplifiers on the polished marble floor and warding spells along each wall. Lord Sol-in-Ar stood with his back against a pillar, features grim but unreadable, and Prince Col and Princess Cora sat on the stairs, looking shell-shocked.

He found King Maxim by the platform where musicians in gold leaf had played each night, conferring with Master Tieren and the head of his guard.

"What do you mean, the city has fallen?" demanded Kell, storming across the marble floor. Between his bloodstained hands and his bare chest on display beneath his open coat, he knew he looked insane. He didn't care. "Why did you call me back?" Tieren tried to block his path, but Kell pushed past. "Do you have a plan?"

"My plan," said the king calmly, "is to stop you from getting yourself killed."

"It was *working*," Kell snarled.

"What was working?" asked Maxim. "Opening a vein over London?"

"If my blood can shield them—"

"How many did you shield, Kell?" demanded the king. "Ten? Twenty? A hundred? There are tens of *thousands* in this city."

Kell felt like he was back in White London, the steel noose cinching around his neck. Helpless. Desperate. "It is *something*—"

"It is *not enough.*"

"Do you have a better idea?"

"Not yet."

"Then, *Sanct,* let me do what I can!"

Maxim took him by the shoulders. "Listen to me," the king said, voice low. "What are Osaron's strengths? What are his weaknesses? What is he doing to our people? Can it be undone? How many questions have you failed to ask because you were too busy being valiant? You have no plan. No strategy. You have not found a crack in your enemy's armor, a place to slide your knife. Instead of devising an attack, you are out there, slashing blindly, not even able to land a blow because you're spending every drop of precious blood protecting others from an enemy we don't know how to best."

Everything in Kell tightened at that. "I was out there trying to protect *your people.*"

"And for every one you shielded, a dozen more were taken by the dark." There was no judgment in Maxim's voice, only grim resolve. "The city has fallen, Kell. It will not rise again without your help, but that does not mean you can save it alone." The king tightened his grip. "I will not lose my sons to this."

Sons.

Kell blinked, shaken by the words as the Maxim released his hold, his anger deflating. "Has Rhy woken?" he asked.

The king shook his head. "Not yet." His attention slid past Kell. "And you."

Kell turned and saw Lila, hair falling over her shattered eye as she scraped blood from under her nails. She looked up at the summons.

"Who are you?" demanded the king.

Lila frowned, started to answer. Kell cut her off.

"This is Miss Delilah Bard."

"A friend to the throne," said Tieren.

"I've already saved your city," added Lila. "*Twice.*" She cocked her head, shifting the dark curtain of hair to reveal the starburst of her shattered eye. Maxim, to his credit, didn't startle. He simply looked at Tieren.

"Is this the one you told me of?"

The head priest nodded, and Kell was left wondering what exactly the *Aven Essen* had said, and how long Tieren had known what she was. The king considered Lila, his gaze moving from her eyes to her bloodstained fingers, before coming to a decision. Maxim raised his chin slightly, and said, "Mark everyone here."

It was not a request, but the order of a king to a subject.

Lila opened her mouth, and for a second Kell thought she might say something awful, but Tieren's hand came down on her shoulder in the universal sign for *Be quiet,* and for once, Lila listened.

Maxim stepped back, voice rising a measure so that others in the hall could overhear. And they *were* listening, Kell realized, several heads already turned carefully to catch the words as the king addressed his *Antari.*

"Holland has been taken to the cells." Only hours before, *Kell* had been the one imprisoned below the palace. "I would have you speak with him. Learn everything you can about the force we're facing." Maxim's expression darkened. "By whatever means."

Kell stiffened.

The cold press of steel.

A collar around his throat.

Skin shredding against a metal frame.

"Your Majesty," said Kell, striving for the proper tone. "It will be done."

Kell's boots echoed on the prison stairs, each step carrying him away from the light and heat of the palace's heart.

Growing up, Rhy's favorite place to hide had been the royal cells. Located directly beneath the guards' hall, carved into one of the massive stone limbs that held the palace up over the river, the cells were rarely filled. They had once been in frequent use, according to Tieren, back when Arnes and Faro were at war, but now they sat abandoned. The royal guards made use of them occasionally, saints knew for what, but whenever Rhy ran off with nothing but a laugh, or a note— *come find me*—Kell started by going to the cells.

They were always cold, the air heavy with the smell of damp stone, and his voice would echo as he called for Rhy—*come out, come out, come out*. Kell had always been better at finding than Rhy was at hiding, and the games usually dissolved into the two boys tucked into a cell, eating stolen apples and playing hands of Sanct.

Rhy always loved coming down here, but Kell thought that what his brother really loved was the going back upstairs afterward, the way he could simply shrug off his surroundings when he was done and trade the dank underbelly for lush robes and spiced tea, having been reminded how lucky he was to be a prince.

Kell had never been fond of the cells back then.

Now he hated them.

Revulsion rose in him with every step, revulsion for the memory of his imprisonment, revulsion for the man now sitting in his place.

Lanterns cast pale light over the space. It glinted where it struck metal, fanned against stone.

Four guards in full armor stood across from the largest cell. The same one Kell had occupied a few hours before. They had their weapons ready, eyes fixed on the shape beyond the bars. Kell took in the way the guards looked at Holland, the venom in their glares, and knew it was the way some wanted to look at *him*. All the fear and anger, none of the respect.

The White *Antari* sat on the stone bench at the back of the cell, shackled hand and foot to the wall behind him. A black blindfold was cinched tight over his eyes, but Kell could tell by the subtle shift of his limbs, the incline of his head, that Holland was awake.

It had been a short trip from the roof to the cell, but the guards had not been gentle. They'd stripped him to the waist to search for weapons, and fresh bruises blossomed along his jaw and across his stomach and chest, the fair skin revealing every abuse, though they'd taken care to clean the blood away. Several fingers looked broken, and the faint stutter of his chest hinted at cracked ribs.

Standing across from Holland, Kell was again taken aback by the changes in the man. The breadth of Holland's shoulders, the lean muscle wrapping his waist, the emotionless set of his mouth, those were all still there. But the newer things—the color in Holland's cheeks, the flush of youth—Osaron had taken those with him when he fled. The *Antari*'s skin looked ashen where it wasn't bruised, and his hair was no longer the glossy black he'd briefly had as king, or even the faded charcoal Kell was more accustomed to—now it was threaded with silver.

Holland looked like someone caught between two selves, the effect eerie, disconcerting.

His shoulders rested against the icy stone wall, but if he felt the cold, he didn't let it show. Kell took in the remains of Athos Dane's control spell, carved into the *Antari*'s front—and ruined by the steel bar Kell himself had driven through his chest—before noticing the web of scars that lined Holland's skin. There was order to the mutilations, as if whoever'd done them had done them carefully. Methodically. Kell knew from experience how easily *Antari* healed. To leave these kinds of scars, the wounds would have to have been very, very deep.

In the end, Holland was the one to break the silence. He couldn't *see* Kell, not through the blindfold, but he must have known it was him, because when the older *Antari* spoke, his voice was laced with disdain. "Come to get your revenge?"

Kell took a slow breath, steadying himself.

"Leave," he said, gesturing to the guards.

They hesitated, eyes flicking between the two *Antari*. One retreated without hesitation, two had the decency to grow nervous, and the fourth looked loath to miss the scene.

"King's orders," warned Kell, and at last they withdrew, taking with them the clank of armor, the echo of boots.

"Do they know?" asked Holland, flexing his ruined fingers. His voice had none of Osaron's echo, only that familiar, gravelly tone. "That you abandoned them? Came to my castle of your own free will?"

Kell flicked his wrist, and the chains around Holland tightened, forcing him back against the cell wall. The gesture earned him nothing—Holland's tone remained cold, unflinching.

"I'll take that as a no."

Even through the blindfold, Kell could *feel* Holland's gaze, the black of his left eye scraping against the black of Kell's right.

He summoned the king's tone as best he could.

"You will tell me everything you know about Osaron."

A gleam of bared teeth. "And then you'll let me go?" sneered Holland.

"What is he?"

A heavy pause, and Kell thought Holland would force him to drag the answers out. But then he answered. "An *oshoc.*"

Kell knew that word. It was Mahktan for *demon,* but what it really meant was a piece of *incarnated* magic. "What are his weaknesses?"

"I do not know."

"How can he be stopped?"

"He can't." Holland twitched the chains. "Does this make us even?"

"*Even?*" snarled Kell. "If I could yet discount the atrocities you committed during the rule of the Danes, it would not change the fact that *you* are the one who set that *oshoc* free. *You* plotted against Red London. *You* lured me into your city. *You* bound me, tortured me, purposefully severed me from my magic, and in so doing *you* nearly killed my brother."

A tilt of the chin. "If it's worth anything—"

"It isn't," snapped Kell. He began to pace, torn between exhaustion and fury, his body aching but his nerves alight.

And Holland, so maddeningly calm. As if he weren't chained to the wall. As if they were standing together in a royal chamber instead of separated by the iron bars of a prison cell.

"What do you want, Kell? An apology?"

He felt his fraying temper finally snap. "What do I *want*? I want to destroy the demon *you've* unleashed. I want to protect my family. I want to save my home."

"So did I. I did what I had to—"

"No," snarled Kell. "When the Danes ruled, they may have forced your hand, but this time, *you* chose. You chose to set Osaron free. You chose to be his vessel. You chose to give him—"

"Life isn't made of choices," said Holland. "It's made of trades. Some are good, some are bad, but they all have a cost."

"You traded away *my* world's safety—"

Holland strained forward suddenly against his chains, and even though his voice didn't rise, every muscle in him tightened. "What do you think *your* London did, when the darkness came? When Osaron's magic consumed his world, and threatened to take ours with it? *You* traded away *our* world's safety for your own, locked the doors and trapped us between the raging water and the rocks. How does it feel now?"

Kell wrapped his will around Holland's skull and forced it back against the wall. The slightest clench in Holland's jaw and the flare of his nostrils were the only signs of pain.

"Hatred is a powerful thing," continued Holland through gritted teeth. "Hold on to it."

And in that moment, Kell *wanted* to. He wanted to keep going, wanted to hear the crack of bone, wanted to see if he could break Holland the way Holland had broken *him* in White London.

But Kell knew he couldn't break Holland.

Holland was already broken. It showed, not in the scars, but in the way he spoke, the way he held himself in the face of pain, too well acquainted with its shape and scale. He was a man hollowed out long before Osaron, a man with no fear and no hope and nothing to lose.

For an instant, Kell tightened his grip anyway—in anger, in spite—and felt Holland's bones groan under the strain.

And then he forced himself to let go.

THREE

FALL
OR
FIGHT

I

Alucard had been dreaming of the sea when he heard the door open. It wasn't a loud sound, but it was so out of place, at odds with the ocean spray and the summer gulls.

He rolled over, lost for a moment in the haze of sleep, his body aching from the abuse of the tournament and his head full of silk. And then, a step, wooden boards groaning underfoot. The sudden, very real presence of another person in the room. *Rhy's* room. And the prince, still unconscious, unarmed, beside him.

Alucard rose in a single, fluid movement, the water from the glass beside the bed rising up and freezing into a dagger against his palm.

"Show yourself."

He held the shard in a fighting stance, ready to strike as the intruder continued his slow march forward. The room around them was dim, a lamp burning just behind the intruder's back, casting him in shadow.

"Down, dog," said an unmistakable voice.

Alucard let out a low curse and slumped back against the side of the bed, heart pounding. "Kell."

The *Antari* stepped forward, light illuminating his grim mouth and narrowed eyes, one blue, the other black. But what caught Alucard's attention, what held it in a vice, was the sigil scrawled over his bare chest. A pattern of concentric circles. An exact replica of the mark over Rhy's heart, the one woven through with iridescent threads.

Kell flicked his fingers, and Alucard's frozen blade flew from his hand, melting back into a ribbon of water as it returned to its glass.

Kell's gaze shifted to the bed, sheets rumpled where Alucard had been lying moments before. "Taking your task seriously, I see."

"Quite."

"I told you to keep him safe, not cuddle."

Alucard spread his hands behind him on the sheets. "I'm more than capable of multitasking." He was about to continue when he registered the pallor of Kell's skin, the blood staining his hands. "What happened?"

Kell looked down at himself, as if he'd forgotten. "The city is under attack," he said hollowly.

Alucard suddenly remembered the pillar of dark magic beyond the window, fracturing across the sky. He spun back toward the balcony, and stiffened at the sight. There was no familiar red light against the clouds. No glow from the river below. When he reached for the door, Kell caught his wrist. Fingers ground against bone.

"Don't," he ordered in his imperious way. "They're warding the palace, to keep it out."

Alucard pulled free, rubbing at the smudge left by Kell's grip. *"It?"*

The *Antari* looked past him. "The infection, or poison, spell, I don't know . . ." He lifted a hand, as if to rub his eyes, then realized it was stained and let it fall. "Whatever it is. Whatever he's done . . . doing. Just stay away from the doors and windows."

Alucard looked at him, incredulous. "The city is being attacked, and we're just going to hole up in the palace and let it happen? There are people out there—"

Kell's jaw clenched. "We cannot save them all," he said stiffly. "Not without a plan, and until we have one—"

"My *crew's* out there. My family, too. And you expect me to just sit and watch—"

"No," snapped Kell. "I expect you to make yourself useful." He pointed at the door. "Preferably somewhere else."

Alucard's eyes went to the bed. "I can't leave Rhy."

"You've done it before," said Kell.

It was a cheap shot, but Alucard still flinched. "I told the queen I'd—"

"Emery," cut in Kell, closing his eyes, and it was only then that he realized how close the magician was to falling over. His face was grey, and it looked like sheer will was keeping him on his feet, but he was beginning to sway. "You're one of the best magicians in this city," said Kell, wincing as if the admission hurt. "Prove it. Go and help the priests. Help the king. Help someone who needs it. You cannot help my brother any more tonight."

Alucard swallowed, and nodded. "All right."

He forced himself to cross the chamber, glancing back only once, to see Kell half sinking, half falling into the chair beside the prince's bed.

The hall beyond Rhy's room was strangely empty. Alucard made it to the stairs before he saw the first servants hurrying past, their arms full of cloth and sand and water basins. Not the tools for binding wounds, but the ones needed for making wards.

A guard rounded the corner, his helmet under his arm. There was a line of blood across his forehead, but he didn't appear wounded, and the mark was too deliberate to be the weary wiping of a brow.

Through a set of wooden doors, Alucard saw the king surrounded by members of his guard, all of them bent over a large map of the city. Runners carried word of new attacks, and with every one, King Maxim placed a black coin atop the parchment.

As Alucard moved through halls, down flights of stairs, he felt like he'd woken from a dream into a nightmare.

Hours before, the palace had brimmed with life. Now the only motions were nervous, halting. The faces masked by shock.

In a trance, his feet found the Grand, the palace's largest ballroom, and stopped cold. Alucard Emery rarely felt helpless, but now he stood in stunned silence. Two nights before, men and women had danced here in pools of light as music played from the gold dais. Two nights before, Rhy had stood here, dressed in red and gold, the shining centerpiece of the ball. Two nights before, this had been a place of laughter and song, crystal glasses and whispered conversation. Now *ostra* and *vestra* huddled together in shock, and white-robed priests stood at every window, hands pressed flat against glass as they wove spells around the palace, shielding it against the poisonous night. He could see their magic, pale and shimmering, as it cast its net over the windows and the walls. It looked fragile compared with the heavy shadows that pushed against the glass, wanting in.

Standing there, at the mouth of the ballroom, Alucard's ears caught slices of information, too thin, and all confused, tangling with one another until he couldn't pick the news apart, sort the real from the fabulous, the truth from the fear.

The city was under attack.

A monster had come to London.

A fog was poisoning the people.

Invading their minds.

Driving them mad.

It was like the Black Night all over again, they said, but worse. That plague had taken twenty, thirty, and passed by touch. This, it seemed, moved on the air itself. It had taken hundreds, maybe even thousands.

And it was spreading.

The tournament magicians stood in clusters, some speaking in low, urgent tones while others simply stared out through the gallery's vaulting windows as tendrils of dark fog wrapped around the palace, blotting out the city in streaks of black.

The Faroans gathered around Lord Sol-in-Ar in tight formation as their general spoke in his serpentine tongue, while the Veskans stood in sullen silence, their prince staring into the night, their princess surveying the room.

The queen caught sight of Alucard and frowned, pulling away from the knot of *vestra* around her.

"Is my son awake?" she said under her breath.

"Not yet, Your Majesty," he answered. "But Kell is with him now."

A long silence, and then the queen nodded, once, attention already shifting away.

"Is it true?" he asked. "That Rhy . . ." He didn't want to shape the words, didn't want to give them life and weight. He'd picked up fragments in the chaos of Rhy's collapse, seen the matching spellwork on Kell's chest.

Someone has wounded you, he'd said nights before, offering to kiss the seal above the prince's heart. But someone had done worse than that.

"He will recover now," she said. "That is what matters."

He wanted to say something else, to tell her he was worried, too (he wondered if she knew—how *much* she knew—about his summer with her son, how much he cared), but she was already moving away, and he was left with the words going sour on his tongue.

"All right then, who's next?" said a familiar voice nearby, and Alucard turned again to see his thief surrounded by palace guards. His pulse quickened until he realized Bard wasn't in any danger.

The guards were *kneeling* around her, and Lila Bard of all people was touching each of their foreheads, as if bestowing a blessing. Head bowed, she almost looked like a saint.

If a saint dressed all in black and carried knives.

If a saint blessed using blood.

He went to her as the guards peeled away, each anointed with a line of red.

Up close, Bard looked pale, shadows like bruises beneath her eyes, jaw clenched as she wrapped a cut in linen.

"Keep some of that in your veins, if you can," he said, reaching out to help her tie the knot.

She looked up, and he stiffened at the unnatural glint in her gaze. The glass surface of her right eye, once a brown that *almost* matched her left, was shattered.

"Your eye," he said dumbly.

"I know."

"It looks . . ."

"Dangerous?"

"Painful." His fingertips drifted to the dried blood caught like a tear in the outer corner of the ruined eye, a nick where a knife had grazed the skin. "Long night?"

She let out a single stifled laugh. "And getting longer."

Alucard's gaze tracked from the guards' marked skin to her stained fingers. "A spell?"

Bard shrugged. "A blessing." He raised a brow. "Haven't you heard?" she added absently. "I'm *aven*."

"You're certainly something," he said as a crack snaked up the nearest window and a pair of older priests rushed toward the novice working to ward the glass. He lowered his voice. "Have you been outside?"

"Yes," she said, features hardening. "It's . . . it's not . . . good . . ." She trailed off. Bard had never been chatty, but he didn't think he'd ever seen her at a loss for words. She took a moment, squinting at the odd gathering that they faced here, and began again, her voice low. "The guards are keeping the people in their homes, but the fog— whatever's *in* the fog—is poisonous. Most fall within moments of contact. They aren't rotting the way they did in the Black Night," she added, "so it's not possession. But they're not themselves, either. And those who fight the hold, they fall to something worse. The priests are trying to learn more, but so far . . ." She blew out a breath, shifting her hair over her damaged eye. "I caught sight of Lenos in the crowd," she added, "and he looked all right, but Tav . . ." She shook her head.

Alucard swallowed. "Has it reached the northern bank?" he asked, thinking of the Emery estate. Of his sister. When Bard didn't answer, he twisted toward the door. "I have to go—"

"You can't," she said, and he expected a reprimand, a reminder there was nothing he could do, but this was Bard—his Bard—and *can't* meant something simple. "The guards are on the doors," she explained. "They've strict orders not to let anyone in or out."

"You never let that stop *you*."

The ghost of a smile. "True." And then, "I could stop you."

"You could try."

And she must have seen the steel in his eyes, because the smile flickered and went out. "Come here."

She tangled her fingers in his collar and pulled his face toward hers, and for a strange, disorienting second he thought she meant to kiss him. The memory of another night flared in his mind—a point made with bodies pressed together, an argument punctuated with a kiss—but now she simply pressed her thumb to his forehead and drew a short line above his brows.

He lifted a hand to his face, but she swatted it away. "It's supposed to shield you," she said, nodding at the windows, "from whatever's out there."

"I thought that's what the palace was for," he said darkly.

Lila cocked her head. "Perhaps," she said, "but only if you plan to stay inside."

Alucard turned to go.

"God be with you," said Bard dryly.

"What?" he asked, confused.

"Nothing," she muttered. "Just try to stay alive."

II

Emira Maresh stood in the doorway to her son's chamber and watched the two of them sleep.

Kell was slumped in a chair beside Rhy's bed, his coat cast off and a blanket around his bare shoulders, his head resting on folded arms atop the bedsheets.

The prince lay stretched out on the bed, one arm draped across his ribs. The color was back in his cheeks, and his eyelids fluttered, lashes dancing the way they did when he dreamed.

In sleep, they both looked so peaceful.

When they were children, Emira used to slip from room to room like a ghost after they'd gone to bed, smoothing sheets and touching hair and watching them fall asleep. Rhy wouldn't let her tuck him in—he claimed it was undignified—and Kell, when she'd tried, had only stared at her with those large inscrutable eyes. He could do it himself, he'd insisted, and so he had.

Now Kell shifted in his sleep, and the blanket began to slip from his shoulders. Emira, unthinking, reached to resettle it, but when her fingers brushed his skin, he started and shot upright as if under attack, eyes bleary, face contorted with panic. Magic was already singing across his skin, flushing the air with heat.

"It's only me," she said softly, but even as recognition settled in Kell's face, his body didn't loosen. His hands returned to his sides, but his shoulders stayed stiff, his gaze landing on her like stones, and Emira's escaped to the bed, to the floor, wondering why he was so much harder to look at when he was awake.

"Your Majesty," he said, reverent, but cold.

"Kell," she said, trying to find her warmth. She meant to go on, meant his name to be the beginning of a question—*Where did you go? What happened to you? To my son?*—but he was already on his feet, already taking up his coat.

"I didn't mean to wake you," she said.

Kell scrubbed at his eyes. "I didn't mean to sleep."

She wanted to stop him, and couldn't. Didn't.

"I'm sorry," he said from the doorway. "I know it's my fault."

No, she wanted to say. And *yes.* Because every time she looked at Kell, she saw Rhy, too, begging for his brother, saw him coughing up blood from someone else's wound, saw him still as death, no longer a prince at all but a body, a corpse, a thing long gone. But he'd come back, and she knew it was Kell's spell that had done it.

She had seen now what Kell had given the prince, and what the prince was without it, and it *terrified* her, the way they were bound, but her son was lying on the bed, alive, and she wanted to cling to Kell and kiss him and say *Thank you, Thank you, thank you.*

She forgave him nothing.

She owed him everything.

And before she could say so, he was gone.

When the door shut behind him, Emira sank into Kell's abandoned seat. Words waited in her mouth, unsaid. She swallowed them, wincing as though they scratched on the way down.

She leaned forward, resting one hand gently over Rhy's.

His skin was smooth and warm, his pulse strong. Tears slid down her cheek and froze as they fell, tiny beads of ice landing in her lap only to melt again into her dress.

"It's all right," she finally managed, though she didn't know if the words were for Kell, or Rhy, or herself.

Emira had never wanted to be a mother.

She'd certainly never planned on being queen.

Before she married Maxim, Emira had been the second child of Vol Nasaro, fourth noble line from the throne behind the Maresh and the Emery and the Loreni.

Growing up, she was the kind of girl who broke things.

Eggs and glass jars, porcelain cups and mirrors.

"You could break a stone," her father used to tease, and she didn't know if she was clumsy or cursed, only that in her hands, things always fell apart. It had seemed a cruel joke when her element proved to be neither steel nor wind, but water—*ice*. Easily made. Easily ruined.

The idea of children had always terrified her—they were so small, so fragile, so easily broken. But then came Prince Maxim, with his solid strength, his steel resolve, his kindness like running water under heavy winter snow. She knew what it meant to be a queen, what it *entailed*, though even then she'd secretly hoped it wouldn't happen, couldn't happen.

But it did.

And for nine months, she'd moved as if cupping a candle in a very strong wind.

For nine months, she'd held her breath, buoyed only by the knowledge that if anyone came for her son, they would have to go through her.

For nine months, she'd prayed to the sources and the nameless saints and the dead Nasaro to lift her curse, or stay its hand.

And then Rhy was born, and he was perfect, and she knew she would spend the rest of her life afraid.

Every time the prince tumbled, every time he fell, she was the one fighting tears. Rhy would spring up with a laugh, rubbing bruises away like dirt, and be off again, charging toward the next catastrophe, and Emira would be left standing there, hands still outstretched as if to catch him.

"Relax," Maxim would say. "Boys don't break so easily. Our son will be as strong as forged steel and thick ice."

But Maxim was wrong.

Steel rusted and ice was only strong until a crack sent it shattering to the ground. She lay awake at night, waiting for the crash, knowing it would come.

And instead came Kell.

Kell, who carried a world of magic in his blood.

Kell, who was unbreakable.

Kell, who could protect her son.

"At first, I *wanted* to raise you as brothers."

Emira didn't know when she had started talking instead of thinking, but she heard her voice echo gently through the prince's chamber.

"You were so close in age, I thought it would be nice. Maxim had always wanted more than one, but I—I couldn't bring myself to have another." She leaned forward. "I worried, you know, that you might not get along; Kell was so quiet and you so loud, like morning and midnight, but you were thick as vines from the start. And it was well enough, when the only danger came from slick stairs and bruised knees. But then the Shadows came and stole you away, and Kell wasn't there because you two were playing one of your games. And after that, I realized you didn't need a brother. You needed a guardian. I tried to raise Kell as a ward, then, not a son. But it was too late. You were inseparable. I thought that maybe as you aged, you would drift, Kell to magic, and you to the crown. You're so different, I hoped that time would carve some space between you. But you grew together instead of apart. . . ."

A flutter of movement on the bed, the shift of legs against sheets, and she was up, brushing the dark curls from his cheek, whispering, "Rhy, Rhy."

His fingers curled in the sheets, his sleep growing shallow, restless. A word escaped his lips, little more than an exhale, but she recognized the sound and shape of Kell's name, before, at last, her son woke up.

III

For a moment, Rhy was caught between sleep and waking, impenetrable darkness and a riot of color. A word sat on his tongue, the echo of something already said, but it melted away, thin as a wafer of sugar.

Where was he?

Where had he been?

In the courtyard, searching for Kell, and then falling, straight through the stone floor and into the dark place, the one that reached for him every time he slept.

It was dark here, too, but the subtle layered dark of a room at night. The red cushions of his bed, with their honeyed trim, were cast in variant shades of grey, the bedsheets mussed beneath him.

Dreams clung to Rhy like cobwebs—dreams of pain, of strong hands holding him up, holding him down, dreams of ice-cold collars and metal frames, of blood on white stone—but he couldn't hold on to their shape.

His body hurt with the memory of hurting, and he collapsed back against the pillows with a gasp.

"Easy," said his mother. "Easy." Tears were spilling down her cheeks, and he reached out to catch one, marveling at the crystal of ice quickly melting in his palm.

He didn't think he'd ever seen her cry.

"What's wrong?"

She let out a stifled sound, something caught between a laugh and a sob and verging on hysterical.

"What's wrong?" she echoed with a shudder. "You left. You were *gone*. I sat here with your *corpse*."

Rhy shivered at that word, the darkness catching, trying to drag his mind back down into the memory of that place without light, without hope, without life.

His mother was still shaking her head. "I thought . . . I thought he healed a wound. I thought he brought you back. I didn't realize he was the only thing keeping you here. That you were . . . that you had really . . ." Her voice hitched.

"I'm here now," he soothed, even though part of him still felt caught somewhere else. He was pulling free of that place, moment by moment, inch by inch. "And where is Kell?"

The queen tensed and pulled away.

"What happened?" pressed Rhy. "Is he safe?"

Her face hardened. "I watched you die because of him."

Frustration hit Rhy in a wave, and he didn't know if it was only his or Kell's as well, but the force was rocking. "I am *alive* again because of him," he snapped. "How can you hate Kell, after all of this?"

Emira rocked back as if struck. "I do not hate him, though I wish I could. You have a blindness when it comes to each other, and it terrifies me. I don't know how to keep you safe."

"You don't have to," said Rhy, getting to his feet. "Kell has done it for you. He's given his life, and saints know what else, to save—to *salvage*—me. Not because I am his prince. But because I am his brother. And I will spend every day of this borrowed life trying to repay him for it."

"He was meant to be your shield," she murmured. "Your shelter. You were never meant to be his."

Rhy shook his head, exasperated. "Kell isn't the only one you fail to understand. My bond with him didn't start with this curse. You wanted him to kill for me, die for me, protect me at all costs. Well, Mother, you got your wish. You simply failed to realize that that kind of love, that bond, it goes both ways. I would kill for him, and I would die for him, and I will protect him however I am able, from Faro and Vesk, from White London, and Black London, and from you."

Rhy went to the balcony doors and threw open the curtains, intending to shower the room in the Isle's red light. Instead, he was met with a wall of darkness. His eyes went wide, anger dissolving into shock.

"What's happened to the river?"

IV

Lila rinsed the blood from her hands, amazed that she had any left. Her body was a patchwork of pain—funny, how it still found ways to surprise her—and under that, a hollowness she knew from hungry days and freezing nights.

She stared down into the bowl, her focus sliding.

Tieren had seen to her calf, where Ojka's knife had gone in; her ribs, where she'd hit the roof; her arm, where she'd drawn blood after blood after blood. And when he was done, he'd touched his fingers to her chin and tipped it up, his gaze a weight, solid but strangely welcome.

"Still in one piece?" he'd asked, and she remembered her ruined eye.

"More or less."

The room had swayed a little, then, and Tieren had steadied her.

"You need to rest," he'd said.

She'd knocked his hand away. "Sleep is for the rich and the bored," she'd said. "I am neither, and I know my limits."

"You might have known them before you came here," he lectured, "before you took up magic. But power has its own boundaries."

She'd brushed him off, though in truth she was tired in a way she'd rarely known, a tired that went down far past skin and muscle and even bone, dragged its fingers through her mind until everything rippled and blurred. A tired that made it hard to breathe, hard to think, hard to be.

Tieren had sighed and turned to go as she dug the stone shard of

Astrid's cheek from her coat pocket. "I guess I've answered the question."

"When it comes to you and questions, Miss Bard," said the priest without looking back, "I think we've only just begun."

Another drop of blood hit the water, clouding the basin, and Lila thought of the mirror in the black market at Sasenroche, the way it had nicked her fingers, taken blood in trade for a future that could be hers. On one side, the promise, on the other, the means. How tempting it had been, to turn the mirror over. Not because she wanted what she'd seen, but simply because there was power in the knowing.

Blood swirled in the bowl between her hands, twisting into almost-shapes before dissolving into a pinkish mist.

Someone cleared their throat, and Lila looked up.

She'd nearly forgotten the boy standing by the door. Hastra. He'd led her here, given her a silver cup of tea—which sat abandoned on the table—filled the basin, then taken up his place by the door to wait.

"Are they afraid I'll steal something, or run away?" she'd asked when it was clear he'd been assigned to mind her.

He'd flushed, and after a moment said bashfully, "Bit of both, I think."

She'd nearly laughed. "Am I a prisoner?" she'd asked, and he'd looked at her with those wide earnest eyes and said, in an English softened by his smooth Arnesian accent, "We are all prisoners, Miss Bard. At least for tonight."

Now he fidgeted, looking toward her, then away, then back again, eyes snagging now on the reddening pool, now on her shattered eye. She'd never met a boy who wore so much on his face. "Something you want to ask me?"

Hastra blinked, cleared his throat. At last, he seemed to find the nerve. "Is it true, what they say about you?"

"What is it they say?" she asked, rinsing the final cut.

The boy swallowed. "That you're the third *Antari*." It gave her a shiver to hear the words. "The one from the *other* London."

"No idea," she said, wiping her arm with a rag.

"I do hope you're like him," the boy pressed on.

"Why's that?"

His cheeks flushed. "I just think Master Kell shouldn't be alone. You know, the only one."

"Last time I checked," said Lila, "you have another in the prison. Maybe we could start bleeding *him* instead." She wrung the rag, red drops falling to the bowl.

Hastra flushed. "I only meant . . ." He pursed his lips, looking for the words, or perhaps the way to say them in her tongue. "I'm glad that he has you."

"Who says he does?" But the words had no bite. Lila was too tired for games. The ache in her body was dull but persistent, and she felt bled dry in more ways than one. She stifled a yawn.

"Even *Antari* need sleep," said Hastra gently.

She waved the words away. "You sound like Tieren."

His face lit up as if it were praise. "Master Tieren is wise."

"Master Tieren is a nag," she shot back, her gaze drifting again to the reflection in the clouded pool.

Two eyes stared up, one ordinary, the other fractured. One brown, the other just a starburst of broken light. She held her gaze—something she'd never been keen to do—and found that, strangely, it was easier now. As if this reflection were somehow closer to the truth.

Lila had always thought of secrets like gold coins. They could be hoarded, or put to use, but once you spent them, or lost them, it was a beast to get your hands on more.

Because of that, she'd always guarded her secrets, prized them above any take.

The fences back in Grey London hadn't known she was a street rat.

The street patrols hadn't known she was a girl.

She herself didn't know what had happened to her eye.

But no one knew it was fake.

Lila dragged her fingers through the water one last time.

So much for that secret, she thought.

And she was running out of ones to keep.

"What now?" she asked, turning toward the boy. "Do I get to

inflict wounds on someone else? Make some trouble? Challenge this Osaron to a fight? Or shall we see what Kell is up to?"

As she ticked off the options, her fingers danced absently over her knives, one of which was missing. Not lost. Simply loaned.

Hastra held the door for her, looking balefully back at the abandoned cup.

"Your tea."

Lila sighed and took up the silver cup, its contents long cold.

She drank, cringing at the bitter dregs before setting it aside, and following Hastra out.

V

Kell didn't realize he was looking for Lila, not until he collided with someone who *wasn't* her.

"Oh," said the girl, resplendent in a green-and-silver dress.

He caught her, steadying them both as the Veskan princess leaned into him instead of away. Her cheeks were flushed, as if she'd been running, her eyes glassy with tears. At only sixteen, Cora still had the long-limbed gait of youth and the body of a young woman. When he first saw her, he'd been struck by that contrast, but now, she looked all child, a girl playing dress-up in a world she wasn't ready for. He still couldn't believe that this was the one Rhy had been afraid of.

"Your Highness."

"Master Kell," she answered breathlessly. "What is going on? They won't tell us anything, but the man on the roof, and that awful fog, now the people in the streets—I saw them, through the window, before Col pulled me away." She spoke quickly, her Veskan accent making her trip over every few words. "What will happen to the rest of us?"

She was flush against him now, and he was grateful he'd stopped at his own room to put on a shirt.

He eased her back gently. "So long as you stay in the palace, you will be safe."

"Safe," she echoed, gaze slanting toward the nearest doors, glass panes frosted with winter chill and streaked with shadow. "I think I'd only feel safe," she added, "with you beside me."

"How romantic," said a dry voice, and Kell turned to see Lila leaning against the wall, Hastra a few strides behind. Cora stiffened in Kell's arms at the sight of them.

"Am I interrupting?" asked Lila.

Cora said "yes" at the same time Kell said "no." The princess shot him a wounded look, then turned her annoyance on Lila. "Leave," she ordered in the imperious tone peculiar to royalty and spoiled children.

Kell cringed, but Lila only raised a brow. "What was that?" she asked, strolling forward. She was half a head taller than the Veskan royal.

To her credit, Cora didn't retreat. "You are in the presence of a princess. I suggest you learn your place."

"And where is that, *Princess*?"

"Beneath me."

Lila smiled at that, one of those smiles that made Kell profoundly nervous. The kind of smile usually followed by a weapon.

"*Sa'tach,* Cora!" Her brother, Col, rounded the corner, his face tight with anger. At eighteen, the prince had none of his sister's childlike features, none of her lithe grace. The last traces of youth lingered in his darting blue eyes, but in every other way he was an ox, a creature of brute strength. "I told you to stay in the gallery. This isn't a game."

A storm cloud crossed Cora's face. "I was looking for the *Antari*."

"And now you have found him." He nodded once at Kell, then took his sister's arm. "Come."

Despite the difference in size, Cora wrenched free, but that was the sum of her defiance. She shot Kell an embarrassed look, and Lila a venomous one, before following her brother out.

"Don't kill the messenger," said Lila when the two were gone, "but I think the princess is trying to get into your"—her gaze trailed Kell up and down—"good graces."

He rolled his eyes. "She's just a child."

"Baby vipers still have fangs. . . ." Lila trailed off, swaying on her feet, the gentle rock of a body trying to find balance. She braced herself against the wall.

"Lila?" He reached to steady her. "Have you slept?"

"Not you, too," she snapped, flicking a hand dismissively at him and then back toward Hastra. "What I need is a stiff drink and a solid plan." The words tumbled out in their usual acerbic way, but she didn't look well. Blood dotted her cheekbones, but it was her eyes—again her eyes—that caught him. One warm and brown, the other a burst of jagged lines.

It looked wrong, and yet right, and Kell couldn't tear his gaze away.

Lila didn't even try. That was the thing about her. Every glance was a test, a challenge. Kell closed the gap between them and brought his hand to her face, the beat of her pulse and power strong against his palm. She tensed at the touch, but didn't pull away.

"You don't look well," he whispered, his thumb tracing her jaw.

"All things considered," she murmured, "I think I'm holding my own. . . ."

Several feet away, Hastra looked like he was trying to melt into the wall.

"Go on," Kell told him without taking his eyes from Lila. "Get some rest."

Hastra shifted. "I can't, sir," he said. "I'm to escort Miss Bard—"

"I'll take that charge," cut in Kell. Hastra bit his lip and retreated several steps.

Lila let her forehead come to rest against his, her face so close the features blurred. And yet, that fractured eye shone with frightening clarity.

"You never told me," he whispered.

"You never noticed," she answered. And then, "Alucard did."

The blow landed, and Kell started to pull away when Lila's eyelids fluttered and she swayed dangerously.

He braced her. "Come on," he said gently. "I have a room upstairs. Why don't we—"

A sleepy flicker of amusement. "Trying to get me into bed?"

Kell mustered a smile. "It's only fair. I've spent enough time in yours."

"If I remember correctly," she said, her voice dreamy with fatigue, "you were on *top* of the bed the entire time."

"And tied to it," observed Kell.

Her words were soft at the edges. "Those were the days. . . ." she said, right before she fell forward. It happened so fast Kell could do nothing but throw his arms around her.

"Lila?" he asked, first gently, and then more urgently. *"Lila?"*

She murmured against his front, something about sharp knives and soft corners, but didn't rouse, and Kell shot a glance at Hastra, who was still standing there, looking thoroughly embarrassed.

"What have you done?" demanded Kell.

"It was just a tonic, sir," he fumbled, "something for sleep."

"You *drugged* her?"

"It was Tieren's order," said Hastra, chastised. "He said she was mad and stubborn and no use to us dead." Hastra lowered his voice when he said this, mimicking Tieren's tone with startling accuracy.

"And what do you plan to do when *she wakes back up*?"

Hastra shrank back. "Apologize?"

Kell made an exasperated sound as Lila nuzzled—actually *nuzzled*—his shoulder.

"I suggest," he snapped at the young man, "you think of something better. Like an escape route."

Hastra paled, and Kell swept Lila up into his arms, amazed at her lightness. She took up so much space in the world—in *his* world—it was hard to imagine her being so slight. In his mind, she was made of stone.

Her head lolled against his chest. He realized then that he'd never seen her sleep—without the edge to her jaw, the crease in her brow, the glint in her glare, she looked startlingly young.

Kell swept through the halls until he reached his room and lowered Lila onto the couch.

Hastra handed him a blanket. "Shouldn't you take off her knives?"

"There's not enough tonic in the world to risk it," said Kell.

He started to drape the blanket over her, then paused, frowning at the holsters that lined Lila's arms and legs.

One of them was empty.

It was probably nothing, he told himself, tucking her in, but the prickle of doubt followed him to his feet, a nagging worry that faded to a whisper as he stepped into the hall.

Probably nothing, he thought as he sagged against the door and scrubbed the dregs of sleep from his eyes.

He hadn't meant to fall asleep earlier, in Rhy's room, had only wanted a moment of quiet, a second to catch his breath. To steady himself for all that was to come.

Now he heard someone clear their throat and looked up to see Hastra, one hand still turning a coin over and over between his fingers.

"Let it go," said Kell.

"I can't," said the former guard.

Kell willed the coin from Hastra's fingers into his. The guard made a small yelp, but didn't try to take it back.

Up close Kell saw it wasn't an ordinary coin. It was of White London make, a wooden disk with the remains of a control spell etched into its face.

What had Hastra said?

It's my fault she found you.

So this was how Ojka had done it.

This was why Hastra blamed himself.

Kell closed his hand over the coin and summoned fire, letting the flames devour the coin. "There," he said, tipping ash from his palm. He pushed himself off the floor, but Hastra's gaze stayed, stuck to the tiles.

"Is the prince truly alive?" he whispered.

Kell pulled back as if struck. "Of course. Why would you ask—"

Hastra's wide brown eyes were tight with worry. "You didn't see him, sir. The way he was, before he came back. He wasn't just gone. It was like he'd . . . *been* gone. Gone for a long time. Like he'd never come back." Kell stiffened, but Hastra kept talking, his voice low but urgent, the color high in his cheeks. "And the queen, she wouldn't leave his body, she kept saying over and over that he would come back, because *you* would come back, and I know you two have the same scar, I know you're bound together, somehow, life to life, and, well, I know it's not my place, I know it's not, but I have to ask. Is it some cruel illusion? Is the real prince—"

Kell brought his hand to the guard's shoulder, and felt the quiver in it, the genuine fear for Rhy's life. For all his foolishness, these people loved his brother.

He pointed down the hall.

"The real prince," he said firmly, "sleeps beyond that door. His heart beats as strongly in his chest as my heart does in mine, and it will until the day I die."

Kell was pulling away when Hastra's voice drew him back, soft, but insistent. "There is a saying in the Sanctuary. *Is aven stran.*"

"*The blessed thread,*" translated Kell.

Hastra nodded eagerly. "Do you know what it means?" His eyes brightened as he spoke. "It's from one of the myths, the Origin of the Magician. Magic and Man were brothers, you see, only they had nothing in common, for each's strength was the other's weakness. And so one day, Magic made a blessed thread, and tied itself to Man, so tightly that the thread cut into their skin. . . ." Here he turned his hands up, flexing his wrists to show the veins, "and from that day, they shared their best and worst, their strength and weakness."

Something fluttered in Kell's chest. "How does the story end?" he asked.

"It doesn't," Hastra said.

"Not even if they part?"

Hastra shook his head. "There's no 'they' anymore, Master Kell. Magic gave so much to Man, and Man so much to Magic, that their edges blurred, and their threads all tangled, and now they can't be pulled apart. They're bound together, you see, life to life. Halves of a whole. If anyone tried to part them, they'd both unravel."

VI

Alucard knew the Maresh palace better than he should have.

Rhy had shown him a dozen ways in and out; hidden doors and secret halls, a curtain pulled aside to reveal a stairwell, a door set flush with the wall. All the ways a friend could sneak into a room, or a lover into a bed.

The first time Alucard had snuck into the palace, he'd been so turned around he'd nearly walked in on *Kell* instead. He *would* have, if the *Antari* had actually been in his rooms, but the chamber was empty, the candlelight dancing over a bed still made, and Alucard had shuddered and slipped back the way he'd come, and fallen into Rhy's arms several minutes later, laughing with relief until the prince pressed a palm over his mouth.

Now he raked his mind, trying to remember the nearest escape. If the doors had been made by—or cloaked with—magic, he'd have seen the threads, but the palace portals were simple, wood and stone and tapestry, forcing him to find his way by touch and memory instead of sight.

A hidden door led from the first floor down into the undercarriage of the palace. Six pillars held the massive structure up, solid bases from which the ethereal arch of the Maresh residence vaulted up against the sky. Six pillars of hollowed rock with a network of tunnels where they met the palace floor.

It was simply a matter of remembering which one to take.

He descended into what he thought was the old sanctuary, and found it converted into a kind of training chamber. The concentric circles of a meditation ring were still set into the floor, but the surfaces bore the scorches and stains befitting a sparring hall.

A lone torch with its enchanted white fire cast the space in shades of grey, and in the colorless haze, Alucard saw weapons scattered on one table and elements on another, bowls of water and sand, shards of stone. Amid them all, a small white flower was growing in a bowl of earth, its leaves spilling over the sides of the pot, a tame thing gone wild.

Alucard took the stairwell on the opposite side of the room, pausing only when he reached the door at the top. Such a thin line, he thought, between inside and out, safe and exposed. But his family, his crew, waited on the other side. He touched the wood, summoning his strength, and the door opened with a groan onto darkness.

Darkness, and before it, a web of light.

Alucard hesitated, face to face with the fabric of the priests' protection spell. It looked like spider silk, but when he passed through, the veil didn't tear; it simply shuddered, and settled back into shape.

Alucard stepped forward into the fog, half expecting it to fold around him. And yet, the shadows wicked off his coat, washed up against his boots and sleeves and collar only to fall away, rebuffed. Retreating with every step, but not far, never far.

His forehead itched, and he remembered Lila's touch, the streak of blood, now dry, across his brow.

It was a thin protection, the shadows trying again and again to find their way in.

How long would it last?

He pulled his jacket close and quickened his pace.

Osaron's magic was *everywhere,* but instead of the threads of spellwork, Alucard saw only heavy shadow, charcoal streaked across the city, the stark *absence* of light like spots across his vision. The darkness *moved* around him, every shadow swaying, dipping, and rolling the way a room did after too many drinks, and woven through it all, the colliding scents of wood fire and spring blossom, snowmelt and poppy, pipe smoke and summer wine. At turns sickly sweet and bitter, and all of it dizzying.

The city was something out of a dream.

London had always been made of sound as much as magic, the music drifting on the air, the singing glass and laughing crowds, the carriages and the bustle of the market.

The sounds he heard now were all wrong.

The wind was up, and on it he heard the hooves of guards on horseback, the clank of metal and the multitude of ghostly voices, an echo of words that all broke down before they reached him, forming a terrible music. Voices, or maybe one voice repeating, looping over and under itself until it seemed like a chorus, the words just out of reach. It was a world of whispers, and part of Alucard wanted to lean in, to listen, to strain until he could make out what it was saying.

Instead, he said the names.

Names of everyone who needed him and everyone he needed and everyone he couldn't—*wouldn't*—lose.

Anisa. Stross. Lenos. Vasry. Jinnar. Rhy. Delilah . . .

The tournament tents sat empty, the fog reaching inside for signs of life. The streets were abandoned, the citizens forced into their homes, as if wood and stone would be enough to stop the spell. Maybe it would. But Alucard doubted it.

Down the road, the night market was on fire. A pair of guards worked furiously to put out the blaze, summoning water from the light-less Isle while two more tried to wrangle a group of men and women. The dark magic scrawled itself across their bodies, smudging out Alucard's vision, engulfing the light of their own energy, blues and greens and reds and purples swallowed up with black.

One of the women was crying.

Another was laughing at the flames.

A man kept making for the river, arms outstretched, while another knelt silently, head tipped back toward the sky. Only the guards' mounts seemed immune to the magic. The horses snorted and flicked their tails, whinnying and stamping hooves at the fog as if it were a snake.

Berras and Anisa waited across the river, the *Night Spire* bobbed in its berth, but Alucard felt himself moving toward the burning market and the guards as a man rushed toward one of them, a metal rod in his hands.

"*Ras al!*" called Alucard, ripping the pole from the man's grip right before it met the guard's neck. It went skittering away, but the sight of it had given the others an idea.

Those on the ground began to rise, their movements strangely fluid, almost coordinated, as if guided by the same invisible hand.

The guard shot toward his horse, but there wasn't time. They were on him, hands tearing blindly at the armor as Alucard surged toward them. A man was beating the guard's helmeted head against the stones, saying, "Let him in, let him in, let him in."

Alucard tore the man off, but instead of letting go, tumbling away, the man held fast to Alucard's arm, fingers digging in.

"Have you met the shadow king?" he asked, eyes wide and swirling with fog, veins edging toward black. Alucard drove his boot into the man's face, tearing himself free.

"Get inside," ordered the second guard, "quickly, before—"

His voice was cut off by the scrape of metal and the wet sound of a blade finding flesh. He looked down at the royal half sword, *his* sword, protruding from his chest. As he slumped to his knees, the woman holding the sword's hilt flashed Alucard a dazzling smile.

"Why won't you let him in?" she asked.

The two guards lay dead on the ground, and now a dozen pairs of poisoned eyes swiveled toward him. Darkness webbed across their skin. Alucard scrambled to his feet and began to back away. Fire was still tearing through the market tents, exposing the metal cords that kept the fabric taut, the steel turning red with heat.

They came at him in a wave.

Alucard swore, and flicked his fingers, and the metal snapped free as they fell on him. The cords snaked through the air, first toward his hands, and then, sharply away. It caught the men and women in its metal grip, coiling around arms and legs, but if they felt its bite or burn, it didn't show.

"The king will find you," snarled one as Alucard lunged for the guard's mount.

"The king will get in," said a second, as he swung up and kicked the horse into motion.

Their voices trailed in his wake.

"All hail the shadow king. . . ."

"Berras?" called Alucard as he rode through unlocked gates. "Anisa?"

His childhood home loomed before him, lit like a lantern against the night.

Despite the cold, Alucard's skin was slick with sweat from riding hard. He'd crossed the Copper Bridge, held his breath for the full stretch as the oily slick of poisoned magic roiled on the surface of the river below. He'd hoped—desperately, dumbly—that the sickness, whatever it was, hadn't reached the northern bank, but the moment his mount's hooves touched solid earth, those hopes crumbled. More chaos. The people moved in mobs, the marked from the *shal* alongside the nobles in their winter fineries, still done up from the last of the tournament balls, all searching out those who hadn't fallen to the spell, and dragging them under.

And through it all, the same haunting chant.

"Have you met the king?"

Anisa. Stross. Lenos.

Alucard spurred the horse on.

Vasry. Jinnar. Rhy. Delilah . . .

Alucard swung down from the borrowed horse and hurried up the steps.

The front door was ajar.

The servants were gone.

The front hall sat empty, save for the fog.

"Anisa!" he called again, moving from the foyer into the library, the library into the dining room, the dining room into the salon. In every room, the lamps were lit, the fires burned, the air stifling with heat. In every room, the low fog twisted around table legs and through chairs, crept the walls like trellis vines. "Berras!"

"For saints' sake, be still," growled a voice behind him.

Alucard spun to find his older brother, one shoulder tipped against the door. A wineglass hung as it always did from his fingers, and his chiseled face held its usual disdain. Berras, ordinary, impertinent Berras.

Relief knocked the air from Alucard's lungs.

"Where are the servants? Where is Anisa?"

"Is that how you greet me?"

"The city is under attack."

"Is it?" Berras asked absently, and Alucard hesitated. There was something wrong with his voice. It held a lightness, bordering on amusement. Berras Emery was never amused.

He should have known then that it was wrong.

All wrong.

"It isn't safe here," said Alucard.

Berras shifted forward. "No, it isn't. Not for you."

The light caught his brother's gaze, snagging on the ropes of fog that shimmered in his eyes, turning them glassy, the beads of sweat beginning to pool in the hollows of his face. Beneath his tan skin, his veins were edging black, and if Berras Emery had had more than an ounce of magic to start with, Alucard would have seen it winking out, smothered by the spell.

"Brother," he said slowly, though the word tasted wrong in his mouth.

Once, Berras would have knocked the term aside. Now he didn't even seem to notice.

"You're stronger than this," said Alucard, even though Berras had never been the master of his temper or his moods.

"Come to claim your laurels?" continued Berras. "One more title to add to the stack?" He lifted his glass and then, discovering it empty, simply let it fall. Alucard caught it with his will before it could shatter against the inlaid floor.

"Champion," drawled Berras, ambling toward him. "Nobleman. Pirate. Whore." Alucard tensed, the last word finding its mark.

"You think I didn't know all along?"

"Stop," he whispered, the word lost beneath his brother's steps. In that moment, Berras looked so much like their father. A predator.

"I'm the one who told him," said Berras, as if reading his mind. "Father wasn't even surprised. Only *disgusted*. 'What a *disappointment*,' he said."

"I'm glad he's dead," snarled Alucard. "I only wish I could have been in London when it happened."

Berras's look darkened, but the lightness in his voice, a hollow ease, remained.

"I went to the arena, you know," he rambled. "I stayed to watch you fight. Every match, can you believe it? I didn't carry your pennant, of course. I didn't come to see you win. I just hoped that someone would beat you. That they would *bury* you."

Alucard had learned how to take up space. He had never felt small, except here, in this house, with Berras, and despite years of practice, he felt himself retreating.

"It would have been worth it," continued Berras, "to see someone knock that smug look off your face—"

A muffled sound from upstairs, the thud of a weight hitting the floor.

"Anisa!" called Alucard, taking his eyes off Berras for an instant.

It was a foolish thing to do.

His brother slammed him back into the nearest wall, a mountain of muscle and bone. Growing up without magic, his brother knew how to use his fists. And he used them well.

Alucard doubled over, the air rushing from his lungs as knuckles cracked into ribs.

"Berras," he said with a gasp. "Listen to—"

"No. You listen to *me,* little brother. It's time to set things straight. I'm the one Father wanted. I'm already the heir of House Emery, but I could be so much *more.* And I will be, once you're gone." His meaty fingers found Alucard's throat. "There is a new king rising."

Alucard had never been one to fight dirty, but he'd spent enough time recently watching Delilah Bard. He brought his hands up swiftly, palm crunching into the base of his brother's nose. A blinder, she'd called that move.

Tears and blood spilled down Berras's face, but he didn't even flinch. His fingers only tightened around Alucard's throat.

"Ber—ras—" gasped Alucard, reaching for glass, for stone, for water. Even *he* wasn't strong enough to call an object to hand without seeing it, and with Berras blocking his way, and his vision tunneling, Alucard found himself reaching futilely for anything and everything. The whole house trembled with the pull of Alucard's power, his carefully honed precision lost in the panic, the struggle for air.

His lips moved, silently summoning, pleading.

The walls shook. The windows shattered. Nails jerked free of boards and wood cracked as it peeled up from the floor. For one desperate instant, nothing happened, and then the world came hurtling in toward a single point.

Tables and chairs, artwork and mirrors, tapestries and curtains, pieces of wall and floor and door all crashed into Berras with blinding force. The massive hands fell away from Alucard's throat as Berras was driven back by the whirlwind of debris twining around his arms and legs, dragging him down.

But still he fought with the blind strength of someone severed from thought, from pain, until at last the chandelier came down, tearing long cracks in the ceiling as it fell and burying Berras in iron and plaster and stone. The whirlwind fell apart and Alucard gasped, hands on his knees. All around him, the house still groaned.

From overhead, nothing. Nothing. And then he heard his sister scream.

He found Anisa in an upstairs room, tucked in a corner with her knees drawn up, her eyes wide with terror. Terror, he soon realized, at something that wasn't there.

She had her hands pressed over her ears, her head buried against her knees, whispering over and over, "I'm not alone, I'm not alone, I'm not alone."

"Anisa," he said, kneeling before her. Her face flushed, veins climbing her throat, darkness clouding her blue eyes.

"Alucard?" Her voice was thin. Her whole body shook. "Make him stop."

"I did," he said, thinking she meant Berras, but then she shook her head and said, "He keeps trying to get in."

The shadow king.

He scanned the air around her, could see the shadows tangling in the green light of her power. It looked like a storm was trapped in the unlit room, the air flickering with mottled light as her magic fought against the intruder.

"It hurts," she whispered, curling in on herself. "Don't leave me. Please. Don't leave me alone with him."

"It's all right," he said, lifting his little sister into his arms. "I'm not going anywhere, not without you."

The house groaned around them as he carried Anisa through the hall.

The walls fissured, and the stairs began to splinter beneath his feet. Some deep damage had been done to the house, a mortal wound he couldn't see but felt with every tremor.

The Emery Estate had stood for centuries.

And now it was coming down.

Alucard *had* ruined it, after all.

It took all his strength to hold the structure up around them, and by the time they crossed the threshold, he was dizzy from the effort.

Anisa's head lolled against his chest.

"Stay with me, Nis," he said. "Stay with me."

He mounted his horse with the aid of a low wall, and kicked the beast into motion, riding through the gate as the rest of the estate came tumbling down.

FOUR

WEAPONS AT HAND

I

White London

Nasi stood before the platform and did not cry.

She was nine winters old, for crow's sake, and had long ago learned to look composed, even if it was fake. Sometimes you had to pretend, everyone knew that. Pretend to be happy. Pretend to be brave. Pretend to be strong. If you pretended long enough, it eventually came true.

Pretending not to be sad was the hardest, but looking sad made people think you were weak, and when you were already a foot too short and a measure too small, and a girl on top of that, you had to work twice as hard to convince them it wasn't true.

So even though the room was empty, save for Nasi and the corpse, she didn't let the sadness show. Nasi worked in the castle, doing whatever needed to be done, but she knew she wasn't supposed to be in here. Knew the northern hall was off limits, the private quarters of the king. But the king was missing, and Nasi had always been good at sneaking, and anyway, she hadn't come to snoop, or steal.

She'd only come to see.

And to make sure the woman wasn't lonely.

Which Nasi knew was ridiculous, because dead people probably didn't feel things like cold, or sad, or lonely. But she couldn't be sure, and if it was her, she would have wanted someone there.

Besides, this was the only quiet room left in the castle.

The rest of the place was plunging into chaos, everyone shouting and searching for the king, but not in here. In here, candles burned, and the heavy doors and walls held in all the quiet. In here, at the center of the chamber, on a platform of beautiful black granite, lay Ojka.

Ojka, laid out in black, hands open at her sides, a blade resting in each palm. Vines, the first things to bloom in the castle gardens, were wound around the platform's edge, a dish of water at Ojka's head and a basin of earth at her feet, places for the magic to go when it left her body. A black cloth was draped over her eyes, and her short red hair made a pool around her head. A piece of white linen had been wrapped tight around her neck, but even in death a line of blackish-red stained through where someone had cut her throat.

Nobody knew what had happened. Only that the king was missing, and the king's chosen knight was dead. Nasi had seen the king's prisoner, the red-haired man with his own black eye, and she wondered if it was his fault, since he was missing, too.

Nasi clenched her hands into fists, and felt the sudden bite of thorns. She'd forgotten about the flowers, wild things plucked from the edge of the castle yard. The prettiest ones hadn't blossomed yet, so she'd been forced to dig up a handful of pale buds studded with vicious thorns.

"*Nijk shöst,*" she murmured, setting the bundle of flowers on the platform, the tail of her braid brushing Ojka's arm as she leaned forward.

Nasi used to wear her hair loose so it covered the scars on her face. It didn't matter that she could barely see through the pale curtain, that she was always tripping and stumbling. It was a shield against the world.

And then one day Ojka passed her in the corridor, and stopped her, and told her to pull the hair off her face.

She hadn't wanted to, but the king's knight stood there, arms crossed, waiting for her to obey, and so she had, cringing as she tied back the strands. Ojka surveyed her face, but didn't ask her what had happened, if she'd been born that way (she hadn't) or caught off-turn in the *Kosik* (she had). Instead, the woman had cocked her head and said, "Why do you hide?"

Nasi could not bring herself to answer Ojka, to tell the king's knight that she hated her scars when Ojka had darkness spilling down one side of her face and a silver line carving its way from eye to lip on the other. When she didn't speak, the woman crouched in front of her and took her firmly by the shoulders.

"Scars are not shameful," said Ojka, "not unless you let them be." The knight straightened. "If you do not wear them, they will wear you." And with that, she'd walked away.

Nasi had worn her hair back ever since.

And every time Ojka had passed her in the halls, her eyes, one yellow, the other black, had flicked to the braid, and she'd nodded in approval, and everything in Nasi had grown stronger, like a starving plant fed water drop by drop.

"I wear my scars now," she whispered in Ojka's ear.

Footsteps sounded beyond the doors, the heavy tread of the Iron Guard, and Nasi pulled back hastily, nearly tipping over the bowl of water when she snagged her sleeve on the vines coiled around the platform.

But she was only nine winters old, and small as a shadow, and by the time the doors opened, she was gone.

II

In the Maresh dungeons, sleep eluded Holland.

His mind drifted, but every time it began to settle, he saw London—*his* London—as it crumbled and fell. Saw the colors fade back to gray, the river freeze, and the castle . . . well, thrones did not stay empty. Holland knew this well. He pictured the city searching for its king, heard the servants calling out his name before new blades found their throats. Blood staining white marble, bodies littering the forest as boots crushed everything he'd started like new grass underfoot.

Holland reached out automatically for Ojka, his mind stretching across the divide of worlds, but found no purchase.

The prison cell he currently occupied was a stone tomb, buried somewhere deep in the bones of the palace. No windows. No warmth. He had lost track of the number of stairs when the Arnesian guards dragged him in, half conscious, mind still gutted from Osaron's intrusion and sudden exit. Holland barely processed the cells, all empty. The animal part of him had struggled at the touch of cold metal closing around his wrists, and in response, they'd slammed his head against the wall. When he'd surfaced, everything was black.

Holland lost track of time—tried to count, but without any light, his mind skipped, stuttered, fell too easily into memories he didn't want.

Kneel, whispered Astrid in one ear.

Stand, goaded Athos in the other.

Bend.

Break.

Stop, he thought, trying to drag his mind back to the cold cell. It kept slipping.

Pick up the knife.

Hold it to your throat.

Stay very still.

He'd tried to will his fingers, of course, but the binding spell held, and when Athos had returned hours—sometimes days—later, and plucked the blade from Holland's hand, and given him permission to move again, his body had folded to the floor. Muscles torn. Limbs shaking.

That is where you belong, Athos had said. *On your knees.*

"*Stop.*" Holland's growl vibrated through the quiet of the prison, answered only by its echo. For a few breaths, his mind was still, but soon, too soon, it all began again, the memories seeping in through the cold stone and the iron cuffs and the silence.

The first time someone tried to kill Holland, he was barely nine years old.

His eye had turned black the year before, pupil widening day by day until the darkness overtook the green, and then the white, slowly poisoning him lash to lid. His hair was long enough to hide the mark, as long as he kept his head down, which Holland always did.

He woke to the hiss of metal, lunged to the side in time to *almost* miss the blade.

It grazed his arm before burying itself in the cot. Holland tumbled to the floor, hitting his shoulder hard, and rolled, expecting to find a stranger, a mercenary, someone marked with the brand of thieves and killers.

Instead, he saw his older brother. Twice his size, with their father's muddy green eyes and their mother's sad mouth. The only blood Holland had left.

"Alox?" he gasped, pain burning up his injured arm. Bright red drops flecked the floor of their room before Holland managed to press his hand over the weeping wound.

Alox stood over him, the veins on his throat already edging toward black. At fifteen, he had taken on a dozen marks, all to help bend will and bind escaping magic.

Holland was on his back on the floor, blood still spilling between his fingers, but he didn't cry out for help. There was no one to cry out *to*. Their father was dead. Their mother had disappeared into the *sho* dens, drowned herself in smoke.

"Hold still, Holland," muttered Alox, dragging the blade free of the cot. His eyes were red with drink or spellwork. Holland didn't move. Couldn't move. Not because the blade was poisoned, though he feared it was. But because every night he'd dreamed of would-be attackers, given them a hundred names and faces, and none of them had ever been Alox.

Alox, who told him stories when he couldn't sleep. Tales of the someday king. The one with enough power to bring the world back.

Alox, who used to let him sit on makeshift thrones in abandoned rooms and dream of better days.

Alox, who had first seen the mark in his eye, and promised to keep him safe.

Alox, who now stood over him with a knife.

"*Vosk*," pleaded Holland now. *Stop.*

"It isn't right," his brother slurred, intoxicated by the knife, the blood, the nearness of power. "That magic isn't *yours*."

Holland's bloody fingers went swiftly to his eye. "But it chose me."

Alox shook his head slowly, ruefully. "Magic doesn't *choose*, Holland." He swayed. "It doesn't belong to those who *have*. It belongs to those who *take*."

With that, Alox brought the knife down.

"*Vosk!*" begged Holland, bloody hands outstretched.

He caught the blade, pushing back with every ounce of strength, not on the weapon itself but on the air, the metal. It still bit in, blood ribboning down his palms.

Holland stared up at Alox, pain forcing the words across his lips.

"*As Staro.*"

The words surfaced on their own, rising from the darkness of his mind like a dream suddenly remembered, and with them, the magic surged up through his torn hands, and around the blade, and wrapped around his brother. Alox tried to pull away, but it was too late. The spell had rolled over his skin, turning flesh to stone as it spread over his stomach, climbed his shoulders, wrapped around his throat.

A single gasp escaped, and then it was over, body to stone in the time it took a drop of blood to hit the floor.

Holland lay there beneath the precarious weight of his brother's statue. With Alox frozen on one knee, Holland could look his brother in the eyes, and he found himself staring up into his brother's face, his mouth open and his features caught between surprise and rage. Slowly, carefully, Holland slid free, inching his body out from beneath the stone. He got to his feet, dizzy from the sudden use of magic, shaking from the attack.

He didn't cry. Didn't run. He simply stood there, surveying Alox, searching for the change in his brother as if it were a freckle, a scar, something he should have seen. His own pulse was settling and something else, something deeper, was beginning to steady, too, as if the spell had turned part of *himself* to stone as well.

"Alox," he said, the word barely an exhale as he reached out and touched his brother's cheek, only to recoil from the hardness. His fingers left a rust-red smear against the marble face.

Holland leaned forward to whisper in his brother's stone ear.

"This magic," he said, putting his hand on Alox's shoulder, "is mine."

He pushed, letting gravity tip the statue until it fell and shattered on the floor.

Footsteps sounded on the prison stairs, and Holland straightened, his senses snapping back to the cell. At first, he assumed the visitor would be Kell, but then he counted the footfalls—three sets.

They were speaking Arnesian, running the words together so Holland couldn't catch them all.

He forced himself still as the lock ground free and his cell door swung open. Forced himself not to lash out when an enemy hand wrapped around his jaw, pinning his mouth shut.

"Let's see . . . eyes . . ."

Rough fingers tangled in his hair and the blindfold came free, and for an instant, the world was gold. Lantern light cast haloes over everything before the man forced his face up.

"Should we carve . . ."

"Doesn't look . . . to me."

They weren't wearing armor, but all three had the stature of palace guards.

The first let go of Holland's jaw and started rolling up his sleeves.

Holland knew what was coming, even before he felt the vicious pull on the chains, shoulders straining as they hauled him to his feet. He held the guard's eyes, right up until the first punch landed, a brutal blow between his collar and his throat.

He followed the pain like a current, tried to ground it.

It really was nothing he hadn't felt before. Athos's cold smile surfaced in Holland's mind. The fire of that silver whip.

No one suffers . . .

He staggered as his ribs cracked.

. . . as beautifully as you.

Blood filled Holland's mouth. He could have spat it in their faces and used the same breath to turn them to stone, leave them broken on the floor. Instead, he swallowed.

He would not kill them.

But he would not give them the satisfaction of display, either.

And then, a glint of steel—unexpected—as a guard drew out a knife. When the man spoke, it was in the common tongue of kings.

"This is from Delilah Bard," he said, driving the dagger toward Holland's heart.

Magic rose in him, sudden and involuntary, the dampening chains too weak to stop the flood as the knife plunged toward his bare chest. The guard's body slowed as Holland forced his will against metal and bone. But before he could stop the blade, it flew from the guard's hand, out of Holland's own control, and landed with a snap against Kell's palm.

The guard spun, shock quickly replaced by fear as he took in the man at the base of the stairs, the black coat blending into shadow, the red hair glinting in the light.

"What is this?" asked the other *Antari,* his voice sharp.

"Master Ke—"

The guard went flying backward and struck the wall between two lanterns. He didn't fall, but hung there, pinned, as Kell turned toward the other two. Instantly they let go of Holland's chains, and he half sat, half fell back against the bench, locking his teeth against the jolt of pain. Kell released his hold on the first guard, and the man went crashing to the floor.

The air in the room was frosting over as Kell considered the knife in his hand. He brought the tip of his finger to the point of the blade and pressed down, drawing a single bead of red.

The guards recoiled as one, and Kell glanced up, as if surprised. "I thought you wanted blood sport."

"*Solase,*" said the first guard, rising to his feet. "*Solase, mas vares.*" The others bit their tongues.

"Go," ordered Kell. "The next time I see any of you down here, you will not leave."

They fled, leaving the cell door open as they went.

Holland, who had said nothing since the first footsteps drew him from reverie, leaned his head back against the stone wall. "My hero."

The blindfold hung around his neck, and for the first time since the roof, their eyes met as Kell reached out and swung the cell door closed between them.

He nodded at the stairs. "How many times has that happened?"

Holland said nothing.

"You didn't fight back."

Holland's swollen fingers curled around the chains as if to say, *How could I?,* and Kell raised a brow as if to say, *Those make a difference?* Because they both knew the simple truth: a prison could not hold an *Antari* unless he let it.

Kell turned his attention back to the blade, clearly recognizing the make. "Lila," he muttered. "Should have realized sooner . . ."

"Miss Bard does not care for me."

"Not since you killed her only family."

"The man in the tavern," said Holland, thoughtfully. "She killed him when she took what wasn't hers. When she led me to her home. If she'd been a better thief, perhaps he would still be alive."

"I'd keep that opinion to yourself," said Kell, "if you want to keep your tongue."

A long silence. In the end, Holland was the one to break it.

"Have you finished sulking?"

"You know," snapped Kell, "you're very good at making enemies. Have you ever tried to make a *friend*?"

Holland cocked his head. "What use are those?" Kell gestured to the cells. Holland didn't rise to the bait. He changed course. "What is happening beyond the palace?"

Kell pressed a palm between his eyes. When he was tired, his composure slipped, the cracks on display. "Osaron is free," he said.

Holland listened, brows drawn, as Kell went on about the blackened river, the poisoned fog. When he was done, he stared at Holland, waiting for some answer to a question he'd never asked. Holland said nothing, and at last Kell made an exasperated sound.

"What does he *want*?" demanded the young *Antari,* clearly resisting the urge to pace.

Holland closed his eyes and remembered Osaron's rising temper, his echo of *more, more, more, we could do more, be more.*

"More," he said simply.

"What does that mean?" demanded Kell.

Holland weighed the words before he spoke. "You asked what he wants," he said. "But for Osaron, it's not about *want* so much as *need.* Fire needs air. Earth needs water. And Osaron needs chaos. He feeds on it, the energy of entropy." Every time Holland had found steady ground, every time things had begun to settle, Osaron had forced them back into motion, into change, into chaos. "He's much like you," he added as Kell paced. "He cannot bear to be still."

The cogs were turning behind Kell's eyes, thoughts and emotions flickering across his face like light. Holland wondered if he knew how much he showed.

"Then I must find a way to *make* him still," said the young *Antari*.

"If you can," said Holland. "That alone won't stop him, but it will force him to be reckless. And if reckless humans make mistakes, then so will reckless gods."

"Do you truly believe that he's a god?"

Holland rolled his eyes. "It doesn't matter what someone is. Only what they *think* they are."

A door ground open overhead, and Holland tensed reflexively, hating the subtle but traitorous rattle of his chains, but Kell didn't seem to notice.

Moments later a guard appeared at the base of the stairs. Not one of Holland's attackers, but an older man, temples silver.

"What is it, Staff?" asked Kell.

"Sir," answered the man gruffly. He held no love for the *Antari* prince. "The king has summoned you."

Kell nodded, and turned to leave. He hesitated at the edge of the room. "Do you care so little for your own world, Holland?"

He stiffened. "My world," he said slowly, "is the *only* thing I care about."

"Yet you stay here. Helpless. Useless." Somewhere deep in Holland, someone—the man he used to be, before Osaron, before the Danes—was screaming. Fighting. He held still, waited for the wave to pass.

"You told me once," said Kell, "that you were either magic's master or its slave. So which are you now?"

The screaming died in Holland's head, smothered by the hollow quiet he'd trained to take its place.

"That's what you don't understand," said Holland, letting the emptiness fold over him. "I have only ever been its slave."

III

The royal map room had always been off limits.

When Kell and Rhy were young, they'd played in every palace chamber and hallway—but never here. There were no chairs in this room. No walls of books. No hearth fire or cells, no hidden doors or secret passages. Only the table with its massive map, Arnes rising from the surface of the parchment like a body beneath a taut sheet. The map spanned the table edge to edge, in full detail, from the glittering city of London at its center to the very edges of the empire. Tiny stone ships floated on flat seas, and tiny stone soldiers marked the royal garrisons stationed at the borders, and tiny stone guards patrolled the streets in troops of rose quartz and marble.

King Maxim told them that the pieces on this board had consequences. That to move a chalice was to make war. To topple a ship was to doom the vessel. To play with the men was to the play with lives.

The warning was a sufficient deterrent—whether or not it was *true*, neither Rhy nor Kell dared chance it and risk Maxim's anger and their own guilt.

The map *was* enchanted, though—it showed the empire as it was; now the river glistened like a streak of oil; now tendrils of fog thin as pipe smoke drifted through the miniature streets; now the arenas stood abandoned, darkness rising like steam off every surface.

What it didn't show were the fallen roaming the streets. It didn't show the desperate survivors pounding on the doors of houses, begging to be let in. It didn't show the panic, the noise, the fear.

King Maxim stood at the map's southern edge, hands braced against the table, head bent over the image of his city. To one side stood Tieren, looking like he'd aged ten years in the course of a single night. To the other stood Isra, the captain of the city guard, a broad-shouldered Londoner with cropped black hair and a strong jaw. Women might be rare in the guard, but if someone questioned Isra's standing, they only did it once.

Two of Maxim's *vestran* council, Lord Casin and Lady Rosec, commanded the map's eastern side, while Parlo and Lisane, the *ostra* who'd organized and overseen the *Essen Tasch,* occupied the west. Each and every one of them looked out of place, still dressed for a winner's ball and not a city under siege.

Kell forced himself up to the map's northern edge, stopping directly across from the king.

"We cannot make sense of it," Isra was saying. "There appear to be two kinds of attack, or rather, two kinds of victim."

"Are they possessed?" asked the king. "During the Black Night, Vitari took multiple hosts, spreading himself like a plague between them."

"This isn't possession," interjected Kell. "Osaron is too strong to take an ordinary host. Vitari ate through every shell he found, but it took hours. Osaron would burn through a shell in seconds." He thought of Kisimyr on the roof, her body cracking and crumbling under Osaron's boot. "There's no point trying to possess them."

Unless, he thought, *they are* Antari.

"Then, by saints," demanded Maxim, "what *is* he doing?"

"It seems like some kind of sickness," said Isra.

The *ostra,* Lisane, shuddered. "He's infecting them?"

"He is creating puppets," said Tieren grimly. "Invading their minds, corrupting them. And if that fails . . ."

"He's taking them by force," said Kell.

"Or killing them in the process," added Isra. "Thinning the pack, weeding out resistance."

"Any wards?" asked the king, looking to Kell. "*Besides Antari* blood?"

"Not yet."

"Survivors?"

A long silence.

Maxim cleared his throat.

"We've no word from either House Loreni or House Emery," started Lord Casin. "Can't your men be mustered—"

"My men are doing everything they can," snapped Maxim. Beside him, Isra shot the lord a cold glare.

"We've sent scouts to follow the fog's line," she continued evenly, "and there *is* a perimeter to Osaron's magic. Right now the spell ends seven measures beyond the city's edge, carving out a circle, but our reports show that it is spreading."

"He's drawing power from every life he claims." Tieren's voice was quiet, but authoritative. "If Osaron is not stopped soon, his shadow will cover Arnes."

"And then Faro," cut in Sol-in-Ar, storming through the doorway. The captain's hand twitched toward her sword, but Maxim stayed her with a look.

"Lord Sol-in-Ar," said the king coolly. "I did not call for you."

"You should have," countered the Faroan as Prince Col appeared at his heels. "Since this matter concerns not only Arnes."

"Do you think this darkness will stop at your borders?" added the Veskan prince.

"If we stop it first," said Maxim.

"And if you do not," said Sol-in-Ar as his dark eyes fell on the map, "it will not matter who fell first."

Who fell first. An idea flickered at the edge of Kell's mind, fighting to take shape amid the noise. The feel of Lila's body sagging against his. Staring at the empty cup cradled in Hastra's hand.

"Very well," said the king. He nodded at Isra to continue.

"The jails are full of those who've fallen," reported the captain. "We've commandeered the plaza, and the port cells, but we're running out of places to put them. We're already using the Rose Hall for those with fever."

"What about the tournament arenas?" offered Kell.

Isra shook her head. "My men won't go onto the river, sir. Not safe. A few tried, and they didn't come back."

"The blood sigils are not lasting," added Tieren. "They fade within hours, and the fallen seem to have discovered their purpose. We've already lost a portion of the guards."

"Call the rest back at once," said the king.

Call the rest.

There it was. "I have an idea," said Kell, softly, the threads of it still drawing together.

"We are caged in," said the Faroan general, sweeping a hand over the map. "And this creature will pick over our bones unless we find a way to fight back."

Make him still. Force him to be reckless.

"I have an idea," said Kell again, louder. This time the room went quiet.

"Speak," said the king.

Kell swallowed. "What if we take away the people?"

"Which people?"

"All of them."

"We can't evacuate," said Maxim. "There are too many poisoned by Osaron's magic. If they were to leave, they'd simply spread the illness faster. No, it must be contained. We still don't know if those lost can be regained, but we must hope it is a sickness and not a sentence."

"No, we can't evacuate them," confirmed Kell. "But every waking body is a potential weapon, and if we want a chance at defeating Osaron, we need him disarmed."

"Speak plainly," ordered Maxim.

Kell drew breath, but was cut off by a voice from the door.

"What's this? No vigil by my bed? I'm offended."

Kell spun to see his brother standing in the doorway, hands in his pockets and shoulder tipped casually against the frame as if nothing were wrong. As if he hadn't spent the better part of the night trapped between the living and the dead. None of it showed, at least, not on the surface. His amber eyes were bright, his hair combed, the ring of burnished gold back where it belonged atop his curls.

Kell's pulse surged at the sight of him, while the king hid his relief *almost* as well as the prince hid his ordeal.

"Rhy," said Maxim, voice nearly betraying him.

"Your Highness," said Sol-in-Ar slowly, "we heard you were hurt in the attack."

"We heard you fell victim to the shadow fog," said Prince Col.

"*We* heard you'd taken ill before the winner's ball," added Lord Casin.

Rhy managed a lazy smile. "Goodness, the rumors fly when one is indisposed." He gestured to himself. "As you can see . . ." A glance at Kell. "I'm surprisingly resilient. Now, what have I missed?"

"Kell was just about to tell us," said the king, "how to defeat this monster."

Rhy's eyes widened even as a ghost of fatigue flitted across his face. He'd only just returned. *Is this going to hurt?* his gaze seemed to ask. Or maybe even, *Are we going to die?* But all he said was, "Go on."

Kell fumbled for his thoughts. "We can't evacuate the city," he said again, turning toward the head priest. "But could we put it to sleep?"

Tieren frowned, knocking his bony knuckles on the table's edge. "You want to cast a spell over London?"

"Over its people," clarified Kell.

"For how long?" asked Rhy.

"As long as we must," retorted Kell, turning back toward the priest. "Osaron has done it."

"He's a god," observed Isra.

"No," said Kell sharply. "He's not."

"Then what exactly *are* we facing?" demanded the king.

"It's an *oshoc*," said Kell, using Holland's word. Only Tieren seemed to understand.

"A kind of *incarnation*," explained the priest. "Magic in its natural form has no self, no consciousness. It simply *is*. The Isle river, for instance, is a source of immense power, but it has no identity. When magic gains a self, it gains motive, desire, will."

"So Osaron is just a piece of magic with an ego?" asked Rhy. "A spell gone awry?"

Kell nodded. "And according to Holland, he feeds on chaos. Right now Osaron has ten thousand sources. But if we took them all away, if he had nothing but his own magic—"

"Which is still considerable—" cut in Isra.

"We could lure him into a fight."

Rhy crossed his arms. "And how do you plan to fight him?"

Kell had an idea, but he couldn't bring himself to voice it, not yet, when Rhy had just recovered.

Tieren spared him. "It could be done," said the priest thoughtfully. "In a fashion. We'll never be able to cast a spell that broad, but we could make a network of many smaller incantations," he rambled, half to himself, "and with an anchor, it could be done." He looked up, pale eyes brightening. "But I'll need some things from the Sanctuary."

A dozen eyes flicked to the map room's only window, where the fingers of Osaron's spell still scratched to get in, despite the morning light. Prince Col stiffened. Lady Rosec fixed her gaze on the floor. Kell started to offer, but a look from Rhy made him pause. The look wasn't refusal. Not at all. It was permission. Unflinching trust.

Go, it said. *Do whatever you must.*

"What a coincidence," said a voice from the door. They turned as one to see Lila, hands on her hips and very much awake. "*I* could use some fresh air."

IV

Lila made her way down the hall, an empty satchel in one hand and Tieren's list of supplies in the other. She'd had the luxury of seeing Kell's shock and Tieren's displeasure register at the same time, for whatever that was worth. Her head was still aching dully from whatever she'd been slipped, but the stiff drink had done its part, and the solid plan—or at least a step—had done the rest.

Your tea, Miss Bard.

It wasn't the first time she'd been drugged, but most of her experience had been of a more . . . investigative nature. She'd spent a month aboard the *Spire* collecting powder for the tapers and ale she intended to take onto the *Copper Thief*, enough to bring down an entire crew. She'd inhaled her share, at first by accident, and then with a kind of purpose, training her senses to recognize and endure a certain portion because the last thing she needed was to faint in the middle of the task.

This time, she'd tasted the powder in the tea the moment it hit her tongue, even managed to spit most of it back into the cup, but by then her senses were going numb, winking out like lights in a strong wind, and she knew what was coming—the shallow, almost pleasant slide before the drop. One minute she'd been in the hall with Kell, and the next her balance was going, floor tipping like a ship in a storm. She'd heard the lilt of his voice, felt the heat of his arms, and then she was gone, down, down, down, and the next thing she knew she was bolting upright on a couch with a headache and a wide-eyed boy watching from the wall.

"You shouldn't be awake," Hastra had stammered as she'd thrown the covers off.

"Is that really the first thing you want to say?" she'd asked, staggering toward the sideboard to pour herself a drink. She hesitated, remembering the bitter tea, but after a few searching sniffs, she found something that burned her nose in a familiar way. She downed two fingers, steadied herself against the counter. The drug was still clinging to her like cobwebs, and she was left trying to drag the edges of her mind back into order, squinting until the blurred lines all hardened into sharp ones.

Hastra was shifting his weight from foot to foot.

"I'm going to do you the favor," she said, setting aside the empty glass, "of assuming this wasn't your idea." She turned on him. "And you're going to do yourself the favor of staying out of my way. And next time you mess with my drink"—she drew a knife, twirled it on her fingers, and brought it up beneath his chin—"I'll pin you to a tree."

The sound of steps hurrying toward her returned Lila to the present.

She spun, knowing it would be him. "Was it your idea?"

"What?" stammered Kell. "No. Tieren's. And what have you done with Hastra?"

"Nothing he won't recover from."

A deep furrow formed between Kell's eyes. Christ, he was an easy mark.

"Come to stop me, or to see me off?"

"Neither." His features smoothed. "I came to give you this." He held out her missing knife, knuckled hilt first. "I believe it's yours."

She took the blade, examining the edge for blood. "Too bad," she murmured, as she slid it back into the sheath.

"While I understand the urge," said Kell, "killing Holland was *not* a helpful notion. We need him."

"Like a dose of poison," muttered Lila.

"He's the only one who knows Osaron."

"And why does he know him so well?" she snapped. "Because he made a *deal* with him."

"I know."

"He let that creature into his head—"

"I know."

"—into his world, and now into yours—"

"I *know*."

"Then *why*?"

"Because it could have been me," said Kell darkly. The words hung between them. "It almost was."

The image came back to her, of Kell lying on the floor before the broken frame, blood pooling rich and red around his wrists. What had Osaron said to him? What had he offered? What had he *done*?

Lila found herself reaching for Kell, and stopped. She didn't know what to say, how to smooth the line between his eyes.

The satchel slipped on her shoulder. The sun was up. "I should go."

Kell nodded, but when she turned away, he caught her hand. The touch was slight, but it pinned her like a knife. "That night on the balcony," he said. "Why did you kiss me?"

Lila's chest tightened. "It seemed like a good idea."

Kell frowned. "That's all?" He started to let go, but she didn't. Their hands hung between them, intertwined.

Lila let out a short, breathless laugh. "What do you want, Kell? A declaration of my affection? I kissed you because I wanted to and—"

His hand tightened around hers, pulling her into him, her free hand splayed against his chest for balance.

"And now?" he whispered. His mouth was inches from her own, and she could feel his heart hammering against his ribs.

"What?" she said with a sly grin. "Do I *always* have to take the lead?" She started to lean in, but he was already there, already kissing her. Their bodies crashed together, the last of the distance disappearing as hips met hips and ribs met ribs and hands searched for skin. Her body sang like a tuning fork against his, like finding like.

Kell's grip tightened, as if he thought she would disappear, but Lila wasn't going anywhere. She could have walked away from almost anything, but she wouldn't have walked away from this. And that itself was terrifying—but she didn't stop, and neither did he. Sparks lit across her lips, and heat burned through her lungs, and the air around them churned as if someone had thrown all the doors and windows open.

The wind rustled their hair, and Kell *laughed* against her.

A soft, dazzling sound, too brief, but wonderful.

And then, too soon, the moment ended.

The wind died away, and Kell pulled back, his breath ragged.

"Better?" she asked, the word barely a hush.

He bowed his head, then let his forehead fall against hers. "Better," he said, and almost in the same moment, "Come with me."

"Where are we going?" she asked as he pulled her up the stairs and into a bedroom. *His* bedroom. Gossamer billowed from the high ceiling in the Arnesian style, a cloudlike painting of night. A sofa spilled cushions, a mirror gleamed in its gold trim, and on a dais stood a bed, dripping with silks.

Lila felt her face go hot.

"This really isn't the time," she started, but then he was pulling her past the fineries to a door and, beyond, into the alcove lined with books, and candles, and a few spare trinkets. Most were too battered to be anything but sentimental. In here, the air smelled less like roses than polished wood and old paper, and Kell spun her around to face the door. There she saw the markings on the wood—a dozen symbols drawn in the ruddy brown of dried blood, each simple but distinct. She'd almost forgotten about his shortcuts.

"This one," he said, tapping a circle quartered by a cross. Lila drew a knife, and nicked her thumb, tracing over the mark in blood.

When she was done, Kell put his hand over hers. He didn't tell her to be safe. He didn't tell her to be careful. He simply pressed his lips to her hair and said, *"As Tascen,"* and then he was gone—the room was gone, the world was gone—and Lila was tipping forward once more into darkness.

V

Alucard rode hard for the docks, Anisa shivering against him.

His sister slid in and out of consciousness, her skin slick and hot to the touch. He couldn't take her to the palace, that much he knew. They'd never let her in now that she was infected. Even though she was fighting it. Even though she hadn't fallen—*wouldn't* fall, Alucard was sure of it.

He had to take her home.

"Stay with me," he told her as they reached the line of ships.

The Isle's current was up, leaving oily streaks against the dock walls and splashing over onto the banks. Here at the river's edge, the magic rolled off the water's surface like steam.

Alucard dismounted, carrying Anisa up the ramp and onto the *Spire*'s deck.

He didn't know if he hoped to find anyone aboard, or feared it, since only the mad and the sick and the fallen seemed to be in the city now.

"Stross?" he called. "Lenos?" But no one answered, and so Alucard took her below.

"Come back," whispered Anisa as the night sky disappeared, replaced by the low wood ceiling of the hold.

"I'm right here," said Alucard.

"Come back," she pleaded again as he lowered her onto his bed, pressed a cold compress to her cheeks. Her eyes drifted open, focused, found his. "Luc," she said, her voice suddenly crisp, clear.

"I'm here," he said, and she smiled, fingers brushing his brow. Her eyes began to flutter shut again, and fear rippled through him, sudden, sharp.

"Hey, Nis," he said, squeezing her hand. "Do you remember the story I used to tell you?" She shivered feverishly. "The one about the place where shadows go at night?"

Anisa curled in toward him, then, the way she used to when he told her tales. A flower to the sun, that's what their mother used to say. Their mother, who'd died so long ago, and taken most of the light with her. Only Anisa held a candle to it. Only Anisa had her eyes, her warmth. Only Anisa reminded Alucard of kinder days.

He lowered himself to his knees beside the bed, holding her hand between his. "A girl was once in love with her shadow," he began, voice slipping into the low, melodic tone befitting stories, even as the *Spire* swayed and the world beyond the window darkened. "All day they couldn't be parted, but when night fell, she was left alone, and she always wondered where her shadow went. She would check all the drawers, and all the jars, and all the places where she liked to hide, but no matter where she looked, she couldn't find it. Until finally the girl lit a candle, to help her search, and there her shadow was."

Anisa murmured incoherently. Tears slipped down her hollowed cheeks.

"You see"—Alucard's fingers tightened around hers—"it hadn't really left. Because our shadows never do. So you see, you're never alone"—his voice cracked—"no matter where you are, or when, no matter if the sun is up, or the moon is full, or there's nothing but stars in the sky, no matter if you have a light in hand, or none at all, you know . . . Anisa? Anisa, stay with me . . . please . . ."

Over the next hour, the sickness burned through her, until she called him father, called him mother, called him Berras. Until she stopped speaking altogether, even in her fevered sleep, and sank deeper, to somewhere dreamless. The shadows hadn't won, but the spring green light of Anisa's own magic was fading, fading, like a fire burning itself out, and all Alucard could do was watch.

He got to his feet. The cabin swayed beneath him as he went to the mantel to pour himself a drink.

Alucard caught his reflection in the ruddy surface of the wine and frowned, tipping the glass. The smudge over his brow, where Lila had streaked a bloody finger across his skin, was gone. Rubbed away by Anisa's fevered hand, or maybe Berras's attack.

How strange, he thought. He hadn't even noticed.

The cabin swayed again before Alucard realized it wasn't the floor tipping.

It was him.

No, thought Alucard, just before the voice slid inside his head.

Let me in, it said as his hands began to tremble. The glass slipped and shattered on the cabin floor.

Let me in.

He braced himself against the mantel, eyes squeezed shut against the creeping vines of the curse as they wound through him, blood and bone.

Let me in.

"No!" he snarled aloud, slamming the doors of his mind and forcing the darkness back. Until then, the voice had been a whisper, soft, insistent, the pulse of magic a gentle but persistent guest knocking at the door. Now, it forced its way in with all its might, prying open the edges of Alucard's mind until the cabin fell away and he was back in the Emery Estate, their father before him, the man's hands brimming with fire. Heat burned along Alucard's cheek from the first lingering blow.

"A disgrace," snarled Reson Emery, the heat of his anger and magic both forcing Alucard back against the wall.

"Father—"

"You've made a fool of yourself. Of your name. Of your house." His hand wrapped around the silver feather that hung from Alucard's neck, flame licking his skin. "And it ends now," he rumbled, tearing the sigil of House Emery from Alucard's throat. It melted in his grip, drops of silver hitting the floor like blood, but when Alucard looked up again, the man standing before him was and was not his father. The image of Reson Emery flickered, replaced by a man made of darkness from head to toe, if darkness were solid and black and caught the light like stone. A crown glittered on the outline of his head.

"I can be merciful," said the dark king, "if you beg."

Alucard straightened. *"No."*

The room rocked violently, and he stumbled forward onto his knees in a cold stone cell, held down as his manacled wrists were forced onto the carved iron block. Embers crackled as the matching poker prodded the fire, and smoke burned Alucard's lungs when he tried to breathe. A man pulled the poker from the coals, its end a violent red, and again Alucard saw the carved features of the king.

"Beg," said Osaron, bringing the iron to rest against the chains.

Alucard clenched his teeth, and would not.

"Beg," said Osaron, as the chains grew hot.

As the heat peeled away flesh, Alucard's refusal became a single, drawn-out scream.

He tore backward, suddenly free, and found himself standing in the hall again, no king, no father, only Anisa, barefoot in a night-gown, holding a burned wrist, their father's fingers like a cuff circling her skin.

"Why would you leave me in this place?" she asked.

And before he could answer, Alucard was dragged back into the cell, his brother Berras now holding the iron and smiling while his brother's skin burned. "You should never have come back."

Around and around it went, memories searing through flesh and muscle, mind and soul.

"Stop," he pleaded.

"Let me in," said Osaron.

"I can be true," said his sister.

"I can be merciful," said his father.

"I can be just," said his brother.

"If you only *let us in*."

VI

"Your Majesty?"

The city was falling.

"Your Majesty?"

The darkness was spreading.

"Maxim."

The king looked up and saw Isra, clearly waiting for an answer to a question he hadn't heard. Maxim turned his attention to the map of London one last time, with its spreading shadows, its black river. How was he supposed to fight a god, or a ghost, or whatever this *thing* was?

Maxim growled, and pushed forcefully away from the table. "I cannot stand here, safe within my palace, while my kingdom dies." Isra barred his way.

"You cannot go out there, either."

"Move aside."

"What good will it do your kingdom, if you die with it? Since when is solidarity a victory of any kind?" Few people would speak to Maxim Maresh with such candor, but Isra had been with him since before he was king, had fought beside him on the Blood Coast so many years ago, when Maxim was a general and Isra his second, his friend, his shadow. "You are thinking like a soldier instead of a king."

Maxim turned away, raking a hand through his coarse black hair.

No, he was thinking *too much* like a king. One who'd been softened by so many years of peace. One whose battles were now fought in ballrooms and in stadium seats with words and wine instead of steel.

How would they have fought Osaron back on the Blood Coast?

How would they have fought him if he were a foe of flesh and blood? With cunning, thought Maxim.

But that was the difference between magic and men—the latter made *mistakes*.

Maxim shook his head.

This monster was magic with a mind attached, and minds could be tricked, bent, even broken. Even the best fighters had flaws in their stance, chinks in their armor . . .

"Move aside, Isra."

"Your Majesty—"

"I've no intention of walking out into the fog," he said. "You know me better than that," he added. "If I fall, I will fall fighting."

Isra frowned but let him pass.

Maxim left the map room, turning not toward the gallery, but away, through the palace and up the stairs to the royal chambers. He crossed the room without pausing to look at the welcoming bed, the grand wood desk with its inlaid gold, the basin of clear water and the decanters of wine.

He'd hoped, selfishly, to find Emira here, but the room was empty.

Maxim knew that if he called for her, she would come, would help in any way she could to ease the burden of what he had to do next— whether that meant working the magic with him, or simply pressing her cool hands to his brow, sliding her fingers through his hair the way she had when they were young, humming songs that worked like spells.

Emira was the ice to Maxim's fire, the cool bath in which to temper his steel. She made him stronger.

But he did not call her.

Instead, he crossed alone to the far wall of the royal chamber where, half hidden by swaths of gossamer and silk, there stood a door.

Maxim brought all ten fingertips to the hollow wood and reached for the metal laid within. He rotated both hands against the door and felt the shift of cogs, the clunk of pins sliding free, others sliding home. It was no simple lock, no combination to be turned, but Maxim Maresh had built this door, and he was the only one who ever opened it.

He'd caught Rhy trying once, when the prince was just a boy.

The prince had a fondness for discovering secrets, whether they belonged to a person or a palace, and the moment he discovered that the door was locked he must have gone and found Kell, dragged the black-eyed boy—still new to his benign breed of mischief—back up into the royal chamber. Maxim had walked in on the two, Rhy urging Kell on as the latter lifted wary fingers to the wood.

Maxim had crossed the room at the sound of sliding metal and caught the boy's hand before the door could open. It wasn't a matter of ability. Kell was getting stronger by the day, his magic blooming like a spring tree, but even the young *Antari*—perhaps the young *Antari* most of all—needed to know that power had its limits.

That rules were meant to be obeyed.

Rhy had sulked and stormed, but Kell had said nothing as Maxim ushered them out. They had always been like that, so different in temper, Rhy's hot and quick to burn, Kell's cold and slow to thaw. Strange, thought Maxim, unlocking the door, in some ways Kell and the queen were so alike.

There was nothing *forbidden* about the chamber beyond. It was simply private. And when you were king, privacy was precious, more so than any gem.

Now Maxim descended the short stone flight into his study. The room was cool and dry and traced with metal, the shelves lined with only a few books, but a hundred memories, tokens. Not of his life in the palace—Emira's gold wedding rose, Rhy's first crown, a portrait of Rhy and Kell in the seasons courtyard—those were all kept in the royal chamber. There were relics of another time, another life.

A half-burned banner and a pair of swords, long and thin as stalks of wheat.

A gleaming helm, not gold, but burnished metal, traced with bands of ruby.

A stone arrowhead Isra had freed from his side in their last battle on the Blood Coast.

Suits of armor stood sentry against the walls, faceless masks tipped down, and in this sanctuary, Maxim threw off the elegant gold-and-crimson cloak, unfastened the chalice pins that held his tunic cuffs, set aside his crown. Piece by piece he shed his kingship, and called up the man he'd been before.

An Tol Vares, they'd called him.

The Steel Prince.

It had been so long since Maxim Maresh had worn that mantle, but there were tasks for kings and tasks for soldiers, and now the latter rolled up his sleeves, took up a knife, and began to work.

VII

The difference of a single day, thought Rhy, standing alone before the windows as the sun rose. One day. A matter of hours. A world of change.

Two days ago, Kell had disappeared, and Rhy had carved five letters into his arm to bring him home. *Sorry.* The cuts were fresh on his skin, the word still burned with movement, and yet it felt like a lifetime ago.

Yesterday his brother had come home, and been arrested, and the prince had fought to see Kell freed, only to lose him again, to lose himself, to lose everything.

And wake to this.

We heard, we heard, we heard.

In darkness, the change was hard to see, but the thin winter light revealed a terrifying scene.

Only hours before, London had brimmed with the cheers of the *Essen Tasch,* the rippling pennants of the final magicians as they fought in the central arena.

Now, all three stadiums floated like sullen corpses on the blackened river, the only sound the steady chant of morning bells coming from the Sanctuary. Bodies bobbed like apples on the surface of the Isle, and dozens—hundreds—more knelt along the riverbank, forming an eerie border. Others moved in packs through the streets of London, searching for those who hadn't fallen, hadn't knelt before the shadow king. The difference of a single day.

He felt his brother coming.

Strange, the way that worked. He'd always been able to tell when Kell was near—sibling intuition—but these days he felt his brother's presence like a cord in reverse, drawing tight instead of slack whenever they were close.

Now the tension thrummed.

The echo in Rhy's chest grew stronger as Kell stepped into the room. He paused in the doorway.

"Do you want to be alone?"

"I am never alone," said the prince absently, and then, forcing himself to brighten, "but I *am* still alive." Kell swallowed, and Rhy could see the apology climbing his brother's throat. "Don't," he said, cutting him off. His attention went back to the world beyond the glass. "What happens, after we put them all to sleep?"

"We force Osaron to face us. And we beat him."

"How?"

"I have a plan."

Rhy raised his fingertips to the glass. On the other side, the fog drew itself into a hand, brushed the window, and then pulled away, collapsing back into mist.

"Is this how a world dies?" he asked.

"I hope not."

"Personally," said Rhy with sudden, hollow lightness, "I'm rather done with dying. It's begun to lose its charm."

Kell shrugged out of his coat and sank into a chair. "Do you know what happened?"

"I know what Mother told me, which means I know what you told her."

"Do you want to know the truth?"

Rhy hesitated. "If it will help you to say it."

Kell tried to smile, failed, and shook his head. "What do you remember?"

Rhy's gaze danced over the city. "Nothing," he said, though in truth, he remembered the pain, and the absence of pain, the darkness like still water folding over him, and a voice, trying to pull him back.

You cannot die . . . I've come so far.

"Have you seen Alucard?"

Kell shrugged. "I assume he's in the gallery," he answered, in a way that said he really didn't care.

Rhy's chest tightened. "You're probably right."

But Rhy knew he wasn't. He had already scanned the Grand Hall as he passed through, searching, searching. The foyer, the ballrooms, the library. Rhy had scoured every room for that familiar shine of silver and blue, the sun-kissed hair, the glint of a sapphire, and found a hundred faces, some known and others foreign, and none of them Alucard.

"He'll turn up," added Kell absently. "He always does."

Just then a shout went up, not from outside, but from within the palace. The crash of doors bursting open somewhere below, a Veskan accent clashing with an Arnesian one.

"*Sanct,*" snarled Kell, shoving himself to his feet. "If the darkness doesn't kill them, their tempers will."

His brother plunged out of the room without looking back, and Rhy stood alone for a long moment, shadows whispering against the glass, before he grabbed Kell's coat, found the nearest hidden door, and slipped through.

The city—*his* city—was full of shadows.

Rhy pulled Kell's coat close about his shoulders and wrapped a scarf around his nose and mouth, the way one might before braving a fire, as if a strip of cloth could keep the magic out. He held his breath as he plunged forward into the sea of fog, but when his body met the shadows, they recoiled, granting Rhy a berth of several feet.

He looked around and, for a moment, felt as if he were a man expecting to drown, only to find the water two feet deep.

And then Rhy stopped thinking altogether, and ran.

Chaos blossomed all around him, the air a tangled mess of sound and fear and smoke. Men and women were trying to drag their neighbors toward the black stretch of the river. Some people staggered and fell, attacked by invisible foes, while others hid behind bolted doors and tried to ward the walls with water, earth, sand, blood.

Still, Rhy moved like a ghost among them. Unseen. Unsensed. No footsteps followed him through the streets. No hands sought to drag him into the river. No mobs tried to sicken him with shadow.

The poisoned fog parted for the prince, slipped around him like water around a stone.

Was it Kell's life shielding him from harm? Or was it the absence of Rhy's own? The fact that there was nothing left for the darkness to claim?

"Get inside," he called to the fevered, but they could not hear him.

"Get back," he shouted at the fallen, but they did not listen.

The madness surged around him, and Rhy tore himself away from the breaking city and turned his sights again to his quest for the captain of the *Night Spire*.

There were only two places Alucard Emery would go: his family estate or his ship.

Logic said he'd go to the house, but something in Rhy's gut sent him in the opposite direction, toward the docks.

He found the captain on his cabin floor.

One of the chairs by the hearth had been toppled, a table knocked clean of glasses, their glittering shards scattered in the rug and across the wooden floor. Alucard—decisive, strong, beautiful Alucard—lay curled on his side, shivering with fever, his warm brown hair matted to his cheeks with sweat. He was clutching his head, breath escaping in ragged gasps as he spoke to ghosts.

"Stop . . . please . . ." His voice—that even, clear voice, always brimming with laughter—broke. "Don't make me . . ."

Rhy was on his knees beside him. "Luc," he said, touching the man's shoulder.

Alucard's eyes flashed open, and Rhy recoiled when he saw them filled with shadows. Not the even black of Kell's gaze, but instead menacing streaks of darkness that writhed and coiled like snakes through his vision, storm blue irises flashing and vanishing behind the fog.

"*Stop,*" snarled the captain suddenly. He struggled up, limbs shaking, only to fall back against the floor.

Rhy hovered over him, helpless, unsure whether to hold him down or try to help him up. Alucard's eyes found his, but looked straight through him. He was somewhere else.

"Please," the captain pleaded with the ghosts. "Don't make me go."

"I won't," said Rhy, wondering who Alucard saw. What he saw. How to free him. The captain's veins stood out like ropes against his skin.

"He'll never forgive me."

"Who?" asked Rhy, and Alucard's brow furrowed, as if he were trying to see through the fog, the fever.

"Rhy—" The sickness tightened its hold, the shadows in his eyes streaking with lines of light like lightning. The captain bit back a scream.

Rhy ran his fingers over Alucard's hair, took his face in his hands. "Fight it," he ordered. "Whatever's holding you, *fight it.*"

Alucard folded in on himself, shuddering. "I can't. . . ."

"Focus on me."

"Rhy . . ." he sobbed.

"I'm here." Rhy Maresh lowered himself onto the glass-strewn floor, lay on his side so they were face-to-face. "I'm here."

He remembered, then. Like a dream flickering back to the surface, he remembered Alucard's hands on his shoulders, his voice cutting through the pain, reaching out to him, even in the dark.

I'm here now, he'd said, *so you can't die.*

"I'm here now," echoed Rhy, twining his fingers through Alucard's. "And I'm not letting go, so don't you dare."

Another scream tore from Alucard's throat, his grip tightening as the lines of black on his skin began to glow. First red, then white. Burning. He was burning from the inside out. And it hurt—hurt to watch, hurt to feel so helpless.

But Rhy kept his word.

He didn't let go.

VIII

Kell stormed toward the western foyer, following the sounds of a brewing fight.

It was only a matter of time before the mood in the palace turned. Before the magicians refused to sit and wait and watch the city fall. Before someone took it in their head to act.

He threw open the doors and found Hastra standing before the western entrance, royal short sword clutched in both hands, looking like a cat facing down a line of wolves.

Brost, Losen, and Sar.

Three of the tournament's magicians—two Arnesians and a Veskan—competitors now aligned against a common foe. Kell expected as much from Brost and Sar, two fighters with tempers to match their size, but Kisimyr's protégé, Losen, was built like a willow, known for his looks as much as his budding talent. Gold rings jingled in his black hair, and he looked out of place between the two oaks. But bruises stained the skin beneath his dark eyes, and his face was grey from grief and lack of sleep.

"Get out of the way," demanded Brost.

Hastra stood resolute. "I cannot let you pass."

"On whose orders?" snapped Losen, his voice hoarse.

"The royal guard. The city guard. The king."

"What is this?" demanded Kell, striding toward them.

"Stay out of it, *Antari*," snarled Sar without turning. She stood even taller than Brost, her Veskan form filling the hall, a pair of axes strapped to her back. She'd fallen to Lila in the opening round, spent the rest

of the tournament sulking and drinking, but now her eyes were full
of fire.

Kell stopped at their backs, relying on their fighters' instincts to
make them turn. It worked, and through the forest of their limbs, he
saw Hastra slump back against the doors.

Kell took in Losen first. "It won't bring Kisimyr back."

The young magician flushed with indignation. Sweat prickled on his
brow, and he swayed a little when he spoke. "Did you see what that
monster did to her?" he said, voice slurring. "I have to—"

"No you don't," said Kell.

"Kisimyr would have—"

"Kisimyr tried, and lost," said Kell grimly.

"You can stay here, hiding in your palace," growled Brost, "but our
friends are out there! Our families!"

"And your bravado cannot help them."

"Veskans do not sit idly by and wait for death," boomed Sar.

"No," said Kell, "your pride carries you right to it."

She bared her teeth. "We will not hide like cowards in this place."

"This place is the only thing keeping you safe."

The air was beginning to shimmer with heat around Brost's clenched
hands. "You cannot keep us here."

"Believe me," said Kell, "there are a dozen other people I'd rather
keep, but you were the only ones lucky enough to be in the palace when
the curse fell."

"And now our city needs us," roared Brost. "We're the best it has."

Kell curled his hand, pricking the base of his palm with the point
of metal he kept against his wrist. He felt the sting, the heat of blood
welling on his skin.

"You're show ponies," he said. "Meant to prance in a ring, and if
you think that's the same thing as battling magic, you're sorely mistaken."

"How dare you—" started Brost.

"Master Kell could fell you all with a single drop of blood,"
announced Hastra from behind them.

Kell stared at the young man with bald surprise.

"I've heard the royal *Antari* has no teeth," cut in Sar.

"We don't want to hurt you, little prince," said Brost.

"But we will," muttered Losen.

"Hastra," said Kell evenly, "leave."

The young man hesitated, torn between abandoning Kell and defying him, but in the end, he obeyed. The eyes of the magicians flicked toward him as he passed, and in that instant, Kell moved.

A breath, and he was behind them, one hand raised to the outer doors.

"*As Staro,*" he said. The locks within the door fell with a heavy clank, and fresh steel bars spread back and forth over the wood, sealing the doors shut.

"Now," said Kell, holding out his bloodied hand, palm up, as if to offer it. "Go back to the gallery."

Losen's eyes widened, but Brost's temper was too high, and Sar was lusting for a fight. When none of them moved, Kell sighed. "I want you to remember," he said, "that I gave you a chance."

It was over quickly.

Within moments, Brost sat on the floor, clutching his face, Losen slumped against the wall, holding bruised ribs, and Sar was out cold, the tails of her blond braids singed black.

The hall was a little worse for wear, but Kell had managed to keep most of the damage confined to the bodies of the three magicians.

Drawn by the noise, the inner doors flew open, and the doorway filled with people—some magicians, others nobles, all straining to see into the foyer. Three magicians laid out, and Kell standing at their center. Just what he needed. A scene. The whispers were starting, and Kell could feel the weight of eyes and words as they landed on him.

"Do you yield?" he asked the crumpled forms, unsure which exactly he was addressing.

A huddle of Faroans looked rather amused as Brost struggled to his feet, still clutching his nose.

A pair of Veskans went to rouse Sar, and while most of the Arnesians hung back, Jinnar, the wind mage with the silver hair, went straight to Losen and helped the grieving youth to his feet.

"Come on," he said, his voice slower and softer than Kell had ever heard it. Tears were streaming silently down Losen's cheeks, and Kell knew they didn't stem from bruised ribs or wounded pride.

"I didn't reach for her on the roof," he murmured. "I didn't . . ."

Kell knelt to clean a drop of blood from the marble floor before it stained, and heard the king's heavy steps before he saw the crowd part around him, Hastra on his heels.

"Master Kell," said Maxim, sweeping his gaze over the scene. "I'll thank you not to bring down the palace." But Kell could sense the approval lacing the king's words. Better a show of strength than a tolerance of weakness.

"Apologies, Your Majesty," said Kell, bowing his head.

The king turned on his heel, and that was that. A mutiny subdued. An instant of chaos restored to order.

Kell knew as well as Maxim how important that was right now, with the city clinging to every shred of power, every sign of strength. As soon as the magicians had been led or carried out, and the hall emptied of spectators, he slumped into a chair along the wall, its cushion still smoking faintly from the incident. He patted it out, then looked up to find his former guard still standing there, warm eyes wide beneath his cap of sun-kissed hair.

"No need to thank me," said Kell, waving his hand.

"It's not that," said Hastra. "I mean, I'm grateful, sir, of course. But . . ."

Kell had a sickening feeling in his stomach. "What is it now?"

"The queen is asking for the prince."

"Last time I checked," said Kell, "that wasn't me."

Hastra looked to the floor, to the wall, to the ceiling, before mustering the courage to look at him again. "I know, sir," he said slowly. "But I can't *find* him."

Kell had felt the blow coming, but it still struck. "You've searched the palace?"

"Pillar to spire, sir."

"Is anyone else missing?"

A hesitation, and then, "Captain Emery."

Kell swore under his breath.

Have you seen Alucard? Rhy had asked, staring out the palace windows. Would he know if the prince had been infected? Would he feel the dark magic swarming in his blood?

"How long?" asked Kell, already moving toward the prince's chambers.

"I'm not certain," said Hastra. "An hour, maybe a little more."

"Sanct."

Kell burst into Rhy's rooms, taking up the prince's gold pin from the table and jabbing it into his thumb, harder than necessary. He hoped that wherever Rhy was, he felt the prick of metal and knew that Kell was coming.

"Should I tell the king?" asked Hastra.

"You came to me," said Kell, "because you have more sense than that."

He knelt, drawing a circle in blood on Rhy's floor, and pressed his palm flat, the gold pin between flesh and polished wood. "Guard the door," he said, and then, to the mark itself, and the magic within, *"As Tascen Rhy."*

The floor fell away, the palace vanished, replaced by an instant of darkness and then, just as swiftly, by a room. The ground rocked gently beneath his feet, and Kell knew before taking in the wooden walls, the portal windows, that he was on a ship.

He found the two of them lying on the floor, foreheads pressed together and fingers intertwined. Alucard's eyes were closed, but Rhy's were open, gaze fixed on the captain's face.

Anger rose in Kell's throat.

"Sorry to interrupt," he snapped, "but this is hardly the time for a lover's—"

Rhy silenced Kell with a look. The amber in his eyes was shot with red, and that's when Kell noticed how pale the captain was, how still.

For a second, he thought Alucard Emery was dead.

Then the captain's eyes drifted wearily open. Bruises stood out beneath them, giving him the gaunt look of a person who'd been ill for a very long time. And something was wrong with his skin. In the low cabin light, silver—not molten bright, but the dull shine of scarred flesh—ribboned at his wrists, his collar, his throat. It traced paths up his cheeks like tears, flashed at his temples. Threads of light that traced the paths where the blue of veins should be, had been.

But there was no curse in his eyes.

Alucard Emery had survived Osaron's magic.

He was alive—and when he spoke, he was still his infuriating self.

"You could have knocked," he said, but his voice was hoarse, his words weak, and Kell saw the darkness in Rhy's expression—not the product of any spell, only fear. How bad had it gotten? How close had he been?

"We have to go," said Kell. "Can Emery stand, or . . ." His voice trailed off as his eyesight sharpened. Across the cabin, something had moved.

A shape, piled on the captain's bed, sat up.

It was a girl. Dark hair fell around her face in sleep-messed waves, but it was her eyes that stilled him. They were not curse-darkened. They were nothing. They were empty.

"Anisa?" started Alucard, struggling to get to his feet. The name stirred something in Kell. A memory of reading scrolls, tucked next to Rhy, in the Maresh library.

Anisa Emery, twelfth in line to the throne, the third child of Reson, and Alucard's younger sister.

"Stay back," ordered Kell, barring the captain's path but keeping his gaze on the girl.

Kell had seen death before, witnessed the moment when a person ceased to be a person and became simply a body, the flame of life extinguished, leaving only a shell. It was as much a feeling as a sight, the sense of missing.

Staring at Anisa Emery, Kell had the horrible sense that he was already looking at a corpse.

But corpses didn't stand.

And she did.

The girl swung her legs out of bed, and when her bare feet hit the floor, the wooden boards began to petrify, color leaching out of the timber as it withered, decayed. Her heart glowed through her chest like a coal.

When she tried to speak, no sound came out, only the crackling of embers, as the thing in her continued to burn.

Kell knew that the girl was already gone.

"Nis?" said her brother again, stepping toward her. "Can you hear me?"

Kell caught the captain's arm and hauled him back just as the girl's fingers brushed Alucard's sleeve. The fabric greyed under her touch. Kell shoved Alucard into Rhy's arms and turned back toward Anisa, reaching out to hold her at bay with his will, and when that didn't work—it wasn't *her* will he was fighting, not anymore, but the will of a monster, a ghost, a self-made god—he bent the ship around them, wood peeling away from the cabin walls to bar her path. She was disappearing from them, board by board, and then suddenly Kell realized he was warring with a second will—Alucard's.

"Stop!" shouted the captain, struggling against Rhy's grip. "We can't leave her, I can't leave her, not again—"

Kell turned and punched Alucard Emery in the stomach.

The captain doubled over, gasping, and Kell knelt before them, quickly drew a second circle on the cabin floor.

"Rhy, now," said Kell, and as soon as the prince's hand met his shoulder, he said the words. The burning girl vanished, the cabin fell away, and they were back in Rhy's room, crouched on the prince's inlaid floors.

Hastra wilted in relief at the sight of them, but Alucard was already fighting to his feet, Rhy straining to hold him back, murmuring "*Solase, solase, solase*" over and over.

I'm sorry, I'm sorry, I'm sorry.

Alucard grabbed Kell by the collar, eyes wide and desperate. "Take me back."

Kell shook his head. "There's no one left on that ship."

"My sister—"

He gripped Alucard's shoulders hard. "Listen to me," he said. "There's *no one left.*"

It must have finally registered, because the fight went out of Alucard Emery. He slumped back onto the nearest sofa, shaking.

"Kell—" started Rhy.

He rounded on his brother. "And you. You're a fool, do you know that? After everything we've been through, you just walked outside? You could have been killed. You could have been poisoned. It's a miracle you didn't fall ill."

"No," said Rhy slowly, "I don't think it is."

Before Kell could stop him, the prince was at the balcony, unlatching the doors. Hastra surged forward, but it was too late. Rhy threw open the doors and stepped out into the fog, Kell reaching him just in time to see the shadows meet the prince's skin—and pull away.

Rhy reached toward the nearest one, and it recoiled from his touch.

Kell did the same. Again, the tendrils of Osaron's magic retreated.

"My life is yours," said Rhy softly, thoughtfully. "And yours is mine." He looked up. "It makes sense."

Footsteps, and then Alucard was there beside them. Kell and Rhy both turned to stop him from stepping out, but the shadows were already pulling away.

"You must be immune," said Rhy.

Alucard looked down at his hands, considering the scars that traced his veins. "And to think, all I had to give up were my good looks."

Rhy managed a ghost of a smile. "I rather like the silver."

Alucard raised a brow. "Do you? Maybe it will start a trend."

Kell rolled his eyes. "If you two are done," he said, "we should show the king."

IX

There were moments when Lila wondered how the hell she'd gotten here.

Which steps—and missteps—she'd taken. A year ago she'd been a thief in another London. A month ago she'd been a pirate, sailing on the open seas. A week ago she'd been a magician in the *Essen Tasch*. And now she was this. *Antari*. Alone, and not alone. Severed, but not adrift. There were too many lives tangled up in hers. Too many people to care about, and once again, she didn't know whether to stay or to run—but the choice would have to wait, because this city was dying and she wanted to save it. And maybe that was a sign she'd already chosen. For now.

Lila looked around the Sanctuary cell, with nothing but its cot and the symbols on the floor. Lila had been here once before, a dying prince draped around her shoulders. The Sanctuary had seemed cold and remote even then, but it was colder now. The hall beyond, once quiet, sat deathly still, her breath the only motion in the air. Pale light burned in sconces along the walls with a steadiness she'd come to recognize as spelled. A gust tore through, strong enough to rustle her coat, but the wind barely stirred the torches. The priests were all gone, most taking refuge while holding up the wards at the palace, and the rest scattered through the city, lost in the fog. Strange, she thought, that they weren't immune, but she supposed that being closer to magic wasn't always a good thing. Not when magic played the devil as well as god.

The Sanctuary's silence felt unnatural—she'd spent years slipping through crowds, carving out privacy in tight quarters. Now, she moved alone through a place meant for dozens, hundreds, a church of sorts that felt wrong without its worshippers, without the soft and steady warmth of their combined magic.

Only stillness, and the voice—voices?—beyond the building urging her to *Come out, come out, or let me in.*

Lila shivered, unnerved, and began to sing beneath her breath as she made her way up the stairs.

"How do you know that the Sarows is coming. . . . "

At the top, the main hall, with its vaulting ceilings and stone pillars, all of it carved from the same flecked stone. Between the columns sat large basins carved from smooth white wood, each brimming with water, flowers, or fine sand. Lila ran her fingers through the water as she walked by, an instinctive benediction, a buried memory from a childhood a world away.

Her steps echoed in the cavernous space, and she cringed, shifting her stride back into that of a thief, soundless even on the stone. The hair bristled on the back of her neck as she crossed the hall and—

A thud, like stone against wood. It came once, and then again, and again.

Someone was knocking on the Sanctuary door.

Lila stood there, uncertain what to do.

"Alos mas en," cried a voice. *Let me in.* Through the heavy wood, she couldn't tell if it belonged to a man or a woman, but either way, they were making too much noise. She'd seen the riots in the streets, the mobs of shadow-eyed men and women attacking those who hadn't fallen, those who tried to fight, drawn to their struggle like cats to mice. And she didn't need them coming *here.*

"Dammit," she growled, storming toward the doors.

They were locked, and she had to lean half her weight on the iron to make it move, knife between her teeth. When the bolt finally slid free and the Sanctuary doors fell open, a man scrambled in, falling to his knees on the stone floor.

"Rensa tav, rensa tav," he stammered breathlessly as Lila forced the doors shut again behind him and spit the blade back into her palm.

She turned, bracing for a fight, but he was still kneeling there, head bowed, and apologizing to the floor.

"I shouldn't have come," he said.

"Probably not," said Lila, "but you're here now."

At the sound of her voice, the intruder's head jerked up, his hood tumbling back to reveal a narrow face with wide eyes unspelled.

Her knife fell back to her side. *"Lenos?"*

The *Spire's* second mate stared up at her. "Bard?"

Lila half expected Lenos to scramble away in fear—he'd always treated her like an open flame, something that might burn him at any moment if he got too close—but his face was merely a mask of shock. Shock, and gratitude. He let out a sob of relief, and didn't even recoil when she hauled him to his feet, though he stared at the place where their hands met even as he said, *"Tas ira . . . "*

Your eye.

"It's been a long night. . . ." Lila glanced at the light streaming in through the windows. "Day. How did you know I was here?"

"I didn't," he said, head ticking side to side in his nervous way. "But when the bells rang, I thought that maybe one of the priests . . ."

"Sorry to disappoint."

"Is the captain safe?"

Lila hesitated. She hadn't seen Alucard, not since marking his forehead, but before she could say as much, the knocking came again at the door. Lila and Lenos spun.

"Let me in," said a new voice.

"Were you alone?" she whispered.

Lenos nodded.

"Let me in," it continued, strangely steady.

Lila and Lenos took a step away from the doors. They were solid, the bolts strong, the Sanctuary supposedly warded against dark magic, but she didn't know how long any of that would hold without the priests.

"Let's go," she said. Lila had a thief's memory, and Tieren's map unfolded in her mind in full detail, revealing the halls, the cells, the study. Lenos followed close at her heels, his lips moving soundlessly in some kind of prayer.

He'd always been the religious one aboard the ship, praying at the first sign of bad weather, the start and end of every journey. She had no idea what or who he was praying *to*. The rest of the crew indulged him, but none of them seemed to put much stock in it, either. Lila assumed that magic was to people here what God was to Christians, and she'd never believed in God, but even if she had, she thought it pretty foolish to think He had time to lend a hand to every rocking ship. And yet . . .

"Lenos," she said slowly, "how are you all right?"

He looked down at himself, as if he wasn't entirely sure. Then he drew a talisman from beneath his shirt. Lila stiffened at the sight of it—the symbol on the front was badly worn, but it had the same curling edges as the sigil on the black stone, and looking at it gave her the same hot-and-cold feeling. In the very center of the talisman, trapped in a bead of glass, hung a single drop of blood.

"My grandmother," he explained, "Helina. She was—"

"*Antari*," cut in Lila.

He nodded. "Magic doesn't get passed on," he said, "so her power's never done me much good." He looked down at the necklace. "Until now." The knocking continued, growing softer as they walked. "The pendant was supposed to go to my older brother, Tanik, but he didn't want it, said it was just a useless trinket, so it went to me."

"Perhaps the gods of magic favor you after all," she said, scanning the halls to either side.

"Perhaps," said Lenos, half to himself.

Lila took the second left and found herself at the doors to the library. They were closed.

"Well," she said, "you're either lucky or blessed. Take your pick."

Lenos cracked a nervous smile. "Which would *you* choose?"

Ear to the wood, she listened for signs of life. Nothing.

"Me?" she said, pushing open the doors. "I'd choose clever."

The doors gave way onto rows of tables, books still open on top, pages rustling faintly in the drafty room.

At the back of the library, beyond the final set of shelves, she found Tieren's study. A towering pile of scrolls sat on the desk. Pots of ink and books lined the walls. A cabinet stood open, showing shelf after shelf of glass jars.

"Watch the door," she said, her fingers tripping over the tinctures and herbs as she squinted at the names, written in a kind of shorthand Arnesian she couldn't read. She sniffed one that looked like it held oil before tipping the mouth of the bottle against the pad of her thumb.

Tyger, Tyger, she sang to herself, stirring the power in her veins, unsheathing it the way she would a knife. She snapped her fingers, and a small flame burst to life in her hand. In its flickering light, Lila scanned the list of supplies, and got to work.

"I think that's it," she said, shouldering the canvas bag. Scrolls threatened to spill out, and vials clattered softly inside, bottles of blood and ink, herbs and sand and other things the names of which made no sense. In addition to Tieren's list, she'd nicked a flask of something called "sleep sweet" and a tiny ampule marked "seer's tea," but she'd left the rest, feeling quite impressed with her restraint.

Lenos stood by the doors, one hand against the wood, and she didn't know if he needed support or was simply listening, the way a sailor sometimes did to a coming storm, not with sound but touch.

"Someone is still knocking," he said softly. "And I think there are more of them now."

Which meant they couldn't go out, not the way they'd come, not without trouble. Lila stepped into the hall and looked around at the branching paths, summoning to mind the map and wishing she'd had time to study more than her own intended path. She snapped her fingers. Fire came to life in her palm, and she held her breath as the flame settled, then began to dance subtly. Lila took off, Lenos on her heels as she followed the draft.

Behind them came the short sound of something rolling from a high shelf.

Lila spun, fire flaring in her hand, in time see the stone orb shatter on the floor.

She braced for an attack that never came. Instead, only a pair of familiar amethyst eyes caught the light.

"Esa?"

Alucard's cat crept forward, hackles raised, but the moment she made toward it, the creature shied away, obviously spooked, and darted through the nearest open door. Lila swore under her breath. She thought of letting it go—she hated the cat, and she was pretty sure the feeling was mutual—but maybe it knew another way out.

Lila and Lenos followed the cat through one door and then a second, the rooms around them turning cold enough to frost. Beyond the third open door they found a kind of cloister, open to the morning air. A dozen arches led onto a garden, not groomed like the rest of the Sanctuary, but wild—a tangle of trees, some winter dead and others summer green. It reminded her of the palace courtyard where she'd found Rhy the day before, only without a shred of order. Flowers bloomed and vines snaked across the path, and beyond the garden—

But beyond the garden, there was *nothing.*

No arches. No doors. The cloisters faced the river, and somewhere beyond the wild foliage, the garden simply ended, dropping away into shadow.

"Esa?" she called, but the cat had darted between hedges and was nowhere to be seen. Lila shivered and swore at the sudden, cutting cold. She was already turning back toward the doors, but she could see the question in Lenos's eyes. The whole crew knew how much the stupid cat meant to Alucard. He'd once jokingly told her that it was a talisman he kept his heart inside, but he'd also confessed that Esa was a gift from his beloved younger sister. Maybe in a way, both were true.

Lila swore and slung the satchel into Lenos's arms. "Stay here."

She turned her collar up against the cold and stormed into the garden, stepping over wild vines and ducking low branches. It was probably some kind of metaphor for the chaos of the natural world—she could almost hear Tieren lecturing her on treading lightly as she drew her sharpest knife and hacked an obnoxious vine aside.

"Here, Esa," she called. She was halfway through the garden when she realized she could no longer see the path ahead. Or behind. It was as though she'd stepped out of London entirely, into a world made of nothing but mist.

"Come back, kitty," she muttered, reaching the garden's edge, "or I swear to god I will throw you into the . . ." Lila trailed off. The garden ended abruptly in front of her, roots trailing onto a platform of pale stone. And at the platform's edge, just as she'd thought, there was no wall, no barrier. Only a sheer drop into the black slick of the Isle below.

"Haven't you heard?"

Lila spun toward the voice and found a girl no taller than her waist standing between her and the garden's edge. A novice dressed in white Sanctuary robes, her dark hair pulled cleanly back into a braid. Her eyes swirled with Osaron's magic, and Lila's fingers tightened on her blade. She didn't want to kill the girl. Not if there was some part of her still inside, trying to get out. She didn't want to, but she would.

The little novice craned her head, staring up at the pale sky. Bruised skin ringed her fingernails and drew dark lines up her cheeks. "The king is calling."

"Is that so?" asked Lila, cheating a step toward the garden.

The mist was thickening around them, swallowing the edges of the world. And then, out of nowhere, it began to snow. A flake drifted down, landing on her cheek, and—

Lila winced as a tiny blade of ice nicked her skin.

"What the hell . . ."

The novice giggled as Lila wiped her cheek with the back of her sleeve as all around her, snowflakes sharpened into knifepoints and came raining down. The fire was in Lila's hands before she thought to call it, and she ducked her head as the heat swept around her in a shield, ice melting before it met her skin.

"Nice trick," she muttered, looking up.

But the novice was gone.

An instant later a small, icy hand slid around Lila's wrist.

"Got you!" said the girl, her voice still filled with laughter as shadow poured from her fingers, only to recoil from Lila's skin. The girl's face fell.

"You're one of *them,*" she said, disgusted. But instead of letting go, her hand vised tighter. The girl was strong—inhumanly strong—black veins coursing over her skin like ropes, and she dragged Lila away from the garden, toward the place where the Sanctuary ended and the marble fell away. Far below, the river stretched in a still black plane.

"Let go of me," warned Lila.

The novice did not. "He's not happy with you, Delilah Bard."

"Let *go.*"

Lila's boots skidded on the slick stone surface. Four strides to the edge of the platform. Three.

"He heard what you said about setting Kell free. And if you don't let him in"—another giggle—"he'll drown you in the sea."

"Well, aren't you creepy," snarled Lila, trying one last time to wrench free. When that didn't work, she drew a knife.

It was barely out of its sheath when another hand, this one massive, caught her wrist and twisted viciously until she dropped the weapon. When Lila turned, trapped now between the two, she found a royal guard, broader than Barron, with a dark beard and the ruined remains of *her* mark on his forehead.

"Have you met the shadow king?" he boomed.

"Oh hell," said Lila as a third figure strode out of the garden. An old woman, barefoot and dressed in nothing but a shimmering night-gown.

"Why won't you let him in?"

Lila had had enough. She threw up her hands and *pushed,* the way she had in the ring so recently. Bodily. Will against will. But what-ever these people were made of now, it didn't work. They simply bent around the force. It moved right through them like wind through wheat, and then they were dragging her again toward the precipitous drop.

Two strides.

"I don't want to hurt you," she lied. At that moment, she wanted to hurt them all quite badly, but it wouldn't stop the monster pulling their strings. She scrambled to think of something.

One stride, and she was out of time. Lila's boot connected with the little girl's chest and sent the novice stumbling away. She then flicked her fingers, producing a second knife, and drove it between the joints of the guard's armor at the knee. Lila expected the man to buckle, to scream, to at least *let go*. He did none of those things.

"Oh, come on," she growled as he pushed her half a step toward the edge, the novice and the woman barring her escape.

"The king wants you to pay," said the guard.

"The king wants you to beg," said the girl.

"The king wants you to kneel," said the old woman.

Their voices all had the same horrible singsong quality, and the ledge was coming up against her heels.

"Beg for your city."

"Beg for your world."

"Beg for your life."

"I don't *beg*," growled Lila, slamming her foot into the blade embedded in the guard's knee. At last his leg buckled, but when he went down, he took her with him. Luckily he fell *away* from the ledge, and she rolled free and came up again, the woman's thin arms already winding around her throat. Lila threw her off, into the approaching novice, and danced back several feet from the edge.

Now, at least, she had the garden behind her and not the stone cliff.

But all three attackers were upright again, their eyes full of shadows and their mouths full of Osaron's words. And if Lila ran, they would simply follow.

Her blood sang with the thrill of the fight and her fingers itched to summon fire, but fire only worked if you cared about getting burned. A body without fear would never slow in the face of flame. No, what Lila needed was something of substance. Of weight.

She looked down at the broad stone platform.

It could work.

"He wants me to kneel?" she said, letting her legs fold beneath her, the cold stone hitting her knees. The fallen watched darkly as she pressed both palms to the marble floor and scoured her memory for a piece of Blake—something, anything to center her mind—but then, suddenly Lila realized she didn't *need* the words. She felt for the pulse in the rock and found a steady thrum, like a plucked string.

The fallen were starting toward her again, but it was too late.

Lila caught hold of the threads and pulled.

The ground shook beneath her. The girl and the guard and the old woman looked down as fissures formed like deep roots in the stone floor. A vicious crack ran edge to edge, severing the ledge from the garden, the fallen souls from Delilah Bard. And then it broke, and the three went tumbling down into the river below with a crash and a wave and then nothing.

Lila straightened, breathless, a defiant smile cracking across her lips as a few last bits of rock tumbled free and fell clattering out of sight. Not the most elegant solution, she knew, but effective.

Within the garden, someone was calling her name.

Lenos.

She turned toward him just as a tendril of darkness wrapped around her leg, and *pulled*.

Lila hit the ground hard.

And kept falling.

Sliding.

Shadow was coiled around her ankle like a stubborn vine—no, like a *hand,* dragging her toward the edge. She skidded over the broken ground, scrambling for something, anything to hold on to as the edge came nearer and nearer, and then she was over, and falling, nothing but black river below.

Lila's fingers caught the edge. She held on with all her strength.

The darkness held on too, pulling her down as the broken edge of the stone platform cut into her palms, and blood welled, and only then, when the first drops fell, did the darkness recoil, and let go.

Lila hung there, gasping, forcing her gashed hands to take her weight as she hauled herself up, hooked one boot on the jagged lip and dragged her body up and over.

She rolled onto her back, hands throbbing, gasping for breath.

She was still lying there when Lenos finally arrived.

He looked around at the broken platform, the streaks of blood. His eyes went saucer wide. "What *happened*?"

Lila dragged herself to a sitting position. "Nothing," she muttered, getting to her feet. Blood was still sliding in fat drops down her fingers.

"This is nothing?"

Lila rolled her neck. "Nothing I couldn't handle," she amended.

That's when she noticed the fluffy white mass in his arms. Esa.

"She came when I called," he said shyly. "And I think we found a way out."

FIVE

ASH AND ATONEMENT

I

"Fascinating," said Tieren, turning Alucard's hands over, tracing a bony finger through the air above his silver-scarred wrists. "Does it hurt?"

"No," said Alucard slowly. "Not anymore."

Rhy watched from his perch on the back of the couch, fingers laced to keep them from shaking.

The king and Kell studied Tieren as Tieren studied the captain, spotting the heavy silence with questions that Alucard tried to answer, even though he was clearly still suffering.

He wouldn't say what it was like, only that he'd been delirious, and in that fevered state, the shadow king had tried to get inside his mind. And Rhy did not betray him by saying more. His hands still ached from clenching Alucard's, his body stiff from his time on the *Spire* floor, but if Kell felt that pain, he said nothing of it, and for that, amid so many things, Rhy was grateful.

"So Osaron *does* need permission," said Tieren.

Alucard swallowed. "Most people, I imagine, give it without knowing. The sickness came on fast. By the time I realized what was happening, he was already inside my head. And the moment I tried to resist . . ." Alucard trailed off. Met Rhy's gaze. "He twists your mind, your memories."

"But now," cut in Maxim, "his magic cannot touch you?"

"So it seems."

"Who found you?" he demanded.

Kell shot a look at Hastra, who stepped forward. "I did, Your Majesty," lied the former guard. "I saw him go, and—"

Rhy cut him off. "Hastra didn't find Captain Emery. *I* did."

His brother sighed, exasperated.

His mother went still.

"Where?" demanded Maxim in a voice that had always made Rhy shrink. Now, he held his ground.

"On his ship. By the time I arrived, he was already ill. I stayed with him to see if he'd survive, and he did—"

His father had flushed red, his mother pale. "You went out there, alone," she said. "Into the fog?"

"The shadows did not touch me."

"You put yourself at risk," chided his father.

"I am in no danger."

"You could have been taken."

"You don't get it!" snapped Rhy. "Whatever part of me Osaron could take, it's already gone."

The room went still. He couldn't bring himself to look at Kell. He could feel the quickening of his brother's pulse, the weight of his stare.

And then the door burst open, and Lila Bard stormed in, trailed by a thin, nervous-looking man holding, of all things, a *cat*. She saw—or felt—the tension humming through the room and stopped. "What did I miss?"

Her hands were bandaged, a deep scratch ran along her jaw, and Rhy watched his brother move toward her as naturally as if the world had simply tipped. For Kell, apparently, it had.

"*Casero*," said the man trailing behind her, his gaunt eyes lighting up at the sight of Alucard. He'd clearly come from beyond the palace, but he showed no signs of harm.

"Lenos," said the captain as the cat leaped down and went to curl around his boot. "Where . . . ?"

"Long story," cut in Lila, tossing the satchel to Tieren, and then, registering the silver scars on Alucard's face: "What happened to *you*?"

"Long story," he echoed.

Lila went to the sideboard to pour herself a drink. "Aren't they all at this point?"

She said it lightly, but Rhy noticed her fingers shaking as she brought the amber liquid to her lips.

The king was staring at the thin and rather scraggly looking sailor. "How did you get into the palace?" he demanded.

The man looked nervously from king to queen to Kell.

"He's my second mate, Your Majesty," answered Alucard.

"That doesn't answer my question."

"We found each other—" started Lila.

"He can speak for himself," snapped the king.

"Maybe if you bothered questioning your people in their own language," she shot back. The room quieted. Kell raised a brow. Rhy, despite himself, almost laughed.

A guard appeared in the doorway and cleared his throat. "Your Majesty," he said, "the prisoner wishes to speak."

Lila stiffened at the mention of Holland. Alucard sank heavily into a chair.

"Finally," said Maxim, starting toward the door, but the guard ducked his head, embarrassed.

"Not with you, Your Majesty." He nodded at Kell. "With him."

Kell looked to Maxim, who nodded brusquely. "Bring me answers," he warned, "or I will find another way to get them."

A shadow crossed Kell's face, but he only bowed and left.

Rhy watched his brother go, then turned to his father. "If Alucard survived, there must be others. Let me—"

"Did you know?" demanded Maxim.

"What?"

"When you left the safety of this palace, did you *know* you were immune to Osaron's magic?"

"I suspected," said Rhy, "but I would have gone either way."

The queen took hold of his arm. "After everything—"

"Yes, after everything," said Rhy, pulling free. "*Because* of everything." He turned to his parents. "You taught me that a ruler suffers with his people. You taught me that he is their strength, their stone. Don't you see? I will never have magic, but finally I have a *purpose*."

"Rhy—" started his father.

"No," he cut in. "I will not let them think the Maresh have abandoned them. I will not hide within a warded palace when I can walk without fear through those streets. When I can remind our people that they are not alone, that I am fighting with them, *for* them. When I may be struck down but rise again and in so doing show them the immortality of hope. That is what I can do for my city, and I will gladly do it. You need not shield me from the darkness. It cannot hurt me anymore. Nothing can."

Rhy felt suddenly wrung out, empty, but in that emptiness lay a kind of peace. No, not peace exactly. Clarity. Resolve.

He looked to his mother, who was clutching her hands together. "Would you have me be your son, or the prince of Arnes?"

Her knuckles went white. "You will always be both."

"Then I will succeed at neither."

He met the king's gaze, but it was the head priest who spoke.

"The prince is right," said Tieren in his soft, steady way. "The royal and city guard are cut in half, and the priests are at their limits trying to keep the palace wards up. Every man and woman immune to Osaron's magic is an ally we cannot forfeit. We need every life we can save."

"Then it's settled," said Rhy. "I will ride out—"

"Not alone," cut in his father, and again, before Rhy could protest, "*No one* goes alone."

Alucard looked up from his seat, pale, exhausted. His hands tightened on the chair, and he started to rise when Lila stepped forward, finishing her drink. "Lenos, put the captain to bed," she said, and then, turning to the king, "I'll go with His Highness."

Maxim frowned. "Why should I trust *you* with my son's safety?"

She tilted her head when she spoke, shifting her dark hair so it framed her shattered eye. In that single defiant gesture, Rhy could see why Kell liked her so.

"Why?" she echoed. "Because the shadows can't touch me, and the fallen won't. Because I'm good with magic, and better with a blade, and I've got more power in my blood than you've got in this whole damned palace. Because I've no qualms about killing, and on top of it all, I've got a knack for keeping your sons—*both* of them—alive."

If Kell had been there, he would have turned white.

As it was, the king went nearly purple.

Alucard let out a small, exhausted sound that might have been a laugh.

The queen stared blankly at the strange girl.

And Rhy, despite everything, smiled.

The prince had only a single suit of armor.

It had never seen battle, never seen anything but a sculptor's eye, cast for the small stone portrait in his parents' chamber, a gift from Maxim to Emira on their tenth anniversary. Rhy had worn the armor just the once—he'd planned to wear it again on the night of his twentieth birthday, but nothing about that night had gone as planned.

The armor was light, too light for a real fight, but perfect for posing, a soft hammered gold with pearl-white trim and a cream-colored cape, and it made the faintest chime whenever he moved, a pleasant sound like a far-off bell.

"Not very subtle, are you?" said Lila when she saw him striding through the palace foyer.

She'd been standing in the doorway, her eyes on the city and the fog still shifting in the late morning light, but at the gentle sound of Rhy's approach, she'd turned, and nearly laughed out loud. And he supposed she had reason to. After all, Lila was dressed in her worn boots and her black high-collared coat, looking with her bandaged hands like a pirate after a hard night, and there *he* was, practically glowing in polished gold, a full complement of silvered guards behind him.

"I've never been fond of subtle," he said.

Rhy imagined Kell shaking his head, exasperation warring with amusement. Perhaps he looked foolish, but Rhy *wanted* to be seen, wanted his people—if they were out there, if they were *in* there—to know their prince was not hiding. That he was not afraid of the dark.

As they descended the palace stairs, Lila's expression hardened, her wounded hands curled into loose fists at her sides. He didn't know what she'd seen at the Sanctuary, but he could tell it hadn't been pleasant, and for all her jaunty posturing, the look on her face now threw him.

"You think this is a bad idea," he said. It wasn't a question. But it sparked something in Lila, rekindled the fire in her eyes and ignited a grin.

"Without a doubt."

"Then why are you smiling?"

"Because," she said, "bad ideas are my favorite kind."

They reached the plaza at the base of the stairs, the flowers that usually lined the steps now sculptures of black glass. Smoke rose from a dozen spots on the horizon, not the simple trails from hearth fires, but the too-dark plumes of burning buildings. Rhy straightened. Lila pulled her jacket close. "Ready?"

"I don't need a chaperone."

"Good thing," she said, setting off. "I don't need a prince tripping on my heels."

Rhy started. "You told my father—"

"That I could you keep alive," she said, glancing back. "But you don't need me to."

Something in Rhy loosened. Because of all the people in his life, his brother and his parents and his guards and even Alucard Emery, Lila was the first—the only—person to treat him like he didn't need saving.

"Guards," he called, hardening his voice. "Split up."

"Your Highness," started one. "We're not to lea—"

He turned on them. "We've too much ground to cover, and last time I checked, we all had a pair of working eyes"—he shot a look at Lila, realizing his error, but she only shrugged—"so put them to use, and *find me my survivors.*"

It was a grim pursuit.

Rhy found too many bodies, and worse, the places where bodies *should* have been but where only a tatter of fabric and a pile of ash were left, the rest blown away by the winter wind. He thought of Alucard's sister, Anisa, burning from the inside out. Thought of what happened to those who lost their battle with Osaron's magic. And what of the fallen? The thousands of people who had *not* fought against the shadow king, but had given in, given way. Were they still in there, prisoners of their own minds? Could they be saved? Or were they already lost?

"*Vas ir,*" he murmured over the bodies he found, and the ones he didn't.

Go in peace.

The streets were hardly empty, but he moved through the masses like a ghost, their shadowed eyes passing over him, through him. He walked in gleaming gold, and still they did not notice. He called to them, but they did not answer. Did not turn.

Whatever part of me Osaron could take, it's already gone.

Did he really believe that?

His boot slid a little on the ground, and, looking down, he saw that a piece of the street had *changed,* from stone to something else, something glassy and black, like the flowers on the stairs.

He knelt, brushing his gloved hand against the smooth patch. It wasn't cold. Wasn't warm, either. Wasn't wet like ice. It wasn't *anything.* Which made no sense. Rhy straightened, perplexed, and kept looking for something, *someone,* he could help.

Silvers, that's what some were calling them, those who'd been burned by Osaron's magic and survived. The priests, it turned out, had discovered a handful already, most rising from the fever beds that lined the Rose Hall.

But how many more waited in the city?

In the end, Rhy didn't find the first silver.

The silver found him.

The young boy came stumbling toward him out of a house and sank to his knees at Rhy's feet. Lines danced like light over his skin, his black hair falling over fever-bright eyes. "*Mas vares.*"

My prince.

Rhy knelt in his armor, scratching the plate as gold met stone. "It's all right," he said as the boy sobbed, tears tracing fresh tracks over the silver on his cheeks.

"All alone," he murmured, breath hitching. "All alone."

"Not anymore," said the prince.

He rose and started toward the house, but small fingers caught his hand. The boy shook his head, and Rhy saw the ash dusting the boy's front, and understood. There was no one else inside the house.

Not anymore.

II

Lila went straight for the night market.

The city around her wasn't empty. It would have been less chilling if it were. Instead, those who'd fallen under Osaron's spell moved through the streets like sleepwalkers carrying out remembered tasks while deep within their dreams.

The night market was a shadow of its former self, half of it burned, and the rest carrying on in that dazed and ghostly way.

A fruit vendor hawked winter apples, his eyes swimming with shadows, while a woman carried flowers, their edges frosting black. The whole thing had a haunted air, a sea of puppets, and Lila kept squinting at the air around them as if looking for the strings.

Rhy moved through the city like a specter, but Lila was like an unwelcome guest. The people looked at her when she passed, their eyes narrowing, but the cuts on her palms were still fresh, and the blood kept them at bay, even as their whispers trailed her through the streets.

Scattered throughout the market, as if someone had splashed inky water onto the ground and let it freeze, were patches of black ice. Lila stepped around them with a thief's sure footing and a fighter's grace.

She was making her way toward Calla's familiar green tent at the end of the market when she saw a man pitch a basin of flaming stones into the river. He was broad and bearded, silver scars tracing his hands and throat.

"You couldn't get me, you monster!" he was screaming. "You couldn't hold me down."

The basin hit the river with a crash, rippling the half-frozen water and sending up a plume of hissing steam.

And just like that, the illusion shattered.

The man selling apples and the woman with flowers and every other fallen in the marketplace broke off and turned toward the man, as if waking from a dream. Only they weren't waking. Instead, it was like the darkness rose inside them, Osaron rousing and turning his head, looking through their eyes. They moved as a single body, one that wasn't theirs.

"Idiot," muttered Lila, starting toward him, but the man didn't seem to notice. Didn't seem to *care*.

"Face me, you coward!" he bellowed as part of the nearest tent tore free and lifted into the air beside him.

The crowd hummed in displeasure.

"How dare you," said a merchant, eyes shining dully as he drew a knife.

"The king will not stand for this," said a second, twining rope between her hands.

The air shook with the sudden urge for violence, and realization struck Lila like a blow—Osaron gained obedience from the fallen, and energy from the fevered. But he had no use for the ones who'd fought free of his spell. And what he couldn't use . . .

Lila ran.

Her injured leg throbbed as she sprinted toward him.

"Look out!" she shouted, her first blade already flying. It caught the nearest attacker in the chest, buried to the hilt, but the merchant's own knife had left his hand before he fell.

Lila tackled the scarred man to the ground as metal sang over their heads.

The stranger looked up at her in shock, but there wasn't time. The fallen were circling them, weapons raised. The man slammed a fist into the ground, and a piece of road as wide as a market stall tipped up into a shield.

He raised another makeshift wall and turned, clearly intending to summon a third, but Lila had no desire to be entombed. She dragged the man to his feet, sprinting into the nearest tent before a steel kettle thudded against the heavy canvas side.

"Keep moving," she called, carving her way through a second tent wall and then a third before the man hauled her to a stop.

"Why did you do that?"

Lila wrenched free. "A thank-you would be nice. I lost my fifth favorite knife out—"

He forced her back against the tent pole. "Why?" he snarled, eyes wide. They were a shocking green, flecked with black and gold.

A swift kick to the ribs with the bottom of her boot, and he went stumbling backward, though not as far as she'd hoped. "Because you were shouting your head off at nothing but shadow and mist. A tip: don't start a fight like that if you want to live."

"I didn't *want* to live." His voice shook as he looked down at his silver-scarred hands. "I didn't want *this*."

"A lot of people would love to trade places."

"That monster took everything. My wife. My father. I fought through it because I thought someone would be waiting for me. But when I woke—when I—" He made a strangled sound. "You should have let me die."

Lila frowned. "What's your name?"

"What?"

"You have a name. What is it?"

"Manel."

"Well, Manel. Dying doesn't help the dead. It doesn't find the lost. A lot of people have fallen. But some of us are still standing. So if you want to give up, walk out that curtain. I won't stop you. I won't save you again. But if you want to put your second chance to better use, come with me."

She turned on her heel and slashed the next tent wall, stepping through, only to slam to a stop.

She'd found Calla's tent.

"What is it?" asked Manel behind her. "What's wrong?"

"This is the last tent," she said slowly. "Go out the flap, and head for the palace."

Manel spat. "The *palace*. The royals hid inside their palace while my family died. The king and queen sat safe on their thrones while London fell and that spoiled prince—"

"Enough," snarled Lila. "That spoiled prince is searching the streets for men like you. He's hunting for the living and burying the dead and doing everything he can to keep one from becoming the other, so you can either help or disappear, but either way, get out."

He looked at her long and hard, then swore beneath his breath and vanished through the tent's flap, bells jingling in his wake.

Lila turned her attention back to the empty shop.

"Calla?" she called, hoping the woman was there, hoping she wasn't. The lanterns that hung in the corners were unlit, the hats and scarves and hoods on the walls casting strange shapes in the dark. Lila snapped her fingers, and the light sparked in her hand, unsteady but bright as she crossed the small tent, searching for any sign of the merchant. She wanted to see the woman's kind smile, wanted to hear Calla's teasing words. She wanted Calla to be far, far away, wanted her to be safe.

Something cracked beneath Lila's boot.

A glass bead, like the ones in the trunk Lila had brought ashore. The box of gold thread and ruby clasps and a dozen other tiny, beautiful things she'd given Calla to pay for the coat, and the mask, and the kindness.

The beads were scattered across the floor in a messy trail that vanished beneath the hem of a second curtain hung near the back of the stall. The light slid beneath, struck gem, and rug, and something solid.

Delilah Bard never read many books.

The few she did had pirates and thieves, and always ended with freedom and the promise of more stories. Characters sailed away. They lived on. Lila always imagined people that way, a series of intersections and adventures. It was easy when you moved through life—through worlds—the way she did. Easy when you didn't care, when people came onto the page and walked away again, back to their own stories, and you could imagine whatever you wanted for them, if you cared enough to write it in your head.

Barron had walked into her life and refused to walk back out, and then he'd gone and died and she had to keep remembering that over and over instead of letting him live on in some version without her.

She didn't want that for Calla.

She didn't want to look behind the curtain, didn't want to know the end of this story, but her hand reached out of its own traitorous accord and pulled the fabric back.

She saw the body on the floor.

Oh, thought Lila dully. *There she is.*

Calla, who had drawn the *i*'s of Lila's name into *e*'s, and always sounded on the verge of laughing.

Calla, who had simply smiled when Lila walked in one night and asked for a man's coat instead of a woman's dress.

Calla, who'd thought Lila was in love with a black-eyed prince, even before Lila really had been. Calla, who wanted Kell to be happy just as a man, not as an *aven.* Who wanted *her*—*Lila*—to be happy.

The box of trinkets Lila had once brought home for the merchant now lay open on its side, spilling a hundred spots of light onto the floor around the woman's head.

Calla was lying on her side, her short, round body curled in on itself, one hand beneath her cheek. But the other hand was pressed over her ear, as if trying to block something out, and for a moment, Lila thought—hoped—she was sleeping. Thought—hoped—she could kneel down and shake the woman gently, and she would get up.

Of course, Calla wasn't a woman anymore. She wasn't even a body. Her eyes—what was left of those warm eyes—were open, the same ruined shade as the rest of her, the chalky grey of hearth ash after the fire's gone and cooled.

Lila's throat closed.

This is why I run.

Because caring was a thing with claws. It sank them in, and didn't let go. Caring hurt more than a knife to the leg, more than a few broken ribs, more than anything that bled or broke and healed again. Caring didn't break you clean. It was a bone that didn't set, a cut that wouldn't close.

It was better not to care—Lila *tried* not to care—but sometimes, people got in. Like a knife against armor, they found the cracks, slid past the guard, and you didn't know how deep they were buried until they were gone and you were bleeding on the floor. And it wasn't fair. Lila hadn't asked to care about Calla. She hadn't wanted to let her in. So why did it still hurt this much?

Lila felt the tears spilling down her cheeks.

"Calla."

She didn't know why she said it that way, soft, as if a soft voice could wake the dead.

She didn't know why she said it at all.

But she didn't have time to wonder. As Lila took a step forward, a gust of winter air cut through the tent, and Calla simply . . . blew apart.

Lila let out a strangled cry and lunged for the curtain, but it was too late.

Calla was already gone.

Nothing but a collapsing pile of ash, and a hundred bits of silver and gold.

Something folded in Lila, then. She sank to the ground, ignoring the bite of the glass beads where they cut into her knees, fingers digging into the threadbare rug.

She didn't mean to summon fire.

It wasn't until the smoke tickled her lungs that Lila realized the tent was catching. Half of her wanted to let it burn, but the rest couldn't bear the thought of Calla's store burning away like her life, nothing left. Never to be seen again.

Lila pressed her hands together, smothering the fire.

She wiped the tears away and got up.

III

Kell stood before Holland's cell, waiting for the man to speak.

He didn't. Didn't even raise his gaze to meet Kell's own. The man's eyes were fixed on something in the distance, beyond the bars, beyond the walls, beyond the city. A cold anger burned in them, but it seemed directed inward as much as out, at himself and the monster who had poisoned his mind, stolen his body.

"You summoned *me,*" said Kell at last. "I assumed you had something to say."

When Holland still didn't answer, he turned to go.

"One hundred and eighty-two."

Kell glanced back. "What?"

Holland's attention was still pointedly somewhere else. "That is the number of people killed by Astrid and Athos Dane."

"And how many killed by *you*?"

"Sixty-seven," answered Holland without hesitation. "Three before I became a slave. Sixty-four before I became a king. And none since." At last, he looked at Kell. "I value life. I've issued death. You were raised a prince, Kell. I watched my whole world wither, day by day, season by season, year by year, and the only thing that kept me going was the hope that I was *Antari* for a reason. That I could do something to help."

"I thought the only thing that kept you going was the binding spell branded into your skin."

Holland cocked his head. "By the time *you* met me, the only thing that kept me going was the thought of killing Athos and Astrid Dane. And then you took that from me."

Kell scowled. "I won't apologize for depriving you of your revenge."

Holland said nothing. Then, "When I asked you what you would have had me do upon waking in Black London, you told me that I should have stayed there. That I should have died. I thought about it. I knew that Athos Dane was dead. I could feel that much." The chains rattled as he reached to tap the ruined branding on his chest. "But *I* wasn't. I didn't know why, but I thought of who'd I'd been, those years before they stripped me down to hate, of what I'd wanted for my world. That's what drove me home. Not fear of death—death is gentle, death is kind—but the hope that I was still capable of something more. And the idea of being free—" He blinked, as if he'd drifted.

The words rang through Kell's chest, echoing chords.

"What will happen to me now?" There was no fear in his voice. There was *nothing* at all.

"I assume you will be tried—"

Holland was shaking his head. "No."

"You're in no place to make demands."

Holland sat forward as far as the chains would let him.

"I don't want a trial, Kell," he said firmly. "I want an execution."

IV

The words landed, as Holland knew they would.

Kell was staring at him, waiting for the twist, the turn.

"An execution?" he said, shaking his head. "Your penchant for self-destruction is impressive, but—"

"It's a matter of practicality," said Holland, letting his shoulders graze the wall, "not atonement."

"I don't follow."

You never do, he thought bleakly.

"How is it done here?" he asked, a false lightness in his voice, as if they were talking of a meal or a dance, and not an execution. "By blade or by fire?"

Kell stared at him blankly, as if he'd never even seen one.

"I imagine," said the other *Antari* slowly, "it would be done by the blade." So Holland was right, then. "How was it done in *your* city?"

Holland had witnessed his first execution on his brother's shoulders. Had followed Alox to the square for years. He remembered the arms forced wide, deep cuts and broken bones and fresh blood caught in basins. "Executions in my London were slow, and brutal, and very public."

Distaste washed across Kell's face. "We don't glorify death with displays."

The chains rattled as Holland sat forward. "This one *needs* to be public. Something out in the open where he can see."

"What are you getting at?"

"Osaron needs a body. He cannot take this world without one."

"Is that so?" challenged Kell. "Because he's doing an impressive job of it so far."

"It's clumsy, broad strokes," said Holland dismissively. "This isn't what he wants."

"You would know."

Holland ignored the jab. "There is no glory in a crown he cannot wear, even if he has not realized it yet. Osaron is a creature of potential. He will never be satisfied with what he has, not for long. And for all his power, all his conjuring, he cannot craft flesh and blood. Not that it will stop him from trying, and poisoning every soul in London in search of a pawn or vessel, but none will do."

"Because he needs an *Antari*."

"And he has only three options."

Kell stiffened. "You knew about Lila?"

"Of course," said Holland evenly. "I'm not a fool."

"Fool enough to play into Osaron's hands," said Kell through clenched teeth. "Fool enough to call for your own execution. To what end? Reduce his options from three to two, and he still—"

"I plan to give him what he wants," said Holland grimly. "I plan to kneel and beg and invite him in. I plan to grant him his vessel." Kell stared in bald disgust. "And then I plan to let you kill me."

Kell's disgust turned to shock, then confusion.

Holland smiled, a cold, rueful twitch of the lips.

"You should learn to guard your feelings."

Kell swallowed, made a thin attempt to mask his features. "As much as I'd like to kill you, Holland, doing so won't kill *him*. Or have you forgotten that magic does not die?"

"Perhaps not, but it can be contained."

"With what?"

"As Tosal."

Kell flinched reflexively at the sound of a blood command, then paled as the realization dawned. "No."

"So you do know the spell?"

"I could turn you to stone. It would be a kinder end."

"I'm not looking for kindness, Kell." Holland tilted his chin up, attention settling on the cell's high ceiling. "I'm looking to finish what I started."

The *Antari* ran a hand through his copper hair. "If Osaron doesn't take the bait. If he doesn't come, then you'll die."

"Death comes for us all," said Holland evenly. "I would simply have mine mean something."

The second time someone tried to kill Holland, he was eighteen, walking home with a loaf of coarse bread in one hand and a bottle of *kaash* in the other.

The sun was going down, the city taking on another shape. It was a risk, to walk with both hands full, but Holland had grown into his frame, long limbs corded with muscle, shoulders broad and straight. He no longer wore his black hair down over his eye. He no longer tried to hide.

Halfway home, he realized he was being followed.

He didn't stop, didn't turn around, didn't even quicken his pace.

Holland didn't go looking for fights, but still they came to him. Trailed him through the streets like strays, like shadows.

He kept walking, now, letting the soft clink of the bottle and the steady tread of his boot form a backdrop for the sounds of the alley around him.

The shuffle of steps.

The soft exhale before a weapon's release.

A blade whistling out of the dark.

Holland dropped the bread and turned, one hand raised. The knife stopped an inch from his throat and hung there in the air, waiting to be plucked. Instead, he twirled his hand and the blade spun on its edge, reversing course. With a flick of his finger, he flung the metal back into the dark, where it found flesh. Someone screamed.

Three more men came out of the shadows. Not by choice— Holland was dragging them forward, their faces contorted as they fought their own bones, his will on their bodies stronger than their own.

He could feel their hearts racing, blood pounding through their veins.

One of the men tried to speak, but Holland willed his mouth shut. He didn't care what they had to say.

All three were young, though a little older than Holland himself, with tattoos already staining their wrists and lips and temples. Blood and word, the sources of power. He had half a mind to walk away and leave them pinned in the street, but this was the third attack in less than a month, and he was getting tired.

He loosened a single pair of jaws.

"Who sent you?"

"Ros . . . Ros Vortalis," stammered the youth through still-clenched teeth.

It wasn't the first time he'd heard the name. It wasn't even the first time he'd heard the name from one of the would-be killers following him home. Vortalis was a thug from the *shal*, a nobody trying to carve a piece of power from a place with too little to spare. A man trying to get Holland's attention in all the wrong ways.

"Why?" he demanded.

"He told us . . . to bring him . . . your head."

Holland sighed. The bread was still on the ground. The wine was beginning to frost. "Tell this *Vortalis* that if he wants my head, he'll have to come for it himself."

With that, he flicked his fingers, and the men went flying backward, just like the knife, slamming into the alley walls with a solid thud. They fell and didn't get back up, and Holland took up the bread, stepped over their bodies—chests still rising—and continued home.

When he got there, he pressed his palm to the door, felt the locks slide free within the wood, and eased it open. There was a slip of paper on the floor, and he was halfway to it when he heard the padding rush of steps, and looked up just in time to catch the girl. She threw her arms around his neck, and when he spun with the weight of her, the skirts of her dress fanned like petals, the edges stained from dancing.

"Hello, Hol," she said sweetly.

"Hello, Tal," he answered.

It had been nine years since Alox attacked him. Nine years trying to survive in a city out for blood, weathering every storm, every fight, every sign of trouble, all the while waiting for something better.

And then, something better came.

And her name was Talya.

Talya, a spot of color in a world of white.

Talya, who carried the sun with her wherever she went.

Talya, so fair that when she smiled, the day grew brighter.

Holland saw her in the market one night.

And next he saw her in the square.

And after that, he saw her everywhere he looked.

She had scars in the corners of her eyes that winked silver in the light, and a laugh that took his breath away.

Who could laugh like that, in a world like this?

She reminded him of Alox. Not the way he'd disappear for hours, or days, come home with blood caking his clothes, but the way her presence could make him forget about the darkness, the cold, the dying world outside their door.

"What's wrong?" she asked as he set her down.

"Nothing," he said, kissing her temple. "Nothing at all."

And perhaps that wasn't strictly true, but there was a startling truth beneath the lie: for the first time in his life, Holland was something like happy.

He stoked the fire with a glance, and Talya pulled him onto the cot they shared, and, then, tearing off pieces of bread and sipping cold wine, she told him the stories of the someday king. Just the way Alox had. The first time, Holland had flinched at the words, but didn't stop her because he liked the way she told them, so full of energy and light. The stories were her favorite—and so he let her talk.

By the third or fourth telling, he'd forgotten why the stories sounded so familiar.

By the tenth, he'd forgotten that he'd first heard them from someone else.

By the hundredth time, he'd forgotten about that other life.

That night, they lay wrapped in blankets, and she ran her fingers through his hair, and he felt himself drifting from the rhythm of the touch and the heat of the fire.

That was when she tried to cut his heart out.

She was fast, but he was faster, the knife's tip sinking only an inch before Holland came to his senses and forced her bodily away. He was up, on his feet, clutching his chest as blood leaked between his fingers.

Talya just stood there in the middle of their tiny room, their *home,* the blade hanging from her fingers.

"Why?" he asked, stunned.

"I'm sorry, Hol. They came to me in the market. Said they'd pay in silver."

He wanted to ask when, ask who, but he never got the chance.

She lunged at him again, tightly, swiftly, all her dancer's grace, and the knife whistled sweetly toward him. It happened so fast. Without thinking, Holland's fingers twitched, and her knife twisted in her grip, freezing in the air even as the rest of her kept moving forward. The blade sank smoothly between her own ribs.

Talya looked at him then with such surprise and indignation, as if she'd thought he'd let her kill him. As if she'd thought he'd simply surrender.

"Sorry, Tal," he said as she tried to breathe, to speak, and couldn't.

She tried to take a step and Holland caught her as she fell, all that dancer's grace gone out of her limbs at the end.

Holland stayed there till she died, then laid her carefully on the floor, got to his feet, and left.

V

"He wants *what*?" said the king, looking up from the map.

"An execution," repeated Kell, still reeling.

As Tosal, those had been Holland's words.

"It must be a trick," said Isra.

"I don't think so," started Kell, but the guard wasn't listening.

"Your Majesty," she said, turning to Maxim. "Surely he wants to draw Osaron in so he can escape. . . ."

As Tosal.

To confine.

Kell had used the blood spell only once in his life, on a bird, a small sunflit he'd caught in the Sanctuary gardens. The sunflit had gone perfectly still in his hands, but it hadn't died. He could feel its heart beating frantically beneath its feathered breast while it lay motionless, as if paralyzed, trapped inside its own body.

When Tieren had found out, the *Aven Essen* was furious. Blood spell or not, Kell had broken the cardinal rule of power: he had used magic to harm a living creature, to alter its life. Kell had apologized profusely, and said the words to dispel what he'd done, to heal the damage, but to his shock and horror, the commands had no effect. Nothing he said seemed to work.

The bird didn't revive.

It just lay there, still as death, in his hands.

"I don't understand."

Tieren shook his head. "Things are not so simple, when it comes to life and death," he'd said. "With minds and bodies, what is done cannot always be undone." And then he'd taken up the sunflit, and brought it to his chest, and broken its neck. The priest had set the lifeless bird back in Kell's hands.

"That," said Tieren grimly, "was a kinder end."

He had never tried the spell again, because he'd never learned the words to undo it.

"Kell."

The king's voice jarred him out of the memory.

Kell swallowed. "Holland did what he did to save his world. I believe that. Now he wants it to be over."

"You're asking us to *trust* him?" challenged Isra.

"No," said Kell, holding the king's gaze, "I'm asking you to trust *me*."

Tieren appeared in the doorway.

Ink stained his fingers, and fatigue hollowed out his cheeks. "You called for me, Maxim?"

The king exhaled heavily. "How long until your spell is ready?"

The *Aven Essen* shook his head. "It is not a simple matter, putting an entire city to sleep. The spell must be broken down into seven or eight smaller ones and then positioned around the city to form a chain—"

"How *long*?"

Tieren made an exasperated sound. "Days, Your Majesty."

The king's gaze returned to Kell. "Can you end it?"

Kell didn't know if Maxim was asking if he had the will or the strength to kill another *Antari*.

I'm not looking for kindness, Kell. I'm looking to finish what I started.

"Yes," he answered.

The king nodded and swept his hand over the map. "The palace wards do not extend to the balconies, do they?"

"No," said Tieren. "It is all we can do to keep them up around the walls, windows, and doors."

"Very well," said the king, letting his knuckles fall to the table's edge. "The north courtyard, then. We'll raise a platform overlooking the Isle, and hold the ritual at dawn, and whether or not Osaron comes . . ." His dark eyes landed on Kell. "Holland dies by your hand."

The words followed Kell into the hall.

Holland dies by your hand.

He sank back against the map room doors, exhaustion winding around his limbs.

It's rather hard to kill an Antari.

By the blade.

A kinder end.

As Tosal.

He pushed off the wood and started for the stairs.

"Kell?"

The queen was standing at the end of the hall, looking out a pair of balcony doors at the shadow of her city. Her eyes met his in the reflection in the glass. There was a sadness in them, and he found himself taking a step toward her before he stopped. He didn't have the strength.

"Your Majesty," he said, bowing before he turned and walked away.

VI

All day Rhy had searched the city for survivors.

In ones and sometimes twos, he found them—shaken, fragile, but alive. Most were startlingly young. Only a few were very old. And just like the magic in their veins, there was no common factor. No bond of blood, or gender, or means. He found a noble girl from House Loreni, still dressed for a tournament ball, an older man in threadbare clothes tucked in an alleyway, a mother in red mourning silks, a royal guard whose mark had failed or simply faded. All now left with the silver veins of a survivor.

Rhy stayed with them only long enough to show they weren't alone, long enough to lead them to the palace steps for shelter, and then he was off again, back into the city, in search of more.

Before dusk, he returned to the *Spire*—he'd known it was too late, but had to see—and found all that was left of Anisa: a small pile of ashes, smoldering on the floor of Alucard's cabin, beyond the cage of warped planks. A few drops of silver from her House Emery ring.

Rhy was crossing the deck in numbed silence when he caught the glint of metal and saw the woman sitting on the deck with her back to a crate and a blade in her hand.

His boots hit the wooden dock with a thud.

The woman didn't move.

She was dressed like a man, like a *sailor,* a black-and-red captain's sash across her front.

At first glance, he could tell she was from the borderlands, the coast where Arnes looked onto Vesk. She had the build of a northerner and the coloring of a local, her rich brown hair worn in two massive braids that coiled like a mane around her face. Her eyes were open, unblinking, but they looked ahead with an intensity that said she was still there, and thin lines of silver shone against her sea-tanned face.

The knife in her hand was slick with blood.

It didn't appear to be hers.

A dozen warnings echoed in Rhy's head—all of them in Kell's voice—as he knelt beside her.

"What's your name?" he asked in Arnesian.

Nothing.

"Captain?"

After several long seconds, the woman blinked, a slow, final gesture.

"Jasta," she said, her voice hoarse, and then, as if the name had sparked something in her, she added, "He tried to drown me. My first mate, Rigar, tried to drag me into that whispering river." She didn't take her eyes off the ship. "So I killed him."

"Are there any others on board?" he asked.

"Half of them are missing," she said. "The others . . ." She trailed off, dark eyes dancing over the vessel.

Rhy touched her shoulder. "Can you stand?"

Jasta's face drifted toward his. She frowned. "Has anyone told you that you look like the prince?"

Rhy smiled. "Once or twice." He held out his hand and helped her to her feet.

VII

The sun had gone down, and Alucard Emery was trying to get drunk.

So far it wasn't working, but he was determined to see it through. He'd even made a little game:

Every time his mind drifted to Anisa—her bare feet, her fevered skin, her small arms around his neck—he took a drink.

Every time he thought of Berras—his brother's cutting tone, the hateful smile, the hands around his throat—he took a drink.

Every time his nightmares rose like bile, or his own screams echoed in his head, or he had to remember his sister's empty eyes, her burning heart, he took a drink.

Every time he thought of Rhy's fingers laced through his, of the prince's voice telling him to *hold on, hold on, hold on to me,* he took a very, very long drink.

Across the room, Lila seemed to be playing her own game; his quiet thief was on her third glass. It took a great deal to shake Delilah Bard, that much he knew, but still, something had shaken her. He might never be able to read the secrets in her face, but he could tell she was keeping them. What had she seen beyond the palace walls? What demons had she faced? Were they strangers or friends?

Every time he asked a question Delilah Bard would never answer, he took a drink, until the pain and grief finally began to blur into something steady.

The room rocked around him, and Alucard Emery—the last surviving Emery—slumped back in the chair, fingering the inlaid wood, the fine gold trim.

How strange it was, to be here, in Rhy's rooms. It had been strange enough when Rhy was stretched out on his bed, but then the details, the room, everything but Rhy himself, had gone out of focus. Now, Alucard took in the glittering curtains, the elegant floor, the vast bed, now made. All signs of struggle smoothed away.

Rhy's amber gaze kept swinging toward him like a pendulum on a heavy rope.

He took another drink.

And then another, and another, in preparation for the ache of want and loss and memory washing over him, a small boat pitching miserably against the waves.

Hold on to me.

That's what Rhy had said, when Alucard was burning from the inside out. When Rhy was lying there beside him in the ship's cabin, hoping desperately that his hands could keep Alucard there, and whole and safe. Keep him from vanishing again, this time forever.

Now that Alucard was alive and more or less upright, Rhy couldn't bring himself to look at his lover, and couldn't bear to look away, so he ended up doing both and neither.

It had been so long since Rhy'd been able to study his face. Three summers. Three winters. Three years, and the prince's heart still cracked along the lines Alucard had made.

They were in the conservatory, Rhy and Alucard and Lila.

The captain sat slumped in a tall-backed chair, silver scars and sapphire stud both winking in the light. A glass hung from one hand, and a fluffy white cat named Esa curled beneath his seat, and his eyes were open but far away.

Over at the sideboard, Lila was pouring herself another drink. (Was this her fourth? Rhy felt he wasn't the one to judge.) However, she was pouring a little too liberally and spilled the last of Rhy's summer wine onto his inlaid floor. There was a time when he would have cared about the stain, but it was gone, that life. It had fallen between the boards like a bit of jewelry, and now lay somewhere out of reach, vaguely remembered but easily forgotten.

"Steady, Bard."

It was the first thing Alucard had said in an hour. Not that Rhy had been waiting.

The captain was pale, his thief ashen, and the prince himself was pacing, his armor cast off like a broken shell onto a corner chair.

By the end of the first day, they'd found twenty-four silvers. Most were being kept in the Rose Hall, treated by the priests. But there were more. He knew there were more. There had to be. Rhy wanted to keep looking, to carry the search into the night, but Maxim had refused. And worse, the remaining royal guards had put him under an unyielding watch.

And what troubled Rhy as much as his own confinement when there were souls still trapped in the city was the sight of the rot spreading through London. A blackness like ice on top of the street stones and splashed across the walls, a film that wasn't a film at all, but a *change.* Rock and dirt and water all being swallowed up, replaced by something that wasn't an element at all, a glossy, dark nothing, a presence and an absence.

He'd told Tieren, pointed out a lone spot at the courtyard's edge, just outside their wards, where the void was spreading like frost. The old man's face had gone pale.

"Magic and nature exist in balance," he'd said, brushing fingers through the air above the pool of black. "This is what happens when that balance fails. When magic overwhelms nature."

The world was *decaying,* he'd explained. Only instead of going soft, like felled branches on a forest floor, it was going hard, calcifying into something like stone that wasn't stone at all.

"Would you stand still?" snapped Lila now, watching Rhy pace. "You're making me dizzy."

"I suspect," said a voice from the door, "that's the wine."

Rhy turned, relieved to see his brother. "Kell," he said, trying to summon something like humor as he tipped his glass at the four guards framing the door. "Is this what you feel like all the time?"

"Pretty much," said Kell, lifting the drink from Lila's hand and taking a long sip. Amazingly, she let him.

"How maddening," said Rhy with a groan. And then, to the men, "Could you at least sit down? Or are you trying to look like coats of armor on my walls?"

They didn't answer.

Kell returned the drink to Lila's hand and then frowned as he noticed Alucard. His brother pointedly ignored the captain's presence and poured himself a very large glass. "What are we drinking to?"

"The living," said Rhy.

"The dead," said Alucard and Lila at the same time.

"We're being thorough," added Rhy.

His attention swung back to Alucard, who was looking out at the night. Rhy realized he wasn't the only one watching the captain. Lila had followed Alucard's gaze to the glass.

"When you look at the fallen," she said, "what do you see?"

Alucard squinted dully, the way he always had when he was trying to picture something. "Knots," he said simply.

"Care to expand?" said Kell, who knew of the captain's gift, and cared for it about as much as he cared for the rest of him.

"You wouldn't understand," murmured Alucard.

"Maybe if you chose the right words."

"I couldn't make them short enough."

"Oh, for Christ's sake," snapped Lila. "If you two could stop bickering for a moment."

Alucard leaned forward in his chair and set the once-more-empty glass on the floor beside his boot, where his cat sniffed it. "This *Osaron*," he said, "is siphoning energy from everyone he touches. His magic, it feeds on ours by . . . *infecting* it. It gets in among the strings of our power, our life, and gets tangled up in our threads until everything is in knots."

"You're right," said Kell after a moment. "I have no idea what you're talking about."

"It must be maddening," said Alucard, "to know I have a power you don't."

Kell's teeth clicked together, but when he spoke, he kept his voice civil, smooth. "Believe it or not, I relish our smallest differences. Besides, I may not be able to see the world the way *you* do, but I can still recognize an asshole."

Lila snorted.

Rhy made an exasperated sound. "Enough," he said, and then, to Kell, "What did our prisoner have to say?"

At the mention of Holland, Alucard's head snapped. Lila sat forward, a glint in her eyes. Kell downed his drink, wincing, and said, "He's to be executed in the morning. A public display."

For a long moment, no one spoke.

And then Lila raised her glass.

"Well," she said cheerfully, "I'll toast to *that*."

VIII

Emira Maresh drifted through the palace like a ghost.

She heard what people said about her. They called her distant, distracted. But in truth, she was simply listening. Not only to them, but to everyone and everything beneath the gilded spires of the roof. Few people noticed the pitchers by every bed, the basins on every table. A bowl of water was a simple thing, but with the right spell, it could carry sound. With the right spell, Emira could make the palace speak.

Her fear of breaking things had taught her well to watch her step, to listen close. The world was a fragile place, full of cracks that didn't always show. One misstep, and they might fissure, break. One wrong move, and the whole of it could come crashing down, a tower of Sanct cards burned to cinders.

It was Emira's job to make sure that her world stayed strong, to shore the fractures, to listen for fresh cracks. It was her duty to keep her family safe, her palace whole, her kingdom well. It was her calling, and if she was careful enough, sharp enough, then nothing bad would happen. That is what Emira told herself.

Only *she had been wrong.*

She'd done everything she could, and Rhy had nearly died. A shadow had fallen on London. Her husband was hiding something. Kell would not look at her.

She hadn't been able to stop the cracks, but now she turned her focus on the rest of the palace.

As she walked the halls, she could hear the priests in the sparring room, the crinkle of scrolls, the drag of ink, the soft murmur as they prepared their spell.

She could hear the heavy tread of guards in armor moving through the lower levels, the deep, guttural voices of Veskans and the sibilant melody of the Faroan tongue in the eastern hall, the murmur of the nobles in the gallery as they sat up still, whispering over tea. Talking about the city, the curse, the king. What was he doing? What *could* he do? Maxim Maresh, gone soft with age and peace. Maxim Maresh, a man against a monster, against a god.

From the Rose Hall, Emira heard the toss and turn of the fevered bodies still trapped in burning dreams, and when she turned her ear to the palace's east wing she heard her son's similarly fitful sleep, echoed in turn by Kell's own restless turnings.

And through it all, the steady whisper against the windows, against the walls, words muffled by the wards, breaking down into the rise and fall and hush of the wind. A voice trying to get in.

Emira heard so many things, but she also heard the absences where sound should be, and wasn't. She heard the muffled hush of those trying too hard to be quiet. In a corner of the ballroom, a pair of guards summoning their courage. In an alcove, a noble and a magician tangled up like string. And in the map room, the sound of a single man standing alone before the table.

She went toward him, but drawing closer, she realized it wasn't her husband.

The man in the map room stood with his back to the door, head bent over the city of London. Emira watched as he reached out a single, dark finger and brought it to rest on the quartz figurine of a royal guard before the palace.

The figurine fell onto its side with the tiny clatter of stone on stone. Emira winced, but the statue did not break.

"Lord Sol-in-Ar," she said evenly.

The Faroan turned, the white gold gems embedded in his profile catching the light. He showed neither surprise at her presence nor guilt at his own.

"Your Majesty."

"Why are you here alone?"

"I was looking for the king," answered Sol-in-Ar in his smooth, susurrant way.

Emira shook her head, eyes darting around the room. It felt askew without Maxim. She scanned the table, as if something might be missing, but Sol-in-Ar had already righted the fallen piece and taken up another from the table's edge. The chalice and sun. The marker of the House Maresh.

The sigil of Arnes.

"I hope it is not out of line," he said, "to say I believe we are alike."

"You and my husband?"

A single shake of the head. "You and I."

Emira's face warmed even as the temperature in the room fell. "How so?"

"We both know much, and say little. We both stand at the side of kings. We are the truth whispered in their ears. The reason."

She said nothing, only inclined her head.

"The darkness is spreading," he added softly, though the words were full of edges. "It must be contained."

"It will be," answered the queen.

Sol-in-Ar nodded once. "Tell the king," he said, "that we can help. If he will let us."

The Faroan started toward the door.

"Lord Sol-in-Ar," she called after him. "Our standard."

He looked down at the carved figure in his hand as if he'd forgotten about it entirely. "Apologies," he said, setting the piece back on the board.

Emira finally found her husband in their chamber, though not in their bed. He'd fallen asleep at her writing desk, slumped forward on the carved wooden table, his head on folded arms atop a ledger, the scent of ink still fresh.

Only the first line was legible beneath his wrinkled sleeve.

To my son, the crown prince of Arnes, when it is time . . .

Emira drew in a sharp breath at the words, then steadied herself. She did not wake Maxim. Did not pull the book from its place beneath his head. She padded silently to the sofa, took up a throw, and settled the blanket over his shoulders.

He stirred briefly, arms shifting beneath his head, the small change revealing not only the next line—*know that a father lives for his son, but a king lives for his people*—but the bandage wrapped around his wrist. Emira stilled at the sight of it, lines of blood seeping through the crisp white linen.

What had Maxim done?

What was he yet planning to do?

She could hear the workings of the palace, but her husband's mind was solid, impenetrable. No matter how hard she listened, all she heard was his heart.

IX

As night fell, the shadows bloomed.

They ran together with the river and the mist and the moonless sky until they were everywhere. *Osaron* was everywhere. In every heartbeat. In every breath.

Some had escaped. For now. Others had been reduced already to dust. It was a necessary thing, like the razing of a forest, the clearing of ground so that new things—*better* things—could grow. A process as natural as the passing of the seasons.

Osaron was the fall, and the winter, and the spring.

And all across the city, he heard the voices of his loyal servants.

How can I serve you?

How can I worship?

Show me the way.

Tell me what to do.

He was in their minds.

He was in their bodies. He whispered in their heads and coursed through their blood. He was in every one of them, and bound to none.

Everywhere, and nowhere.

It was enough.

And it was *not* enough.

He wanted *more*.

SIX

EXECUTION

I

Grey London

Ned Tuttle woke to a very bad feeling.

He'd recently moved out of his family's house in Mayfair and into the room above the tavern—*his* tavern—that magical place once called the Stone's Throw, and rechristened the Five Points.

Ned sat up, listening intently to the silence. He could have sworn someone was speaking, but he couldn't hear the voice anymore, and, as the moments ticked past, he couldn't be sure if it had ever been real, or simply the dregs of sleep clinging to him, the urge to listen to an echo of some peculiar dream.

Ned had always had vivid dreams.

So vivid he couldn't always tell when something had truly happened or when he'd simply dreamed it. Ned's dreams had always been strange, and sometimes they were wonderful, but lately, they'd grown . . . disturbing, skewing darker, more menacing.

Growing up, his parents had written off his dreams as simply an effect of his reading too many novels, disappearing for hours—sometimes days—into fictional and fantastical worlds. In his youth, he'd seen the dreams as a sign of his sensitivity to the *other,* that aspect of the world most people couldn't see—the one even *Ned* couldn't see—but that he believed in, fervently, determinedly, doggedly, right up until the day he met Kell and learned for certain that the *other* was real.

But tonight, Ned had been dreaming of a forest made of stone. Kell was in the dream, too, had been at one point but wasn't anymore, and now Ned was lost, and every time he called out for help, the whole forest echoed like an empty church, but the voices that came back weren't his. Some of them were high and others low, some young and sweet, and others old, and there at the center, a voice he couldn't quite make out, one that bent around his ears the way light sometimes bent around a corner.

Now, sitting up in the stiff little bed, he had the strangest urge to call out, the way he had in the forest, but some small—well, not as small as he'd like—part of him feared that just like in the forest, someone *else* would call back.

Perhaps the sound had come from the tavern downstairs. He swung his long legs over the side of the bed, slid his feet into his slippers, and stood, the old wooden floor groaning beneath his toes.

He moved in silence, only that *creak-creak-creak* following him across the room, and then the *oomph* as he ran into the dresser, the *eek* of the metal lantern rocking, almost tipping, then *humph*ing back into place, followed by the *shhhh* of tapers rolling of the table.

"Bugger," muttered Ned.

It would have been dreadfully handy, he thought, if he could simply snap his fingers and summon a bit of fire, but in four straight months of trying, he'd barely managed to shift the pieces in Kell's kit of elements, so he fumbled on his robe in the dark and stepped out onto the stairs.

And shivered.

Something was most certainly strange.

Ordinarily Ned loved strange things, lived in the hope of spying them, but this was a type of strange bordering on *wrong*. The air smelled of roses and woodsmoke and dying leaves, and when he moved it felt like he was wading through a warm spot in a cold pool, or a cold spot in a warm one. Like a draft in a room when all the doors were shut, the windows latched.

He knew this feeling, had sensed it once before in the street outside the Five Points, back when it was the Stone's Throw and he was still waiting for Kell to return with his promised dirt. Ned had seen a cart crash, heard the driver rant about a man he'd crushed. Only there was no body left behind, no man, only smoke and ash and the faint frisson of magic.

Bad magic.

Black magic.

Ned returned to his room and fetched his ceremonial dagger—he'd bought it from a patron the week before, the handle etched with runes around a pentagram of inlaid onyx.

My name is Edward Archibald Tuttle, he thought, gripping the dagger, *I am the third of that name, and I am not afraid.*

The *creak-creak-creak* followed him down the warping stairs, and when he reached the bottom, standing in the darkened tavern with only the *thud-thud* of his heart, Ned realized where that feeling of strangeness was coming from.

The Five Points was too quiet.

A heavy, muffled, *unnatural* quiet, as if the room were filled with wool instead of air. The last embers in the hearth smoldered behind their grate, the wind blew through the boards, but none of it made any sound.

Ned went to the front door and threw back the bolt. Outside, the street was empty—it was the darkest hour, that time before the first streaks of dawn—but London was never truly still, not this close to the river, and so he was instantly greeted by the *clop-clop* of carriages, the distant trills of laughter and song. Somewhere near the Thames, the scrape of a fiddle, and much closer, the sound of a stray cat, yowling for milk or company or whatever stray cats wanted. A dozen sounds that made up the fabric of his city, and when Ned closed the door again, the noises followed him, sneaking in through the crack beneath the door, around the sill. The pressure ebbed, the air in the tavern thinning, the spell broken.

Ned yawned, the sense of strangeness already slipping away as he climbed the stairs. Back in his room, he cracked the window despite the cold, and let the sounds of London drift in. But as he crawled back into bed and pulled the covers up, and the world settled into silence, the whispers came again. And as he sank back into that place between waking and sleep, those elusive words finally took shape.

Let me in, they said.

Let me in.

II

Voices rang out past Holland's cell just after midnight.

"You're early," said the guard nearest the bars.

"Where's your second?" asked the one on the wall.

"The king needs men on the steps," answered the interloper, "what with the scarred fellows coming in." His voice was muffled by his helm.

"We've got orders."

"So do I," said the new guard. "And we're running thin."

A pause, and in that pause, Holland felt a strange thing happen. It was like someone took the air—the energy in the air—and pulled on it. Shallowly. A tug of will. A shifting of scales. A subtle exertion of control.

"Besides," the new guard was saying absently, "what would you rather be doing? Staring at this piece of filth, or saving your friends?"

The balance tipped. The men roused from their places. Holland wondered if the new guard knew what he'd done. It was the kind of magic forbidden in this world, and worshipped in his own.

The new guard watched the others climb the stairs, and swayed ever so slightly on his feet. When they were gone, he leaned back against the wall facing Holland's cell, the metal of his armor scraping stone, and drew a knife. He toyed with it absently, fingertips on the tip, tossing and catching and tossing it again. Holland felt himself being studied, and so he studied in return. Studied the way the new guard tipped his head, the speed of his fingers on the knife, the scent of another London wafting in his blood.

Her blood.

He should have recognized that voice, even through the stolen helm. Maybe if he'd slept—how long had it been?—maybe if he wasn't bloody and broken and behind bars. He still should have known.

"Delilah," he said evenly.

"Holland," she answered.

Delilah Bard, the *Antari* of Grey London, set her helmet on the table beneath a hook holding the jailer's keys. Her fingers danced absently across their teeth. "Your last night . . ."

"Did you come to say farewell?"

She made a humming sound. "Something like that."

"You're a long way from home."

Her gaze flicked toward him, quick and sharp as a sliver of steel. "So are you." One of her eyes had the glassy sheen that came with too much drink. The other, the false one, had been shattered. It hung together by a shell of glass, but the inside was a starburst of color and cracks.

Lila's knife vanished back into its sheath. She pulled off the gauntlets, one by one, and set them on the table, too. Even drunk, she moved with the fluid grace of a fighter. She reminded him of Ojka.

"Ojka," she echoed, as if reading his mind.

Holland stilled. "What?"

Lila tapped her cheek. "The redhead with the scar and the face leaking black. She did this—tried to drive a knife into my eye—right before I cut her throat."

The words were a dull blow. Just a small flame of hope flickering out inside his chest. Nothing left. Ash over embers. "She was following orders," he said hollowly.

Lila lifted the keys from their hook. "Yours or Osaron's?"

It was a hard question. When had they been different? Had they ever been the same?

He heard the clang of metal, and Holland blinked to find the cell door falling open, Lila stepping in. She pulled the door shut behind her, snapped the lock back into place.

"If you came to kill me—"

"No," she sneered. "That can wait till morning."

"Then why are you here?"

"Because good people die, and bad people live, and it doesn't seem very fair, does it, Holland?" Her face crinkled. "Of all the people you could kill, you chose someone who actually mattered to me."

"I had to."

Her fist hit him like a brick, hard enough to crack his head sideways and make the world go momentarily white. When his vision cleared, she was standing over him, knuckles bleeding.

She tried to strike him again, but this time Holland caught her wrist.

"Enough," he said.

But it wasn't. Her free hand swung up, fire dancing across her knuckles, but he caught that, too.

"Enough."

She tried to pull free, but his hands vised tighter, finding the tender place where bones met. He pressed down, and a guttural sound escaped her throat, low and animal.

"It does nothing to dwell on what's been taken from you," he snarled. *"Nothing."*

Over seven years, Holland's life had been distilled to one desire. To see Athos and Astrid Dane suffer. And Kell had stolen that from him. Stolen the look in Astrid's eyes as he drove the dagger through her heart. Stolen Athos's expression as he took him apart piece by piece.

No one suffers as beautifully as you do.

Seven years.

Holland shoved Lila back. She stumbled, her shoulders hitting the bars. For a moment, the cell was filled with only the sounds of ragged breathing as they stared at one another across the narrow space, two beasts caged together.

And then, slowly, Lila straightened, flexing her hands.

"If you want your revenge," he said, "take it."

One of us should have it, he thought, closing his eyes. He took a steadying breath and began to count his dead, starting with Alox and ending with Ojka.

But when he opened his eyes again, Delilah Bard was gone.

They came to collect him just after dawn.

In truth, he didn't know the hour, but he could feel the palace stirring overhead, the subtle warming of the world beyond the prison's pillar. With so many years of cold, he'd learned to sense the smallest shifts in warmth, knew how to mark the passing of a day.

The guards came and freed Holland from the wall, and for a moment, he was bound by nothing but two hands before they wrapped the chains around his wrists, his shoulders, his waist. The heavy metal was hobbling, and it took all his strength to keep his feet, to climb the stairs, his stride reduced to a halting step.

"*On vis och,*" he told himself.

Dawn to dusk. A phrase that meant two things in his native tongue. *A fresh start. A good end.*

The guards marched Holland up and through the palace halls, where men and women gathered to watch him pass. They led him out onto a balcony, a large space stripped bare except for a broad wooden platform, freshly constructed, and on it, a block of stone.

On vis och.

Holland felt the change as soon as he stepped outside, the prickling magic of the palace wards giving way to nothing but crisp air and light so bright it stung his eyes.

The sun was rising on a frigid day, and Holland, still stripped to the waist beneath the chains, felt the icy air bite viciously into his skin. But he had long ago learned not to give others the satisfaction of his suffering. And though he knew he stood at the center of a performance—had in fact orchestrated it himself—Holland could not bring himself to shiver and beg. Not in front of these people.

The king was present, and the prince, as well as four more guards, their foreheads marked with blood, and a handful of magicians, similarly stained—a young, silver-haired man, the wind jostling around his limbs; a pair of dark-skinned twins, their faces set with gems; a blond man built like a wall. There, beside them, his skin scarred by silver lines, stood an almost-familiar man with a blue gem above one eye; an old man in white robes, a drop of crimson on his brow; Delilah Bard, her shattered brown eye catching the light.

And last—just there, on the platform, beside the stone block—stood Kell, a long sword in his hands, its broad point resting on the ground.

Holland's steps must have slowed, because one of the guards drove a gauntlet into his back, forcing him forward, up the two short steps onto the newly built dais. He came to a stop and straightened, looking out at the darkened river beyond the balcony.

So like Black London.

Too like Black London.

"Second thoughts?" asked Kell, gripping the sword.

"No," said Holland, staring past him. "Just taking a moment to enjoy the view."

His gaze flicked to the young *Antari,* took in the way he held the sword, one hand around the hilt and the other resting on the blade, pressing down just hard enough to draw a line of blood.

"If he does not come—" started Holland.

"I'll make it quick."

"Last time, you missed my heart."

"I won't miss your head," answered Kell. "But I hope it doesn't come to that."

Holland started to speak but forced the words down.

They served no purpose.

Still, he thought them.

I hope it does.

The king's voice thundered through the cold morning.

"Kneel," ordered the ruler of Arnes.

Holland stiffened at the word, his mind stuttering into another day, another life, cold steel and Athos's smooth voice—but he let the weight of the memories, as well as the present weight of chains, pull him down. He kept his eyes on the river, the darkness moving just beneath the surface, and when he spoke, his voice was low, the words meant not for the crowd on the balcony, or for Kell, but for the shadow king.

"Help me."

The words were nothing but a breath of fog. To the gathered crowd, it might have looked like a prayer, given to whatever gods they thought he worshipped. And in a way, it was.

"*Antari,*" said the king, addressing him not by name, or even title, only by what he was, and Holland wondered if Maxim Maresh even knew his given name.

Vosijk, he almost said. *My name is Holland Vosijk.*

But it didn't matter now.

"You are guilty of grievous sins against the empire, guilty of practicing forbidden magic, of inciting chaos and ruin, of bringing war. . . ."

The king's words washed around him as Holland tipped his head back toward the sky. Birds flew high overhead, while shadows threaded through the low clouds. Osaron was there. Holland gritted his teeth and forced himself to speak, not to the men around him, not to the king or Kell, but to the presence lurking, listening.

"Help me."

"You are sentenced to death by the blade for your crimes, your body committed to fire. . . ."

He could feel the *oshoc*'s magic weaving through his hair, brushing against his skin, but still it did not come.

"If you have any words, speak them now, but know that your fate is sealed."

He heard a new voice, then, like a vibration in the winter air.

Beg.

Holland went still.

"Have you nothing to say?" demanded the king.

Beg.

Holland swallowed, and did something he'd never done, not in seven years of slavery and torture.

"Please," he begged, first softly, and then louder. "Please. I will be yours."

The darkness laughed but did not come.

Holland's pulse began to race, the chains suddenly too tight.

"*Osaron,*" he called out. "This body is yours. This life—what's left of it—is yours—"

The guards were on either side of him now, gauntleted fists forcing Holland's head forward onto the block.

"Osaron," he growled, fighting their grip for the first time.

The laughter continued, ringing through his head.

"Gods don't need bodies, but kings do! How will you rule without a head for your crown?"

Kell was beside him now, both hands on the sword's hilt.

"End it," ordered the king.

Wait, thought Holland.

"Kill him," said Lila.

"Be still," demanded Kell.

Holland's vision narrowed to the wood of the platform.

"Osaron!" he bellowed as Kell's sword sang upward.

It never came down.

A shadow swept over the balcony. One moment the sun was there, and the next, they were plunged into shade, and everyone looked up in time to see the wave of black water crest overhead and come crashing down.

Holland twisted sideways, still clinging to the stone block as the river slammed onto the platform. One of the guards was knocked over the edge, down into the roiling surf below, while the other held on to Holland.

The icy torrent knocked the blade from Kell's hands and sent him backward across the dais, a shard of ice pinning his sleeve to the floor as the guards dove to cover the king and prince. The wave hit the steps between the platform and the balcony and splashed up, swirling first into a column, before its edges smoothed and pulled together into the shape of a man.

A king.

Osaron smiled at Holland.

"*Do you see?*" he said in his echoing way. "*I can be merciful.*"

Someone was moving across the balcony. The silver-haired magician came surging forward, the air like knives around him.

Osaron didn't take his eyes off Holland, but he flicked his watery fingers and a spike of ice materialized, launching toward the magician's chest. The man actually smiled as he spun around the shard, the movement light as air before shattering it with a single sharp gust.

Silver hair and swirling robes danced again toward Osaron, a blur, and then the magician slashed, one hand surrounded by a blade of wind. Osaron's watery form parted around the magician's wrist, then vised closed. The airborne magician slammed to a stop, pinned in the icy core of Osaron's form. Before he could break free, the shadow king drove his own hand through the magician's chest.

His fingers went clean through, icy black points glistening with streams of red.

"Jinnar!" screamed someone as the wind suddenly died atop the platform, and the magician collapsed, lifeless, to the ground.

Osaron shook the blood from his fingers as he climbed the steps.

"*Tell me, Holland,*" he said. "*Do I look in need of a body?*"

Using their distraction, Kell tore the icy shard free of his sleeve and threw it hard at the shadow king's back. Holland was grudgingly, fleetingly, impressed—but it passed right through Osaron's watery form. He turned, as if amused, to face Kell.

"*It will take more than that,* Antari."

"I know," said Kell, and Holland saw the ribbon of blood swirling in the column of water that formed Osaron's chest the moment before Kell said, "*As Isera.*"

And just like that, Osaron *froze.*

It happened in an instant, the shadow king replaced by a statue rendered in ice.

Holland met Kell's gaze through the frozen surface of Osaron's torso.

He saw it first, relief turning to horror as the dead magician—Jinnar—rose to his feet. His eyes were black—not shadowed, but solid—his skin already beginning to burn with the strength of his new host. And when he spoke, a smooth, familiar voice poured out.

"*It will take more than that,*" said Osaron again, silver hair steaming.

Bodies were rising around him, and Holland understood too late. The wave. The water. "Kell!" he shouted. "The blood marks—"

He was cut off by a fist as the nearest guard drove a gauntleted hand into his ribs, the crimson smear on his helmet washed away by the first swell of the river. "Kneel before the king."

The silver-scarred man and the Maresh prince both surged forward, but Kell stopped them with a jagged slash of his arm, a wall of ice surging up and cutting them off from the platform and Osaron.

Osaron, who now stood between Holland and Kell in his stolen host, his skin flaking away like curls of burning paper.

Holland forced himself up despite the weight of chains. "What a poor substitute you've chosen," he said, drawing the *oshoc*'s attention as Kell shifted forward, blood dripping from his fingers. "How quickly it crumbles." His voice was low amid the surge of chaos, dripping with disdain. "It is not a body for a king."

"*You would still offer yours instead,*" mused Osaron. His shell was dying fast, lit by a bloodred glow that cracked along his skin.

"I do," said Holland.

"*Tempting,*" said Osaron. His black eyes burned inside his skull. In a flash, he was at Holland's side. "*But I'd rather watch you fall.*"

Holland felt the push before he saw the hand, felt the force against his chest and the sudden weight of gravity as the world shifted and the platform disappeared, and the chains pulled him over the edge and down, down, down into the river below.

III

Kell saw Holland fall.

One moment the *Antari* was there, at the edge, and the next he was gone, plunging down into the river with no magic at hand, only the cold, dead weight of the spelled iron around him. The balcony was chaos, one guard on his knees, fighting the fog, while Lila and Alucard squared off against the animated corpse of Jinnar, who was now nothing more than charred bone.

There wasn't time to think, to wonder, to question.

Kell dove.

The drop was farther than it seemed.

The impact knocked the air from Kell's lungs, jarring his bones, and he gasped as the river closed over him, ice-cold and black as ink.

Far below, almost out of sight, a pale form sank to the bottom of the tainted water.

Kell swam down toward Holland, lungs aching as he fought the press of the river—not only the weight of water, but Osaron's magic, leaching heat and focus as it tried to force its way in.

By the time he reached Holland, the man was on his knees on the river floor, his lips moving faintly, soundlessly, his body weighed down by the shackles at his wrists and the steel chains around his waist and legs. The *Antari* struggled to his feet but couldn't manage any further. After a brief struggle he lost his battle with gravity and sank back to his knees, driving up a cloud of silt as the irons hit the riverbed.

Kell hovered in front of him, his own coat heavy with water, its weight enough to keep him under. He drew his dagger, slicing skin before he realized the futility—the instant the blood welled, it vanished, dissipated by the current. Kell swore, sacrificing a thin stream of air as Holland struggled to hold on to the last of his own. Holland's black hair floated in the water around his face, his eyes closed, a resignation to his posture, as if he would rather drown than return to the world above.

As if he meant to end his life here, at the bottom of the river.

But Kell couldn't let him do that.

Holland's eyes flashed open as Kell took hold of his shoulders, crouching to reach his wrists where they were weighted to the river floor. The *Antari* shook his head minutely, but Kell didn't let go. His whole body ached from the cold and the lack of air, and he could see Holland's chest stuttering as he fought the urge to breathe in.

Kell wrapped his hands around the iron shackles and pulled, not with muscle but with magic. Iron was a mineral, somewhere between stone and earth on the spectrum of elements. He couldn't unmake it, but he could—with enough effort—change its shape.

Transmuting an element was no small feat, even in a workroom with ample time and focus; doing it underwater surrounded by dark magic while his chest screamed and Holland slowly drowned was something else entirely.

Focus, Master Tieren chided in his head. *Unfocus.*

Kell squeezed his eyes shut and tried to remember Tieren's instructions.

Elements are not whole unto themselves, the Aven Essen *had said, but parts, each a knot on the same, ever-circling rope, one giving way onto the next and the next. There is a natural pause, but no seam.*

It had been years since he'd learned to do this; ages since he'd stood in the head priest's study with a glass in each hand, following the lines of the element spectrum as he poured the contents back and forth, turning a cup of water into sand, sand into rock, rock into fire, fire into air, air into water. On and on, slowly, painstakingly, the action never as natural as the theory. The priests could do it—they were so attuned to the subtleties of magic, the boundaries between elements porous in their hands—but Kell's magic was too loud, too bright, and half the time he faltered, shattering the glass or spilling contents that were now half rock, half glass.

Focus.

Unfocus.

The iron was cold under his hands.

Unyielding.

Knots on a rope.

Holland was dying.

The watery world swirled darkly.

Focus.

Unfocus.

Kell's eyes flashed open. He met Holland's gaze, and as the metal began to soften in his hands, something flashed across the magician's face, and Kell realized suddenly that Holland's resignation had been a mask, veiling the panic beneath. The cuffs gave way beneath Kell's desperate fingers, turning from iron to sand, silt that formed a cloud and then dissolved in the river's current.

Holland lurched forward in the sudden absence of chains. He rose up, the need for air propelling him toward the surface.

Kell pushed off the river floor to follow.

Or tried to.

He lifted a few feet, only to be wrenched back down, held fast by a sudden, unseen force. The last of Kell's air escaped in a violent stream as he fought the water's hold. The force tightened around his legs, tried to crush the strength from his limbs, his chest, dragging his arms out to his sides in a gruesome echo of the steel frame in the White London castle.

The water before Kell shifted and swirled, the current bending around the outlines of a man.

Hello again, Antari.

Too late, Kell understood. That last moment on the balcony, when Osaron had looked not at Holland, but at him. Pushing Holland into the river, knowing Kell would save him. They'd set a trap for the shadow king, and he'd set one for them. For *him.*

After all, Kell was the one who'd resisted, the one who'd refused to yield.

Now will you kneel?

The invisible bonds forced Kell to the river floor. His lungs flamed as he tried to push back against the river. Tried, and failed. Panic tore through him.

Now will you beg?

He closed his eyes and tried to fight against the need for air that screamed through his chest, drowning his senses. His vision flickered with spots of white light and hollow black.

Now will you let me in?

IV

Lila saw Kell vanish over the balcony's edge.

At first, she thought he must have been knocked over, that surely he wouldn't have *willingly* jumped into the black water, not for Holland, but then she remembered his words—*it could have been me*—and she realized, with icy clarity, that Kell hadn't told her the truth. The execution was a farce. Holland was never supposed to die.

It had all been a trap, and Osaron hadn't taken the bait, and now Holland was sinking to the bottom of the Isle, and Kell was going with him.

"Fucking hell," muttered Lila, shrugging out of her coat.

On the balcony, Jinnar had collapsed, body crumbling to muddy ash, while those who'd fallen to Osaron's spell were being subdued. A pair of silver-scarred guards fought to regain order while a third fought the fever raging through him. The king shoved past his own guard, scouring the balcony, while Alucard shielded Rhy, who had one hand to his chest as if he couldn't breathe.

Because, of course, he *couldn't* breathe. Kell wasn't the only one drowning.

Lila turned, mounted the balcony edge, and jumped.

The water cut like knives. She sputtered, shocked by the pain and the cold, and she was going to *kill* someone when this was over.

Without the weight of her coat, her body rebelled, trying with every stride to lift her toward the surface, toward air, toward life. Instead she swam down, lungs burning, icy water stinging her open eyes, toward the shape on the river floor. She expected it to be Holland, weighed down by chains. But the figure was thrashing freely, his hair a tangled cloud.

Kell.

Lila kicked toward him when a hand caught her arm. She twisted around behind her to see Holland, now free of chains.

She brought up her boot to kick him away, but the water gripped it and his fingers tightened as he forced her back around to face the struggling figure on the river floor.

For a sick, frozen moment she thought he wanted her to watch Kell die.

But then she saw it, the faint outline of something—*someone*—hovering in the water before him.

Osaron.

Holland pointed at himself and then the shadow king. He pointed at her and then Kell. And then he let go, and she understood.

They dove as one, but Holland reached the bottom first, landing in a plume of silt that caught the edges of the shadow king like dust catching light.

Lila reached Kell's side in the cover of the clouded water and tried to pull him up, pull him free, but Osaron's will held firm. She flung a desperate hand toward Holland, a speechless plea, and the magician spread his arms and *shoved.*

The river recoiled, flung away in every direction, carving out a column of air with Kell and Lila at its center. Kell and Lila, but not Holland.

Lila drew in a deep breath, lungs aching, while Kell collapsed to the river floor, gasping and heaving up water.

Get him out, mouthed Holland, hands trembling from the force of holding the river—and *Osaron*—at bay.

With what? Lila wanted to say. They might be able to breathe, but they were still standing at the bottom of the river, Kell only half conscious and Lila with all her strength but none of his skill. She couldn't craft wings of air, couldn't sculpt a set of stairs from ice. Her gaze went to the silt floor.

The column of air swayed around them.

Holland was losing his hold.

Shadows grew, curling in the water around the faltering *Antari,* like roaming limbs, fingers, mouths.

She wanted to leave him, but Kell had brought them here, to this point, all for Holland's bloody life. *Leave him. Save him. Damn him.* Lila snarled and, keeping one hand on Kell's sleeve, thrust the other out toward the column, widening the circle until Holland staggered forward, safely within.

Safe being a relative thing.

Holland drew in ragged breaths, and Kell, finally recovering his senses, pressed his palms to the damp river floor. It began to rise, a disk of earth beneath their feet surging toward the surface as the column collapsed below.

They broke the surface and scrambled onto the riverbank beneath the palace, dropping to the ground soaked and half frozen, but alive.

Holland was the first to recover, but before he was even halfway to his feet, Lila had a knife against his throat.

"Steady now," she said, her own limbs shaking.

"Wait—" Kell began to speak, but the king and his men were already on them, the guards forcing Holland back to his knees on the icy bank. When they realized he was no longer chained, half of them lunged forward, blades drawn, the other half away. But Holland made no move to strike. Lila kept her knife out all the same until the king's men had hauled their prisoner back toward the cells. In their wake, Rhy came storming down the riverbank. The prince's jaw was set, his cheeks red, as if he'd almost drowned. Because, of course, he had.

Kell saw him coming.

"Rhy—"

The prince slammed his fist into his brother's face.

Kell staggered backward to the ground, and the prince reeled back in mirrored pain, cradling his own cheek.

Rhy grabbed Kell by the soaking collar of his coat. "I've made my peace with death," he said, jabbing a finger at Holland's retreating form. "But I refuse to die for *him.*"

With that, Rhy shoved his brother away again. Kell's mouth opened and closed, a fleck of blood at the corner of his lip, but the prince turned and marched back toward the palace.

Lila brushed herself off.

"You had that coming," she said before leaving Kell on the bank, soaked and shivering and alone.

V

"Gods don't need bodies, but kings do."

Osaron *seethed* at the words echoing through his mind. Weeds to be torn out at the root. After all, he was a god. And a god did not need a body. A shell. A *cage*. A god was everywhere.

The river rippled, and from it rose a drop, a shimmering black bead that stretched and lengthened until it had a form, limbs, fingers, a face. Osaron stood on the surface of the water.

Holland was *wrong*.

A body was merely a tool, a thing to be used, discarded, but it was never *needed*.

Osaron had wanted to kill Holland slowly, to tear out his mortal heart—a heart he *knew,* a heart he'd listened to for months.

He had given Holland so much—a second chance, a city reborn— and all he'd asked for in return was *cooperation*.

They'd made a deal.

And Holland would pay for breaking it.

The insolence of these Antari.

As for the *other* two—

He hadn't decided yet how to use them.

Kell was a temptation.

A gift given, and then lost, a body to break in—or simply break.

And the girl. Delilah. Strong and sharp. So much fight. So much promise. So much *more* that she could be.

He wanted—

No.

But then—

It was a different thing, for a god to want, and a human to need.

He didn't *need* these playthings, these shells.

Did not need to be *confined*.

He was everywhere.

(It was enough.)

It was—

Osaron looked down at his form sculpted of dark water, and was reminded of another body, another world.

Missing—

No.

But something *was* missing.

He drifted up from the surface of the water, rose into the air to survey the city that would become *his* city, and frowned. It was midday, and yet London sulked in shadow. The mists of his power shimmered, twisted, coiled, but beneath their blanket, the city looked *dull*.

The world—his world—should be beautiful, bright, filled with the light of magic, the song of power.

It *would* be, once the city stopped fighting. Once they all bowed, all kneeled, all recognized him as king, then he could make the city what it would be, what it *should* be. Progress was a process, change took time, a winter before every spring.

But in the meantime—

Missing—

What was missing—

He spun in place, and there it was.

The royal palace.

Somewhere inside, the defiant huddled, hiding behind their wards as if wards would outlast *him*. And they would fall, in time, but it was the palace itself that shone in his gaze, rising above the blackened river like a second sun, casting its spokes of reddish light into the sky even now, its echo dancing on the mirror-dark surface of the river.

Every ruler needed a palace.

He'd had one once, of course, at the center of his first city. A beautiful thing sculpted from want and will and sheer potential. Osaron had told himself he would not repeat that place, would not make the same mistakes—

But that was the wrong word.

He'd been young, learning, and though the city had fallen, it wasn't the *palace's* doing. Wasn't *his* doing. It was theirs, the people's, with their flawed minds, their brittle shapes—and yes, he'd given them the power, but he knew better now, knew the power must be his and his alone, and it had been *such* a splendid palace. The dark heart of his kingdom.

It would do better here.

Right here.

Then, perhaps, this place would feel like home.

Home.

What a strange idea.

But still. Here. This.

Osaron had risen high into the air now, far above the shimmering black expanse of the river, the lifeless arenas, hulking skeletons of stone and wood topped with their lions and serpents and birds of prey, their bodies empty, their banners still whipping in the breeze.

Right here.

He spread his hands and pulled on the strings of this world, on the threads of power in the stadium stones and the water below, and the massive silhouettes began to draw together, groaning as they came free from their bridges and holds.

In his mind, the palace took shape, smoke and stone and magic prying loose, rearranging into something else, something more. And, as in his mind, so in the world below. His new palace lengthened like a shadow, rising up instead of out, tendrils of mist climbing the sides like vines, smoothing into polished black stone like new flesh over old bones. Overhead, the stadium banners rose like smoke before hardening into a crown of glossy spires above his creation.

Osaron smiled.

It was a start.

VI

Kell had always been a fan of silence.

He craved those too-rare moments when the world calmed and the chaos of life in the palace gave way to easy, comfortable stillness.

This was *not* that kind of silence.

No, this silence was a hollow, sulking thing, a heavy quiet broken only by the drip of river water hitting the polished floor, and the fire crackling in the hearth, and the shuffle of Rhy's restless steps.

Kell sat in one of the prince's chairs, a cup of scalding hot tea in one hand, his bruised jaw in the other, his hair a mess of damp red streaks, beads of river water trickling down his neck. While Tieren tended to his bruised lungs, Kell took stock of the damage—two guards were dead, as well as another Arnesian magician. Holland was back in the cells, the queen was in the gallery, and the king stood across the room by the prince's hearth, his face shadowed, gaunt. Hastra was by the doors, Alucard Emery—a shade Kell seemingly couldn't be rid of—sat on the couch with a glass of wine, while his shipmate, Lenos, hovered like a shadow at his back. Blood and ash still stained Alucard's front. Some of it was his, but the rest belonged to Jinnar.

Jinnar—who'd taken it upon himself to fight, and failed.

The single best wind worker in Arnes, reduced to a burning puppet, a pile of ash.

Lila was lounging on the floor, her back against Alucard's sofa, and the sight of her sitting there—near the damned privateer instead of Kell—stoked the fire in Kell's aching chest.

The minutes ticked past, and his damp hair finally began to dry, yet no one spoke. Instead the air hummed with the frustration of things unsaid, of fights gone dormant.

"Well," said the prince at last, "I think it's safe to say that didn't go as planned."

The words broke the seal, and suddenly the room was filled with voices.

"Jinnar was my *friend*," said Alucard, glaring at Kell, "and he's dead because of you."

"Jinnar is dead because of himself," said Kell, shaking off Tieren's attentions. "No one forced him onto that balcony. No one told him to attack the shadow king."

Lila scowled. "You should have let Holland drown."

"Why didn't you?" interjected Rhy.

"After all," she went on, "wasn't it supposed to be an *execution*? Or did you have other plans? Ones you didn't share with us."

"Yes, Kell," chimed Alucard. "Do enlighten us."

Kell shot the captain a frigid look. "Why are you here?"

"Kell," said the king in a low, stern way. "Tell them."

Kell ran a hand through his frizzing hair, frustrated. "Osaron needs permission to take an *Antari* shell," he said. "The plan was for Holland to let Osaron in, and for me to then kill Holland."

"I knew it," said Lila.

"So did Osaron, it seems," said Rhy.

"During the execution," continued Kell, "Holland was trying to draw Osaron in. When Osaron appeared, I assumed it had worked, but then when he pushed Holland into the river . . . I didn't think—"

"No," snapped Rhy, "you didn't."

Kell held his ground. "He *might* have let Holland drown, *or* he might have simply been trying to get him away from us before claiming his shell, and if you think Osaron is bad without a body, you should have seen him in Holland's. I didn't realize he was after *me* until it was too late."

"It was the right thing to do," said the king. Kell looked at him, stunned. It was the closest Maxim had come to taking Kell's side in *months*.

"Well," said Rhy peevishly, "Holland is still alive, and Osaron is still free, and we still have no idea how to stop him."

Kell pressed his palms to his eyes. "Osaron still needs a body."

"He doesn't seem to think so," said Lila.

"He'll change his mind," said Kell.

Rhy stopped pacing. "How do you know?"

"Because right now, he can afford to be stubborn. He has too many options." Kell looked to Tieren, who had remained silent, still as stone. "Once you put the city to sleep, he'll run out of bodies to play with. He'll get restless. He'll get angry. And then we'll have his attention."

"And what do we do *then*?" said Lila, exasperated. "Even if we can convince Osaron to take the body we give him, we have to be fast enough to trap him in it. It's like trying to catch lightning."

"We need another way to contain him," said Rhy. "Something better than a body. Bodies come with minds, and those, as we know, can be manipulated." He plucked a small silver sphere off a shelf, and stretched it out between his fingers. The sphere was made of fine metal cords woven in such a way that they drew apart, expanding into a large orb of delicate filaments, and folded back together, collapsing into a dense ball of tightly coiled silver. "We need something stronger. Something permanent."

"We would need an Inheritor," said Tieren softly.

The room looked to the *Aven Essen,* but it was Maxim who spoke. He was turning red. "You told me they didn't exist."

"No," said Tieren. "I told you I would not help you *make* one."

The priest and the king locked stares for long enough that Rhy spoke up. "Anyone want to explain?"

"An Inheritor," said Tieren slowly, addressing the room, "is a device that transfers magic. And even if it could be made, it is by its very nature corrupt, an outright defiance of cardinal law and an *interference*"—Maxim stiffened at this—"with the natural order of magical selection."

The room went quiet. The king's face was rigid with anger, Rhy's own features set but pale, and understanding settled in Kell's chest. A device to transfer magic would be able to grant it to those without.

What wouldn't a father do for a son born without power? What wouldn't a king do for his heir?

When the prince spoke, his voice was careful, even. "Is that really possible, Tieren?"

"In *theory*," answered the priest, crossing to an ornate desk that stood in the corner of the room. He pulled a piece of parchment from the drawer, produced a pencil from one of the many folds of his white priest robes, and began to draw.

"Magic, as you know, does not follow blood. It chooses the strong and the weak as it will. As is *natural*," he added, casting a stern look at the king. "But some time ago, a nobleman named Tolec Loreni wanted a way to pass on not only his land and his titles, but also his power to his beloved eldest son." The sketch on the page began to take shape. A metal cylinder shaped like a scroll, the length embossed with spell-work. "He designed a device that could be spelled to take and hold a person's power until the next of kin could lay claim to it."

"Hence, *Inheritor*," said Lila.

Rhy swallowed. "And it actually worked?"

"Well, no," said Tieren. "The spell killed him instantly. But"—he brightened—"his niece, Nadina, had a rather brilliant mind. She perfected the design, and the first Inheritor was made."

Kell shook his head. "Why have I never heard of this? And if they worked, why aren't they still used?"

"Power does not like being forced into lines," said Tieren pointedly. "Nadina Loreni's Inheritor worked. But it worked on *anyone*. *For* anyone. There was no way to control *who* claimed the contents of an Inheritor. Magicians could be *persuaded* to relinquish the entirety of their power to the device, and once it was surrendered to the Inheritor, it was anyone's to claim. As you can imagine, things got . . . messy. In the end, most of the Inheritors were destroyed."

"But if we could find the Loreni designs," said Lila, "if we could re-create one—"

"We don't need to," said Alucard, speaking up at last. "I know exactly where to find one."

VII

"What do you mean you *sold* it?" Kell snapped at the captain.

"I didn't know what it *was*."

This had been going on for several minutes now, and Lila poured herself a fresh drink as the room around her hummed with Kell's anger, the king's frustration, Alucard's annoyance.

"I didn't recognize the magic," Alucard was saying for the third time. "I'd never seen anything like it before. I knew it was rare, but that was all."

"You *sold* an *Inheritor*," repeated Kell, drawing out the words.

"Technically," said Alucard, defensively, "I didn't *sell* it. I offered it in trade."

Everyone groaned at that.

"Who did you give it to?" demanded Maxim. The king didn't look well—dark bruises stood out beneath his eyes, as though he hadn't slept in days. Not that any of them had, but Lila liked to think she wore fatigue rather well, given her sheer amount of practice.

"Maris Patrol," answered Alucard.

The king reddened at the name. No one else seemed to notice. Lila did. "You know them."

The king's attention snapped toward her. "What? No. Only by reputation."

Lila knew a lie, especially a bad one, but Rhy cut in.

"And what reputation is that?"

The king wasn't the one to answer. Lila noticed that, too.

"Maris runs the *Ferase Stras,*" said Alucard.

"The Going Waters?" translated Kell, assuming Lila didn't know the words. She did. "I've never heard of it," he added.

"I'm not surprised," said the captain.

"*Er an merst . . .*" started Lenos, speaking up for the first time. *It's a market.* Alucard shot the man a look, but the shipmate kept going, his voice soft, the accent rural Arnesian. "It caters to sailors of a special sort, looking to trade in . . ." He finally caught the captain's look and trailed off.

"You mean a black market," offered Lila, tipping her drink toward the captain. "Like Sasenroche."

The king raised a brow at that.

"Your Majesty," started Alucard. "It was before I served the crown—"

The king held up a hand, clearly not interested in excuses. "You believe the Inheritor is still there?"

Alucard nodded once. "The head of the market took a shine to it. Last I saw, it was around Maris's neck."

"And where is this *Ferase Stras*?" asked Tieren, pushing a piece of parchment toward them. On it, he'd outlined a rough map of the empire. No labels, just the drawn borders of land. The sight tickled something in the back of Lila's mind.

"That's the thing," said Alucard, running a hand through his messy brown curls. "It moves around."

"Can you find it?" demanded Maxim.

"With a pirate's cipher, sure," answered Alucard, "but I don't have one anymore. On the honor of Arnes, I swear—"

"You mean it was confiscated when you were arrested," said Kell.

Alucard shot him a venomous look.

"A pirate's cipher?" asked Lila. "Is that a kind of sea map?"

Alucard nodded. "Not all sea maps are made equal, though. They all have the ports, the paths to avoid, the best places and times for making deals. But a pirate's cipher is designed to keep secrets. To the passing eye, the cipher's practically useless, nothing but lines. Not even a city named." He glanced at Tieren's rough map. "Like that."

Lila frowned. There it was again, that tickle, only now it took shape.

Behind her eyes, another room in another London in another life. A map with no markings spread across the table in the attic of the Stone's Throw, weighted down by the night's take.

She must have lowered her guard, let the memory show in her face, because Kell touched her arm. "What is it?"

She drew a finger around the rim of her glass, trying not to betray the emotion in her voice. "I had a map like that once. Nicked it from a shop when I was fifteen. Didn't even know what it was—the parchment was all rolled up, bound with string—but it just kind of . . . *pulled* at me, so I took it. Weird thing was, after all that, I never thought to sell the thing. I suppose I liked the idea of a map with no names, no places, nothing but land and sea and promise. My map to anywhere, that's what I called it. . . ."

Lila realized the room had gone quiet. They were all staring at her, the king and the captain, the magician and the priest and the prince. "What?"

"Where is it now," said Rhy, "this map to anywhere?"

Lila shrugged. "Back in Grey London, I suspect, in a room at the top of the Stone's Throw."

"No," said Kell gently. "It's not there anymore."

The knowledge hit her like a blow. A last door slamming closed. "Oh . . ." she said, a little breathless, "well . . . I should have figured someone would—"

"I took it," cut in Kell. And then, before she could ask him why, he added, hurriedly, "It just caught my eye. It's like you said, Lila, the map has a kind of pull to it. Must be the spellwork."

"Must be," said Alucard dryly.

Kell scowled at the captain, but went to fetch the map.

While he was gone, Maxim lowered himself into a chair, fingers gripping the cushioned arms. If anyone else noticed the strain in the monarch's dark eyes, they said nothing, but Lila watched as Tieren moved too, taking up a place behind the king's chair. One hand came to rest on Maxim's shoulder, and Lila saw the king's features softening, some pain or malady eased by the priest's touch.

She didn't know why the sight made her nervous, but she was still trying to shake the prickle of unease when Kell returned, map in hand. The room gathered around the table, all but the king, while Kell unfurled his prize, weighting the edges. One side was stained with long-dry blood. Lila's fingers drifted toward the stain, but she stopped herself and shoved her hands instead in the pockets of her coat, fingers curling around her timepiece.

"I went back once," said Kell softly, head tipped toward hers. "After Barron . . ."

After Barron, he said. As if Barron had been a simple thing, a marker in time. As if Holland hadn't cut his throat.

"Nick anything else?" she asked, voice tight. Kell shook his head. "I'm sorry," he said, and she didn't know if he was sorry for taking the map, or for not taking more, or for simply reminding Lila of a life—a death—she wanted so badly to forget.

"Well," asked the king, "*is* it a cipher?"

Alucard, on the other side of the table, nodded. "It appears to be."

"But the doors were sealed centuries ago," said Kell. "How would an Arnesian pirate's cipher even come to *be* in Grey London?"

Lila blew out a breath. "Honestly, Kell."

"What?" he snapped.

"You weren't the first *Antari,*" she said, "and I'll bet you weren't the first to break the rules, either."

Alucard raised a brow at the mention of Kell's past crimes, but had the sense for once to say nothing. He kept his attention fixed on the map, running his fingers back and forth as if searching for a clue, a hidden clasp.

"Do you even know what you're doing?" asked Kell.

Alucard made a sound that was neither a yes nor a no, and might have been a curse.

"Spare a knife, Bard?" he said, and Lila produced a small, sharp blade from the cuff of her coat. Alucard took the weapon and briskly pierced his thumb, then pressed the cut to the corner of the paper.

"Blood magic?" she asked, sorry she'd never known how to unlock the map's secrets, never even known it had secrets to unlock.

"Not really," said Alucard. "Blood is just the ink."

Under his hand, the map was *unfolding*—that was the word that came to mind—crimson spreading in thin lines across the paper, illuminating everything from ports and cities to the serpents marking the seas and a decorative band around the edge.

Lila's pulse quickened.

Her map to anywhere became a map to *everywhere*—or, at least, everywhere a pirate might want to go.

She squinted, trying to decipher the blood-drawn names. She picked out *Sasenroche*—the black market carved into the cliffs at the place where Arnes and Faro and Vesk all met—and a town on the cliffs named *Astor,* as well as a spot at the northern edge of the empire marked only by a small star and the word *Is Shast.*

She remembered that word from the tavern in town, with its two-fold meaning.

The Road, or *the Soul.*

But nowhere could she find the *Ferase Stras.*

"I don't see it."

"Patience, Bard."

Alucard's fingers skimmed the edge of the map, and that's when she saw that the border wasn't simply a design, but three bands of small, squat numbers trimming the paper. As she watched, the numbers seemed to *move.* It was a fractional progress, slow as syrup, but the longer she stared, the more certain she was—the first and third lines were shifting to the left, the middle to the right, to what end she didn't know.

"*This,*" said Alucard proudly, tracing the lines, "is the pirate's cipher."

"Impressive," said Kell, voice dripping with skepticism. "But can you *read* it?"

"You'd better hope so."

Alucard took up a quill and began the strange alchemy of transmuting the shifting symbols of the map's trim into something like coordinates: not one set, or two, but three. He did this, keeping up a steady stream of conversation not with the room, but with himself, the words too low for Lila to hear.

By the hearth, the king and Tieren fell into muted conversation.

By the windows, Kell and Rhy stood side by side in silence.

Lenos perched nervously on the sofa's edge, fiddling with his medallion.

Only Lila stayed with Alucard and watched him translate the pirate's cipher, all the while thinking she had so much left to learn.

VIII

It took the better part of an hour for the captain to crack the code, the air in the room growing tenser with every minute, the quiet taut as sails in a strong wind. It was a thief's quiet, coiled, lying in wait, and Lila kept having to remind herself to exhale.

Alucard, who could usually be counted on to disrupt any silence before it grew oppressive, was busy scratching numbers on a slip of paper and snapping at Lenos whenever the man began to hover.

Tieren had left shortly after the captain started, explaining that he had to help his priests with their spell, and King Maxim had risen to his feet several minutes later looking like a corpse revived.

"Where are you going?" Rhy asked as his father turned toward the door.

"There are other matters to attend to," he said in a distracted way.

"What could be more—"

"A king is not one man, Rhy. He does not have the luxury of valuing one direction and ignoring the rest. This Inheritor, *if* it can be found, is but a single course. It is my task to chart them all." The king left with only the short command to summon him when the damned business of the map was done.

Rhy now sprawled across the couch, one arm over his eyes, while Kell seemed to be sulking against the hearth and Hastra stood at attention with his back to the door.

Lila tried to focus on these men, their slow movements like ticking cogs, but her own attention kept flicking back to the window, to those tendrils of fog that coiled and uncoiled beyond the glass, taking shape and falling apart, cresting, then crashing like waves against the palace.

She stared at the fog, searching for shapes in the shadows the way she sometimes did in clouds—a bird, ship, a pile of gold coins—before she realized that the shadows were indeed taking the shape of something.

Hands.

The revelation was unsettling.

Lila watched as the darkness drew together into a sea of fingers. Mesmerized, she lifted her own hand to the cold glass, the warmth of her touch steaming the window around her fingertips. Just beyond the window, the nearest shadows drew into a mirror image, palm pressed to hers, the seam of glass suddenly too thin, humming as wall and ward strained and shuddered between them.

Her brow furrowed as she flexed her fingers, the shadow hand mimicking with a child's slow way, close but not in time, a fraction off the beat.

She moved her hand back and forth.

The shadows followed.

She tapped her fingers soundlessly on the glass.

The other hand echoed.

She was just beginning to curl her fingers into a rude gesture when she saw the greater darkness—the one beyond the wave of hands, the one that rose from the river, blanketed the sky—begin to move.

At first, she thought they were coalescing into a column, but soon that column began to grow wings. Not the kind you found on a sparrow or a crow. The kind of wings that formed on a *castle*. Buttresses, towers, turrets, unfolding like a flower in sudden, violent bloom. As she watched, the shadows shimmered and hardened into glassy black stone.

Lila's hand fell away from the glass. "Am I losing my wits," she said, "or is there another palace floating on the river?"

Rhy sat up. Kell was at her shoulder in an instant, peering out through the fog. Parts of it were still blossoming, others dissolving into mist, caught in a never-ending process of being made and remade. The whole thing seemed at once very real and utterly impossible.

"*Sanct,*" swore Kell.

"That fucking monster," growled the prince, now at Lila's other side, "is playing blocks with my arenas."

Lenos hung back, his eyes wide with either horror or awe as he stared at the incredible palace, but Hastra abandoned his place by the door, surging forward to see.

"By the nameless saints . . ." he whispered.

Lila called over her shoulder. "Alucard, come see this."

"A little busy," muttered the captain without looking up. Judging by the crease between his brows, the cipher wasn't proving quite as simple as he'd hoped. "Blasted numbers, sit *still,*" he muttered, leaning closer.

Rhy kept shaking his head. "Why?" he said sadly. "Why did he have to use the arenas?"

"You know," said Kell, "that's really not the most important aspect of this situation."

Alucard made a triumphant sound and set the quill aside. "There."

Everyone turned back toward the table except for Kell. He stayed by the window, visibly appalled by the shift in focus. "Are we just going to ignore the shadow palace, then?" he asked, sweeping his hand at the specter beyond the glass.

"Not at all," said Lila, glancing back. "In fact, shadow palaces are where I draw the line. Which is why I'm keen to find this Inheritor." She took in the map. Frowned.

Lenos looked down at the parchment. "*Nas teras,*" he said softly. *I don't see it.*

The prince cocked his head. "Neither do I."

Lila leaned in. "Maybe you should draw an *X,* for dramatic effect."

Alucard blew out an indignant breath. "You're quite an ungrateful bunch, you know that?" He took up a pencil and, plucking a very expensive-looking book from a shelf, used its spine to draw a line across the map's surface. Kell finally drifted over as Alucard drew a second, and a third, the lines intersecting at odd angles until they formed a small triangle. "There," he said, adding a little *X* with a flourish at the center.

"I think you've made a mistake," said Kell dryly. The *X* was, after all, not on the coast, or inland, but in the Arnesian Sea.

"Hardly," said Alucard. "*Ferase Stras* is the largest black market *on water.*"

Lila broke into a smile. "It's not a market, then," she said. "It's a *ship.*"

Alucard's eyes were bright. "It's both. And now," he added, tapping the paper, "we know where to find it."

"I'll summon my father," said Rhy as the others pored over the map. According to Alucard's calculations, the market wasn't far this time of year, sitting somewhere between Arnes and the northwest edge of Faro.

"How long to reach it?" asked Kell.

"Depends on the weather," said Alucard. "A week, perhaps. Maybe less. Assuming we don't run into trouble."

"What kind of trouble?"

"Pirates. Storms. Enemy ships." And then, with a sapphire wink: "It is the sea, after all. Do try to keep up."

"We still have a problem," said Lila, nodding at the window. "Osaron has a hold on the river. His magic is keeping the ships in their berths. Nothing in London is likely to sail, and that includes the *Night Spire.*"

She saw Lenos straighten at this, the man's thin form shifting from foot to foot.

"Osaron's strength isn't infinite," Kell was saying. "His magic has limits. And right now, his power is still focused largely on the city."

"Well, then," sniped Alucard. "Can't you magic the *Spire* out of London?"

Kell rolled his eyes. "That's not how my power works."

"Well what good are you, then?" muttered the captain.

Lila watched Lenos duck out of the room. Neither Kell nor Alucard seemed to notice. They were too busy bickering.

"Fine," said Alucard, "I'll need to get beyond Osaron's sphere, and *then* find a ship."

"You?" said Kell. "I'm not leaving the fate of this city in *your* hands."

"I'm the one who found the Inheritor."

"And you're the one who lost it."

"A trade isn't the same thing as a—"

"I'm not letting you—"

Alucard leaned across the desk. "Do you even know how to sail, *mas vares?*" The honorific was said with serpentine sweetness. "I didn't think so."

"How hard can it be," snarled Kell, "if they let someone like you do it?"

A glint of mischief flashed in the captain's eyes. "I'm rather good with hard things. Just ask—"

The blow caught Alucard across the cheek.

Lila hadn't even seen Kell move, but the captain's jaw was marked with red.

It was an insult, she knew, for one magician to strike another with a bare fist.

As if they weren't worth the use of power.

Alucard flashed a feral grin, blood staining his teeth.

The air hummed with magic and—

The doors swung open, and they all turned, expecting the king or the prince returning. Instead there was Lenos, holding a woman by the elbow, which made a strange picture, since the woman was twice his weight and didn't look the type to be easily led. Lila recognized her as the captain who'd greeted them on the docks before the tournament.

Jasta.

She had to be half Veskan, broad as she was. Her hair plumed in two massive braids around her face, dark eyes threaded with gold, and despite the winter cold she wore nothing but trousers and a light tunic rolled to the elbows, revealing the silver lines of fresh scars along her skin. She'd survived the fog.

Alucard and Kell trailed off at the sight of her.

"*Casero Jasta Felis,*" said the woman, by way of grudging introduction.

"*Van nes,*" said Lenos, nudging the captain forward. *Tell them.*

She shot him a look Lila recognized—one she'd doled out a dozen times. A look that said, quite simply, that the next time the sailor laid a hand on her, he'd lose a finger.

"*Kers la?*" demanded Kell.

Jasta crossed her arms, scars flashing in the light. "Some of us are wanting to leave the city." She spoke the common tongue, and her accent had the rumble of a big cat, dropping letters and slurring syllables so that Lila missed every third word if she wasn't careful. "I might have mentioned something about a ship, down in the gallery. Your fellow heard me, and now I am here."

"The ships in London will not sail," said the king, appearing behind her, Rhy at his side. He spoke the captain's tongue like a man who'd mastered Arnesian but did not relish the taste. Jasta took a formal step to the side, bowing her head a fraction. "*Anesh,*" she said, "but then, my ship is not here. It is docked at Tanek, Your Majesty."

Alucard and Lila both straightened at that. Tanek was the mouth of the Isle, the last port before the open sea.

"Why wouldn't you sail it into London?" asked Rhy.

Jasta shot the prince a wary look. "She is a sensitive skiff. Private-like."

"A pirate ship," said Kell, bluntly.

Jasta flashed a sharp-toothed grin. "Your words, Prince, not mine. My ship, she carries all kinds. Fastest skiff on the open seas. To Vesk and back in nine days flat. But if you are asking, no, she does not sail the red and gold."

"Now she does," said the king pointedly.

After a moment, the captain nodded. "It is dangerous, but I could lead them to the ship. . . ." She trailed off.

For a moment Maxim looked irritated. Then his gaze narrowed and his demeanor cooled. "What is it you want?"

Jasta gave a short bow. "The favor of the crown, Your Majesty . . . and a hundred *lish.*"

Alucard hissed through his teeth at the sum, and Kell glowered, but the king was evidently not in the mood to negotiate. "Done."

The woman raised a brow. "I should have asked for more."

"You should have asked for none," said Kell. The pirate ignored him, dark eyes sweeping the room. "How many will go?"

Lila wasn't about to miss this. She raised her hand.

So did Alucard and Lenos.

And so did *Kell*.

He did this while holding the king's gaze, as if daring the monarch to say no. But the king said nothing, and neither did Rhy. The prince only stared at his brother's raised hand, his face unreadable. Across the room, Alucard folded his arms and scowled at Kell.

"This can't possibly go wrong," he muttered.

"You could stay behind," snapped Kell.

Alucard snorted, Kell seethed, Jasta watched, amused, and Lila poured herself another drink.

She had a feeling she was going to need it.

IX

Rhy heard Kell coming.

One moment he was alone, staring out at the ghostly mirage of the shadow palace—the strange impostor of his *home*—and the next he found his brother's reflection in the glass. Kell's coat was no longer royal red but black and high-collared, silver buttons running down the front. It was the coat he wore whenever he carried messages to other Londons. A coat meant for traveling. For leaving.

"You always wanted to travel beyond the city," said Rhy.

Kell ducked his head. "This isn't what I had in mind."

Rhy turned toward him. Kell was standing before the mirror, so Rhy could see his own face repeated. He tried—and failed—to force his features smooth, tried—and failed—to keep the sadness from his voice. "We were supposed to go together."

"And one day we will," said Kell, "but right now, I can't stop Osaron by sitting here, and if there's a chance that he's after the *Antari* instead of the city, if there's a chance we can draw him away—"

"I know," said Rhy, in a way that said *Stop.* In a way that said *I trust you.* He slumped into a chair. "I know you thought it was just a line, but I had it all planned out. We could have left after the season's end, toured the island first, gone from the mist-strewn valleys up to Orten and down through the Stasina forests to the cliffs at Astor, then taken a ship over to the mainland." He leaned back, let his gaze escape to the ceiling with its folds of color. "Once we landed, we'd have hit Hanas first, then gone by carriage to Linar—I heard the capital there will one day rival London—and the market in Nesto, near the Faroan border, is said to be made of glass. I figured we'd pick up a ship there, stop at the point of Sheran, where the water's barely a seam between Arnes and Vesk—so narrow you can walk across it—and we'd be back in time for the dawn of summer."

"Sounds like quite an adventure," said Kell.

"You're not the only restless soul," said Rhy, getting to his feet. "I suppose it's time now?"

Kell nodded. "But I brought you something." He dug a hand into his pocket and came up with two gold pins, each emblazoned with the chalice and rising sun of the House Maresh. The same pins they'd worn during the tournament—Rhy with pride, and Kell under duress. The same pin Rhy had used to carve a word into his arm, its twin the one Kell had used to bring Rhy and Alucard back from the *Night Spire.*

"I've done my best to spell the two together," explained his brother. "The bond should hold, no matter the distance."

"I thought my way was rather clever," said Rhy, rubbing his forearm, where he'd carved the word into his skin.

"This one requires far less blood." Kell came forward, and fastened the pin over his brother's heart. "If something worrisome happens, and you need me to come back, simply take hold of the pin and say 'tol.'"

Tol.

Brother.

Rhy managed a rueful smile. "And what if I get lonely?"

Kell rolled his eyes, pinning the second pendant to the front of his coat.

Rhy's chest tightened.

Don't go, he wanted to say, even though that wasn't fair, wasn't right, wasn't princely. He swallowed. "If you don't come back, I'll have to save the day without you and steal all the glory for myself."

A short laugh, a ghost of a smile, but then Kell brought a hand to Rhy's shoulder. It was so light. So heavy. He could feel the tether tighten, the shadows lap at his heels, the darkness whisper through his head.

"Listen to me," said his brother. "Promise me you won't go after Osaron. Not until we're back."

Rhy frowned. "You can't expect me to hide in the palace until it's over."

"I don't," said Kell. "But I expect you to be smart. And I expect you to trust me when I say I have a plan."

"It would help if you shared it."

Kell chewed his lip. A dreadful habit. Hardly princely. "Osaron can't see us coming," he said. "If we go storming in, demanding a fight, he'll know we've got a card to play. But if we come to save one of ours—"

"I'm to be a lure?" said Rhy, pretending to be aghast.

"What?" teased Kell. "You've always liked people fighting for you."

"Actually," said the prince, "I prefer people fighting *over* me."

Kell's grip tightened on his sleeve, and the humor died on the air. "Four days, Rhy. We'll make it back in that. And then you can get yourself into trouble, and—"

Behind them someone cleared their throat.

Kell's eyes narrowed. His hand fell from Rhy's arm.

Alucard Emery was waiting in the doorway, his hair pinned back, a blue traveling cloak fastened around his shoulders. Rhy's body ached at the sight of him. Standing there, Alucard didn't look like a nobleman, or a triad magician, or even the captain of a ship. He looked like a stranger, like someone who could slip into a crowd, and disappear. *Is this what he looked like that night?* wondered Rhy. *When he snuck out of my bed, out of the palace, out of the city?*

Alucard stepped forward into the room, those thin silver scars dancing in the light.

"Are the horses ready?" asked Kell coolly.

"Almost," answered the captain, plucking at his gloves.

A brief silence fell as Kell waited for Alucard to leave, and while Alucard did not.

"I was hoping," the captain said at last, "to have a word with the prince."

"We need to go," said Kell.

"I won't be long."

"We don't—"

"Kell," said Rhy, giving his brother a short, gentle nudge toward the door. "Go on. I'll be here when you get back."

Kell's arms were a sudden circle around Rhy's shoulders, and then, just as quickly, they were gone, and Rhy was left dizzy from their weight, and then the loss of it. A flutter of black fabric, and the door was swinging shut behind Kell. A strange, irrational panic rose in Rhy's throat, and he had to fight the urge to call his brother back or run after him. He held his ground.

Alucard was watching the place where Kell had been as if the *Antari* had left his shadow behind. Some visible trace now lingering between them.

"I always hated how close you two were," he murmured. "Now I suppose I should be thankful for it."

Rhy swallowed, dragging his gaze from the door. "I suppose I should be, too." His attention fell on the captain. For all their time together in the last few days, they'd hardly spoken. There was Alucard's delirium aboard the ship, and the flickering memories of Alucard's hand, his voice a tether in the dark. The *Essen Tasch* had been a flurry of witty quips and stolen looks, but the last time they'd been together in this room, *alone* in this room, Rhy's back had been up against the mirror, the captain's lips against his throat. And before that . . . before that . . .

"Rhy—"

"Leaving?" he cut in, straining to keep the words light. "At least this time you came to say good-bye."

Alucard winced at the jab, but didn't retreat. Instead, he closed the gap between them, Rhy fighting back a shiver as the captain's fingers found his skin. "You were with me, in the dark."

"I was returning a favor." Rhy held his gaze. "I believe we're even now."

Alucard's eyes were searching his face, and Rhy felt himself flush, his body singing with the urge to pull Alucard's mouth to his, to let the world beyond this room disappear.

"You'd better go," he said breathlessly.

But Alucard didn't pull away. A shadow had crossed the captain's face, something like sadness in his eyes. "You haven't asked me."

The words sank like a stone in Rhy's chest, and he staggered under the weight. A too-heavy reminder of what had happened three summers ago. Of going to bed in Alucard's arms, and waking up alone. Alucard gone from the palace, from the city, from his life.

"What?" he said, his voice cool, but his face burning. "You want me to ask you why you left? Why you chose the open sea over my bed? A criminal's brand over my touch? I didn't ask you, Alucard, because I don't want to hear them."

"Hear what?" asked Alucard, cupping Rhy's cheek.

He knocked the hand away. "The excuses." Alucard drew breath to speak, but Rhy cut him off. "I know what I was to you—a piece of fruit to be picked, a summer fling."

"You were more than that. You *are*—"

"It was only a season."

"That's not—"

"*Stop,*" said Rhy with all the quiet force of a royal. "Just. Stop. I've never cared for liars, Luc, and I care even less for fools, so don't make me feel like more of one. You caught me off guard on the Banner Night. What happened between us, happened . . ." Rhy tried to steady his breathing, then sliced a hand through the air dismissively. "But now it's done."

Alucard caught Rhy's wrist, head bowed to hide those storm blue eyes as he said, under his breath, "What if I don't want it to be done?"

The words landed like a blow, the air leaving his lungs in a jagged exhale. Something burned through him, and it took Rhy a moment to realize what it was. *Anger.*

"What right have you," he said softly, imperiously, "to want *anything* of me?"

His hand splayed across Alucard's chest, a touch once warm, now full of force as he pushed Alucard away. The captain caught himself and looked up, startled, but made no motion to advance. Alucard was standing on the wrong side of the line. He might have been a noble, but Rhy was a prince, untouchable unless he *wanted* to be touched, and he'd just made it clear that he didn't.

"Rhy," Alucard said, clenching his fists, all playfulness gone. "I didn't want to leave."

"But you did."

"If you would only listen—"

"No." Rhy was fighting back another deep, internal tremor. The tension between love and loss, holding on and letting go. "I am not a toy anymore. I am not a foolish youth." He forced the waver from his words. "I am the crown prince of Arnes. The future king of this empire. And if you want another audience with me, a chance to explain yourself, then you must earn it. Go. Bring me back this Inheritor. Help me save my city. Then, Master Emery, I will consider your request."

Alucard blinked rapidly, obviously stricken. But after a long moment, he drew himself up to his full height. "Yes, Your Highness." He turned and crossed the room with steady strides, his boots echoing Rhy's heart as it pounded in his chest. For the second time, he watched someone precious walk away. For the second time, he held his ground. But he could not help the urge to soften the blow. For both of them.

"And, Alucard," he called, when the captain had reached the door. Alucard glanced back, his features pale but set as Rhy said, "Do try not to kill my brother."

A small, defiant smile flickered across the captain's face. Laced with humor, with hope.

"I'll do my best."

SEVEN

SETTING SAIL

I

No wonder Lila hated good-byes, thought Kell. It would have been so much easier to simply *go*. His brother's heart still echoed in his chest as he descended the inner palace stairs, but the threads between them slackened a little with every step. What would it feel like when they were cities apart? When days and leagues stretched between them? Would he still know Rhy's heart?

The air went suddenly cold around him, and Kell looked up to find Emira Maresh barring his path. Of course, it had been too simple. After all this, the king would grant him leave, but the queen would not.

"Your Majesty," he said, expecting accusations, a rebuke. Instead, the queen's gaze fell on him, not a glancing blow, but something soft, solid. They were a cyclone of green and gold, those eyes, like leaves caught in a fall breeze. Eyes that had not held his in weeks.

"You are leaving, then," she said, the words caught between question and observation.

Kell held his ground. "I am, for now. The king has given me permission—"

Emira was already shaking her head, an inward gesture as if trying to clear her own mind. There was something in her hands, a piece of fabric twisted in her grip. "It is poor luck," she said, holding out the cloth, "to leave without a piece of home."

Kell stared at the offering. It was a square of crimson, the kind stitched to children's tunics, embroidered with two letters: *KM*.

Kell Maresh.

He'd never seen it before, and he frowned, confused by that second initial. He'd never considered himself a Maresh. Rhy's brother, yes, and once upon a time, their adopted son, but never this. Never family.

He wondered if it was some kind of peace offering, newly fashioned, but the fabric looked old, worn by someone else's touch.

"I had it made," said Emira, fumbling in a way she rarely did, "when you first came to the palace, but then I couldn't . . . I didn't think it was . . ." She trailed off, and tried again. "People break so easily, Kell," she said. "A hundred different ways, and I was afraid . . . but you have to understand that you are . . . have always been . . ."

This time, when she trailed off, she didn't have the strength to start again, only stood there, staring down at the swatch of cloth, thumb brushing back and forth across the letters, and he knew this was the moment to reach out, or walk away. It was his choice.

And it wasn't fair—he shouldn't *have* to choose—she should have come to him a dozen times, should have listened, should have, should have, but he was tired, and she was sorry, and in that moment, it was enough.

"Thank you," said Kell, accepting the square of cloth, "my queen."

And then, to his surprise, she reached out and placed her other hand against his face, the way she had so many times, when he'd returned from one of his trips, a silent question in her eyes. *Are you all right?*

But now, the question altered, *Will we be all right?*

He nodded once, leaning into her touch.

"Come home," she said softly.

Kell found her gaze again. "I will."

He was the first to pull away, the queen's fingers slipping from his jaw to his shoulder to his sleeve as he left. *I will come back,* he thought, and for the first time in a long time, he knew it was the truth.

Kell knew what he had to do next.

And knew Lila wouldn't be happy about it.

He headed toward the royal cells, and was nearly there when he felt the gentle smoothing of his pulse, the blanket of calm around his shoulders that came with the priest's presence. Kell's steps faltered but didn't stop as Tieren fell in step beside him. The *Aven Essen* said nothing, and the silence dragged like water around Kell's limbs.

"It's not what you think," he said. "I'm not running away."

"I never said you were."

"I'm not doing this because I want to go," continued Kell. "I would never—" He stumbled over the words—there was a time when he would have, when he *had*. "If I thought the city would be safer with me in it—"

"You're hoping to lure the demon away." It wasn't a question.

At last, Kell's steps dragged to a stop. "Osaron *wants,* Tieren. It is his nature. Holland was right about that. He wants change. He wants power. He wants whatever *isn't*. We made an offering, and he scorned it, tried to claim my life instead. He doesn't want what he has, he wants to *take* what he doesn't."

"And if he chooses not to follow you?"

"Then you put the city to sleep." Kell set off again, determined. "Deprive him of every puppet, every person, so that when we return with the Inheritor, he has no choice but to face us."

"Very well. . . ." said Tieren.

"Is this where you tell me to be safe?"

"Oh," said the priest, "I think the time for that is gone."

They walked together, Kell stopping only when he reached the door that led down into the prison. He brought his hand to the wood, fingers splayed across the surface.

"I keep wondering," he said softly, "if all of it is my fault. Where does it start, Tieren?" He looked up. "With Holland's choice, or with mine?"

The priest looked at him, eyes bright within his tired face, and shook his head. For once, the old man didn't seem to have the answer.

II

Delilah Bard did *not* like horses.

She'd never liked them, not when she only knew them for their snapping teeth, and their flicking tails, and their stomping hooves, and not when she found herself on the back of one, the night racing past so fast it blurred around her, and not now as she watched a pair of silver-scarred guards saddle up three for their ride to the port.

As far as she was concerned, nothing with so little brain should have so much force.

Then again, she could say the same about half the tournament magicians.

"If you look at animals like that," said Alucard, clapping her on the shoulder, "it's no wonder they hate you."

"Yes, well, then the feeling is mutual." She glanced around. "No Esa?"

"My cat dislikes horses almost as much as you do," he said. "I left her in the palace."

"God help them all."

"Chatter chatter," said Jasta in Arnesian, her mane of hair pulled back beneath a traveling hood. "Do you always prattle on in that high tongue?"

"Like a songbird," preened Alucard, looking around. "Where's His Highness?"

"I'm right here," said Kell, without rising to the jab. And when Lila turned toward him, she saw why. He wasn't alone.

"*No,*" she snarled.

Holland stood a step behind Kell, flanked by two guards, his hands bound in iron beneath a grey half cloak. His eyes met hers, one a dazzling green, the other black. "Delilah," he said by way of greeting.

Beside her, Jasta went still as stone.

Lenos turned white.

Even Alucard looked uncomfortable.

"*Kers la?*" growled Jasta.

"What is he doing here?" echoed Lila.

Kell's brow furrowed. "I can't leave him in the palace."

"Of course you can."

"I won't." And with those two words, she realized it wasn't only the *palace's* safety he was worried about. "He comes with us."

"He's not a pet," she snapped.

"See, Kell," said Holland evenly. "I told you she wouldn't like it."

"*She's* not the only one," muttered Alucard.

Jasta snarled something too low and slurred for her to hear.

"We're wasting time," said Kell, moving to unlock Holland's manacles.

Lila had a knife out before key touched iron. "He stays chained."

Holland held up his cuffed hands. "You do realize, Delilah, that these won't stop me."

"Of course not," she said with a feral grin. "But they'll slow you down long enough that *I* can."

Holland sighed. "As you wish," he said, just before Jasta slammed her fist into his cheek. His head snapped sideways and his boots slid back a step, but he didn't fall.

"Jasta!" called Kell as the other *Antari* flexed his jaw and spit a mouthful of blood into the dirt.

"Anyone else?" asked Holland darkly.

"I wouldn't mind a go—" started Alucard, but Kell cut him off.

"Enough," he snapped, the ground rumbling faintly with the order. "Alucard, since you volunteered, Holland can ride with you."

The captain sulked at the assignment, even as he hauled the chained *Antari* up onto the horse.

"Try anything . . ." he growled.

"And you'll kill me?" finished Holland dryly.

"No," said Alucard with a vicious smile. "I'll let Bard have you."

Lenos saddled up with Jasta, this pairing just as comical, her massive frame making the sailor seem even smaller and more skeletal. He hinged forward and patted the horse's flank as Kell swung up into his own saddle. He was infuriatingly elegant on horseback, with the regal posture that only came, Lila expected, from years of practice. It was one of those moments that reminded her—as if she could ever forget—that Kell was in so many ways a prince. She made a mental note to tell him sometime, when she was next particularly cross.

"Come on," he said, holding out his hand. And this time, when he pulled her up, he seated her before him instead of behind, one arm wrapping protectively around her waist.

"Don't stab me," he whispered in her ear, and she wished it were full night so no one could see the color rising in her cheeks.

She cast a last look up at the palace, the dark, distorted echo stretching like a shadow at its side.

"What if Osaron follows us?" she asked.

Kell glanced back. "If we're lucky, he will."

"You've an odd notion of luck," said Jasta, kicking her horse into motion.

Lila's own mount lurched forward beneath her, and so did her stomach. *This is not how I die,* she told herself as, in a thunder of hooves and fogging breath, the horses plunged into the night.

III

It was a palace fit for a king.

Fit for a *god*.

A place of promise, potential, power.

Osaron strode through the great hall of his newest creation, his steps landing soundlessly on polished stone. The floor flickered beneath each stride, grass and blossom and ice born with every step, fading behind him like footsteps on sand.

Columns rose up from the floor, growing more like trees than marble pillars, their stone limbs branching up and out, flowering with dark-hued glass and fall leaves and beads of dew, and in their shining columns he saw the world as it could be. So many possible transformations, such infinite potential.

And there, at the heart of the great hall, his throne, its base throwing roots, its back surging into crownlike spires, its arms spread like an old friend waiting to be embraced. Its surface shone with an iridescent light, and as Osaron climbed the steps, mounted the platform, took his seat, the whole palace sang with the rightness of his presence.

Osaron sat at the center of this web and felt the strings of the city, the mind of each and every servant tethered to his by threads of magic. A tug here, a tremor there, thoughts carrying like movement along a thousand lines.

In each devoted life, a fire burned. Some flames were dull and small, barely kindling, while others shone bright and hot, and those he summoned now, called them forward from every corner of the city.

Come, he thought. *Kneel at my feet like children, and I will raise you. As men. As women. As chosen.*

Beyond the palace walls, bridges began to bloom like ice over the river, hands extended to usher them in.

My king, they said, rising from their tables.

My king, they said, turning from their work.

Osaron smiled, savoring the echo of those words, until a new chorus interrupted them.

My king, whispered his subjects, *the bad ones are leaving.*

My king, they said, *the bad ones are fleeing.*

The ones who dared to refuse you.

The ones who dare defy you.

Osaron steepled his fingers. The *Antari* were leaving London.

All of them? he asked, and the echo came.

All of them. All of them. All of them.

Holland's words came back to him, an unwelcome intrusion.

"How will you rule without a head for your crown?"

Words quickly swallowed by his clamoring servants.

Shall we chase them?

Shall we stop them?

Shall we drag them down?

Shall we bring them back?

Osaron rapped his fingers on the arm of the throne. The gesture made no sound.

Shall we?

No, thought Osaron, his command rippling through the minds of thousands like a vibration along a string. He sat back in his sculpted throne. *No. Let them go.*

If it was a trap, he would not follow.

He did not need them.

He did not need their minds, or their bodies.

He had *thousands.*

The first of those he'd summoned was entering the hall, a man striding toward him with a proud jaw and a head held high. He came to a stop before the throne, and knelt, dark head bowed.

"*Rise,*" commanded Osaron, and the man obeyed. "*What is your name?*"

The man stood, broad shouldered and shadow eyed, a silver ring in the shape of a feather circling one thumb.

"My name is Berras Emery," said the man. "How may I serve you?"

IV

Tanek came into sight shortly after dark.

Alucard didn't like the port, but he knew it well. For three years, it was as close to London as he'd dared to come. In many ways it was *too* close. The people here knew the name Emery, had an idea of what it meant.

It was here he learned to be someone else—not a nobleman, but the jaunty captain of the *Night Spire*. Here he first met Lenos and Stross, at a game of Sanct. Here he was reminded, again and again and again, of how close—how far—he was from home. Every time he returned to Tanek, he saw London in the tapestries and trappings, heard it in the accents, smelled it in the air, that scent like woods in spring, and his body ached.

But right now, Tanek seemed nothing like London. It was bustling in a surreal way, oblivious to the danger lurking inland. The berths were filled with ships, the taverns with men and women, the greatest danger a pickpocket or a winter chill.

In the end, Osaron hadn't taken their halfhearted bait, and so the shadow of his power had ended an hour back, the weight of it lifting like the air after a storm. The strangest thing, thought Alucard, was the *way* it stopped. Not suddenly, but slowly, over the course of a click, the spellwork tapering so that by the end of its reach, the few people they met had no shadows in their eyes, nothing but a bad feeling, an urge to turn back. Several times they passed travelers on the road who seemed lost, when in fact they'd simply waded to the edge of the spell, and stopped, repelled by a thing they couldn't name, couldn't remember.

"Don't say anything," Kell had warned when they'd passed the first bunch. "The last thing we need is panic spreading beyond the capital."

A man and woman stumbled past now, arm in arm and laughing drunkenly.

Word clearly hadn't reached the port.

Alucard hauled Holland down from the horse, setting him roughly on the ground. The *Antari* hadn't said a word since they'd left, and the silence made Alucard nervous. Bard didn't talk much either, but hers was a different kind of quiet, present, inquisitive. Holland's silence hung in the air, made Alucard want to speak just to break it. Then again, maybe it was the man's magic that set him on edge, silver threads splintering the air like lightning.

They handed the horses off to a stablehand whose eyes widened at the royal emblem blazoned on the harnesses.

"Keep your heads down," said Kell as the boy led the mounts away.

"We are hardly inconspicuous," said Holland finally, his voice like rough-hewn rock. "Perhaps, if you unchained me—"

"Not likely," said Lila and Jasta, the same words overlapping in different tongues.

The air had warmed a fraction despite the thickening dark, and Alucard was looking around for the source of that warmth when he heard the approach of armored boots and caught the gleam of metal.

"Oh, look," he said. "A welcome party."

Whether it was because of the royal horses or the sight of the strange entourage, a pair of soldiers was heading straight toward them.

"Halt!" they called in Arnesian, and Holland had the sense to fold his cuffed hands beneath his cloak; but at the sight of Kell, the two men paled, one bowing deeply, the other murmuring what might have been a blessing or a prayer, too low for him to make out.

Alucard rolled his eyes at the display as Kell adopted an imitation of his usual arrogance, explaining that they were here on royal business. Yes, everything was well. No, they did not need an escort.

At last, the men retreated to their post, and Lila gave her own mocking bow in Kell's direction.

"*Mas vares,*" she said, then straightened sharply, the humor gone from her face. With a gesture that was at once casual and frighteningly quick, she freed a knife from her belt.

"What is it?" asked Kell and Alucard at once.

"Someone's been following us," she said.

Kell's brows went up. "You didn't think to mention that before?"

"I could have been wrong," she said, twirling the blade in her fingers, "but I'm not."

"Where are—"

Before Kell could finish, she spun, and threw.

The knife sang through the air, eliciting a yelp as it embedded itself in a post a few inches above a crop of brown curls threaded with gold. A boy stood, back pressed to the post and empty hands raised in immediate surrender. On his forehead was a mark in blood. He was dressed in ordinary clothes, no red and gold trim, no symbols of the House Maresh emblazoned on his coat, but Alucard still recognized him from the palace.

"Hastra," said Kell darkly.

The young man ducked out from under Lila's blade. "Sir," he said, dislodging the knife.

"What are you doing here?"

"Tieren sent me."

Kell groaned, and muttered under his breath, "Of course he did." Then, louder, "Go home. You have no business here."

The boy—and he really was just a boy, in manner as well as age—straightened at that, puffing up his narrow chest. "I'm your guard, sir. What is that worth if I don't guard you?"

"You're not my guard, Hastra," said Kell. "Not anymore."

The boy flinched but held his ground. "Very well, sir. But if I am not a guard, then I am a priest, and my orders come from the *Aven Essen* himself."

"Hastra—"

"And he's really very hard to please, you know—"

"Hastra—"

"And you do owe me a favor, sir, since I did stand by you, when you snuck out of the palace and entered the tournament—"

Alucard's head whipped around. "You did *what*?"

"Enough," cut in Kell, waving his hand.

"*Anesh*," said Jasta, who hadn't been following the conversation and didn't seem to care. "Come, go, I don't care. I'd rather not stand here on display. Bad for my reputation to be seen with black-eyed princes and royal guards and nobles playing dress-up."

"I'm a privateer," said Alucard, affronted.

Jasta only snorted and started toward the docks. Hastra hung back, his wide brown eyes still leveled expectantly on Kell.

"Oh, come on," said Lila. "Every ship needs a pet."

Kell threw up his hands. "Fine. He can stay."

"Who were you?" demanded Alucard as they walked along the docks, passing ships of every size and color. The thought of *Kell* entering the tournament—his tournament—was madness. The thought that Alucard had had the chance to fight him—that maybe he *had*—was maddening.

"It doesn't matter," said Kell.

"Did we fight?" But how could they have? Alucard would have seen the silver thread, would have known—

"If we had," said Kell pointedly, "I would have won."

Annoyance flared through Alucard, but then he thought of Rhy, the tether between the two, and anger swallowed indignation.

"Do you have any idea how foolish that was? How dangerous for the prince?"

"Not that it's any of your business," said Kell, "but the whole thing was Rhy's idea." That two-toned gaze cut his way. "I don't suppose you tried to stop *Lila*?"

Alucard glanced over his shoulder. Bard brought up the rear of the party, Holland a pace ahead of her. The other *Antari* was looking at the ships the way Lila had looked at the horses, with a mixture of discomfort and disdain.

"What's the matter," she was saying, "can't swim?"

Holland's lips pursed. "It is a little harder with chains on." His attention went back to the boats, and Alucard understood. He recognized the look in his eyes, a wariness bordering on fear.

"You've never been on a ship, have you?"

The man didn't answer. He didn't need to.

Lila let out a small, malicious laugh. As if she'd known half a thing about ships when Alucard first took her on.

"Here we are," said Jasta, coming to a stop beside something that might—in certain places—qualify as a ship, the way some cottages might qualify as mansions. Jasta patted the boat's side the way a rider might a horse's flank. Its name ran in silver stenciling along the white hull. *Is Hosna. The Ghost.*

"She's a bit small," said the captain, "but whip fast."

"A bit small," echoed Lila dryly. The *Ghost* was half the length of the *Night Spire,* with three short sails and a Faroanesque hull, narrow and feather sharp. "It's a *skiff.*"

"It's a runner," clarified Alucard. "They don't hold much, but there are few things faster on the open sea. It won't be a cozy ride, by any stretch, but we'll reach the market quickly. Especially with three *Antari* keeping wind in our sails."

Lila looked longingly at the ships to either side, towering vessels with dark wood and gleaming sails.

"What about that one?" she said, pointing to a proud ship two berths down.

Alucard shook his head. "It isn't ours."

"It *could* be."

Jasta shot her a look, and Lila rolled her eyes. "Kidding," she said, even though Alucard knew she wasn't. "Besides," she added, "wouldn't want something *too* pretty. Pretty things tend to draw greedy eyes."

"Speaking from experience, Bard?" he teased.

"Thank you, Jasta," cut in Kell. "We'll bring her back in one piece."

"Oh, I'll be making sure of it," said the captain, striding up the boat's narrow ramp.

"Jasta—"

"My vessel, my rules," she said, arms akimbo. "I can get you wherever you're going in half the time, and if you're on some mission to save the kingdom, well, it is my kingdom, too. And I wouldn't mind having the crown on my side next time *I'm* in troubled waters."

"How do you know our motives are so honorable?" said Alucard. "We could just be fleeing."

"*You* could be," she said, and then, jabbing a finger at Kell, "but *he* isn't." With that she stomped onto the deck and they had little choice but to follow her aboard.

"Three *Antari* get on a boat," singsonged Alucard, as if it were the beginning of a tavern joke. He had the added delight of seeing both Kell and Holland try to balance as the deck bobbed under the sudden weight. One looked uncomfortable, the other ill, and Alucard could have assured them that it wouldn't be so bad once they were out at sea, but he wasn't feeling generous.

"Hano!" called Jasta, and a young girl's head appeared above a stack of crates, her black hair pulled into a messy bun.

"*Casero!*" She swung up onto the crate, legs dangling over the edge. "You're back early."

"I have some cargo," said Jasta.

"*Sha!*" said Hano delightedly.

There was a thud and a muffled curse from somewhere on board, and a moment later an old man shuffled out from behind another crate, rubbing his head. His back was bent like a hook, his skin dark and his eyes a milky white.

"*Solase,*" he mumbled, and Alucard couldn't tell if he was apologizing to them or to the crates he'd thudded into.

"That's Ilo," said Jasta, nodding at the blind man.

"Where's the rest of your crew?" asked Kell, looking around.

"This is it," said Jasta.

"You let a little girl and a blind man guard a ship full of stolen merchandise," said Alucard.

Hano giggled and held up a purse. *Alucard's* purse. A moment later Ilo held up a blade. It was Kell's.

The magician flicked his fingers, and the blade snapped hilt first back into his hand, a display that earned him an approving clap from the girl. Alucard reclaimed his purse with a similar flourish and went so far as to let the leather retie itself onto his belt. Lila patted herself down, making sure she still had all her knives, and smiled in satisfaction.

"The map," prompted Jasta. Alucard handed it over.

The captain unfurled the paper, clicking her tongue. "Going Waters, then," she said. It was no surprise to anyone that Jasta, given her particular interests, was familiar with the market.

"What's in these boxes?" asked Kell, resting a hand on one lid.

"A little of this, a little of that," said the captain. "Nothing that will bite."

Hastra and Lenos were already unwinding the ropes, the young guard cheerfully following the sailor's lead.

"Why are you in chains?" asked Hano. Alucard hadn't seen the girl hop down from her perch, but now she stood directly in front of Holland, hands on her hips in a mimic of Jasta's own stance, her black bun coming roughly to the *Antari*'s ribs. "Did you do a bad thing?"

"Hano!" called Jasta, and the girl flitted away again without waiting for an answer. The boat came unmoored, rocking beneath them. Bard smiled, and Alucard felt his balance shift, and then return.

Holland, meanwhile, tipped his head back and drew a deep, steadying breath, eyes up to the sky as if that would keep him from being ill.

"Come on," said Kell, taking the other *Antari*'s arm. "Let's find the hold."

"I don't like that one," said Alucard as Bard came to stand at his side.

"Which one?" she asked dryly, but she cut him a glance, and must have seen something in his face because she sobered. "What do you see when you look at Holland?"

Alucard drew in a breath, and blew it out in a cloud. "This is what magic looks like," he said twirling his fingers through the plume. Instead of dispersing, the pale air twisted and coiled into thin ribbons of mist against the seamless stretch of night and sea.

"But Holland's magic is . . ." He splayed his fingers, and the ribbons of fog splintered, frayed. "He isn't weaker for it. If anything, his light is brighter than yours or Kell's. But the light is uneven, unsteady, the lines all broken, re-formed, like bones that didn't set. It's . . ."

"Unnatural?" she guessed.

"Dangerous."

"Splendid," she said, folding her arms against the cold. A yawn escaped, like a silent snarl through clenched teeth.

"Get some rest," he said.

"I will," said Bard, but she didn't move.

Alucard turned automatically toward the wheel before remembering he wasn't the captain of this ship. He hesitated, like a man who's gone through a door to fetch something, only to forget what he'd come for. At last, he went to help Lenos with the sails, leaving Bard at the ship's rail.

When he looked back ten, fifteen, twenty minutes later, she was still there, eyes trained on the line where water met sky.

V

Rhy rode out as soon as they were gone.

There were too many souls to find, and the thought of staying in the palace another minute made him want to scream. Soon the dark would be upon them, upon him, the fall of night and the confinement. But for now, there was still light, still time.

He took two men, both silvers, and set out into the city, trying to keep his attention from drifting to the eerie palace floating next to his, the strange procession of men and women climbing its steps, trying to keep himself from dwelling on the strange black substance that turned stretches of road into glossy, icelike streaks and climbed bits of wall like ivy or frost. *Magic overwhelming nature.*

He found a couple hunkered down in the back of their house, too afraid to leave. A girl wandering, dazed and coated in the ash of someone else, family or friend or stranger, she wouldn't say. On the third trip, one of the guards came galloping toward him.

"Your Highness," called the man, blood mark smearing with the sweat on his brow as he reined in his horse. "There's something you need to see."

They were in a tavern hall.

Two dozen men, all dressed in the gold and red of the royal guard. And all sick. All dying. Rhy knew each and every one, by face if not by name. Isra had said that some of them were missing. That the blood marks had failed. But they hadn't vanished. They were *here.*

"Your Highness, wait!" called the silver as Rhy plunged forward into the hall, but he was not afraid of the smoke or the sickness. Someone had pushed the tables and chairs out of the way, cleared the space, and now his father's men—his men—were lying on the floor in rows, spaces here and there where a few had risen up, or fallen forever.

Their armor had been stripped off and set aside, propped like a gallery of hollow spectators along the walls as, on the floor, the guards sweated and writhed and fought demons he couldn't see, the way Alucard had aboard the *Spire*.

Their veins stood out black against their throats, and the whole hall smelled vaguely of burning skin as the magic scorched its way through them.

The air was thick with something like dust.

Ash, realized Rhy.

All that was left of those who'd burned.

One man was slumped against the wall by the doors, sweat sheening his face, the sickness just beginning to set in.

His beard was trimmed short, his hair streaked with grey, and Rhy recognized him at once. Tolners. A man who'd served his father before he was king. A man assigned to serve *Rhy*. He'd seen the guard this morning in the palace, safe and well within the wards.

"What have you done?" he asked, grabbing the guard by the collar. "Why did you leave the palace?"

The man's vision slid in and out of focus. "Your Majesty," he rasped. Trapped in the fever's hold, he mistook Rhy for his father. "We are—the royal guard. We—do not hide. If we are not—strong enough—to brave the dark—we do not—deserve to serve—" he broke off, wracked by a sudden, violent chill.

"You fool," snapped Rhy, even as he eased Tolners back into his chair and pulled the man's coat close around his shivering form. Rhy turned on the room of dying guards, raking an ash-slicked hand through his hair, feeling furious, helpless. He couldn't save these men. Could only watch as they fought, failed, died.

"We are the royal guard," murmured a man on the floor.

"We are the royal guard," echoed two more, taking it up as a chant against whatever darkness fought to take them.

Rhy wanted to yell, to curse, but he couldn't, because he knew the things he had done in the name of strength, knew what he was doing even now, walking the cursed streets, combing the poisoned fog, knew that even if Kell's magic hadn't shielded him, he would have gone again, and again, for his city, his people.

And so Rhy did what he had done for Alucard on the *Spire* floor.

He did the only thing he could.

He *stayed*.

Maxim Maresh knew the value of a single *Antari*.

He had stood before the windows and watched *three* ride away from the palace, the city, the monster poisoning its heart. He had weighed the odds, known it was the right decision, the strategy with the highest odds, and yet he could not help but feel that his best weapons were suddenly out of reach. Worse, that he had loosened his grip, let them fall, and now stood facing a foe without a blade.

His own wasn't ready—it was still being forged.

Maxim's reflection hung suspended in the glass. He did not look well. He felt worse. One hand rested against the window, shadows contouring to his fingers in a ghostly mimic, a morbid echo.

"You let him leave," said a gentle voice, and the *Aven Essen* materialized in the glass behind him, a specter in white.

"I did," said Maxim. He had seen his son's body on the bed, chest still, cheeks hollow, skin grey. The image was burned like light against his eyes, an image he would never forget. And he understood, now more than ever, that Kell's life was Rhy's, and if he could not guard it himself, he would see it sent away. "I tried to stop Kell once. It was a mistake."

"He might have stayed this time," said Tieren carefully, "if you'd asked instead of ordered."

"Perhaps." Maxim's hand fell away from the glass. "But this city is no longer safe."

The priest's blue eyes were piercing. "The world might prove no safer."

"I cannot do anything about the dangers in the world, Tieren, but I can do something about the monster here in London."

He began to cross the room, and made it three steps before it tipped violently beneath him. For a terrible instant his vision dimmed, and he thought he would fall.

"Your Majesty," said Tieren, catching his arm. Beneath his tunic, the fresh line of cuts ached, the wounds deep, flesh and blood carved away. A necessary sacrifice.

"I'm well," he lied, pulling free.

Tieren gave him a scornful look, and he regretted showing the priest his progress.

"I cannot stop you, Maxim," said Tieren, "but this kind of magic has consequences."

"When will the sleeping spell be ready?"

"If you are not careful—"

"When?"

"It is difficult to make such a spell, harder still to stretch it over a city. The very nature of it toes the line of the obscene, to put a body and mind to rest is still a manipulation, an exertion of one's will over—"

"When?"

The priest sighed. "Another day. Maybe two."

Maxim straightened, nodded. They would last that long. They had to. When he began to walk again, the ground held firm beneath his feet.

"Your Majesty—"

"Go and finish your own spell, Tieren. And let me finish mine."

VI

By the time Rhy returned to the palace, the light was gone and his armor was painted grey with ash. More than half of the men in the hall had died; the surviving few now marched in his wake, helms beneath their arms, faces gaunt from fever and lit by lines of silver that trailed like tears down this cheeks.

Rhy climbed the front steps in exhausted silence.

The silvered guards stationed at the palace doors said nothing, and he wondered if they'd known—they *had* to have known, letting so many of their own pass through into the fog. They wouldn't meet their prince's gaze, but they met one another's, exchanging a single nod that might have been pride or solidarity, or something else Rhy couldn't read.

His second guard, Vis, was standing in the front hall, clearly waiting for word of Tolners. Rhy shook his head and pushed past him, past everyone, heading for the royal baths, needing to be clean, but as he walked his armor seemed to tighten around him, cutting into his throat, binding his ribs.

He couldn't breathe, and for an instant he thought of the river, of Kell trapped beneath the surface while he'd gasped for air above, but this wasn't an echo of his brother's suffering. His own chest was heaving itself against the armor plate, his own heart pounding, his own lungs coated with the ash of dead men. He had to be rid of it.

"Your Highness?" said Vis as he fought to strip off the armor. The pieces tumbled to the floor, clanging and sending up plumes of dust.

But his chest was still lurching, and his stomach, too, and he barely reached the nearest basin before he was sick.

He clutched the edges of the bowl, dragging in ragged breaths as his heart finally slowed. Vis stood nearby, holding the discarded helmet in his hands.

"It's been a long day," said Rhy shakily, and Vis didn't ask what was wrong, didn't say anything, and for that, Rhy was grateful. He wiped his mouth with a shaking hand, straightened, and continued toward the royal baths.

He was already unbuttoning his tunic when he reached the doors and saw that the room beyond wasn't empty.

Two servants draped in silver and green stood along the far wall, and Cora perched on the stone rim of the large bath set into the floor, dipping a comb into the water and running it through her long, loose hair. The Veskan princess was wearing only a robe, open at the waist, and Rhy knew her people weren't prudish when it came to bodies, but still he blushed at the sight of so much fair skin.

His shirt still half buttoned, his hands slid back to his sides.

Cora's blue eyes drifted up.

"*Mas vares,*" she said in halting Arnesian.

"*Na ch'al,*" he responded hoarsely in Veskan.

The comb came to rest in her lap as she took in his ash-streaked face. "Do you want me to go?"

He honestly didn't know. After hours of holding his head up, of being strong while other men fought and died, he couldn't put on another show, couldn't pretend that everything was all right, but the thought of being alone with his thoughts, with the shadows, not the ones outside the palace walls, but the ones that came for *him* at night . . .

Cora was starting to rise when he said, "*Ta'ch.*"

Don't.

She sank back to her knees as two of his own servants came forward and began to undress him with quick, efficient motions. He expected Cora to look away, but she watched steadily, a curious light in her eyes as they freed the last of his armor, unlaced his boots, unfastened the buttons at cuff and collar with hands steadier than his. The servants peeled away the tunic, exposing his bare, dark chest, smooth except for the line at his ribs, the swirling scar over his heart.

"Clean the armor," he said softly. "Burn the cloth."

Rhy stepped forward, then, a silent command that he'd see to the rest himself.

He left his trousers on and padded barefoot straight down the beautiful inlaid steps and into the bath, the warm water embracing his ankles, his knees, his waist. The clear pool fogged around him, a clouded train of ash in his wake.

He waded to the center of the bath and went under, folding to his knees on the basin floor. His body tried to rise, but he forced all the air from his lungs and dug his fingertips into the grate on the bath floor, and held on until it hurt, until the water smoothed around him, and the world began to tunnel, and no more ash came off his skin.

And when at last he rose, breaking the surface with a ragged gasp, Cora was there, robe discarded on the edge of the bath, her long blond hair held up by some deft motion of the comb. Her hands floated from the surface of the bath like lilies.

"Can I help?" she asked, and before he could answer, she was kissing him, her fingertips brushing his hips beneath the water. Heat flared through him, simple and physical, and Rhy fought to keep his senses as the girl's hands caught the laces of his trousers and began to drag them loose.

He tore his mouth free.

"I thought you had a fondness for my brother," he rasped.

Cora flashed a mischievous smile. "I have a fondness for many things," she said, pulling him close again. Her hand slid over him, and he felt himself rising as she pressed into him, her mouth soft and searching against his, and part of Rhy wanted to let her, to take her, to lose himself the way he had so many times after Alucard left, to hold off the shadows and the nightmares with the simple, welcome distraction of another body.

His hands drifted up to her shoulders.

"*Ta'ch,*" he said, easing her back.

Her cheeks colored, hurt crossing her face before indignation. "You do not want me."

"No," he said gently. "Not like this."

Her gaze flicked down to the place where her fingers still rested against him, her expression coy. "Your body and your mind seem to disagree, my prince."

Rhy flushed and took a step back through the water. "I'm sorry." He continued to retreat until his back hit the stone side of the bath. He sank onto a bench.

The princess sighed, letting her arms drift absently through the water in a childlike way, as if those fingers hadn't just been questing deftly across his skin. "So it's true," she mused, "what they say about you?"

Rhy tensed. He had heard most of the rumors, and all of the truths, heard men speak about his lack of powers, about whether he deserved to be king, about who shared his bed, and who didn't, but still he forced himself to ask. "What do they say, Cora?"

She drifted toward him—wisps of blond hair escaping her bun in the bath's heat—and came to rest beside him on the bench, legs tucked up beneath her. She crossed her arms on the edge of the bath, and leaned her head on top, and just like that, she seemed to shed the last of her seduction and become a girl again.

"They say, Rhy Maresh, that your heart is taken."

He tried to speak, but he didn't know what to say. "It's complicated," he managed.

"Of course it is." Cora trailed her fingers through the water. "I was in love once," she added, as if it were an afterthought. "His name was Vik. I loved him the way the moon loves the stars—that is what we say, when a person fills the world with light."

"What happened?"

Her pale blue eyes drifted up. "You are the sole heir to your throne," she said. "But I am one of seven. Love is not enough."

The way she said it, as if it were a simple, immutable truth, made his eyes burn, his throat tighten. He thought of Alucard, not the way he'd been when Rhy sent him away, or even as he was on the Banner

Night, but the Alucard who'd lingered in his bed that first summer, lips playing against his skin as he whispered the words.

I love you.

Cora's fingers stilled, splaying on the water's surface, and Rhy noticed the deep scratches circling her wrist, the bruised skin. She caught him looking and flicked her hand, a motion of dismissal.

"My brother has a temper," she said absently. "Sometimes he forgets his strength." And then, a small, defiant smile. "But he always forgets mine."

"Does it hurt?"

"It is nothing that won't heal." She shifted. "Your scars are far more interesting."

Rhy's fingers went to the mark over his heart, but he said nothing, and she asked nothing, and they settled into an easy quiet, steam rising in tendrils around them, the patterns swirling in the mist. Rhy felt his mind drifting, to shadows, and dying men, to blades between ribs, and cold, dark places slick with blood, and beyond, beyond, the silence, thick as cotton, heavy as stone.

"Do you have the gift?"

Rhy blinked, the visions dissolving back into the baths. "What gift?"

Cora's fingers curled through the steam. "In my country, there are those who look into the fog and see things that are not there. Things that haven't happened yet. Just now, you looked like you were seeing something."

"Not seeing," said Rhy. "Just remembering."

They sat for ages in the bath, eager to leave neither the warmth nor the company. They perched side by side on the stone bench at the basin's edge, or on the cooler tile of its rim, and spoke—not about the past, or their respective scars. Instead, they shared the present. Rhy told her about the city beyond the walls, about the curse cast over London, its strange and spreading transmutation, about the fallen, and the silvers. And Cora told him about the claustrophobic palace with its maddening nobles, the gallery where they gathered to worry, the corners where they huddled to whisper.

Cora had the kind of voice that rang out through a room, but when she spoke softly, there was a music to it, a melody that he found lulling. She wove stories about this lord and that lady, calling them by their clothes since she didn't always know their names. She spoke of the magicians, too, with their tempers and their egos, recounted whole conversations without a stutter or a stop.

Cora, it seemed, had a mind like a gem, sharp and bright, and buried beneath childish airs. He knew why she did it—it was the same reason he played a rake as much as a royal. It was easier, sometimes, to be underestimated, discounted, dismissed.

". . . And then he actually did it," she was saying. "Swallowed a glass of wine and lit a spark, and poof, burned half his beard off."

Rhy laughed—it felt easy, and wrong, and so very needed—and Cora shook her head. "Never dare a Veskan. It turns us stupid."

"Kell said he had to knock one of your magicians out cold to keep her from charging into the fog."

Cora cocked her head. "I haven't seen your brother all day. Where has he gone?"

Rhy leaned his head back against the tiles. "To find help."

"He's not in the palace?"

"He's not in the city."

"Oh," she said thoughtfully. And then her smile was back, lazy on her lips. "And what about this?" she asked, producing Rhy's royal pin.

He shot upright. "Where did you get that?"

"It was in your trouser pocket."

He reached for it, and she pulled playfully out of reach.

"Give it *back*," he demanded, and she must have heard the warning in his voice, the sudden, shocking cold of the command, because she didn't resist, didn't play any games. Rhy's hand closed over the water-warmed metal. "It's late," he said, rising out of the bath. "I should go."

"I didn't mean to upset you," she said, looking genuinely hurt.

He ran a hand through damp curls. "You didn't," he lied as a pair of servants appeared, wrapping a robe around his bare shoulders. Anger burned through him, but only at himself for letting his guard slip, letting his focus drift. He should have left long ago, but he hadn't wanted to face the shadows that came with sleep. Now his body ached, his mind blurring with fatigue. "It's been a long day, and I'm tired."

Sadness washed across Cora's face.

"Rhy," she mewed, "it was only a game. I wouldn't have kept it."

He knelt on the bath's tiled edge, tipped her chin, and kissed her once on the forehead. "I know," he said.

He left her sitting alone in the bath.

Outside, Vis was slumped in a chair, weary but awake.

"I'm sorry," said Rhy as the guard rose beside him. "You shouldn't have waited. Or I shouldn't have stayed."

"It's all right, sir," said the man groggily, falling into step behind him.

The palace had gone quiet around them, only the murmur of the guards on duty filling the air as Rhy climbed the stairs, pausing outside Kell's room before remembering he wasn't there.

His own chamber stood empty, the lamps lit low, casting long shadows on every surface. A collection of tonics glittered on the sideboard— Tieren's concoctions for nights when it got bad—but the warmth of the bath still clung to his limbs and dawn was only a few hours away, so Rhy set his pin on the table and fell into the bed.

Only to be assaulted by a ball of white fur.

Alucard's cat had been sleeping on his pillow, and gave an indignant chirp when Rhy landed on the sheets. He didn't have the energy to evict the cat—its violet eyes were daring him to try—so Rhy slumped back, content to share the space. He threw an arm over his eyes and was surprised to feel the soft weight of a paw prodding his arm before curling up against his side. He slid his fingers absently through the creature's fur, letting the soft rumble of its purr and the faint, lingering scent of the captain—all sea breeze and summer wine—pull him down into sleep.

VII

There was a moment, when a ship first put out to sea.

When the land fell away and the world stretched wide, nothing but water and sky and freedom.

It was Lila's favorite time, when anything could happen and nothing yet had. She stood on the deck of the *Ghost* as Tanek parted around them, and the wild night opened its arms.

When she finally went below, Jasta was waiting at the base of the stairs.

"*Avan,*" said Lila casually.

"*Avan,*" rumbled Jasta.

It was a narrow hall, and she had to sidestep the captain in order to get by. She was halfway past when Jasta's hand shot out and closed around her throat. Lila's feet left the floor and then she was hanging, pinned roughly against the wall. She scrambled for purchase, too stunned to summon magic or reach her blade. By the time she finally freed the one she kept strapped to her ribs, the captain's hand had withdrawn and Lila was sagging back against the wall. One leg buckled before she managed to catch herself.

"What the everloving hell was that for?"

Jasta just stood there, looking down at Lila as if she hadn't just tried to strangle her. "That," said the captain, "was for insulting my ship."

"You've got to be kidding me," she snarled.

Jasta simply shrugged. "That was a warning. Next time, I throw you over."

With that, the captain held out her hand. It seemed a bad idea to take it, but a worse idea to refuse. Before Lila could decide, Jasta reached down and hauled her upright, gave her a sturdy pat on the back, and walked away, whistling as she went.

Lila watched the woman go, rocked by the sudden violence, the fact that she hadn't seen it coming. She holstered her blade with shaking fingers, and went to find Kell.

He was in the first cabin on the left.

"Well, this is cozy," she said, standing in the doorway.

The cabin was half the size of a closet, and about as welcoming. With just enough space for a single cot, it reminded Lila a bit too much of the makeshift coffin she'd been buried in by a bitter Faroan during the tournament.

Kell was sitting on the cot, turning a royal pin over in his fingers. When he saw her, he tucked it in his pocket.

"Room for another?" she asked, feeling like a fool even as she said it. There were only four cabins, and one was being used as a cell.

"I think we can make do," said Kell, rising to his feet. "But if you'd rather . . ."

He took a step toward the door, as if to go. She didn't want him to.

"Stay," she said, and there it was, that flickering smile, like an ember, coaxed with every breath.

"All right."

A single lantern hung from the ceiling, and Kell snapped his fingers, pale fire dancing above his thumb as he reached up to light the wick. Lila turned in a careful circle, surveying the cubby. "A bit smaller than your usual accommodations, *mas vares*?"

"Don't call me that," he said, pulling her back toward him, and she was about to say it again just to tease him when she saw the look in his eyes and relented, running her hands along his coat.

"All right."

He pulled her close, brushing his thumb against her cheek, and she knew he was looking at her eye, the spiral of fractured glass.

"You really didn't notice?"

Color spread across his fair cheeks, and she wondered, absently, if his skin freckled in the summer. "I don't suppose you'd believe me if I said I was distracted by your charm?"

Lila let out a low, sharp laugh. "My knives, perhaps. My quick fingers. But not my charm."

"Wit, then. Power."

She flashed a wicked smile. "Go on."

"I was distracted by everything about you, Lila. I still am. You're maddening, infuriating, incredible." She'd ben teasing, but he clearly wasn't. Everything about him—the set of his mouth, the crease in his brow, the intensity in that blue eye—was dead serious. "I have never known what to make of you. Not since the day we met. And it terrifies me. You terrify me." He cupped her face in both hands. "And the idea of you walking away again, vanishing from my life, that terrifies me most of all."

Her heart was racing, banging out that same old song—*run, run, run*—but she was tired of running, of letting things go before she had the chance to lose them. She pulled Kell closer.

"Next time I walk away," she whispered into his skin, "come with me." She let her gaze drift up to his throat, his jaw, his lips. "When this is all over, when Osaron is gone and we've saved the world again, and everyone else gets their happily ever after, come with me."

"Lila," he said, and there was so much sadness in his voice, she suddenly realized she didn't want to hear his answer, didn't want to think of all the ways their story could end, of the chance that none of them would make it out alive, intact. She didn't want to think beyond this boat, this moment, so she kissed him, deeply, and whatever he was going to say, it died on his lips as they met hers.

VIII

Holland sat on the cot with his back against the cabin wall.

Beyond the wooden boards, the sea splashed against the ship's hull, and the rocking of the floor beneath him made him dizzy every time he moved. The iron cuff around Holland's wrist wasn't helping—the manacles been spelled to dampen magic, the effect like a wet cloth over a fire, not enough to douse his flame, but enough to make it smoke, like a cloud smothering his senses.

He was kept off balance by the second cuff, no longer around his wrist but clamped to a hook in the cabin wall.

And worse, he wasn't alone.

Alucard Emery was leaning in the doorway with a book in one hand and a glass of wine in the other (the thought of both made Holland ill) and every now and then his dark blue eyes flicked up, as if to make sure the *Antari* was still there, safely tethered to the wall.

Holland's head ached. His mouth was dry. He wanted air. Not the stale air of the cabin cell, but the fresh air above, whistling across the deck.

"If you set me free," he said, "I could help propel the ship."

Alucard licked his thumb and turned a page. "If I set you free, you could kill us all."

"I could do that from here," said Holland casually.

"Words that do not help your cause," said the captain.

A small window was embedded in the wall above Holland's head. "You could at least open that," he said. "Give us both some air."

Alucard looked at him long and hard before finally tucking the book under his arm. He downed the last of the wine, set the empty glass on the ground, and came forward, leaning over him to unlock the hatch.

A gust of cold air spilled in, and Holland filled his lungs as a spray of water sloshed against the hull and through the open window, spilling into the cabin.

Holland braced for the icy spray, but it never hit him.

With a flick of his wrist and a murmur of words, the water sprang up, circling Alucard's fingers once before hardening into a thin but vicious blade. His hand tightened on the hilt as he brought the knife's ice edge to rest against Holland's throat.

He swallowed, testing the blade's bite as he met Alucard's gaze.

"It would be a foolish thing," he said slowly, "to draw my blood."

Flexing his wrist, Holland felt the splinter of wood he'd slipped under the manacle, point digging into the base of his palm. It wouldn't take much pressure. A drop, a word, and the cuffs would melt away. But it wouldn't set him free.

Alucard's smile sharpened, and the knife dissolved back into a ribbon of water dancing in the air around him.

"Just remember something, *Antari*," he said, twirling his fingers and the water with them. "If this ship sinks, you will sink with it." Alucard straightened, shooing the sea spray back out the open window. "Any other requests?" he asked, the picture of hospitality.

"No," said Holland coolly. "You've already done so much."

Alucard cracked an icy smile and opened his book again, obviously content with his post.

The third time Death came for Holland, he was on his knees.

He crouched beside the stream, blood dripping from his fingertips in fat red drops as the Silver Wood rose around him. Twice a year he went there, a place up the river where the Sijlt branched off through a grove of trees growing up from the barren ground in shades of burnished metal—neither wood nor stone nor steel. Some said the Silver Wood had been made by a magician's hand, while

others said it was the place where magic made its final stand before withdrawing from the surface of the world.

It was a place where, if you stood still, and closed your eyes,
you could smell the echoes of summer. A memory of natural magic
worn into the wood.

Holland bowed his head. He didn't pray—didn't know who to
pray to, or what to say—only watched the frosted waters of the
Sijlt swirl beneath his outstretched hand, waiting to catch each drop
as it fell. A dash of crimson, a cloud of pink, and then gone, the
pale surface of the stream returning to its usual whitish grey.

"What a waste of blood," said a voice behind him casually.

Holland didn't startle. He'd heard the steps coming from the
edge of the grove, boots landing on dry grass. A short, sharp knife
lay on the bank beside him, and Holland's fingers drifted toward
it, only to find it wasn't there. He rose to his feet, then, and turned
to find the stranger holding his weapon in both hands. The man
was half a head shorter than Holland, and two decades older,
dressed in a faded grey that almost passed for black, with dusty
brown hair and dark eyes flecked with amber.

"Nice blade," said the intruder, testing its tip. "Gotta keep them
sharp."

Blood dripped from Holland's palm, and the man's eyes flicked
to the vivid red before smiling broadly. "*Sot,*" he said easily, "I didn't
come looking for trouble."

He sank onto a petrified log and drove the knife into the hard
earth at his feet before lacing his fingers and leaning forward,
elbows on his knees. One hand was covered in binding spells, an
element scrawled along each finger. "Nice view."

Holland still said nothing.

"I come here sometimes, to think," continued the man, drawing a rolled paper from behind his ear. He looked at the end, unlit,
then held it toward Holland.

"Help a friend out?"

"We're not friends," said Holland.

The man's eyes danced with light. "Not yet."

When Holland didn't move, the man sighed and flicked his own fingers, producing a small coin-sized flame that danced above his thumb. It was no small feat, this display of natural magic, even with the spellwork scrawled on his skin. He took a long drag. "My friends call me Vor."

The name settled like a stone in Holland's chest. "Vortalis."

The man brightened. "You remember," he said. Not *you've heard of me,* or *you know,* but you *remember.*

And Holland did. Ros Vortalis. He was a legend in the Kosik, a story in the streets and the shadows, a man who used his words as much as his weapons, and one who always seemed to get his way. A man known across the city as the Hunter, named for tracking down whoever and whatever he wanted, and for never leaving without his quarry. A man who had been hunting *Holland* for years.

"You have a reputation," said Holland.

"Oh," said Vortalis, exhaling, "we both have those. How many men and women walk the streets of London without weapons at hand? How many end fights without lifting a finger? How many refuse to join the gangs or the guard—"

"I'm not a thug."

Vortalis cocked his head. His smile vanished. "What are you, then? What's the point of you? All the magic in that little black eye, and what do you use it for? Emptying your veins into a frozen river? Dreaming of a nicer world? Surely there are better uses."

"My power has never brought me anything but pain."

"Then you're using it wrong." With that he stood and put the end of his taper out against the nearest tree.

Holland frowned. "This is a sacred—"

He didn't get the chance to finish the admonition, for that was when Vortalis moved, so fast it had to be a spell, something scrawled somewhere beneath his clothes—but then again, spells only *amplified* power. They didn't make it from scratch.

His fist was inches from Holland's face when Holland's will ground against flesh and bone, forcing Vortalis to a stop. But it wasn't enough. The man's fist trembled in the air, warring with the hold, and then it came crashing through, like a brick through glass, and slammed into Holland's jaw. The pain was sudden, bright, Vortalis beaming as he danced backward out of Holland's range. Or tried to. The stream shot up behind him and surged forward. But just before it caught Vortalis in the back, he moved again, sidestepping a blow he couldn't have seen before Holland finally lost patience and sent two spears of ice careening toward the man from opposite sides.

He dodged the first, but the second took him in the stomach, the spear spinning on its axis so it shattered broadside across the man's ribs instead of running him through.

Vortalis fell backward with a groan.

Holland stood, waiting to see if the man would get back up. He did, chuckling softly as he rocked forward to his knees.

"They told me you were good," said Vortalis, rubbing his ribs. "I've a feeling you're even better than they know."

Holland's fingers curled around his drying blood. Vortalis picked up a shard of ice, handling it less like a weapon than an artifact. "As it is, you could have killed me."

And Holland could have. Easily. If he hadn't turned the spear, it would have gone straight through flesh and muscle, broken against bone, but there was Alox in his head, stone body shattering against the floor, and Talya, slumping lifeless against her own knife.

Vortalis got to his feet, holding his side. "Why didn't you do it?"

"You weren't trying to kill *me*."

"The men I sent were. But you didn't kill them, either."

Holland held his gaze.

"You got something against killing?" pressed Vortalis.

"I've taken lives," answered Holland.

"That's not what I asked."

Holland fell silent. He clenched his fists, focused on the line of pain along his palm. At last, he said, "It's too easy."

"Killing? Of course it is," said Vortalis. "Living with it, that's the hard part. But sometimes, it's worth it. Sometimes, it's *necessary*."

"It wasn't necessary for me to kill your men."

Vortalis raised a brow. "They could have come after you again."

"They didn't," said Holland. "You just kept sending new ones."

"And you kept letting them live." Vortalis stretched, wincing faintly at his injured ribs. "I'd say you have a death wish, but you don't seem all that keen to die." He walked to the edge of the grove, his back to Holland as he looked out over the pale expanse of the city. He lit another taper, stuck the end between his teeth. "You know what I think?"

"I don't care—"

"I think you're a romantic. One of those fools waiting for the someday king to come. Waiting for the magic to return, for the world to wake up. But it doesn't work like that, Holland. If you want change, you have to make it." Vortalis waved dismissively at the stream. "You can empty your veins into that water, but it won't change a thing." He held out his hand. "If you really want to save this city, help me put that blood to better use."

Holland stared at the man's spell-covered hand. "And what use would that be?"

Vortalis smiled. "You can help me kill a king."

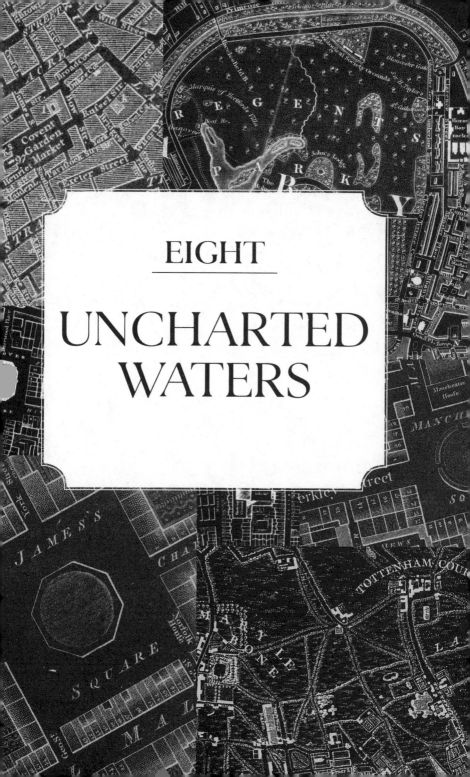

EIGHT

UNCHARTED WATERS

I

The coffee tasted like muck, but it kept Alucard's hands warm.

He hadn't slept, nerves sharpened to knife points by the foreign ship and the traitor magician and the fact that every time he closed his eyes, he saw Anisa burning, saw Jinnar crumbling to ash, saw himself reaching out as if there were a damned thing he could do to save his sister, his friend. Anisa had always been so bright, Jinnar had always been so strong, and it had meant nothing in the end.

They were still dead.

Alucard climbed the steps to the deck and took another swig, forgetting how bad the brew really was. He spit the brown sludge over the rail and wiped his mouth.

Jasta was busy tying off a rope against the mainmast. Hastra and Hano were sitting on a crate in the shade of the mainsail, the young guard cross-legged and the sailor girl perched like a crow, leaning forward to see something cupped in his hands. It looked, of all things, like the leafy green beginnings of an acina blossom. Hano made a delighted sound as the thing slowly unfurled before her eyes. Hastra was surrounded by the thin white threads of light particular to those rare few who held the elements in balance. Alucard wondered briefly why the young guard was not instead a priest. The air around Hano was a nest of dark blue spirals: a wind magician in the making, like Jinnar—

"Careful, now," said a voice. "A sailor's no good without a full set of fingers."

It was Bard. She was standing near the prow, teaching Lenos a trick with one of her knives. The sailor watched, eyes wide, as she took the blade between her fingertips and flipped it up into the air, and by the time she caught it handle side, the knife's edge was on fire. She gave a bow, and Lenos actually flashed a nervous smile.

Lenos, who'd come to Alucard on her first night aboard the *Spire* and warned that she was an omen. As if Alucard didn't already know.

Lenos, who'd named her the Sarows.

The first time Alucard had seen Delilah Bard, she'd been standing on his ship, bound at the wrists and frizzing the air with silver. He'd only ever met one magician who glowed like that, and that one had a black eye and an air of general disdain that spoke louder than any words. Lila Bard, however, had two average brown eyes, and nothing to say for herself, nothing to say for the corpse of Alucard's crewmember, stretched out there on the plank. Had offered a single broken sentence:

Is en ranes gast.

I am the best thief.

And as he'd stood there, taking in her dagger smile, her silver lines of light, Alucard had thought, *Well, you're certainly the strangest.*

The first bad decision he'd made was taking her aboard.

The second was letting her stay.

From there, the bad decisions seemed to multiply like drinks during a game of Sanct.

That first night, in his cabin, Lila sat across from Alucard, her magic tangled, a snarled knot of power never used. And when she asked him to teach her, he'd nearly choked on his wine. Teach an *Antari* magic? But Alucard had. He'd groomed the coil of power, smoothed it as best he could, and watched the magic flow through clear channels, brighter than anything he'd ever seen.

He'd had his moments of clarity, of course.

He'd thought of selling her to Maris at the *Ferase Stras.*

Thought of killing her before she decided to kill him.

Thought of leaving her, betraying her, dreamed up a dozen ways to wash his hands of her. She was trouble—even the crew knew it, and they couldn't see the word written in knotted silver above her head.

But for all of that, he *liked* her.

Alucard had taken a dangerous girl and made her positively lethal, and he knew that combination was likely to be the end of him, one way or another. So when she'd betrayed him, attacking a competitor before the *Essen Tasch*, stealing their place even though she had to know what it would mean for *him, his crew*, his *ship* . . . Alucard hadn't truly been surprised. If anything, he'd been a bit relieved. He'd always known *Antari* were selfish, bullheaded magicians. Lila was simply proving his instinct right.

He thought it would be easy then, to be rid of her, to take back his ship, his order, his life. But nothing about Bard was easy. That silver light had snagged him, gotten his own blue and green all tangled up.

"You *knew*."

Alucard hadn't heard Kell coming, hadn't noticed the silver stirring the air outside his thoughts, but now the other magician stood beside him, following his gaze to Bard. "We look different to you, don't we?"

Alucard crossed his arms. "Everyone looks different to me. No two threads of magic are the same."

"But you knew what she was," said Kell, "from the moment you saw her."

Alucard tipped his head. "Imagine my surprise," he said, "when a cutpurse with a silver cloud killed one of my men, joined up with my crew, and then asked *me* to teach *her* magic."

"So it's *your* fault she entered the *Essen Tasch*."

"Believe it or not," said Alucard, echoing Kell's words about Rhy from the night before, "it was her idea. And I tried to stop her. Valiantly, but it turns out she's rather stubborn." His gaze flicked toward Kell. "Must be an *Antari* trait."

Kell gave a grunt of annoyance and turned away. Always storming off. That was definitely an *Antari* habit.

"Wait," said Alucard. "Before you go, there's something—"

"No."

Alucard bristled. "You don't even know what I was going to say."

"I know it was probably about Rhy, so I know I don't want to hear it, because if you say one more thing about how my brother was in bed, I'm going to break your jaw."

Alucard laughed softly, sadly.

"Is that *funny*?" snarled Kell.

"No . . ." said Alucard, trailing off. "You're just so easy to rile. You really can't fault me for doing it."

"No more than you will be able to fault me for hitting you when you go too far."

Alucard raised his hands. "Fair enough." He began to rub the old scars that circled his wrists. "Look, all I wanted to say was—that I never meant to hurt him."

Kell gave him a disparaging look. "You treated him like a fling."

"How would you know?"

"Rhy was in love with you, and you *left* him. You made him think . . ." An exasperated sigh. "Or have you forgotten, that you ran from London long before I ever tried to cast you out?"

Alucard shook his head, eyes escaping to the steady blue line of the sea. His jaw locked, body revolting against the truth. The truth had claws, and they were sunk into his chest. It would be easier to let it go unsaid, but when Kell turned again to go, he forced it up.

"I *left*," he said, "because *my* brother found out where I was spending my nights—who I was spending them *with*."

Alucard kept his eyes on the water, but he heard Kell's steps drag to a stop. "Believe it or not, not all families are willing to put aside propriety to indulge a royal's taste. The Emerys have old notions. Strict ones." He swallowed. "My brother, Berras, told my father, who beat me until I couldn't stand. Until he broke my arm, my shoulder, my ribs. Until I blacked out. And then he had Berras put me out to sea. I woke up in a ship's hold, the captain ten *rish* richer with the order not to return to London until his crew had *set me right*. I made it off that ship the first time it docked, with three *lin* in my pocket and a fair bit of magic in my veins, and no one to welcome me home, so no, I didn't turn back. And that's my fault. But I didn't know what I meant to him." He tore his gaze from the sea and met Kell's eyes.

"I never wanted to leave," he said. "And if I'd known Rhy loved me then as much as I love him, I would never have stayed away."

They stood surrounded by the sea spray and the crack of sails.

For a long minute, neither spoke.

At last, Kell sighed. "I still can't stand you."

Alucard laughed with relief. "Oh, don't worry," he said. "The feeling's mutual."

With that, the captain left the *Antari* and made his way to his thief. Lenos had left her standing alone at the rail, and she was now using her blade to scrape dirt from beneath her nails, gaze trained on something distant.

"Coin for your thoughts, Bard."

She glanced his way, and a smile touched the corner of her mouth.

"I never thought we'd never share a deck again."

"Well, the world is full of surprises. And shadow kings. And curses. Coffee?" Alucard asked, offering the cup. She took one look at the brown sludge and said, "I'll pass."

"Don't know what you're missing, Bard."

"Oh, I do. I made the mistake of trying some this morning."

Alucard made a sour face and tipped the rest of the drink out over the side. Ilo was making the *Spire*'s usual cook look like a palace chef. "I need a real meal."

"I'm sorry," teased Lila, "when did someone exchange my stalwart captain for a whining noble?"

"When did someone exchange my best thief for a thorn in the ass?"

"Ah," she said, "but I've always been one of those."

Lila tipped her face toward the sun. Her hair was getting long, the dark strands brushing her shoulders, her glass eye winking in the crisp winter light.

"You love the sea," he said.

"Don't you?"

Alucard's hand tightened on the rail. "I love pieces of it. The air on the open water, the energy of a crew working together, the chance for adventure and all that. But . . ." He sensed her attention sharpening, and stopped. For months they'd walked a careful line between outright lie and truth by omission, caught in a stalemate, neither willing to tip their hand. They'd doled out truths like precious currency, and only ever in trade.

Just now, he'd almost gone and told her something for free.

"But?" she prodded with a thief's light touch.

"Do you ever get tired of running, Bard?"

She cocked her head. "No."

Alucard's gaze went to the horizon. "Then you haven't left enough behind."

A chill breeze cut through, and Lila crossed her arms on the rail and looked down at the water below. She frowned. "What is that?"

Something bobbed on the surface, a piece of driftwood. And then another. And another. The boards floated past in broken shards, the edges burned. An unpleasant chill went through Alucard.

The *Ghost* was sailing through the remains of a ship.

"That," said Alucard, "is the work of Sea Serpents."

Lila's eyes widened. "Please tell me you're talking about mercenaries and not giant ship-eating snakes."

Alucard raised a brow. "Giant ship-eating snakes? Really?"

"What?" she challenged. "How am I supposed to know where to draw the line in this world?"

"You can draw it well before giant ship-eating snakes. . . . You see this, Jasta?" he called.

The captain squinted in the direction he was pointing. "I see it. Looks maybe a week old."

"Not old enough," muttered Alucard.

"You wanted the fastest route," she called, turning back to the wheel as a large piece of hull floated past, part of the name still painted on its side.

"So what are they, then," asked Lila, "these Sea Serpents?"

"Swords for hire. They sink their own ships right before they attack."

"As a distraction?" asked Lila.

He shook his head. "A message. That they won't be needing them anymore, that once they're done killing everyone aboard and dumping the bodies in the sea, they'll take their victims' boat instead and sail away."

"Huh," said Lila.

"Exactly."

"Seems like a waste of a perfectly good ship."

He rolled his eyes. "Only you would mourn the vessel instead of the sailors."

"Well," she said matter-of-factly, "the ship certainly didn't do anything wrong. The *people* might have deserved it."

II

When Kell was young and couldn't sleep, he'd taken to wandering the palace.

The simple act of walking steadied something in him, calmed his nerves and stilled his thoughts. He'd lose track of time, but also space, look up and find himself in a strange part of the palace with no memory of getting there, his attention turned inward instead of out.

He couldn't get nearly as lost on the *Ghost*—the whole of the ship was roughly the size of Rhy's chambers—but he was still surprised when he looked up and realized he was standing outside Holland's makeshift cell.

The old man, Ilo, was propped in a chair in the doorway, silently whittling a piece of black wood into the shape of a ship by feel alone, and doing a rather decent job. He seemed lost in his task, the way Kell had been moment before, but now Ilo rose, sensing his presence and reading in it a silent dismissal. He left the small wooden carving behind on the chair. Kell glanced into the small room, expecting to see Holland staring back, and frowned.

Holland was sitting on the cot with his back to the wall, his head resting on his drawn-up knees. One hand was cuffed to the wall, the chain hanging like a leash. His skin had taken on a greyish pallor— the sea clearly wasn't agreeing with him—and his black hair, Kell realized, was streaked with new bright silver, as if shedding Osaron had cost him something vital.

But what surprised Kell most was the simple fact that Holland was *asleep.*

Kell had never seen Holland lower his guard, never seen him re-laxed, let alone unconscious. And yet, he wasn't entirely *still*. The mus-cles in the other *Antari*'s arms twitched, his breath hitching, as though he were trapped in a bad dream.

Kell held his breath as he lifted the chair out of the way and stepped into the room.

Holland didn't stir when Kell neared, nor when he knelt in front of the bed.

"Holland?" said Kell quietly, but the man didn't shift.

It wasn't until Kell's hand touched Holland's arm that the man woke. His head snapped up and he pulled suddenly away, or tried to, his shoulders hitting the cabin wall. For a moment his gaze was wide and empty, his body coiled, his mind somewhere else. It lasted only a sec-ond, but in that sliver of time, Kell saw fear. A deep, trained fear, the kind beaten into animals who'd once bitten their masters, Holland's careful composure slipping to reveal the tension beneath. And then he blinked, once, twice, eyes focusing.

"Kell." He exhaled sharply, his posture shifting back into a mimicry of calm, control, as he wrestled with whatever demons haunted his sleep. "*Vos och?*" he demanded brusquely in his own tongue. *What is it?*

Kell resisted the urge to retreat under the man's glare. They'd hardly spoken since he had arrived in front of Holland's cell and told him to get up. Now he said only, "You look ill."

Holland's dark hair was plastered to his face with sweat, his eyes feverish. "Worried for my health?" he said hoarsely. "How touching." He began to fiddle absently with the manacle around his wrist. Beneath the iron, his skin looked red, raw, and before Kell had fully decided, he was reaching for the metal.

Holland stilled. "What are you doing?"

"What does it look like?" said Kell, producing the key. His fingers closed around the cuff, and the cold metal with its strange numbing weight made him think of White London, of the collar and the cage and his own voice screaming—

The chains fell away, manacle hitting the floor hard and heavy enough to mark the wood.

Holland stared down at his skin, at the place where the metal cuff had been. He flexed his fingers. "Is that a good idea?"

"I suppose we'll see," said Kell, retreating to sit in the chair against the opposite wall. He kept his guard up, hand hovering over a blade even now, but Holland made no motion to attack, only rubbed his wrist thoughtfully.

"It's a strange feeling, isn't it?" said Kell. "The king had me arrested. I spent some time in that cell. In those chains."

Holland raised a single dark brow. "How long did you spend in chains, Kell?" he asked, voice dripping with scorn. "Was it a few hours, or an entire day?"

Kell went silent, and Holland shook his head ruefully, a mocking sound caught in his throat. The *Ghost* must have caught a wave, because it rocked, and Holland paled. "Why am I on this ship?" When Kell didn't answer, he went on. "Or perhaps the better question is, why are *you* on this ship?"

Kell still said nothing. Knowledge was a weapon, and he had no intention of arming Holland, not yet. He expected the other magician to press the issue, but instead he settled back, face tipped to the open window.

"If you listen, you can hear the sea. And the ship. And the people on it." Kell tensed, but Holland continued. "That Hastra, he has the kind of voice that carries. The captains, too, both of them like to talk. A black market, a container for magic . . . it won't be long before I've pieced it all together."

So he wasn't dropping it.

"Enjoy the challenge," said Kell, wondering why he was still there, why he'd come in the first place.

"If you're planning an attack against Osaron, then let me *help*." The other *Antari*'s voice had changed, and it took Kell a moment to realize what he heard threaded through it. Passion. Anger. Holland's voice had always been as smooth and steady as a rock. Now, it had fissures.

"Help requires trust," said Kell.

"Hardly," countered Holland. "Only mutual interest." His gaze burned through Kell. "Why did you bring me?" he asked again.

"I brought you along so you wouldn't cause trouble in the palace. And I brought you as bait, in the hopes that Osaron would follow us." It was a partial truth, but the telling of it and the look in Holland's eyes loosened something in Kell. He relented. "That container you heard about—it's called an Inheritor. And we're going to use it to contain Osaron."

"How?" demanded Holland, not incredulous, but intense.

"It's a receptacle for power," explained Kell. "Magicians used them once to pass on the entirety of their magic by transferring it into a container."

Holland went quiet, but his eyes were still fever bright. After a long moment he spoke again, his voice low, composed. "If you want me to use this Inheritor—"

"That isn't why I brought you," cut in Kell, too fast, unsure if Holland's guess was too far from or too close to the truth. He'd already considered the dilemma—in fact, had tried to think of nothing else since leaving London. The Inheritor required a sacrifice. It would be one of them. It had to be. But he didn't trust it to be Holland, who'd fallen once before, and he didn't want it to be Lila, who didn't fear anything, even when she should, and he knew Osaron had his sights set on *him,* but he had Rhy, and Holland had no one, and Lila had lived without power, and he would rather die than lose his brother, himself . . . and around and around it went in his head.

"Kell," said Holland sternly. "I own my shadows, and Osaron is one of them."

"As Vitari was mine," replied Kell.

Where does it start?

He got to his feet before he could say more, before he seriously began to entertain the notion. "We can argue over noble sacrifices when we have the device in hand. In the meantime . . ." He nodded at Holland's chains. "Enjoy the taste of freedom. I'd give you leave to walk the ship, but—"

"Between Delilah and Jasta, I wouldn't make it far." Holland rubbed his wrists again. Flexed his fingers. He didn't seem to know what to do with his hands. At last he crossed his arms loosely over his chest, mimicking Kell's own stance. Holland closed his eyes, but Kell could tell he wasn't resting. His guard was up, his hackles raised.

"Who were they?" Kell asked softly.

Holland blinked. "What?"

"The three people you killed before the Danes."

Tension rippled through the air. "It doesn't matter."

"It mattered enough for you to keep track," said Kell.

But Holland's face had retreated back behind its mask of indifference, and the room filled with silence until it drowned them both.

III

Vortalis had always wanted to be king—not the *someday* king, he told Holland, but the *now* king. He didn't care about the stories. Didn't buy into the legends. But he knew the city needed order. Needed strength. Needed a leader.

"Everyone wants to be king," said Vortalis.

"Not me," said Holland.

"Well, then you're either a liar or a fool."

They were sitting in a booth at the Scorched Bone. The kind of place where men could talk of regicide without raising any brows. Now and then the attention drifted toward them, but Holland knew it had less to do with the topic and more to do with his left eye and Vortalis's knives.

"A pretty pair we make," the man had said when they first entered the tavern. "The *Antari* and the Hunter. Sounds like one of those tales you love," he'd added, pouring the first round of drinks.

"London *has* a king," said Holland now.

"London *always* has a king," countered Vortalis. "Or queen. And how long has that ruler been a tyrant?"

They both knew there was only one way the throne changed hands—by force. A ruler wore the crown as long as they could keep it on their head. And that meant every king or queen had been a killer first. Power required corruption, and corruption rewarded power. The people who ended up on that throne had always paved the way with blood.

"It takes a tyrant," said Holland.

"But it doesn't have to," argued Vortalis. "You could be my might, my knight, my power, and I could be the law, the right, the order, and together, we could more than take this throne," he said, setting down his cup. "We could *hold* it."

He was a gifted orator, Holland would give him that. The kind of man who stoked passion the way an iron did coals. They had called him the Hunter, but the longer Holland was in his presence, the more he thought of him as the Bellows—he'd told him once, and the man had chuckled, said he was indeed full of air.

There was an undeniable charm about the man, not merely the youthful airs of one who hadn't seen the worst the world has to offer, but the blaze of someone who managed to believe in change, in spite of it.

When Vortalis spoke to Holland, he always met both eyes, and in that flecked gaze, Holland felt like he was being *seen*.

"You know what happened to the last *Antari*?" Vortalis was saying now, leaning forward into Holland's space. "I do. I was there in the castle when Queen Stol cut his throat and bathed in his blood."

"What were you doing in the castle?" wondered Holland.

Vortalis gave him a long, hard look. "That's what you take away from my story?" He shook his head. "Look, our world needs every drop of magic, and we've got kings and queens spilling it like water so they can have a taste of power, or maybe just so it can't rise against them. We got where we are because of fear. Fear of Black London, fear of magic that wasn't ours to control, but that's no way forward, only down. I could have killed you—"

"You could have tried—"

"But the world *needs* power. And men who aren't afraid of it. Think what London could do with a leader like that," said Vortalis. "A king who cared about his people."

Holland ran a finger around the rim of his glass, the ale itself untouched, while the other man drained his second cup. "So you want to kill our current king."

Vortalis leaned forward. "Doesn't everyone?"

It was a valid question.

Gorst—a mountain of a man who'd carved his way to the throne with an army at his back and turned the castle into a fortress, the city into a slum. His men rode the streets, taking everything they could, everything they wanted, in the name of a king who pretended to care, who claimed he could resurrect the city even while he drained it dry.

And every week, King Gorst opened throats in the blood square, a tithe to the dying world, as if that sacrifice—a sacrifice that wasn't even his—could set the world to rights. As if the spilling of *their* blood was proof of *his* devotion to his cause.

How many days had Holland stood at the edge of that square, and watched, and thought of cutting Gorst's throat? Of offering *him* back to the hungry earth?

Vortalis was giving him a weighted look, and Holland understood. "You want *me* to kill Gorst." The other man smiled. "Why not kill him yourself?"

Vortalis had no problem killing—he hadn't earned his nickname by abstaining from violence—and he was really very good at it. But only a fool walked into a fight without his sharpest knives, Vortalis explained, leaning closer, and Holland was uniquely suited to the task. "I know you're not fond of the practice," he'd added. "But there's a difference between killing for purpose and killing for sport, and wise men know that some must fall so others can rise."

"Some throats are meant to be opened," said Holland dryly.

Vortalis flashed a cutting grin. "Exactly. So you can sit around waiting for a storybook ending, or you can help me write a real one."

Holland rapped his fingers on the table. "It won't be easy to do," he said thoughtfully. "Not with his guard."

"Like rats, those men," said Vortalis, producing a tightly rolled paper. He lit the end in the nearest lantern. "No matter how many I kill, more scurry out to take their place."

"Are they loyal?" asked Holland.

Smoke poured from the man's nostrils in a derisive snort. "Loyalty is either bought or earned, and as far as I can tell, Gorst has neither the riches nor the charm to merit his army. These men, they fight for him, they die for him, they wipe his ass. They have the blind devotion of the cursed."

"Curses die with their makers," mused Holland.

"And so we return to the point. The death of a tyrant and a curse-maker, and why you're so suited for the job. According to one of the few spies I've managed, Gorst keeps himself at the top of the palace, in a room guarded on all four sides, locked up like a prize in his own treasure chest. Now, is it true," Vortalis said, his eyes dancing with light, "that the *Antari* can make doors?"

Three nights later, at the ninth bell, Holland walked through the castle gate, and disappeared. One step took him across the threshold, and the next landed in the middle of the royal chamber, a room brimming with cushions and silks.

Blood dripped from the *Antari*'s hand, where he still clutched the talisman. Gorst wore so many, he hadn't even noticed it was missing, pinched by Vortalis's spy within the castle. Three simple words—*As Tascen Gorst*—and he was in.

The king sat before a blazing fire, gorging himself on a feast of fowl and bread and candied pears. Across the city, people wasted away, but Gorst's bones had long been swallowed up by his constant feasting.

Occupied by his meal, the king hadn't noticed Holland standing there behind him, hadn't heard him draw his knife.

"Try not to stab him in the back," Vortalis had advised. "After all, he *is* the king. He deserves to see the blade coming."

"You have a very odd set of principles."

"Ah, but I do have them."

Holland was halfway to the king when he realized Gorst was not dining alone.

A girl, no more than fifteen, crouched naked at the king's side like an animal, a pet. Unlike Gorst, she had no distraction, and her head drifted up at the movement of Holland's steps. At the sight of him, she began to scream.

The sound cut off sharply as he pinned the air in the girl's lungs, but Gorst was already rising, his massive form filling the hearth. Holland didn't wait—his knife went whipping toward the king's heart.

And Gorst *caught* it.

The king plucked the weapon from the air with a sneer while the girl still clawed at her throat. "Is that all you have?"

"No," said Holland, bringing his palms together around the brooch.

"*As Steno,*" he said, opening his hands as the brooch shattered into a dozen shards of metal. They flew through the air, fast as light, driving through cloth and flesh and muscle.

Gorst let out a groan as blood blossomed against the white of his tunic, stained his sleeves, but still he did not fall. Holland forced the metal deeper, felt the pieces grind against bone, and Gorst sank to his knees beside the girl.

"You think it is that easy—to kill—a king?" he panted, and then, before Holland could stop him, Gorst lifted Holland's knife, and used it to slit the girl's throat.

Holland staggered, letting go of her voice as blood splashed onto the floor. Gorst was running his fingers through the viscous pool. He was trying to write a spell. Her life had been worth nothing more than the meanest ink.

Anger flared in Holland. His hands splayed out, and Gorst was wrenched back and up, a puppet on strings. The tyrant let out a guttural roar as his arms were forced wide.

"You think you can rule this city?" he rasped, bones straining against Holland's hold. "You try, and see—how long—you last."

Holland whipped the fire from the hearth, a ribbon of flame that wrapped around the king's throat in a burning collar. At last, Gorst began to keen, screams dragging into whimpers. Holland stepped forward, through the wasted girl's blood, until he was close enough that the heat of the burning coil was licking his skin.

"It's time," he said, the words lost beneath the sounds of mortal anguish, "for a new kind of king."

"*As Orense,*" said Holland when it was done.

The flames had died away, and the chamber doors fell open one after the other, Vortalis striding into the room, a dozen men in his wake. Across the front of their dark armor they already bore his chosen seal—an open hand with a circle carved into its palm.

Vortalis himself wasn't dressed for battle. He wore his usual dark grey, the only spots of color the spectrum of his eyes and the blood he tracked like mud into the room.

The bodies of Gorst's guards littered the hall behind him.

Holland frowned. "I thought you said the curse would lift. They wouldn't have to die."

"Better safe than sorry," said Vortalis, and then, seeing Holland's face, "I didn't kill the ones that begged."

He took one look at Gorst's body—the bloody wounds, the burn around his neck—and whistled under his breath. "Remind me never to cross you."

Gorst's meal still sat before the hearth and Vortalis took up the dead king's glass, dumped the contents in the fire with a hiss, and poured himself a fresh drink, swishing the wine to cleanse the vessel.

He raised the glass to his men. "*On vis och,*" he said. "The castle is ours. Take down the old banners. By dawn, I want the whole city to know the tyrant no longer sits on the throne. Take his stores, and this shitty wine, and see it spread from the *das* to the Kosik. Let the people know there's a new king in London, and his name is Ros Vortalis."

The men erupted into cheers, pouring out through the open doors, past and around and over the bodies of the old guard.

"And find somebody to clean up that mess!" Vortalis called after them.

"You're in a fine mood," said Holland.

"You should be too," chided Vortalis. "This is how change happens. Not with a whisper and a wish like in those tales of yours, but with a well-executed plan—and, yes, a bit of blood, but that's the way of the world, isn't it? It's our turn now. I will be this city's king, and you can be its valiant knight, and together we will build something better." He raised the glass to Holland. *"On vis och,"* he said again. "To new dawns, and good ends, and loyal friends."

Holland folded his arms. "I'm amazed you have any left, after sending so many after me."

Vortalis laughed. Holland hadn't heard a laugh like that since Talya, and even then, her laugh had been the sweet of poison berries, and Vortalis's was the open rolling of the sea.

"I never sent you friends," he said. "Only enemies."

IV

Lenos was standing at the *Ghost*'s stern, toying with one of the little carved ships Ilo left everywhere, when a bird flew past.

He looked up, worried. The sudden appearance could only mean one thing—they were approaching land. Which wouldn't be a problem if they weren't meant to be heading straight for Maris's market, in the middle of the sea. The sailor hurried to the prow as the *Ghost* glided serenely toward a port that rose on the shoreline.

"Why are we docking?"

"It is easier to chart the course from here," said Jasta. "Besides, supplies are low. We left in a hurry."

Lenos cast a nervous glance at Alucard, who was climbing the steps. "Aren't we still in a hurry?" asked Lenos,

"Won't take long," was all Jasta said.

Lenos shielded his eyes against the sun—it had already passed its apex and was now sinking toward the horizon—and squinted at the line of ships tethered to the docks.

"Port of Rosenal," offered Alucard. "It's the last stop of any interest before the northern bay."

"I don't like this," grumbled the *Antari* prince as he joined them on deck. "Jasta, we—"

"We unload the crates and restock," insisted the captain as she and Hano uncoiled the ropes and threw them over. "One hour, maybe two. Stretch your legs. We'll be out of port by nightfall, and to the market by late morning."

"I for one could use a meal," said Alucard, unhitching the ramp. "No offense meant, Jasta, but Ilo cooks about as well as he sees."

The ship drifted to a stop as two dock hands caught the ropes and tied them off. Alucard set off down the ramp without a backward glance, Bard on his heels.

"*Sanct,*" muttered Jasta under her breath. Kell and Lenos both turned toward her. Something was wrong, Lenos felt it in his gut.

"You coming?" called Lila, but Kell called back, "I'm staying on the ship." And then he spun on Jasta. "What is it?"

"You need to get off," said the *Ghost*'s captain. *"Now."*

"Why?" asked Kell, but Lenos had already seen the trio headed their way down the dock. Two men and a woman, all in black, and each with a sword hanging at their waist. A nervous prickle ran through him.

Kell finally noticed the strangers. "Who are they?"

"Trouble," spat Jasta, and Lenos turned to warn Alucard and Bard, but they were already halfway down the dock, and the captain must have seen the danger, too, because he threw his arm casually around Lila's shoulder, angling her away.

"What's going on?" demanded Kell as Jasta spun on her heel and started for the hold.

"They shouldn't be here, not this early in the year."

"Who *are* they?" demanded Kell.

"This is a private port," said Lenos, his long legs easily keeping pace, "run by a man named Rosenal. Those are his swords. Normally they don't dock until summer, when the weather holds and the sea is full. They are here to check the cargo, search for contraband."

Kell shook his head. "I thought this ship *dealt* in contraband."

"It does," said Jasta, descending the steps in two strides and taking off down the hold. "Rosenal's men take a cut. Convenient, too, since the only ships that come here do not fly royal colors. But they are early."

"I still don't understand why we have to *go,*" said Kell. "Your cargo is your problem—"

Jasta turned on him, her form filling the hall. "Is it? Not in London anymore, princeling, and not everyone outside the capital is friend to the crown. Out here, coin is king, and no doubt Rosenal's men would love to ransom a prince, or sell *Antari* parts to the *Ferase Stras*. If you want to make it there intact, get the traitor magician and go."

Lenos saw the other man go pale.

Steps sounded on deck, and Jasta snarled and took off again, leaving Kell to snag a pair of caps from the hooks in the hall and pull one down over his copper hair. Holland couldn't have heard Jasta's warning through the floor, but the stomping must have said enough, because he was already on his feet when they arrived.

"I assume there's a problem." Lenos's stomach cramped with worry at the sight of him free, but Kell just pushed the second cap into the *Antari*'s hands.

"Jasta?" called a new voice overhead.

Holland tugged the cap down, his black eye lost beneath the brim's shadow as the captain nudged them both out of the cabin toward the window at the back of the ship. She threw it open, revealing a short ladder that plunged toward the water below.

"Go. Now. Come back in an hour or two." Jasta was already turning away as one of the figures reached the stairs leading down into the hold. A pair of black boots came into sight and Lenos threw his narrow frame in front of the window.

Behind him, Kell climbed through.

He waited for the splash, but heard nothing but a rush of breath, an instant of silence, and then the muted thud of boots hitting dock. Lenos glanced over his shoulder to see Holland leap from the ladder and land in an elegant crouch beside Kell just before Rosenal's sellswords came stomping into the hold.

"What's this now?" said the woman when she saw Lenos, limbs spread across the opening. He managed an awkward smile.

"Just airing out the hold," he said, turning to swing the window shut. The sellsword caught his wrist and shoved him aside.

"That so?" Lenos held his breath as she stuck her head out the window, scanning the water and the docks.

But when she drew back into the hold, he saw the answer in her bored expression and sagged with relief.

She'd seen nothing strange.

The *Antari* were gone.

V

Lila had a bad feeling about Rosenal.

She didn't know if it was the port town itself that disturbed her, or the fact that they were being followed. Probably the latter.

At first, she thought it might be nothing, an echo of nerves from that close call back on the docks, but as she climbed the hill to the town, the certainty settled like a cloak around her shoulders, awareness scratching at her neck.

Lila had always been good at knowing when she wasn't alone. People had a presence, a weight in the world. Lila had always been able to sense it, but now she wondered if maybe it was the magic in their blood she'd been hearing all along, ringing like a plucked string.

And by the time they reached the rise, Kell either sensed it, too, or he simply felt her tensing beside him.

"Do you think we're being followed?" he asked.

"Probably," offered Holland blandly. The sight of him loose, unchained, turned her stomach.

"I always assume I'm being followed," she said with false cheer. "Why do you think I have so many knives?"

Kell's brow furrowed. "You know, I honestly can't tell if you're joking."

"Some towns have fog," offered Alucard, "and some have bad feelings. Rosenal simply has a bit of both."

Lila slid her arm free of Kell's, senses pricking. The town overlooking the port was a tight nest of streets, squat buildings huddled against the icy wind. Sailors hurried from doorway to doorway, hoods and collars up against the cold. The town was riddled with alleys, the dregs of light thin and the shadows deep enough to swallow the places where a person might wait.

"Gives it a strange kind of charm," continued the captain, "that sense of being watched . . ."

Her steps slowed before the mouth of a winding street, the familiar weight of a knife falling into her grip. The bad feeling was getting worse. Lila knew the way a heart raced when it was chasing someone, and the way it stuttered when it was being chased, and right now her heart felt less like predator and more like prey, and she didn't like it. She squinted into the lidded dark of the alley but saw nothing.

The others were getting ahead of her, and Lila was just turning to catch up when she saw it. There, in the hollow where the road curved away—the shape of a man. The sheen of rotting teeth. A shadow wrapped around his throat. His lips were moving, and when the wind picked up it carried the broken edge of a melody.

A song she'd hummed a hundred times aboard the *Spire*.

How do you know when the Sarows is coming?

Lila shivered and took a step forward, drawing her fingertip along the oil-slicked edge of her knife.

Tyger, Tyger—

"Bard!"

Alucard's voice cut through the air, scattering her senses. They were waiting, all of them, at the top of the road, and by the time Lila looked back at the alley, the road was empty. The shadow was gone.

Lila slumped back in the rickety old chair and folded her arms. Nearby a woman climbed into the lap of her companion, and three tables down a fight broke out, Sanct cards spilling onto the floor as a table overturned between the brawling men. The tavern was all stale liquor and jostling bodies and cluttered noise.

"Not the most savory lot," observed Kell, sipping his drink.

"Not the worst, either," said the captain, setting down a round of drinks and a heaping tray of food.

"Do you really plan to eat all that?" asked Lila.

"Not by myself, I don't," he said, nudging a bowl of stew her way. Her stomach growled and she took up the spoon, but focused her gaze on Holland.

He was sitting in the back of the booth, and Lila on the outside edge, as far from him as possible. She couldn't shake the feeling he was watching her beneath that brimmed cap, even though every time she checked, his attention was leveled on the tavern behind her head. His fingers traced absent patterns in a pool of spilled ale, but his green eye twitched in concentration. It took her several long seconds to realize he was counting the bodies in the room.

"Nineteen," she said coolly, and Alucard and Kell both looked at her as if she'd spoken out of turn, but Holland simply answered, "Twenty," and despite herself, Lila swiveled in her seat. She did a swift count. He was right. She'd missed one of the men behind the bar. Dammit.

"If you have to use your eyes," he added, "you're doing it wrong."

"So," said Kell, frowning at Holland before turning toward Alucard. "What do you know about this floating market?"

Alucard took a swig of his ale. "Well, it's been around about as long as its owner, Maris, which is to say a long damn time. There's a running line that the same way magic never dies, it never really disappears, either. It just ends up in the *Ferase Stras*. It's a bit of a legend among the seaborne—if there's something you want, the Going Waters has it. For a price."

"And what did you buy," asked Lila, "the last time you were there?"

Alucard hesitated, lowering the glass. It always amazed her, the things he chose to guard.

"Isn't it obvious?" said Kell. "He bought his sight."

Alucard's eyes narrowed. Lila's widened. "Is that true?"

"No," said her captain. "For your information, Master Kell, I've always had this gift."

"Then what?" pressed Lila.

"I bought my father's death."

The table went still, a pocket of silence in the noisy room. Kell's mouth hung open. Alucard's clenched shut. Lila stared.

"That's not possible," murmured Kell.

"These are open waters," said Alucard, pushing to his feet. "Anything is possible. And on that note . . . I've got an errand to run. I'll meet you back at the ship."

Lila frowned. There were a hundred shades between a truth and lie, and she knew them all. She could tell when someone was being dishonest, and when they were only saying one word for every three.

"*Alucard*," she pressed. "What are you—"

He turned, hands in his pockets. "Oh, I forgot to mention—you'll each need a token to enter the market. Something valuable."

Kell set his cup down with a crack. "You could have told us this before we left London."

"I could have," said Alucard. "It must have slipped my mind. But don't worry, I'm sure you'll think of *something*. Perhaps Maris will settle for your coat."

Kell's knuckles were white on the handle of his cup as the captain strode away. By the time the door swung shut, Lila was already on her feet.

"Where are *you* going?" snapped Kell.

"Where do you think?" She didn't know how to explain—they had a deal, she and Alucard, even if they would never say it. They watched each other's back. "He shouldn't go alone."

"Leave him," muttered Kell.

"He has a way of getting lost," she said, buttoning her coat. "I'm—"

"I said *stay*—"

It was the wrong thing to say.

Lila bristled. "Funny thing, Kell," she said coldly. "That sounded like an order." And before he could say anything else, Lila turned up her collar against the wind and marched out.

Within minutes, Lila lost him.

She didn't want to admit it—she'd always prided herself on being a clever tail, but the streets of Rosenal were narrow and winding, full of hidden breaks and turns that made it too easy to lose sight—and track—of whoever you were trying to follow. It made sense, she supposed, in a town that catered mostly to pirates and thieves and the sort who didn't like to be tracked.

Somewhere in that maze, Alucard had simply disappeared. Lila had given up any attempts at stealth after that, let her steps fall loud, even called his name, but it was no use; she couldn't find him.

The sun was setting fast over the port, the last light quickly giving way to shadow. In the twilight, the edges between light and dark began to blur, and everything was rendered in flattened layers of grey. Dusk was the only time Lila truly felt the absence of her second eye.

If it had been a little darker, she would have hauled herself up onto the nearest roof and scanned the town that way, but there was just enough daylight to turn the act into display.

She stopped at the intersection of four alleys, certain she'd already come this way, and was about to give up—to turn back toward the tavern and her waiting drink—when she heard the voice.

That *same* voice, its melody carrying on the breeze.

How do you know when the Sarows is coming . . .

A flick of her wrist, and a knife dropped into her palm, her free hand already reaching for the one beneath her coat.

Footsteps sounded, and she turned, bracing for the attack.

But the alley was empty.

Lila started to straighten just as a weight hit the ground behind her—boots on stone—and she spun, jumping back as a stranger's blade sang through the air, narrowly missing her stomach.

Her attacker smiled that rotting grin, but her eyes went to the tattoo of the dagger across his throat.

"Delilah Bard," he growled. "Remember me?"

She twirled her blades. "Vaguely," she lied.

In truth, she did. Not his name, that she'd never caught, but she knew the tattoo worn by the cutthroats of the *Copper Thief.* They had sailed under Baliz Kasnov, a ruthless pirate she'd murdered—somewhat carelessly—weeks before, as part of a bet with the crew of the *Night*

Spire. They'd scoffed at the idea that she could take an entire ship herself.

She'd proven them wrong, won the bet, even spared most of the Thieves.

Now, as two more men dropped from the rooftops behind him, and a third emerged from the lengthening shadows, she decided that act of mercy had been a mistake.

"Four on one hardly seems fair," she said, putting her back to the wall as two more men slunk toward her, tattoos like dark and jagged wounds beneath their chins.

That made six.

She'd counted them once before, but then she'd been counting down instead of up.

"Tell you what," said the first attacker. "If you beg, we'll make it quick."

Lila's blood sang the way it always did before a fight, clear and bright and hungry. "And why," she said, "would I want to rush your deaths?"

"Cocky bitch," growled the second. "I'm gonna fu—"

Her knife hissed through the air and embedded itself in his throat. Blood spilled down his front as he clawed at his neck and toppled forward, and she made it under the next man's guard before the body hit the ground, driving her serrated blade up through his chin before the first blow caught her, a fist to the jaw.

She went down hard, spitting blood into the street.

Heat coursed through her limbs as a hand grabbed her by the hair and hauled her to her feet, a knife under her chin.

"Any last words?" asked the man with the rotting teeth.

Lila held up her hands, as if in surrender, before flashing a vicious smile.

"*Tyger, Tyger,*" she said, and the fire roared to life.

VI

Kell and Holland sat across from each other, swathed in a silence that only thickened as Kell tried to drown his annoyance in his drink. Of all the reasons for Lila to leave, of all the people for her to go with, it had to be Emery.

Across the room a group of men were deep in their cups and singing a sea shanty of some kind.

" . . . *Sarows is coming, is coming, is coming aboard . . .* "

Kell finished his glass, and reached for hers.

Holland was drawing his fingers through a spill on the table, the glass in front of him untouched. Now that they were back on solid ground, the color was returning to his face, but even dressed down in winter greys with a cap pulled over his brow, there was something about Holland that drew the eye. The way he held himself, perhaps, mixed with the faintest scent of foreign magic. Ash and steel and ice.

"Say something," Kell muttered into his drink.

Holland's attention flicked toward him, then slid pointedly away. "This Inheritor . . ."

"What about it?"

"I should be the one to use it."

"Perhaps." Kell's answer was simple, blunt. "But I don't trust you." Holland's expression hardened. "And I'm certainly not letting Lila try her hand. She doesn't know how to *use* her power, let alone how to survive getting rid of it."

"That leaves you."

Kell looked down into the last of his ale. "That leaves me."

If the Inheritor worked as Tieren suggested, the device absorbed a person's magic. But Kell's magic was all that bound Rhy's life to his. He'd learned that from the collar, the horrible severing of power from body, the stutter of Rhy's failing heart. Would it be like that? Would it hurt that much? Or would it be easy? His brother had known what he would do, had given his assent. He'd seen it in Rhy's eyes when they parted. Heard it in his voice. Rhy had made his peace long before he said good-bye.

"Stop being selfish."

Kell's head snapped up. "What?"

"Osaron is *mine,*" said Holland, finally taking up his drink. "I don't give a damn about your self-sacrificing notions, your need to be the hero. When the time comes for one of us to destroy that monster, it is going to be *me.* And if you try to stop me, Kell, I'll remind you the hard way which of us is the stronger *Antari.* Do you understand?"

Holland met Kell's eyes over the glass, and beyond the words and the bravado, he saw something else in the man's gaze.

Mercy.

Kell's chest ached with relief as he said, "Thank you."

"For what?" said Holland coldly. "I'm not doing this for *you.*"

⸶

In the end, Vortalis had named himself the Winter King.

"Why not summer," Holland asked, "or spring?"

Vortalis snorted. "Do you feel warmth on the air, Holland? Do you see the river running blue? We are not in the spring of this world, and certainly not in the summer. Those are the seasons for your someday king. This is winter, and we must survive it."

They were standing side by side on the castle balcony while the banners—the open hand turned out on its dark field—snapped in the wind. The gates stood open, the grounds filling edge to edge as people gathered to see the new king, and waited for the castle doors to open so they could make their cases and their claims. The air buzzed with excitement. Fresh blood on the throne meant new chances for the streets. The hope that *this* ruler would succeed where so many had failed before him, that he would be the one to restore what was lost—what began to die when the doors first closed—and breathe life back into the embers.

Vortalis wore a single ring of burnished steel in his hair to match the circle on his banner. Beyond that, he looked like the same man who'd come to Holland months ago, deep in the Silver Wood.

"The outfit suits you," said the Winter King, gesturing to Holland's half cloak, the silver pin bearing Vortalis's seal.

Holland took a step back from the balcony's edge. "Last time I checked, *you* are king. So why am *I* on display?"

"Because, Holland, ruling is a balance between hope and fear. I may have a *way* with people, but you have a way of *frightening* them. I draw them like flies, but you keep that at bay. Together we are a welcome and a warning, and I would have each and every one of them know that my black-eyed knight, my sharpest sword, stands firmly beside me." He shot Holland a sidelong glance. "I'm quite aware of our city's penchant for regicide, including the bloody pattern we continued in order to stand here today, but, selfish as it seems, I'm not keen to go out as Gorst did."

"Gorst didn't have *me*," said Holland, and the king broke into a smile.

"Thank the gods for that."

"Am I supposed to call you king now?" asked Holland.

Vortalis blew out a breath. "You are supposed to call me friend."

"As you wish . . ." A smile stole across Holland's lips at the memory of their meeting in the Silver Wood. "Vor."

The king smiled at that, a broad, bright gesture so at odds with the city around them. "And to think, Holland, all it took was a crown and—"

"Köt Vortalis," cut in a guard behind them.

Vor's face closed, the open light replaced by the hardened planes befitting a new king. "What is it?"

"There is a boy requesting an audience."

Holland frowned. "We haven't opened the doors yet."

"I know, sir," said the guard. "He didn't come by the door. He just . . . *appeared*."

The first thing Holland noticed was the boy's red coat.

He was standing in the throne hall, craning his head toward the vaulted bones of the castle ceiling, and that coat—it was such a vivid color, not a faded red like the sun at dusk, or the fabrics worn in summer, but a vibrant crimson, the color of fresh blood.

His hair was a softer shade, like autumn leaves, muted, but not faded by any stretch, and he wore crisp black boots—true black, as dark as winter nights—with gold clasps that matched his cuffs, every inch of him sharp and bright as a glare on new steel. Even stranger than his appearance was the scent that drifted off him, something sweet, almost cloying, like crushed blossoms left to rot.

Vortalis gave a low whistle at the sight of him, and the boy turned, revealing a pair of mismatched eyes. Holland stilled. The boy's left eye was a light blue. The right was solid black. Their gazes met, and a strange vibration lanced through Holland's head. The stranger couldn't be more than twelve or thirteen, with the unmarked skin of a royal and the imperious posture to match, but he was undeniably *Antari*.

The boy stepped forward and started speaking briskly, in a foreign tongue, the accent smooth and lilting. Vortalis bore a translation rune at the base of his throat, the product of times abroad, but Holland bore nothing save an ear for tone, and at the blankness in his gaze the boy stopped and started again, this time in Holland's native tongue.

"Apologies," he said. "My Mahktahn is not perfect. I learned it from a book. My name is Kell, and I come bearing a message from my king."

His hand went into his coat, and across the room the guards surged forward, Holland already shifting in front of Vor, when the boy drew out, of all things, a *letter*. That same sweet scent drifted off the envelope.

Vortalis looked down at the paper and said, "I am the only king here."

"Of course," said the boy *Antari*. "*My* king is in another London."

The room went still. Everyone knew, of course, about the other Londons, and the worlds that went with them. There was the one far away, a place where magic held no sway. There was the broken one, where magic had devoured everything. And then there was the cruel one, the place that had sealed its doors, forcing Holland's world to face the dark alone.

Holland had never been to this other place—he knew the spell to go there, had found the words buried in his mind like treasure in the months after he'd turned Alox to stone—but travel needed a token the way a lock needed a key, and he'd never had anything with which to cast the spell, to buy his way through.

And yet, Holland had always assumed that other world was like *his*. After all, both cities had been powerful. Both had been vibrant. Both had been cut off when the doors sealed. But as Holland took in this *Kell,* with his bright attire, his healthy glow, he saw the hall as the boy must—dingy, coated with the film of frost-like neglect, the mark of years fighting for every drop of magic, and felt a surge of anger. Was *this* how the other London lived?

"You are a long way from home," said Vor coolly.

"A long way," said the boy, "and a single step." His gaze kept flicking back toward Holland, as if fascinated by the sight of another *Antari*. So they were rare in his world, too.

"What does your king want?" asked Vor, declining to take the letter.

"King Maresh wishes to restore communication between your world and mine."

"Does he wish to open the doors?"

The boy hesitated. "No," he said carefully. "The doors cannot be opened. But this could be the first step in rebuilding the relationships—"

"I don't give a damn about relationships," snapped the Winter

King. "I am trying to rebuild a *city*. Can this *Maresh* help me with that?"

"I do not know," said Kell. "I am only the messenger. If you write it down—"

"Hang the message." Vortalis turned away. "You found your way in," he said. "Find it back out."

Kell lifted his chin. "Is that your final answer?" he asked. "Perhaps I should return in a few weeks, when the *next* king takes the throne."

"Careful, boy," warned Holland.

Kell turned his attention—and those unnerving eyes, so strange and so familiar—toward him. He produced a coin, small and red, with a gold star at the center. A token. A key. "Here," he said. "In case your king changes his mind."

Holland said nothing, but flexed his hand, and the coin whipped out of the boy's grip and into his own, his fingers closing silently over the metal.

"It's *As Travars*," added Kell. "In case you didn't know."

"Holland," said Vortalis from the door.

Holland was still holding Kell's gaze. "Coming, my *king*," he said pointedly, breaking away.

"Wait," called the boy, and Holland could tell by his tone that the words were meant not for Vor, but for him. The *Antari* jogged toward him, steps ringing like bells from his gold clasps.

"What?" demanded Holland.

"It's nice," said Kell, "to meet someone like me."

Holland frowned. "I am not like you," he said, and walked away.

VII

For a while, Lila held her own.

Flame and steel against blind strength, a thief's cunning against a pirate's might.

She might have even been winning.

And then, quite suddenly, she wasn't.

Six men became four, but four was still a good deal more than one.

A knife slid along her skin.

A hand wrapped around her throat.

Her back slammed against the wall.

No, not a wall, she realized, a *door*. She had hit it hard enough to crack the wood, bolts and pins jangling in their grooves. An idea. She threw up her hands, and the nails shuddered free. Some struck only air or stone, but others found flesh, and two of the Copper Thieves staggered back, clutching their arms, stomachs, heads.

Without its pins, the door gave way behind her, and Lila tumbled backward, rolling into a crouch inside a shabby hall and heaving the door back up before pressing her blood-slicked fingers to the wood.

"As Steno," she said, thinking that was the word Kell had taught her for *seal,* but she was wrong. The whole door *shattered* like a pane of glass, wooden splinters raining down, and before she could summon them back up, she was hauled into the street. Something hit her in the stomach—a fist, a knee, a boot—and the air left her lungs in a violent breath.

She summoned the wind—it tore through the alley and whipped around her, forcing the men back as she took a running step, pushed off the wall, and leaped for the edge of the roof.

She almost made it, but one of them caught her boot and jerked her back. She fell, hitting the street with brutal force. Something cracked inside her chest.

And then they fell on her.

Holland was proving horrible company.

Kell had tried to keep the conversation alive, but it was like stoking coals after a bucket of water had been poured on them, nothing but fragile wisps of smoke. He'd finally given up, resigned himself to the uncomfortable quiet, when the other *Antari* met his gaze across the table.

"At the market tomorrow," he said. "What will you offer?"

Kell raised a brow. His own mind had just been drifting over the question.

"I was thinking," he said, "of offering you."

It was said in jest, but Holland only stared at him, and Kell sighed, relenting. He'd never been very good at sarcasm.

"It depends," he answered honestly, "on whether Maris cares for cost or worth." He patted down his pockets, and came up with a handful of coins, Lila's kerchief, his royal pin. The look on Holland's face mirrored the worry in Kell's gut—none of these things were good enough.

"You *could* offer the coat," said Holland.

But the thought made Kell's chest hurt. It was *his,* one of the only things in his life not bestowed by the crown, or bartered for, not given because of his position, but won. Won in a simple game of cards.

He put the trinkets away, and instead dug the cord out from under his shirt. On the end hung the three coins, one for each world. He unknotted the cord and slid the last coin out onto his palm.

His Grey London token.

George III's profile was on the front, his face rubbed away from use.

Kell had given the king a new *lin* with every visit, but he still had the same shilling George had given him on his very first trip. Before the age and the madness wore him away, before his son buried him in Windsor.

It cost almost nothing, but it was worth a great deal to him.

"I hate to interrupt whatever reverie you're having," said Holland, nodding at the window, "but your friend has returned."

Kell turned in his seat, expecting Lila, but instead he found Alucard strolling past. He had a vial in his hand, and was holding it up to the light of a lantern. The contents glittered faintly like white sand, or finely broken glass.

The captain looked their way and flashed an impatient summons that a little too closely resembled a rude gesture.

Kell sighed, shoving to his feet.

The two *Antari* left the tavern, Alucard a block ahead, his stride brisk as he headed for the docks. Kell frowned, scanning the streets.

"Where's Lila?" called Kell.

Alucard turned, brows raised. "Bard? I left her with you."

Dread coiled through him. "And she followed *you* out."

Alucard started shaking his head, but Kell was heading for the door, Holland and the captain close on his heels.

"Split up," said Alucard as they spilled out onto the street. He took off down the first street, but when Holland started down another, Kell caught his sleeve.

"Wait." His mind spun, torn between duty and panic, reason and fear.

Letting the White London *Antari* out of his chains was one thing.

Letting him out of Kell's sight was another.

Holland looked down at the place where the younger *Antari* gripped him. "Do you want to find her or not?"

Rhy's voice echoed in Kell's head, those warnings about the world beyond the city, the value of a black-eyed prince. An *Antari*. He'd told Kell what the Veskans thought of him, and the Faroans, but he hadn't said enough about their own people, and Kell, fool that he was, hadn't thought about the risk of ransom. Or worse, knowing Lila.

Kell snarled, but let go. "Don't make me regret this," he said, taking off at a run.

VIII

Lila sagged against the wall, gasping for breath. She was out of knives, and blood was running into her eye from a blow to the temple, and it hurt to breathe, but she was still on her feet.

It would take more than that, she thought, shoving off the wall and stepping over the bodies of the six men now lying dead in the street.

There was a hollow feeling in her veins, like she'd used up everything she had. The ground swayed beneath her and she braced herself against the alley wall, leaving a smear of red as she went. One foot in front of the other, every breath a jagged tear, her pulse heavy in her ears, and then something that wasn't her pulse.

Footsteps.

Someone was coming.

Lila dragged her head up, wracking her tired mind for a spell as the steps echoed against the alley walls.

She heard a voice calling her name, somewhere far behind her, and turned just in time to watch someone drive a knife between her ribs.

"This is for Kasnov," snarled the seventh Thief, forcing the weapon in to the hilt. It tore through her chest and out her back and for a moment—only a moment—she felt nothing but the warmth of the blood. But then her body caught up, and the pain swallowed everything.

Not the brisk bright pain of grazed skin but something deep. Severing.

The knife came free, and her legs folded beneath her.

She tried to breathe, choked as blood rose in her throat. Soaked her shirt.

Get up, she thought as her body slumped to the ground.

This isn't how I die, she thought, *this isn't—*

She retched blood into the street.

Something was wrong.

It hurt.

No.

Kell.

Get up.

She tried to rise, slipped in something slick and warm.

No.

Not like this.

She closed her eyes, tried desperately to summon magic.

There wasn't any left.

All she had was Kell's face. And Alucard's. Barron's watch. A ship. The open sea. A chance at freedom.

I'm not done.

Her vision slipped.

Not like this.

Her chest rattled.

Get up.

She was on her back now, the Thief circling like a vulture. Above him, the sky was turning colors like a bruise.

Like the sea before a . . . what?

He was getting closer, crouching down, burying a knee in her wounded chest and she couldn't breathe and this wasn't how it happened, and—

A blur of motion, quick as a knife, at the edge of her sight, and the man was gone. The beginnings of a shout cut off, the distant sound of a weight hitting something solid, but Lila couldn't raise her head to see, couldn't . . .

The world narrowed, the light slipping from the sky, then blotted out altogether by the shadow kneeling over her, pressing a hand to her ribs.

"Hold on," said a low voice as the world darkened. Then: "Over here! Now!"

Another voice.

"Stay with me."

She was so cold.

"Stay . . ."

It was the last thing she heard.

IX

Holland knelt over Lila's body.

She was deathly pale, but he had been quick enough; the spell had taken hold in time. Kell was at Lila's other side, distraught, face pale under crimson curls, checking her wounds as if he doubted Holland's work.

If he'd gotten there first, he could have healed her himself.

Holland hadn't thought it wise to wait.

And now there were more pressing problems.

He'd caught the slow-moving shadows flitting over the wall at the end of the alley. He rose to his feet.

"Stay with me," Kell was murmuring to Lila's bloody form, as if that would do any good. "Stay with—"

"How many blades do you have?" Holland cut in.

Kell's eyes never left Lila, but his fingers went to the sheath on his arm. "One."

Holland rolled his eyes. "Brilliant," he said, pressing his palms together. The gash he'd made in his hand wept a fresh line of red.

"*As Narahi,*" he murmured.

Quicken.

Magic flared at his command, and he moved with a speed he rarely showed and had certainly never seen fit to show *Kell.* It was a hard piece of magic under any circumstances, and a grueling spell when done to one's self, but it was worth it as the world around him *slowed.*

He became a blur, pale skin and grey cloak knifing through the dark. By the time the first man crouching on the roof above had drawn his knife, Holland was behind him. The man looked wide eyed at the place where his target had been as Holland lifted his hands and, with an elegant motion, snapped the man's neck.

He let the limp body fall to the alley stones and followed quickly after, putting his back to Kell—who'd finally caught the scent of danger—as three more shadows, glinting with weapons, dropped from the sky.

And just like that, their fight began.

It didn't last long.

Soon three more bodies littered the ground, and the winter air around the two *Antari* surged with exhaustion and triumph. Blood ran from Kell's lip, and Holland's knuckles were raw, and they'd both lost their hats, but otherwise they were intact.

It was strange, fighting beside Kell instead of against him, the resonance of their styles, so different but somehow in sync—unnerving.

"You've gotten better," he observed.

"I had to," said Kell, wiping the blood from his knife before he sheathed it. Holland had the strange urge to say more, but Kell was already moving to Lila's side again as Alucard appeared at the mouth of the alley, a sword in one hand and a curl of ice in the other, clearly ready to join the fight.

"You're late," said Holland.

"Did I miss all the fun?" asked the magician, but when he saw Lila in Kell's arms, her limp body covered in blood, every trace of humor left his face. *"No."*

"She'll live," said Holland.

"What happened? Saints, Bard. Can you hear me?" said Alucard as Kell took up his useless chant again, as if it were a spell, a prayer.

Stay with me.

Holland leaned against the alley wall, suddenly tired.

Stay with me.

He closed his eyes, memories rising like bile in his throat.

Stay with me.

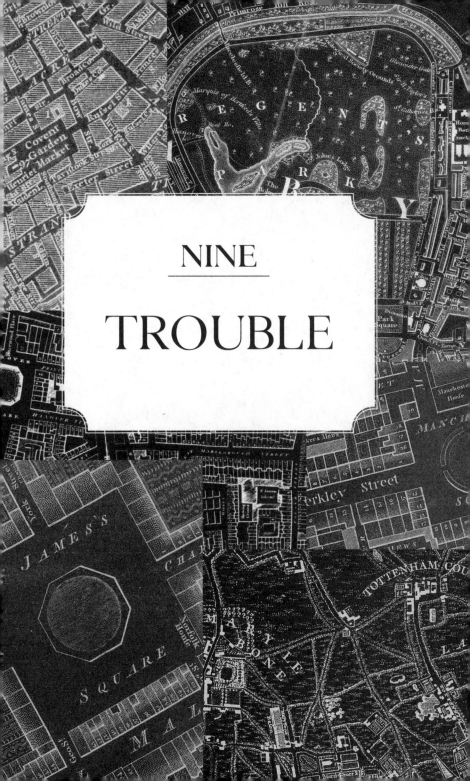

NINE

TROUBLE

I

Tieren Serense had never been able to see the future.

He could only see himself.

That was the thing so many didn't understand about scrying. A man could not gaze into the stream of life, the heart of magic, and read it as if it were a book. The world spoke its own language, as indecipherable as the chirping of a bird, the rustling of leaves. A tongue meant not even for priests.

It is an arrogant man that thinks himself a god.

And an arrogant god, thought Tieren, looking to the window, that thinks himself a man.

So when he poured the water into the basin, when he took up the vial of ink and tipped three drops into the water, when he stared into the cloud that bloomed beneath the surface, he was not trying to see the future. He wasn't looking out at all, but in.

A scrying dish, after all, was a mirror for one's mind, a way to look in at one's self, to pose questions that only the self could answer.

Tonight Tieren's questions revolved around Maxim Maresh. Around the spell his king was weaving, and how far the *Aven Essen* should let him go.

Tieren Serense had served Nokil Maresh when he was king, had watched his only son, Maxim, grow, had stood beside him when he married Emira, and been there to usher Rhy into the world, and Kell into the palace. He had spent his life serving this family.

Now, he did not know how to save it.

The ink spread through the basin, turning the water grey, and in the shudder of its surface, he felt the queen before he saw her. A blush of cold in the room behind him.

"I hope you won't mind, Your Majesty," he said softly. "I borrowed one of your bowls."

She was standing there, arms folded across her front as if chilled, or guarding something fragile behind her ribs.

Emira, who never confided in him, never sought out his waiting ear, no matter how many times he offered. Instead, he'd learned of her through Rhy, through Maxim, through Kell. He'd learned of her through watching her watch the world with those wide, dark eyes that never blinked for fear of missing something.

Now those wide, dark eyes went to the shallow bowl between his hands. "What did you see?"

"I see what all reflections show," he answered wearily. "Myself."

Emira bit her lip, a gesture he'd seen Rhy make a hundred times. Her fingers tightened around her ribs. "What is Maxim doing?"

"What he believes is right."

"Aren't we all?" she whispered.

Thin tears slid down her cheeks, and she dashed them away with the back of her hand. It was only the second time he'd ever seen Emira cry.

The first had been more than twenty years ago, when she was new to the palace.

He'd found her in the courtyard, her back up against a winter tree, arms wrapped around herself as if she were cold, even though two rows away the summer was in bloom. She stood perfectly still, save for the silent shudder of her chest, but he could see the storm behind her eyes, the strain in her jaw, and he remembered thinking, then, that she looked old for one so young. Not aged, but worn, weary from the weight of her own mind. Fears, after all, were heavy things. And whether or not Emira voiced them, Tieren could feel them on the air, thick as rain right before it falls.

She wouldn't tell him what was wrong, but a week later Tieren heard the news, watched Maxim's face glow with pride while Emira stood at his side, steeling herself against the declaration as if it were a sentence.

She was pregnant.

Emira cleared her throat, eyes still trained on the clouded water. "May I ask you something, Master Tieren?"

"Of course, Your Highness."

Her gaze shifted toward him, two dark pools that hid their depths. "What do you fear most?"

The question took him by surprise, but the answer rose to meet it. "Emptiness," he said. "And you, my queen?"

Her lips quirked into a sad smile. "Everything," she said. "Or so it feels."

"I do not believe that," said Tieren gently.

She thought. "Loss, then."

Tieren curled a finger around his beard. "Love and loss," he said, "are like a ship and the sea. They rise together. The more we love, the more we have to lose. But the only way to avoid loss is to avoid love. And what a sad world that would be."

II

Lila opened her eyes.

At first all she saw was sky. That same bruised sunset she'd been staring at a moment before. Only the moment was gone, and the colors had bled away, leaving a heavy blanket of night. The ground was cold beneath her but dry, a coat bunched up beneath her head.

"It shouldn't take this long," a voice was saying. "Are you sure—"

"She'll be fine."

Her head spun, fingers drifting over her ribs to the place where the blade had gone in. Her shirt was sticky with blood, and she cringed reflexively, expecting pain. The *memory* of pain sang through her, but it was nothing but an echo, and when she took a testing breath, crisp air filled her lungs instead of blood.

"Fucking Copper Thieves," said a third voice. "Should have killed them months ago, and stop pacing, Kell, you're making me dizzy."

Lila closed her eyes, swallowed.

When she blinked, vision sliding in and out of focus, Kell was kneeling over her. She looked up into his two-toned eyes, and realized they weren't his eyes at all. One was black. The other emerald green.

"She's awake." Holland straightened, blood dripping from a gash along his palm.

A copper tang still filled her mouth, and she rolled over and spit onto the stones.

"Lila," said Kell, so much emotion in her name, and how could she ever have thought that cold, steady voice belonged to him? He crouched beside her, one hand beneath her back—she shivered at the sudden visceral memory of the blade scraping over bone, jutting out beneath her shoulder blade—as he helped her sit up.

"I told you she'd be fine," said Holland, folding his arms.

"She still looks pretty rough," said Alucard. "No offense, Bard."

"None taken," she said hoarsely. She looked up into their faces—Kell pale, Holland grim, Alucard tense—and knew it must have been a near thing.

Leaning on Kell, she got to her feet.

Ten Copper Thieves lay sprawled on the alley floor. Lila's hands shook as she took in the scene, and then kicked the nearest corpse as hard as she could. Again and again and again, until Kell took her by the arms and pulled her in, the breath leaving her lungs in broken gasps, even though her chest was healed.

"I miscounted," she said into his shoulder. "I thought there were six. . . ."

Kell brushed the tears from her cheek. She hadn't realized she was crying.

"You were only at sea for four months," he said. "How many enemies did you *make*?"

Lila laughed, a small, jagged hiccup of a laugh, as he pulled her closer.

They stood there like that for a long moment, while Alucard and Holland walked among the dead, freeing Lila's knives from chests and legs and throats.

"And what have we learned from this, Bard?" asked the captain, wiping a blade on a corpse's chest.

Lila looked down at the bodies of the men she'd once spared aboard the *Copper Thief*.

"Dead men can't hold grudges."

They made their way back to the ship in silence, Kell's arm around her waist, though she no longer needed him for support. Holland walked in front with Alucard, and Lila kept her eyes on the back of his head.

He hadn't had to do it.

He could have let her bleed out in the street.

He could have stood and watched her die.

That's what she would have done.

She told herself that's what she would have done.

It isn't enough, she thought. *It doesn't make up for Barron, for Kell, for me. I haven't forgotten.*

"*Tac,*" said Jasta as they made their way up the dock. "What happened to *you?*"

"Rosenal," said Lila blandly.

"Tell me we're ready to sail," said Kell.

Holland said nothing, but made his way straight toward the hold. Lila watched him go.

I still don't trust you, she thought.

As if he could feel the weight of her gaze, Holland glanced back over his shoulder.

You do not know me, his gaze seemed to say.

You do not know me at all.

III

"I've been thinking about the boy," said Vor.

They were sitting at a low table in the king's room, he and Holland, playing a round of Ost. It was a game of strategy and risk, and it was Vortalis's favorite way to unwind, but no one would play him anymore—the guards were tired of losing the game, and their money—so Holland always ended up across the board.

"Which boy?" he asked, rolling the chips in his palm.

"The messenger."

It had been two years since that visit, two long years spent trying to rebuild a broken city, to carve a shelter in the storm. Trying—and failing. Holland kept his voice even. "What of him?"

"Do you still have the coin?" asked Vor, even though they both knew he did. It sat in his pocket always, the metal worn from use. They did not speak of Holland's absences, of the times he disappeared, only to return smelling too sweetly of flowers instead of ash and stone. Holland never stayed, of course. And he was never gone long. He hated those visits, hated seeing what his world could have been, and yet he couldn't keep himself from going, from seeing, from knowing what was on the other side of the door. He couldn't look away.

"Why?" he asked now.

"I think it's time to send a letter."

"Why now?"

"Don't play the fool," said Vor, letting his chips fall to the table. "It doesn't suit you. We both know the stores are thinning and the days grow shorter. I make laws, and people break them, I make order and they turn it into chaos." He ran a hand through his hair, fingers snagging on the ring of steel. His usual poise faltered. With a snarl he flung the crown across the room. "No matter what I do, the hope is rotting, and I can hear the whispers starting in the streets. New blood, they call. As if that will fix what is broken, as if shedding enough will bring the magic in this world to heel."

"And you would fix this with a *letter*?" demanded Holland.

"I would fix it any way I can," countered Vor. "Perhaps their world was once like ours, Holland. Perhaps they know a way to *help*."

"They're the ones who sealed us off, who live in splendor while we rot, and you would go begging—"

"I would do anything if I thought it would truly help my world," snapped Vortalis, "and so would you. That is why you're here beside me. Not because you are my sword, not because you are my shield, not because you are my friend. You are here with me because we will *both* do whatever we can to keep our world alive."

Holland looked hard at the king then, hard, took in the grey threading his dark hair, the permanent furrow between his brows. He was still charming, still magnetic, still smiled when something delighted him, but the act now drew deep lines in his skin, and Holland knew the spells across Vor's hands weren't enough to bind the magic anymore.

Holland set a chip on the board, as though they were still playing. "I thought I was here to keep your head on your shoulders."

Vortalis managed a strained laugh, a farce of humor. "That, too," he said, and then, sobering: "Listen to me, Holland. Of all the ways to die, only a fool chooses pride."

A servant entered with a loaf of bread, a bottle of *kaash,* a pile of thin cigars. Despite the crown, the castle, Vor was still a man of habit.

He took up a tightly rolled paper, and Holland snapped his fingers, offering the flame.

Vor sat back and examined the burning end of the taper. "Why didn't you want to be king?"

"I suppose I'm not arrogant enough."

Vor chuckled. "Maybe you're a wiser man than I am." He took a long drag. "I'm beginning to think that thrones make tyrants of us all."

He blew out the smoke, and coughed.

Holland frowned. The king smoked ten times a day, and never seemed to suffer for it.

"Are you well?"

Vor was already waving the question away, but as he leaned forward to pour himself a drink, he put too much weight on the table's edge and it upset, the Ost chips raining down onto the stone floor as he fell.

"Vortalis!"

The king was still coughing, a deep, wracking sound, clawing at his chest with both hands as Holland folded over him. On the floor nearby, the cigar still burned. Vor tried to speak, but managed only blood.

"*Kajt*," swore Holland as he clutched a shard of glass until it bit into his hand, blood welling as he tore open Vor's tunic and pressed his palm against the king's chest, and commanded him to *heal*.

But the toxin had been too fast, the king's heart too slow. It wasn't working.

"Hold on, Vor. . . ." Holland splayed both hands against his friend's heaving chest, and he could feel the poison in his blood, because it wasn't poison after all but a hundred tiny slivers of spelled metal, tearing the king apart from within. No matter how fast Holland tried to heal the damage, the shards made more.

"Stay with me," the *Antari* ordered, with all the force of a spell, while he drew the metal shards free, his king's skin soaking first with sweat and then blood as the metal slivers pierced vein and muscle and flesh before rising in a dark red mist into the air above Vor's chest.

"*As Tanas*," said Holland, closing his fist, and the shards drew together into a cloud of steel before fusing back into a solid piece, cursework scrawled along its surface.

But it was too late.

He was too late.

Beneath the spelled steel, beneath Holland's hand, the king had gone still. Blood matted his front, flecked his beard, shone in his open, empty eyes.

Ros Vortalis was dead.

Holland staggered to his feet, the cursed steel falling from his fingers, landing among the abandoned Ost chips. It didn't roll, but splashed softly in the pool of blood. Blood that already slicked Holland's hands, misted his skin.

"Guards," he said once, softly, and then, raising his voice in a way he never did, "*Guards!*"

The room was too still, the castle too quiet.

Holland called again, but no one came. Part of him knew they weren't coming, but shock was singing him, tangled up with grief, making him clumsy, slow.

He forced himself up, turned from Vor's body, drawing the blade his king—his friend—had given him the day they stood on the balcony, the day Vor became the Winter King, the day Holland became his knight. Holland left his king and stormed through the doors, into an eerily silent castle.

He called out to the guards again, but of course they were already dead.

Bodies slumped forward on tables and against walls, halls empty and the world reduced to the *drip drip drip* of blood and wine on pale stone floors. It must have happened in minutes. Seconds. The time it took to light a cigarette, to draw a breath, exhale a plume of cursed smoke.

Holland didn't see the spell written on the floor.

Didn't feel the room slow around him until he'd crossed the line of magic, his body dragging suddenly as if through water instead of air.

Somewhere, echoing off the castle walls, someone laughed.

It was a laugh so unlike Talya's, so unlike Vor's. No sweetness, no richness, no warmth. A laugh as cold and sharp as glass.

"Look, Athos," said the voice. "I've caught us a prize."

Holland tried to turn, dragging his body toward the sound, but he was too slow, and the knife came from behind, a barbed blade that sank deep into his thigh. Pain lit his mind like light as he staggered to one knee.

A woman danced at the edges of his sight. White skin. White hair. Eyes like ice.

"Hello, pretty thing," she said, twisting the knife until Holland actually screamed. A sound that rang out through the too-quiet castle, only to be cut off by a flash of silver, a slash of pain, a whip closing around his throat, stealing air, stealing everything. A swift tug, and Holland was forced forward, onto his hands and knees, his throat on fire. He couldn't breathe, couldn't speak, couldn't spell the blood now dripping to the floor beneath him.

"Ah," said a second voice. "The infamous Holland." A pale shape strode forward, winding the handle of the whip around his fingers. "I was hoping you would survive."

The figure stopped at the edge of the spell, and sank onto his haunches in front of Holland's buckled form. Up close, his skin and hair were the same white as the woman's, his eyes the same frigid blue.

"Now," said the man with a slow smile. "What to do with *you?*"

Alox was dead.

Talya was dead.

Vortalis was dead.

But Holland wasn't.

He was strapped into a metal frame, his skin fever-hot and his limbs splayed like a moth mid-flight. Blood dripped to the stone floor, a dark red pool beneath his feet.

He could have cast a hundred spells, with all that blood, but his jaw was strapped shut. He'd woken with the vice around his head, teeth forced together so hard the only thing he could manage was a guttural sound, a groan, a sob of pain.

Athos Dane swam in his vision, those cold blue eyes and that curled mouth, a smile lurking beneath the surface like a fish under thin ice.

"I want to hear your voice, Holland," said the man, sliding the knife under his skin. "Sing to me." The blade sank deeper, probing for nerves, biting into tendons, slipping between bones.

Holland shuddered against the pain, but didn't scream. He never did. It was small consolation in the end, some quicksilver hope that if he didn't break, Athos would give up and simply kill him.

He didn't *want* to die. Not in the beginning. For the first few hours—days—he'd fought back, until the metal frame had cut into his skin, until the pool of blood was large enough to see himself in, until the pain became a blanket, and his mind blurred, deprived of food, of sleep.

"Pity," mused Athos when Holland made no sound. He turned to a table that held, among so many gruesome things, a bowl of ink, and dipped his bloodstained knife, coating the crimson steel black.

Holland's stomach turned at the sight of it. Ink and blood, these were the stuff of *curses*. Athos returned to him and splayed a hand over Holland's ribs, clearly savoring the hitching breath, the stuttering heart, the smallest tells of terror.

"You think you know," he said quietly, "what I have planned for you." He lifted the knife, brought the tip to the pale, unbroken skin over Holland's heart, and smiled. "You have no idea."

When it was done, Athos Dane took a step back to admire his work.

Holland slumped in the metal frame, blood and ink spilling down his ruined chest. His head buzzed with magic, even though some vital part of him had been stripped away.

No, not stripped away. Buried.

"Are you finished?"

The voice belonged to the other Dane. Holland dragged his head up.

Astrid was standing in the doorway behind her brother, arms folded lazily across her front.

Athos, with his sated smile, flicked his blade as if it were a brush. "You cannot rush an artist."

She clicked her tongue, that icy gaze raking over Holland's mutilated chest as she drew near, boots clicking sharply over stone.

"Tell me, brother," she said, playing her cool fingers up Holland's arm. "Do you think it wise to keep this pet?" She traced a nail along his shoulder. "He might bite."

"What good is a beast that *cannot*?"

Athos slid his knife along Holland's cheek, slicing the leather strap of the vice around his mouth. Pain sang through his jaw as it slackened, teeth aching. Air rushed into his lungs, but when he tried to speak, to summon the spells he'd kept ready on his tongue, they froze in his throat so suddenly he choked on them and nearly retched.

One wrist came free of its cuff, and then another, and Holland staggered forward, his screaming limbs nearly buckling beneath the sudden weight while Athos and Astrid stood there, simply *watching*.

He wanted to kill them both.

Wanted to, and could not.

Athos had carved the lines of the curse one by one, sunk the rules of the spell into his skin with steel and ink.

Holland had tried to close his mind to the magic, but it was already inside him, burning through his chest, driven like a spike through flesh and mind and soul.

The chains of the spell were stiff, articulated things. They coiled through his head, weighed heavy as iron around every limb.

Obey, they said, not to his mind, his heart—only his hands, his lips.

The command was written on his skin, threaded through his bones.

Athos cocked his head and gestured absently.

"Kneel."

When Holland made no motion to obey, a block of stone struck him in the shoulders, a sudden, vicious, invisible weight forcing him forward. He fought to keep his feet, and the binding spell crackled through his nerves, ground against his bones.

His vision went white, and something too close to a scream escaped his aching mouth before his legs finally folded, shins meeting the cold stone floor.

Astrid clapped her hands once, pleased.

"Shall we test it?"

A sound, half curse, half cry, rang through the room as a man was dragged in, hands bound behind his back. He was bloody, beaten, his face more broken than not, but Holland recognized him as one of Vor's. The man staggered, was righted. The moment he saw Holland, something shifted in him. Fell. His mouth opened.

"Traitor."

"Cut his throat," instructed Athos.

The words rippled through Holland's limbs.

"No," he said hoarsely. It was the first word he'd managed in days, and it was useless, his fingers moving even before his mind could register. Red blossomed at the man's throat and he went down, his last words drowned in blood.

Holland stared at his own hand, the knife's edge crimson.

They left they body where it fell.

And brought another in.

"No," snarled Holland at the sight of him. A boy from the kitchens, hardly fourteen, who looked at him with wide, uncertain eyes. "Help," he begged.

Then they brought another.

And another.

One by one, Athos and Astrid paraded the remains of Vor's life before Holland, instructing him again and again to cut their throats. Every time, he tried to fight the order. Every time, he failed. Every time, he had to look them in their eyes and see the hatred, the betrayal, the anguished confusion before he cut them down.

The bodies piled. Athos watched. Astrid grinned.

Holland's hand moved on its puppet string.

And his mind screamed until it finally lost its voice.

IV

Lila couldn't sleep.

The fight kept spinning through her head, dark alleys and sharp knives, her heart racing until she was sure the sound would wake Kell. Halfway through the night she shoved up from the cot, crossed the tiny cabin in two short strides, and sank against the opposite wall, one blade resting on her knee, a small but familiar comfort.

It was late, or early, that dense dark time before the first shreds of day, and cold in the cabin—she pulled her coat down from its hook and shrugged it on, shoving her free hand in her pocket for warmth. Her fingers brushed stone, silver, silver, and she thought of Alucard's words.

You'll need a token to enter. Something valuable.

She searched her meager possessions for something precious enough to buy her entrance. There was the knife she'd taken from Fletcher, with its serrated blade and knuckled hilt, and then the one she'd won from Lenos, with its hidden catch that split one blade into two. There was the bloodstained shard of white marble that had once been part of Astrid Dane's face. And last, a warm and constant weight in the bottom of her pocket, there was Barron's timepiece. Her only tether to the world she'd left. The life she'd left. Lila knew, with bone-deep certainty, that the knives wouldn't be enough. That left her key to White London, and her key to Grey. She closed her eyes, clutching the two tokens until it hurt, knowing which was useless, and which would buy her passage.

Behind her eyes, she saw Barron's face the night she returned to the

Stone's Throw, the smoke from the burning ship still rising at her back. Heard her own voice offering the stolen watch up as payment. She felt the heavy warmth of his hand as he closed her fingers over the time-piece, told her to keep it. She'd left it behind, though, the night she followed Kell, more a token of gratitude than anything, the only good-bye she could manage. But the watch had come back to her at Holland's hands, stained with Barron's blood.

It was a part of her past now.

And holding on to it wouldn't bring him back.

Lila returned the tokens to her coat and let her head fall back against the cabin wall.

On the cot, Kell shifted in his sleep.

Overhead, the muffled sound of someone walking on the deck.

The gentle slosh of the sea. The rock of the ship.

Her eyes were just drifting shut when she heard a short, pained gasp. She jerked forward, alert, but Kell was still asleep. It came again and she was on her feet, knife at the ready as she followed the sound across the narrow corridor to the cabin where they were keeping Holland.

He was on his back on the cot, not chained, not even guarded, and dreaming—badly, it seemed. His teeth were clenched, his chest rising and falling in a staccato way. His whole body shuddered, fingers digging into the thin blanket beneath him. His mouth opened and a breath hitched in his throat. The nightmare wracked him like a chill, but he never made a sound.

Lying there, trapped within his dreams, Holland looked . . . exposed.

Lila stood, watching. And then she felt herself step into the room.

The boards beneath her creaked, and Holland tensed in his sleep. Lila held her breath, hovering for an instant before she crossed the narrow space and reached out and—

Holland shot forward, his fingers vising around her wrist. Pain shot up Lila's arm. There was no electricity, no magic, only skin on skin and the grind of bones.

His eyes were feverish as they found hers in the dark.

"What do you think you're doing?" The words hissed out like wind through a crack.

Lila pulled free. "You were having a bad dream," she snapped, rubbing her wrist. "I was going to wake you up."

His eyes flicked to the knife in her other hand. She'd forgotten it was there. She forced herself to sheath it.

Now that he was awake, Holland's face was a mask of calm, his stress betrayed only by the rivulet of sweat that slid down his temple, tracing a slow line along cheek and jaw. But his eyes followed her as she retreated to the doorway.

"What?" she said, crossing her arms. "Afraid I'll kill you in your sleep?"

"No."

Lila watched him. "I haven't forgotten what you did."

At that, Holland closed his eyes. "Neither have I."

She hovered, unsure what to say, what to do, tethered by the inability to do either. She had a feeling Holland wasn't trying to sleep, wasn't trying to dismiss her, either. He was giving her a chance to attack him, testing her resolve not to do it.

It was tempting—and yet somehow it wasn't, and that angered her more than anything. Lila huffed and turned to go.

"I did save your life," he said softly.

She hesitated, turned back. "It was one time."

The slight arching of one brow, the only movement in his face. "Tell me, Delilah, how many times will it take?"

She shook her head in disgust. "The man in the Stone's Throw," she said. "The one with the watch. The one whose throat you cut, he didn't deserve to die."

"Most people don't," said Holland calmly.

"Did you ever consider sparing his life?"

"No."

"Did you even hesitate before you killed him?"

"No."

"Why not?" she snarled, the air trembling with her anger.

Holland held her gaze. "Because it was easier."

"I don't—"

"Because if I stopped I would think, and if I thought, I would re-member, and if I remembered, I would—" He swallowed, the small-est rise in his throat. "No, I did not hesitate. I cut his throat, and added his death to the ones I count every day when I wake." His eyes hard-ened on her. "Now tell me, Delilah, how many lives have you ended? Do you know the number?"

Lila started to answer, then stopped.

The truth—the infuriating, maddening, sickening truth—was that she didn't.

Lila stormed back to her own cabin.

She wanted to sleep, wanted to fight, wanted to quell the fear and anger rising in her throat like a scream. Wanted to banish Holland's words, carve out the memory of the knife between her ribs, smother the terrible instant that reckless energy of danger turned to cold fear.

She wanted to forget.

Kell was halfway to his feet, coat in one hand, when she came in.

Wanted to feel . . .

"There you are," he said, his hair mussed from sleep. "I was just coming to look for—"

Lila caught him by the shoulders and pressed her mouth against his.

"—*you*," he finished, the word nothing but a breath between her lips.

. . . This.

Kell returned the kiss. Deepened it. That current of magic like a spark across her lips.

And then his arms were folding around her, and in that small ges-ture, she understood, felt it down to her bones, that draw, not the elec-tric pulse of power but the thing beneath it, the weight she'd never understood. In a world where everything rocked and swayed and fell away, this was solid ground.

Safe.

Her heart was beating hard against her ribs, some primal part of her saying *run,* and she *was* running, just not away. She was tired of running away. So she was running into Kell.

And he caught her.

His coat fell to the floor, and then they were half stepping, half stumbling back through the tiny room. They missed the bed, but found the wall—it wasn't that far—and when Lila's back met the hull of the ship, the whole thing seemed to rock beneath them, pressing Kell's body into hers.

She gasped, less from the sudden weight than from the sense of him against her, one leg between hers.

Her hand slid beneath his shirt with all the practiced grace of a thief. But this time she *wanted* him to feel her touch, her palms gliding over his ribs and around his back, fingertips digging into his shoulder blades.

"Lila," he rasped into her ear as the ship righted, swung the other way, and they tumbled back onto the cot. She pulled his body down with hers, and he caught himself on his elbows, hovering over her. His lashes were strands of copper around his black and blue eyes. She'd never noticed before. She reached up and brushed the hair out of his face. It was soft—feathery—where the rest of him was sharp. His cheekbone scraped against her palm. His hips cut into hers. Their bodies sparked against each other, the energy electric across their skin.

"Kell," she said, the word something between a whisper and a gasp.

And then the door burst open.

Alucard stood in the doorway, soaking wet, as if he'd just been dumped in the sea, or the sea had been dumped over him. *"Stop fucking with the ship."*

Kell and Lila stared at him in stunned silence, and then burst into laughter as the door slammed shut.

They fell back against the cot, the laughter trailing off, only to rise again out of the silence full force. Lila laughed until her body ached, and even when she thought she was done, the sound came on like hiccups.

"Hush," Kell whispered in her hair, and that nearly set her off again as she rolled toward him on the narrow cot, squeezing in so she wouldn't fall off. He made room, one arm beneath his head and the other wrapped around her waist, pulling her in against him.

He smelled like roses.

She remembered thinking that, the first time they met, and even now, with the salty sea and the damp wood of the ship, she could smell it, the faint, fresh garden scent that was his magic.

"Teach me the words," she whispered.

"Hm?" he asked sleepily.

"The blood spells." She propped her head on her hand. "I want to know them."

Kell sighed in mock exhaustion. "Now?"

"Yes, now." She rolled onto her back, eyes trained on the wooden ceiling. "What happened in Rosenal—I don't plan on letting it happen again. Ever."

Kell lifted himself onto one elbow above her. He looked down at her for a long, searching moment, and then a mischievous grin flickered across his face.

"All right," he said. "I'll teach you."

His copper lashes sank low over his two-toned eyes. "There's *As Travars,* to travel between worlds."

She rolled her eyes. "I know that one."

He lowered himself a fraction, bringing his lips to her ear.

"And *As Tascen,*" he continued, breath warm. "To move within a world."

She felt a shiver of pleasure as his lips brushed her jaw. "And *As Hasari,*" he murmured. "To heal."

His mouth found hers, stealing a kiss before he said, "*As Staro.* To seal." And she would have let him linger there, but his mouth continued downward.

"*As Pyrata.*"

A breath against the base of her throat.

"To burn."

His hands sliding beneath the fabric of her shirt.

"*As Anasae.*"

A blossom of heat between her breasts.

"To dispel."

Above her navel.

"As Steno."

One hand unlacing the ties of her slacks.

"To break."

Guiding them off.

"As Orense."

His teeth skimming her hip bone.

"To open . . ."

Kell's mouth came to rest between her legs, and she arched against him, fingers tangling in his auburn curls as heat rolled through her. Sweat prickled across her skin. She blazed inside, and her breath grew ragged, one hand clenched in the sheets over her head as something like magic rose inside her, a tide that swelled and swelled until she couldn't hold it in.

"Kell," she moaned as his kiss deepened. Her whole body trembled with the power, and when she finally let go, it crashed down in a wave at once electric and sublime.

Lila collapsed back against the sheets with something between a laugh and a sigh, the whole cabin buzzing in the aftermath, the sheets singed where she'd gripped them.

Kell rose, fitting himself beside her once again.

"Was that a good enough lesson?" he asked, his own breath still uneven.

Lila grinned, and then rolled on top of him, straddling his waist. His eyes widened, his chest rising and falling beneath her. "Well," she said, guiding his hands over his head. "Let's see if I remember it all."

They lay pressed together in the narrow cot, Kell's arm looped around her. The heat of the moment was gone, replaced by a pleasant, steady warmth. His shirt was open, and she brought her fingertips to the scar over his heart, tracing the circles absently until his eyes drifted shut.

Lila knew she wouldn't sleep. Not like this, body to body in the bed. She usually slept with her back to a wall.

Usually slept with a knife on her knee.

Usually slept *alone*.

But soon, the ship was quiet, the small skiff rocking gently on the current, and Kell's breathing was low and even, his pulse a lulling beat against her skin, and for the first time in as long as she could remember, Lila fell well, and truly, and soundly, asleep.

V

"Sanct," muttered Alucard, "it's getting *worse.*"

He spit Ilo's latest batch of dawn coffee over the side of the ship. Jasta called out from the wheel, her words lost on the breeze, and he wiped his mouth with the back of his hand and looked up to see the Going Waters take shape on the horizon.

First only a specter, and then, slowly, a ship.

When he'd first set out for Maris's infamous vessel, he'd done so expecting to find something like the port of Sasenroche or London's night market, only set at sea. *Is Feras Stras* was neither. It was indeed a ship—or rather, several, growing together like coral atop the crisp blue sea. Squares of canvas stretched here and dipped there, turning the network of decks and masts into something that resembled a nest of tents.

The whole thing looked unstable, a house of cards waiting to fall, swaying and bobbing in the winter breeze. It had the worn air of something that had lasted a very long time, that only grew, not torn down and rebuilt by whim or by wind, but added to in layers like paint.

But there was a strange elegance to the madness, an order to the chaos, made more severe by the quiet shrouding the ship. There were no shouts from any of the decks. No layered voices echoing on the breeze. The whole affair sat silently atop the waves, a ramshackle estate bathing in the sun.

It had been nearly two years since Alucard had last seen Maris's craft, and the sight of it still left him strangely awed.

Bard appeared beside him at the rail.

She let out a low whistle, her eyes wide with the same hungry light.

A low boat was already drawn up beside the floating market, and as the *Ghost* slowed, Alucard could make out a man, skeletal thin and leathered by the sun and the sea, being escorted from Maris's ship.

"Wait!" he was saying. "I paid my due. Let me keep looking. I'll find something else!"

But the men on his arms seemed oblivious to his pleas and protestations as they heaved him bodily overboard. He fell several feet before landing on the deck of his own small craft, groaning in pain.

"A word of advice," said Alucard lightly. "When Maris says leave, you leave."

"Don't worry," said Bard. "I'll be on my best behavior."

It wasn't a comforting notion. As far as he could see, she only had one kind of behavior, and it usually ended with several dead bodies.

In Jasta's hands, the *Ghost* slowed, drawing up beside the *Ferase Stras*. A plank was shifted into place between the *Ghost* and the brim of the floating market, which led onto a covered platform with a simple wooden door. They crossed the plank one at a time, Jasta in the front, then Lila and Kell, with Alucard bringing up the rear. After an hour's disagreement, the decision was made to leave Holland behind with Hastra and Lenos.

The remaining *Antari* was cuffed again, but some silent accord must have been struck between Holland and Kell, because he'd been granted freedom to move aboard the ship—Alucard had walked into the galley that morning and seen the magician sitting at the narrow table holding a cup of *tea*. Now Holland stood on the deck, leaning against the mast in the shadow of the mainsail, arms crossed as much as his chains would allow, head tipped toward the sky.

"Do we knock?" asked Lila, grinning at Alucard, but before she could reach out and rap her knuckles on the door, it swung open and a man stepped forward, dressed in trim white clothes. That, more than anything, made the scene surreal. Life at sea was a painting done primarily in muted shades—the sun and salt leached color, the sweat and grime wore whites to grey. Yet the man stood in the midst of the sea spray and mid-morning light, spotless in his milk-colored slacks and spotless tunic.

On his head, the man wore something between a headscarf and a helm. It circled his head and swept down over his brow and across his high cheeks. The gap between showed his eyes, which were the lightest shade of brown, fringed by long black lashes. He was lovely. Had always been lovely.

At the sight of Alucard, the figure cocked his head. "Didn't I just get rid of you?"

"Good to see you, too, Katros," he said cheerfully.

The man's gaze swept past Alucard to the others, pausing an instant on each before he held out a tan hand. "Your tokens."

They gave them up: Jasta, a small metal sphere full of holes that whistled and whispered; Kell, a Grey London coin; Lila, a silver watch; and Alucard, the vial of dreamsquick he'd picked up at Rosenal. Katros vanished behind the door, and the four stood in silence on the platform for several long minutes before he returned to let them in.

Kell passed through the door first, vanishing into the shadowed space beyond, followed by Bard with her brisk, soundless step, and then Jasta—but as the captain of the *Ghost* started forward, Katros blocked her way.

"Not this time, Jasta," he said evenly.

The woman scowled. "Why not?"

Katros shrugged. "Maris chooses."

"My gift was good."

"Perhaps," was all he said.

Jasta let out something that might have been a curse, or merely a growl, too low for Alucard to parse. They were roughly the same size, she and Katros, even counting the helm, and Alucard wondered what would happen if she tried to force her way through. He doubted it would end well for any of them, so he was relieved when she threw up her hands and skulked back onto the *Ghost*.

Katros turned toward him, a wry smile nocked like an arrow on his lips. "Alucard," he said, weighing the captain with those light eyes. And then, at last, "Come in."

VI

Kell stepped into the room, and drew up short.

He'd expected a contradiction of space, an interior as strange and mysterious as the ship's facade.

Instead, he found a room roughly the same size of Alucard's cabin aboard the *Night Spire,* though far more cluttered. Cabinets bulged with trinkets, cases brimmed with books, and massive chests hugged every wall, some locked and others open (and one trembling as if something inside was both alive and wanted to get out). There were no windows, and with so much clutter, Kell would have expected the room to smell stuffy, moth-eaten, but he was surprised to find the air crisp and clear, the only scent a faint but pleasant one, like old paper.

A broad table sat in the center of the room with a large white hound—though really it looked less like a dog and more like a pile of books shoved under a shaggy rug—snoring gently beneath it.

And there, behind the table, sat Maris.

The king of the floating market, who turned out to be a *queen.*

Maris was old, old as anyone Kell had ever seen, her skin dark even by Arnesian standards, its surface cracked into a hundred lines like tree bark. But like the sentry at the door, her clothing—a crisp white tunic laced to the throat—lacked even the smallest crease. Her long silver hair was pulled back off her weathered face and spilled between her shoulders in a narrow sheet of metal. She wore silver in both ears, and on both hands, one of which held their tokens while the other curled its bony fingers around the silver head of a cane.

And around her neck—along with three or four other silver chains—hung the Inheritor. It was the size of a small scroll, just as Tieren had said, not a cylinder exactly, but a thing of six or eight sides—he couldn't tell from here—all short and flat and shaped to form a column, each facet intricately patterned and its base tapered to a spindle's point.

When they were all there—all save Jasta, who'd apparently been turned back—Maris cleared her throat.

"A pocket watch. A coin. And a vial of sugar." Her voice held none of the frailty of age—it was rich and low and scornful. "I must admit, I'm disappointed."

Her gaze lifted, revealing eyes the color of sand. "The watch isn't even spelled, though I do suppose that's half the charm. And is this blood? Well, that's the other half for you. Though I do enjoy an object with a story. As for the coin, yes, I can tell it's not from here, but rather worn out, isn't it? As for the dreamsquick, Captain Emery, at least you remembered, needless as it is two years after the point. But I must say, I expected more from two *Antari* magicians and the victor of the *Essen Tasch*—yes, I know, word does travel quickly, and Alucard, I suppose I owe you a congratulations, though I doubt you've had much time to celebrate, what with the shadows looming over London."

All of this was said without a pause, or, as far as Kell could tell, the need for breath. But that wasn't what unnerved him most. "How do you know about the state of London?"

Maris's attention drifted toward him, and she began to answer, then squinted. "Ah," she said, "it seems you've found my old coat." Kell's hands rose defensively to his collar, but Maris waved it away. "If I wanted it back, I wouldn't have lost it. Thing's got a mind of its own, I think the spellwork must be fraying. Still eating coins and spitting out lint? No? It must like you."

Kell never got a word in edgewise, as Maris seemed more than content to carry on her conversations without a partner. He wondered if the old woman was a little daft, but her pale eyes flicked from target to target with all the speed and accuracy of a well-thrown knife.

Now that attention landed on Lila. "Aren't you a trinket," said Maris.

"But I'm betting a devil to hold on to. Has anyone told you, you've something in your eye?" Her hand tipped, letting the tokens tumble roughly to the table. "The watch must be yours, my darling traveler. It smells of ash and blood instead of flowers."

"It's the most precious thing I own," said Lila through gritted teeth.

"*Owned,*" corrected Maris. "Oh, don't look at me like that, dearie. *You* gave it up." Her fingers tightened on the cane, eliciting a crackle of ligament and bone. "You must want something more. What brings a prince, a noble, and a stranger to my market? Have you come with a single prize in mind, or are you here to browse?"

"We only want—" started Kell, but Alucard clapped a hand on his shoulder.

"To help our city," said the captain.

Kell shot him a confused look but had the sense to say nothing.

"You're right, Maris," continued Alucard. "A shadow has fallen over London, and nothing we have can stop it."

The old woman rapped her nails on the table. "And here I thought London wanted nothing to do with *you,* Master Emery."

Alucard swallowed. "Perhaps," he said, casting a dark look Kell's way. "But I still care for it."

Lila's attention was still leveled on Maris. "What are the rules?"

"This is a black market," she said. "There are no rules."

"This is a ship," countered Lila. "And every ship has rules. The captain sets them. Unless, of course, you're *not* the captain of this ship."

Maris flashed her teeth. "I am captain and crew, merchant and law. Everyone aboard works for me."

"They're family, aren't they?" said Lila.

"Stop talking, Bard," warned Alucard.

"The two men who threw the other overboard, they take after you, and the one guarding the door—Katros, was it?—has your eyes."

"Perceptive," said Maris, "for a girl with only one of her own." The woman stood, and Kell expected to hear the creak and pop of old bones settling. Instead, he heard only a soft exhale, the rustle of cloth as it settled. "The rules are simple enough: your token buys you access to this market; it buys you nothing more. Everything aboard has a price, whether or not you elect to pay it."

"And I assume we can only choose one thing," said Lila.

Kell recalled the man thrown overboard, the way he'd called out for another chance.

"You know, Miss Bard, there *is* such a thing as being sharp enough to cut yourself."

Lila smiled, as if it were a compliment.

"Lastly," continued Maris with a pointed look her way, "the market is warded five ways to summer against acts of magic and theft. I encourage you not to try and pocket anything before it's yours. It will not go well."

With that, Maris took her seat, opened a ledger, and began to write.

They stood there, waiting for her to say more, or to excuse them, but after several uncomfortable moments, during which the only sound was the rattling of one trunk, the slosh of the sea, and the scratch of her quill, Maris's bony fingers drifted to a second door set between two stacks of boxes.

"Why are you still here?" she said without looking up, and that was all the dismissal they got.

"Why are we even bothering with the ship?" asked Kell as soon as they were through the door. "Maris has the only thing we need."

"Which is the last thing you're going *tell* her," snapped Alucard.

"The more you want something from someone," added Lila, "the less they'll want to part with it. If Maris finds out what we actually *need,* we'll lose what power we have to bargain." Kell crossed his arms and looked about to counter, but she pressed on. "There are three of us, and only one Inheritor, which means the two of you need to find something else to buy." Before either of the men could protest, she cut them off. "Alucard, you can't ask for the Inheritor back, you're the one who gave it to her, and Kell, no offense, but you tend to make people angry."

Kell's brow furrowed. "I don't see how that—"

"Maris is a *thief*," said Lila, "and a bloody good one by the look of this ship, so she and I have something in common. Leave the Inheritor to me."

"And what are *we* supposed to do?" asked Kell, gesturing to himself and the captain.

Alucard made a sweeping gesture across the market, the sapphire twinkling above his eye. "Shop."

VII

Holland still hated being at sea—the dip and swell of the ship, the constant sense of imbalance—but moving around helped, somewhat. The manacles still emitted their dull, muffling pressure, but the air on deck was crisp and fresh, and if he closed his eyes, he could almost imagine he was somewhere else—though where he'd be, Holland didn't really know.

His stomach panged, still hollowed out from his first hours aboard, and he reluctantly made his way back down into the hold.

The old man, Ilo, stood at the narrow counter in the galley, rinsing potatoes and humming to himself. He didn't stop when Holland entered, didn't even soften his tune, just carried on as if he didn't know the magician was there.

A bowl of apples sat in the center of the table, and Holland reached out, chains scraping the wood. Still the cook didn't move. So the gesture was pointed, thought Holland, turning to go.

But his way was blocked.

Jasta stood in the doorway, half a head taller than Holland, her dark eyes leveled on him. There was no kindness in that gaze, and no sign of the others behind her.

Holland frowned. "That was fast. . . ."

He trailed off at the sight of the blade in her hand. One manacled wrist leaned on the table, the apple in his other hand, a short length of chain between. He'd lost the splinter he'd kept between metal and skin, but a paring knife sat on the counter nearby, its handle within reach. He didn't move toward it, not yet.

It was a narrow room, and Ilo was still washing and humming as if nothing were amiss, pointedly ignoring the rising tension.

Jasta held her blade loosely, with a comfort that gave Holland pause.

"Captain," he said carefully.

Jasta looked down at her knife. "My brother is dead," she said slowly, "because of you. Half my crew is gone because of you."

She stepped toward him.

"My city is in peril because of you."

He held his ground. She was close now. Close enough to use the blade before he could stop her without things getting messy.

"Perhaps two *Antari* will be enough," she said, bringing the tip of the knife to rest against his collar. Her gaze held his as she pressed down, testing, the knife sinking just enough to draw blood before a new voice echoed down the hall. Hastra. Followed by Lenos. Steps tumbling briskly down the stairs.

"Perhaps," she said again, stepping back, "but I'm not willing to risk it."

She turned and stormed out. Holland rocked back against the counter, wiping the blood from his skin as Hastra and Lenos appeared and Ilo took up another song.

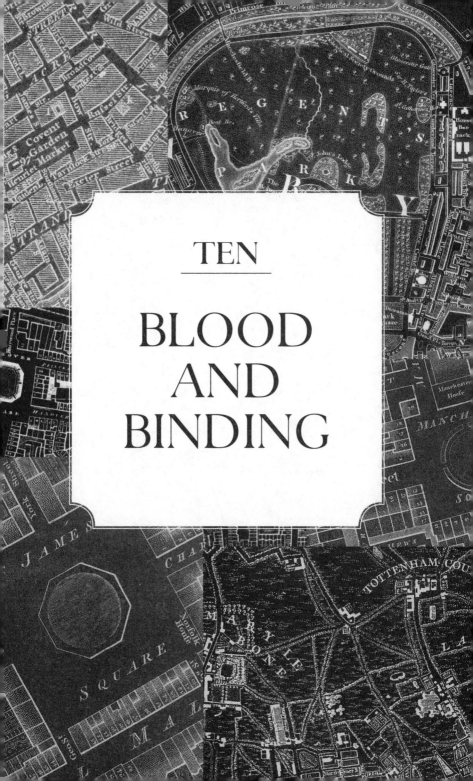

TEN

BLOOD
AND
BINDING

I

Grey London

Ned Tuttle woke to the sound of someone knocking.

It was late morning, and he'd fallen asleep at a table in the tavern, the grooves of the table's pentagram now etched like sheet folds into the side of his face.

He sat up, lost for a moment between where he was and where he'd been.

The dreams were getting stranger.

Every time, he found himself somewhere else—on a bridge overlooking a black river, looking up at a palace of marble and crimson and gold—and every time he was lost.

He'd read about men who could walk through dreams. They could project themselves into other places, other times—but when they walked, they were able to speak to people, and learn things, and they always came away wiser. When *Ned* dreamt, he just felt more and more alone.

He moved like a ghost through crowds of men and women who spoke languages he'd never heard, whose eyes swam with shadows and whose edges burned with light. Sometimes they didn't seem to see him, and other times they did, and those were worse, because then they'd reach for him, claw at him, and he'd have to run, and every time he ran, he ended up lost.

And then he'd hear that particular voice; the murmur and the susurrus, low and smooth and steady as water over rocks, the words muffled by some unseen veil between them. A voice that reached just like those shadow hands, wrapping fingers around his throat.

Ned's temples were pounding in time with the door as he reached for the glass on the table that had so recently served as his bed. Realizing the glass was empty, he swore and took up the bottle just beyond his fingers, swigging in a way that would have earned him a reproach if he were still at home. The table itself was scattered with parchment, ink, the elemental kit he'd bought from the gentleman who'd bought it from Kell. This last item rattled sporadically as if possessed (and it *was,* the bits of bone and stone and drops of water trying to get out). Ned thought groggily that it might have been the source of the knocking, but when he put his hand firmly on the box, the sound still echoed from the door.

"Coming," he called hoarsely, pausing a moment to steady his aching head, but when he rose and turned toward the tavern door, his jaw dropped.

The door was knocking *itself,* rocking forward and back in its frame, straining against the bolt. Ned wondered if there was a strong wind outside, but when he threw the shutters, the tavern sign hung still as death in the early morning light.

A shiver passed through him. He had always known this place was special. He'd heard the rumors from patrons back when he was one of them, and now they'd lean forward on their stools and ask *him,* as if he knew any more than they.

"Is it true . . ." they'd start, followed by a dozen different questions.

"That this place is haunted?"

"That it's built on a ley line?"

"That it sits in two worlds?"

"That it belongs to neither?"

Is it true, is it true, and Ned only knew that whatever it was, it had drawn him, and now it was drawing something else.

The door kept up its phantom knocking as Ned stumbled up the stairs and into his room, searching through the drawers until he found his biggest bundle of sage and his favored book of spells.

He was halfway down the stairs again when the noise stopped.

Ned returned to the tavern, crossing himself for good measure, and set the book on the table, turning through the pages until he found one to banish negative forces.

He went to the hearth, stoked the last embers of the night's fire, and touched the end of the sage bundle until it caught.

"I banish the darkness," he intoned, sweeping the sage through the air. "It is not welcome," he went on, tracing the windows and doors. "Begone foul spirits, and demons, and ghosts, for this is a place of . . ."

He trailed off as the smoke from the sage curled through the air around him and began to make *shapes*. First mouths, and then eyes, nightmarish faces drawing themselves in the pale plumes around him.

That wasn't supposed to happen.

Ned fumbled for a piece of chalk and dropped to his knees, drawing a pentagram on the tavern floor. He climbed inside, wishing he had a bit of salt, too, but unwilling to venture out behind the bar as all around him the grotesque faces swelled and fell apart and swelled again, their mouths yawning wide, as if laughing, or screaming—but the only sound that came out was *that voice*.

The one from his dream.

It was up close and far away, the kind of voice that seemed to be coming from the other room and another world at once.

"What are you?" Ned demanded, voice trembling.

"*I am a god,*" it said. "*I am a king.*"

"What do you want?" he said, because everyone knew that spirits had to tell the truth. Or was that fae? Christ . . .

"*I am just,*" said the voice. "*I am merciful. . . .*"

"What is your name?"

"*Worship me, and we will do great things. . . .*"

"Answer me."

"*I am a god. . . . I am a king. . . .*"

That's when Ned realized that, whatever it was, *wherever* it was, the voice wasn't talking to *him*. It was reciting its lines, repeating the words as one might a spell. Or a summoning.

Ned began to back out of the pentagram, his foot slipping on something smooth. Looking down, he saw a small patch of black on the old wooden floor, the size of a large coin. He thought at first that he had missed a spill, the remnants of someone's drink frozen in the recent cold snap. But the room wasn't really cold enough, and when Ned touched the strange dark slick, neither was it. He tapped it once with his nail and it sounded almost like glass, and then, before his eyes, the patch began to *spread*.

The knocking started up again, but this time a very human voice beyond the door called out, "Oy, Tuttle! Open up!"

Ned looked from the door, to the thinning smoke faces still hanging in the air, to the patch of creeping darkness on the floor, and called back, "We're closed!"

The words were met by a grumbled curse and the scuff of boots, and as soon as the man was gone, Ned was up, propping a chair against the locked door for good measure before he returned to the open book and started looking for a stronger spell.

II

It didn't matter that Alucard had been to the market once before. And it didn't matter that he had a compass in his head from years at sea, and a knack for learning paths. Within minutes, Alucard Emery was lost. The floating market was a maze of stairs and cabins and corridors, all of them empty of people and full of treasure.

There were no merchants here, calling out their wares. This was a private collection, a pirate's hoard on display. Only the rarest and strangest and most forbidden objects in the world made it onto Maris's ship.

It was a marvel nothing had ever been lost—or lifted, though not, he'd heard, for lack of trying. Maris had a fearful reputation, but a reputation carried only so far, and inevitably, drunk either on power or cheap wine, a thief would get it in their head to try to steal from the queen of the *Ferase Stras*.

As she'd warned, it never ended well.

Most of the stories involved missing limbs, though a few of the more outlandish tales involved entire crews scattered over land and sea in pieces so small no one ever found more than a thumb, a heel.

It made sense—when you had a wealth of black magic at your fingertips, you also had a wealth of ways to keep it safe. The market wasn't simply warded against light fingers. It was warded, he knew, against *intent*. You couldn't draw a knife. Couldn't reach for a thing you didn't mean to purchase. Some days, when the wards were fickle, you couldn't even think about stealing.

Unlike most magicians, Alucard was fond of Maris's wards, the way they muted everything. Without the noise of other magic, the treasures shone—his eyes could pick out the strands of power clinging to each artifact, the signatures of the magicians who'd spelled them. In a place without merchants to tell him what an object *did,* his sight came in handy. A spell was, after all, a kind of tapestry, woven from the threads of magic itself.

But it didn't stop him from getting lost.

In the end, it had taken Alucard half an hour to find the room of mirrors.

He stood there, surrounded by artifacts of every shape and size— some made of glass, and others polished stone, ones that reflected his own face, and ones that showed him other times and other places and other people—scanning the spellwork until he found the right one.

It was a lovely, oval thing with an onyx rim and two handles like a serving tray. Not an ordinary mirror, by any stretch, but not strictly forbidden, either. Only very rare. Most reflective magic showed what was in your mind, but a mind could invent almost anything, so a reflector could be fooled into showing a tale instead of the truth.

Reaching into the past—reflecting things not as they were remembered, or rewritten, but as they *were,* as they'd really happened—that was a very special kind of magic.

He slid the mirror into its case, a sleeve like a sheath but made of delicately carved onyx, and went to face Maris.

He was on his way back to the captain's chamber when his eyes snagged on the familiar threads of *Antari* magic. At first he thought he was simply catching sight of Kell, whose iridescence always trailed behind him like a coat, but when he rounded the corner, the magician was nowhere to be seen. Instead, the threads of magic were spilling from a table where they wrapped around a ring.

It was old, the metal fogged with age, and wide, the length of one full knuckle, and it sat on a table with a hundred others, each in an open box—but where the rest were woven with threads of blue and green, gold and red, this one was knotted with that unsteady color, like oil and water, that marked an *Antari.*

Alucard took it up, and went to find Kell.

III

Despite a wealth of natural magic, and years of rigorous study alongside the *Aven Essen,* Kell didn't know everything there was to know about spells. He *knew* that, but it was still disconcerting to be surrounded by so much *evidence* in support of the fact. In Maris's market, Kell didn't even *recognize* half the objects, let alone the enchantments woven through them. When the spellwork was written on an object's surface, he could usually make it out, but most of the talismans bore nothing but a design, a flourish. Now and then he could *feel* their intent, not a specific purpose so much as a general sense, but that was all.

He could tell the *Feras Stras* was a place where most people came with an object in mind, a goal, and the longer he wandered without one, the more he began to feel lost.

Which was likely why he found the room of knives so comforting. It was the kind of place Lila would gravitate to; the smallest weapon was no longer than his palm, the largest greater than the spread of his arms.

He knew Maris didn't deal in ordinary weapons, but as he squinted at the spellwork shorthand carved into the hilts and blades—every magician had their own dialect—he was still taken aback by the variety.

Swords to cut wounds that would not heal.

Knives to bleed truth instead of blood.

Weapons that channeled power, or stole it, or killed with a single stroke, or—

A low whistle behind him as Alucard appeared at the entrance.

"Picking out a gift?" asked the captain.

"No."

"Good, then take this." He dropped a ring into Kell's hand.

Kell frowned. "I'm flattered, but I think you're asking the wrong brother."

An exasperated sound escaped the man's throat. "I don't know what it *does,* but it's . . . like you. And I don't mean pompous and infuriating. The magic surrounding that ring—it's *Antari.*"

Kell straightened. "Are you sure?" He squinted at the band. It bore no seals, no obvious spellwork, but the metal hummed faintly against his skin, resonating. Up close, the silver was grooved, not in patterns but in rings. Tentatively, Kell slipped it onto his finger. Nothing happened—not that anything would, of course, since the ship was warded. He let the band slide back off into his palm.

"If you want it, buy it yourself," he said, handing it to Alucard. But the captain shied away.

"I can't," he said. "There's something else I need."

"What could you possibly need?"

Alucard looked purposefully away. "Time is wasting, Kell. Just take it."

Kell sighed and lifted the ring again, holding it between both hands and turning it slowly in search of markings or clues. And then, the strangest thing happened. He pulled gently, and part of the ring *came away* in his hand.

"Just perfect," said Alucard, looking around, "now you've gone and broken it."

But Kell didn't think he had. Instead of holding two broken pieces of one ring, he was now holding two *rings,* the original somehow unchanged, as if it hadn't given up half of itself to make the second, which was an exact replica of its brother. The two bands both thrummed in his hands, singing against his skin. Whatever they were, they were strong.

And Kell knew they'd need every drop of strength they could muster.

"Come on," he said, sliding both rings into his pocket. "Let's go see Maris."

They found Lila still standing outside the woman's door. Kell could tell it had taken a feat of self-restraint for her to stay put, with so many treasures strewn across the ship. She fidgeted, hands in the pockets of her coat.

"Well?" asked Alucard. "Did you get it?"

She shook her head. "Not yet."

"Why not?"

"I'm saving the best for last."

"Lila," chided Kell, "we only have one chance—"

"Yes," she said, straightening. "So I guess you'll have to trust me."

Kell shifted his weight. He wanted to trust her. He *didn't,* but he wanted to. For the moment, it would have to be enough.

At last, she flashed a small, sharp smile. "Hey, want to make a bet?"

"No," said Kell and Alucard at the same time.

Lila shrugged, but when he held the door for her, she didn't follow.

"Trust," she said again, leaning on the rail as if she had nowhere else to be. Alucard cleared his throat, and Maris was waiting, and finally Kell had no choice but to leave Lila there, staring hungrily out at the market.

Inside, Maris was sitting at her desk, paging through the ledger. They stood there, silently waiting for her to look up at them. She didn't.

"Go on, then," she said, turning the page.

Alucard went first. He stepped forward and produced, of all things, a *mirror.*

"You've got to be joking," growled Kell, but Maris only smiled.

"Captain Emery, you always have had a knack for finding rare and precious things."

"How do you think I found you?"

"Flattery is no payment here."

The sapphire above Alucard's eye winked. "And yet, like coin, it never hurts."

"Ah," she countered, "but like coin, I have no interest in it, either."
She put down the ledger and held one hand out, across the table, but
to the side, her fingers drifting toward a large sphere in a stand beside
the desk. At first, Kell had taken the object for a globe, its surface raised
and dented with impressions that could have been land and sea. But
now he saw that it was something else entirely.

"Five years," she said.

Alucard let out a small, audible gasp, as if he'd taken a blow to the
ribs. "Two."

Maris steepled her fingers. "Do I look like the kind of person
who haggles?"

The captain swallowed. "No, Maris."

"You're young enough to bear the cost."

"Four."

"Alucard," she warned.

"A lot can be done with a year," he countered. "And I have already
lost three."

She sighed. "Very well. Four."

Kell still didn't understand, not until Alucard set the mirror on the
desk's edge and went to the sphere. Not until he placed his hands in
the grooves on either side as the dial turned, ticking up from zero to
four.

"Do we have a deal?" she asked.

"Yes," answered Alucard, bowing his head.

Maris reach out and pulled a lever on the sphere's stand, and Kell
watched in horror as a shudder wracked the captain's body, shoulders
hunched against the strain. And then it was done. The device let go,
or he did, and the captain took up his bounty and retreated, cradling
the mirror against his chest.

His face had altered slightly, the hollows in his cheeks deepen-
ing, the faintest creases showing at the corners of his eyes. He'd aged
a fraction.

Four *years*.

Kell's attention snapped back to the sphere. It was, like the Inheritor around Maris's neck, like so many things here, a forbidden kind of

magic. Transferring power, transferring *life,* these things contradicted nature, they—

"And you, princeling?" said Maris, her pale eyes dancing in her dark face.

Kell tore his gaze from the sphere and dug the rings from his coat pocket, and came up with one instead of two. He froze, afraid he'd somehow dropped the second, or worse, that the coat had eaten it the way it sometimes did with coins, but Maris didn't seem concerned.

"Ah," she said as he placed the object on the desk, "*Antari* binding rings. Alucard, your little *talent* is quite a nuisance sometimes."

"How do they work?" asked Kell.

"Do I look like a set of instructions?" She sat back. "Those have been sitting in my market for a very long time. Fickle things, they take a certain touch, and you could say that touch has all but died off, though between my boat and yours, you've managed quite a collection." Shock rattled through him. Kell started to speak, but she waved a hand. "The third *Antari* means nothing to me. My interests are bounded by this ship. But as for your purchase." She steepled her fingers. "Three."

Three years.

It could have been more.

But it could have been less.

"My life is not my own," he said slowly.

Maris raised a brow, the small gesture causing the wrinkles to multiply like cracks across her face. "That is your problem, not mine."

Alucard had gone silent behind him, his eyes open but vacant, as if his mind were somewhere else.

"What good is this to you," pressed Kell, "if no one else can use it?"

"Ah, but *you* can use it," she countered, "and therein lies its worth."

"If I refuse, we both end up empty-handed. As you said, Maris, I am a dying breed."

The woman considered him over her fingertips. "Hm. Two for making a valid point," she said, "and one for annoying me. The cost stays at three, Kell Maresh." He started to back away when she added, "It would be wise of you to take this deal."

And there was something in her gaze, something old and steady, and he wondered if she saw something he couldn't. He hesitated, then moved to the sphere and placed his fingers in the grooves.

The dial ticked down from four to three.

Maris pulled the lever.

It did not hurt, not exactly. The orb seemed to suddenly bind to his hands, holding them in place. His pulse surged in his head, and there was a short, dull ache in his chest, as if someone were drawing the air from his lungs, and then it was done. Three years, gone in three seconds. The sphere released him, and he closed his eyes against a shallow wave of dizziness before taking up the ring, now rightfully his. Bought and paid for. He wanted to be free of this room, this ship. But before he could escape, Maris spoke again, voice heavy as stone.

"Captain Emery," she said. "Give us the room."

Kell turned to see Alucard vanish through the door, leaving him alone with the ancient woman who'd just robbed him of three years of life.

She rose from the table, knuckles whitening on her cane as she used it to lever her old body up, then crossed behind the sphere.

"Captain?" he prompted, but she didn't speak, not yet. He watched as the old woman splayed one hand across its top. She murmured a few words, and the surface of the metal glowed, a tracery of light that withdrew line by line beneath her fingers. When it was gone, Maris exhaled, shoulders loosening as if a weight had been lifted.

"*Anesh*," she said, wiping her hands. There was a new ease to her motions, a straightness to her spine. "Kell Maresh," she said, turning the name over on her tongue. "The prize of the Arnesian crown. The *Antari* raised as royalty. We've met before, you and I."

"No, we haven't," said Kell, even though the sight of her tickled something in his mind. Not a memory, he realized, but the absence of one. The place where a memory should be. The place where it was *missing*.

He'd been five years old when he was given to the royal family, deposited at the palace with nothing but a sheathed knife, the letters *KL* carved into its hilt, and a memory spell burned into the crook of his arm, his short life before that moment erased.

"You were young," she said. "But I thought by now you might remember."

"You knew me before?" His head spun at the thought. "How?"

"I deal in rare things, *Antari*. There are few things rarer than you. I met your parents," continued Maris. "They brought you here."

Kell felt dizzy, ill. "Why?"

"Perhaps they were greedy," she said absently. "Perhaps they were afraid. Perhaps they wanted what was best. Perhaps they wanted only to be rid of you."

"If you know the answer—"

"Do *you* really want to know?" she cut in.

He started to say *yes,* the word automatic, but it stuck in his throat. How many years had he lain awake in bed, thumb brushing the scar at his elbow, wondering who he was, who he'd *been,* before?

"Do you want to know the last thing your mother said? What the initials stand for on your father's knife? Do you want to know who your true family was?"

Maris rounded her desk and took her seat with a slow precision that belied her age. She took up a quill and scribbled something on a slip of parchment, folding it twice into a small, neat square. She held it out between two aged fingers.

"To remove the spell I put on you."

Kell stared at the paper, his vision sliding in and out. He swallowed. "What is the price?"

A smile played across the woman's old mouth. "This one, and this one alone, is free. Call it a debt now paid, a kindness, or a closing door. Call it whatever you want, but expect nothing more."

He willed his body forward, willed his hand not to tremble as it reached for the paper.

"You still have that crease between your eyes," she said. "Still the same sad-faced boy you were that day."

Kell closed his fist around the slip of paper. "Is that all, Maris?"

A sigh escaped like steam between her lips. "I suppose." But her voice followed him through the door. "Strange thing about forgetting spells," she added as he hovered on the threshold, caught between shadow and sharp light. "Most will fade on their own. Stuck on at first, sure as stone. But over time, they slide right off. Unless we don't *want* to let them go. . . ."

With that, a gust of wind cut through, and the door to Maris's market swung shut behind him.

IV

The market called to Delilah Bard.

She couldn't see the threads of magic like Alucard, couldn't read the spells like Kell, but the pull was there all the same, enticing as new coins, fine jewels, sharp weapons.

Temptation: that was the word for it, the urge to let herself look, touch, take.

But that shine, that unspoken promise—of strength, of power—reminded Lila of the sword she'd found back in Grey London, the way Vitari's magic had called to her through the steel, singing of promise. Almost everything in her life had changed since that night, but she still didn't trust that kind of blind, bottomless want.

So she waited.

Waited until the sounds beyond the door had stopped, waited until Kell and Alucard were gone, waited until there was no one and nothing left to stop her, until Maris was alone, and the want in Lila's chest had cooled into something hard, sharp, usable.

And then she went in.

The old woman was at her desk, cupping Lila's watch in one gnarled hand as if it were a piece of ripened fruit as she drew a nail across the crystal surface.

It is not Barron, Lila told herself. *That watch is not him. It's just a thing, and things are meant to be used.*

The dog heaved a sigh beneath Maris's feet, and it must have been a trick of the light, because the queen of the market looked . . . younger. Or, at least, a few wrinkles shy of ancient.

"Nothing strike your fancy, dearie?" she said without looking up.

"I know what I want."

Maris set the watch down, then, with a surprising degree of care. "And yet, your hands are empty."

Lila pointed at the Inheritor hanging from the woman's throat. "That's because you're wearing my prize."

Maris's hand drifted up. "This old piece?" she demurred, twirling the Inheritor between her fingers as if it were a simple pendant.

"What can I say?" said Lila casually. "I have a weakness for antiquated things."

A smile split the old woman's face, the innocence shed like a skin. "You know what it is."

"A smart pirate keeps her best treasure close."

Maris's sandy eyes drifted back to the silver watch. "A valid point. And if I refuse?"

"You said everything had a price."

"Perhaps I lied."

Lila smiled and said without malice, "Then perhaps I'll just cut it from your wrinkled neck."

A gravelly laugh. "You wouldn't be the first to try, but I don't think that would go well for either of us." She traced the hem of her white tunic. "You wouldn't believe how hard it is to get blood out of these clothes." Maris took up the watch again, weighing it in her palm. "You should know, I don't often take things without power, but then few people realize that memory casts its own spell, that it writes itself on an object just like magic, waiting to be picked over—or picked apart—by clever fingers. Another city. Another home. Another life. All bound up in something as simple as a cup, a coat, a silver watch. The past is a powerful thing, don't you think?"

"The past is the past."

A withering look. "Lies don't write themselves on me, Miss Bard."

"I'm not lying," said Lila. "The past is the past. It doesn't live in any one thing. It certainly doesn't live in something that can be given away. If it did, I would have just handed you everything I was, everything I am. But you can't have that, not even for a look around your market."

Lila tried to slow her heartbeat before continuing. "What you *can* have is a silver watch."

Maris's gaze held hers. "A pretty speech." She lifted the Inheritor over her head and set it on the desk beside the timepiece. Her face betrayed no strain, but when the object hit the wood, it made a solid sound, as if it weighed a great deal more than it seemed, and the woman's shoulders seemed lighter for the lack of it. "What will you give me?"

Lila cocked her head. "What do you *want*?"

Maris leaned back and crossed her legs, one white boot resting on the dog's back. It didn't seem to mind. "You'd be surprised how rarely people ask. They come here assuming I'll want their money or power, as if I've any need for either."

"Why run this market, then?"

"Someone has to keep an eye on things. Call it a passion, or a hobby. But as to the question of payment . . ." She sat forward. "I'm an old woman, Miss Bard—older than I look—and I really want only one thing."

Lila lifted her chin. "And what is that?"

She spread her hands. "Something I don't already have."

"A tall order, by the looks of this place."

"Not really," said Maris. "You want the Inheritor. I'll sell it to you for the price of an eye."

Lila's stomach turned. "You know," she said, fighting to keep her tone airy, "I need the one I have."

Maris chuckled. "Believe it or not, dearie, I'm not in the business of blinding my customers." She held out her hand. "The broken one will do."

Lila watched the lid of the small black box close over her glass eye.

The cost had been higher, the loss greater, than she realized when she first agreed. The eye had always been useless, its origins as strange and lost to her as the accident that took her real one. She'd wondered about it, of course—the craftwork so fine it must have been stolen—but for all that, Lila wasn't sentimental. She'd never been particularly attached to the ball of glass, but the moment it was gone, she felt suddenly wrong, exposed. A deformity on display, an absence made visible.

It is only a thing, she told herself again, *and things are meant to be used.*

Her fingers tightened on the Inheritor, relishing the pain as it cut into her palm.

"The instructions are written on the side," Maris was saying. "But perhaps I should have mentioned that the vessel is empty." The woman's expression went coy, as if she'd managed a trick. As if she thought Lila was after the remains of someone else's power instead of the device itself.

"Good," she said simply. "That's even better."

The woman's thin lips curled with amusement, but if she wanted to know more, she didn't ask. Lila started toward the door, combing the hair over her missing eye.

"A patch will help," said Maris, setting something on the table. "Or perhaps this."

Lila turned back.

The box was small and white and open, and at first, it looked empty, nothing but a swatch of crushed black velvet lining its sides. But then the light shifted and the object caught the sun, glinting faintly.

It was a sphere roughly the size and shape of an eye.

And it was solid black.

"Everyone knows the mark of an *Antari,*" explained Maris. "The all-black eye. There was a fashion, oh, about a century ago—those who'd lost an eye in battle or by accident and found themselves in need of a false one would don one of blackened glass, passing themselves off as more than they were. The fashion ended, of course, when those ambitious, misguided few discovered that an *Antari* is much more than a marking. Some were challenged to duels they could not win, some were kidnapped or murdered for their magic, and some simply couldn't stand the pressure. As such, these eyes became quite rare," said Maris. "Almost as rare as you."

Lila didn't realize she'd crossed the room until she felt her fingers brush the smooth black glass. It seemed to sing beneath her touch, as if wanting to be held. "How much?"

"Take it."

Lila looked up. "A gift?"

Maris laughed softly, the sound of steam escaping a kettle. "This is the *Ferase Stras,*" she said. "Nothing is free."

"I've already given you my left eye," growled Lila.

"And while an eye for an eye is enough for some—for this," she said, nudging the box toward Lila, "I'll need something more precious."

"A heart?"

"A favor."

"What kind of favor?"

Maris shrugged. "I suppose I'll know when I need it. But when I call you, you will come."

Lila hesitated. It was a dangerous deal, she knew, the kind villains coaxed from maidens in fairy tales, and devils from lost men, but she still heard herself answer, a single binding word.

"Yes."

Maris's smile cracked wider. "*Anesh,*" she said. "Try it on."

When she had it in, Lila stood before the mirror, blinking fiercely at her changed appearance, the startling difference of a shadow cast across her face, a pit of darkness so complete it registered as absence. As if a piece of her were missing—not an eye, but an entire self.

The girl from Grey London.

The one who picked pockets and cut purses and froze to death on winter nights with only pride to keep her warm.

The one without a family, without a world.

This new eye looked startlingly strange, wrong, and yet right.

"There," said Maris. "Isn't that better?"

And Lila smiled, because it was.

V

The slip of paper Maris had given Kell still blazed against his palm, but he kept his fist closed tight around it as he and Alucard stood, waiting, beyond the door.

He was worried that if they crossed the platform and left the ship, they wouldn't be allowed back on, and given Lila's tendency for trouble, Kell wanted to stay close.

But then the door swung open and Lila stepped through, the Inheritor clutched in her hand. And yet it wasn't the scroll-like device that caught his attention. It was Lila's smile, a dazzling, happy smile, and just above, a sphere of glossy black where shattered brown had been. Kell sucked in a breath.

"Your eye," he said.

"Oh," said Lila with a smirk, "you noticed."

"Saints, Bard," said Alucard. "Do I want to know how much *that* cost?"

"Worth every penny," she said.

Kell reached out and tucked the hair behind Lila's ear so he could see it better. The eye looked stark and strange and utterly right. His own gaze didn't clash against it, the way it did with Holland's, and yet, now that it was there, her eyes divided into brown and black, he couldn't imagine ever thinking she was ordinary. "It suits you."

"Not to interrupt . . ." said Alucard behind them.

Lila tossed him the Inheritor as if it were a mere coin, a simple to-ken instead of the entire goal of their mad mission, their best—and maybe only—chance of saving London. Kell's stomach dropped, but Alucard snatched the talisman from the air just as easy.

He crossed the plank between the market and the *Ghost,* Lila falling in step behind him, but Kell lingered. He looked down at the paper in his hand. It was nothing but parchment, yet it could have weighed more than stone, the way it rooted him to the wooden floor.

Your true family.

But what did that mean? Was family the ones you were born to, or the ones who took you in? Did the first years of his life weigh more than the rest?

Strange thing about forgetting spells.

Rhy was his brother.

They fade on their own.

London was his home.

Unless we don't let go.

"Kell?" called Lila, looking over her shoulder with those two-toned eyes. "You coming?"

He nodded. "I'm right behind you."

His fingers closed over the paper, and with a brush of heat, it caught fire. He let it burn, and when the note was nothing but ashes, he tipped them over the side, letting the wind catch them before they ever hit the sea.

The crew stood on deck, gathered around a wooden crate—the make-shift table where Kell had set the bounty for which he'd paid three years.

"Tell me again," said Lila, "why, with a ship full of shiny things, you bought yourself a ring."

"It's not just a ring," he protested with far more certainty than he felt.

"Then what is it?" asked Jasta, arms crossed, still clearly bitter from being turned away.

"I don't exactly know," he said, defensively. "Maris called it a *binding* ring."

"No," corrected Alucard. "Maris called it binding *rings*."

"There's more than one?" asked Holland.

Kell took up the loop of metal and pulled, the way he had before, one ring becoming two the way Lila's knives did, only these had no hidden clasp. It wasn't an illusion. It was magic.

He set the newly made second ring back atop the crate, wondering at the original. Perhaps two was the limit of its power, but he didn't think it was.

Again Kell held the ring in both hands, and again he pulled, and again it came apart.

"That one never gets smaller," noted Lila, as Kell tried to make a fourth ring. It didn't work. There was no resistance, no rebuff. The refusal was simple and solid, as if the ring simply had no more to give.

All magic has limits.

It was something Tieren would say.

"And you're sure it's *Antari*-made?" asked Lenos.

"That's what *Alucard* said," said Kell, cutting him a look.

Alucard threw up his hands. "*Maris* confirmed it. She called them *Antari* binding rings."

"All right," said Lila. "But what do they *do*?"

"That she wouldn't say."

Hastra took up one of the spell-made rings and squinted through it, as if expecting to see something beside Kell's face on the other side.

Lenos poked at the second with his index finger, startling a little when it rolled away, not a specter, but a solid band of metal.

It tumbled right off the crate, and Holland caught it as it fell, his chains rattling against the wood.

"Would you take these foolish things off?"

Kell looked to Lila, who frowned back but didn't threaten mutiny. He slipped the original ring on his finger so he wouldn't drop it as he undid the manacles. They fell away with a heavy thud, everyone on deck tensing at the sudden sound, the knowledge that Holland was free.

Lila plucked the third ring from Hastra's grip.

"A little plain, aren't they?" She started to put it on, then cut a look at Holland, who was still considering the band of metal in his palm. Her eyes narrowed in distrust—they were *binding* rings, after all—but the moment Holland returned his ring to the crate, Lila flashed Kell a wicked grin.

"Shall we see what they do?" she asked, already sliding the silver band onto her finger.

"Lila, wait—" Kell started tugging his own ring off, but he was too late. The moment the band crossed her knuckle, it hit him like a blow.

Kell let out a short, breathless cry and doubled over, bracing himself against the crate as the deck tilted violently beneath him. It wasn't pain, but something just as deep. As if a thread in the very center of his being had pulled suddenly tight, and his whole self thrummed with the sudden tension of the cord.

"*Mas vares,*" Hastra was saying, "what's wrong?"

Nothing was *wrong.* Power coursed through him, so bright it lit the world, every one of his senses singing with the strain. His vision blurred, overwhelmed by the sudden surge, and when he managed to focus, to look at Lila, he could almost *see* the threads running between them, a metallic river of magic.

Her eyes were wide, as if she saw it, too.

"Huh," said Alucard, gaze flicking along the lines of power. "So that's what Maris meant."

"What is it?" asked Jasta, unable to see.

Kell straightened, the threads humming beneath his skin. He wanted to try something, so he reached, not with his hands, but with his will, and drew a fraction of Lila's magic toward him. It was like drinking light, warm and lush and startlingly bright, and suddenly anything felt possible. Was this what the world looked like to Osaron? Was this how it *felt* to be invincible?

Across the deck, Lila frowned at the shifting balance.

"That's mine," she said, wrenching the power back. As quick as it had come, the magic was gone, not just Lila's borrowed stake but his natural well, and, for a terrifying moment, Kell's world went black. He staggered and fell to his hands and knees on the deck. Nearby, Lila let out a sound that was part shock, part triumph, as she claimed his power as her own.

"Lila," he said, but his voice was unsteady, weak, swallowed by the whipping wind and the rocking ship and that sudden, gutting absence of strength, too like the cursed collar and the metal frame. Kell's whole body shook, his vision flickered, and through the spotted dark he saw her bring her hands together and, with nothing but a smile, summon an arc of flame.

"*Lila, stop,*" he gasped, but she didn't seem to hear him. Her gaze was empty, elsewhere, her attention consumed by the gold-red light of the fire as it grew and grew around her, threatening to brush the wooden boards of the *Ghost,* rising toward the canvas sail. A shout went up. Kell tried to rise, but couldn't. His hands tingled with heat, but he couldn't pull the ring from his finger. It was stuck, fused in place by whatever spellwork bound the two of them together.

And then, as sudden as the gain of Lila's magic, the loss of his, a new wave of magic surged through his veins. It wasn't coming from Lila, who still stood at the burning center of her own world. It was a third source, sharp and cold but just as bright. Kell's vision focused and he saw *Holland,* the final ring on his hand, its presence flooding the paths between them with fresh magic.

Kell's own power came back like air into starved lungs as the other *Antari* peeled away thread after thread of Lila's magic, the fire in her hands shrinking as the power was drawn away, divided between them, the air around Holland's hands dancing with tendrils of stolen flame.

Lila blinked rapidly, waking from the power's thrall. Startled, she dragged the ring from her finger, and nearly toppled over from the sudden spike and subsequent loss of power. As soon as the band was free of her hand, it melted away, first dissolving into a ribbon of silver mist and then—nothing.

Without her presence, the connection shuddered and shortened, drawing taut between Kell and Holland, the light of their collective power dimming a fraction. Again Kell tried to wrench the ring from his finger. Again he couldn't. It wasn't until *Holland* withdrew his own band, the echo of Kell's original, that the spell broke and his ring came free, tumbling to the wooden deck and rolling several feet before Alucard stopped it with the toe of his boot.

For a long moment, no one spoke.

Lila was leaning heavily against the rail, the deck scorched beneath her feet. Holland braced one hand against the mast for balance. Kell shivered, fighting the urge to be sick.

"What—" gasped Lila, "—the bloody hell—just happened?"

Hastra whistled softly to himself as Alucard knelt and retrieved the abandoned ring. "Well," he mused. "I'd say that was worth three years."

"Three years of what?" asked Lila, swaying as she tried to straighten. Kell glared at the captain, even as he sagged back against a stack of crates.

"No offense, Bard," continued Alucard, scuffing his boot where Lila had scorched the deck. "But your form could use some work."

Kell's head was pounding so loudly, it took him a moment to realize Holland was talking, too.

"This is how we do it," he was saying quietly, his green eye fever-bright.

"Do what?" asked Lila.

"This is how we catch Osaron." Something crossed Holland's face. Kell thought it *might* have been a smile. "This is how we *win*."

VI

Rhy sat atop his mount, squinting through the London fog for signs of life.

The streets were too still, the city too empty.

In the last hour, he hadn't found a single survivor. He'd hardly seen anyone at all, for that matter. The cursed, who'd moved like echoes through the beat of their lives, had withdrawn into their homes, leaving only the shimmering mist and the black rot spreading inch by inch over the city.

Rhy looked to the shadow palace, sitting like oil atop the river, and for a moment he wanted to spur his horse up the icy bridge to the doors of that dark, unnatural place. Wanted to force his way in. To face the shadow king himself.

But Kell had said to wait. *I have a plan,* he'd said. *Do you trust me?*

And Rhy did.

He turned the horse away.

"Your Highness," said the guard, meeting him at the mouth of the road.

"Have you found any more?" asked Rhy, heart sinking when the man shook his head.

They rode back toward the palace in silence, only the sound of their horses ringing through the deserted streets.

Wrong, said his gut.

They reached the plaza, and he slowed his horse as the palace steps came into view. There at the base of the stairs stood a young woman with a bunch of flowers in her hand. Winter roses, their petals frosty white. As he watched, she knelt and placed the bouquet on the steps. It was such an ordinary gesture, the kind of thing a commoner would have done on a normal winter day, an offering, a thanks, a prayer, but it wasn't a normal winter day, and everything about it was out of place against the backdrop of fog and barren streets.

"*Mas vares?*" said the guard as Rhy dismounted.

Wrong, beat his heart.

"Take the horses and get inside," he ordered, starting forward on foot across the plaza. As he drew near, he could see the darkness splashed like paint across the other flowers, dripping onto the pale polished stone beneath.

The woman didn't look up, not until he was nearly at her side, and then she rose and tipped her chin to the palace, revealing eyes that swirled with fog, veins traced black with the shadow king's curse.

Rhy stilled, but didn't retreat.

"All things rise and all things fall," she said, her voice high and sweet and lilting, as if reciting a bit of song. "Even castles. Even kings."

She didn't notice Rhy—or so he thought, until her hand shot out, thin fingers clutching the armor plate of his forearm so hard it buckled. "He sees you now, hollow prince."

Rhy tore free, stumbling back against the steps.

"Broken toy soldier."

He got to his feet again.

"Osaron will cut your threads."

Rhy kept his back to the palace as he retreated up, one step, two.

But on the third stair, he stumbled.

And on the fourth, the shadows came.

The woman gave a manic little laugh, wind rippling her skirts as Osaron's puppets poured from the houses and the shops and the alleys, ten, twenty, fifty, a hundred. They appeared at the edge of the palace plaza, holding iron bars, axes, and blades, fire and ice and rock. Some were young and others old, some tall and others little more than children, and all of them under the shadow king's spell.

"There can be only one castle," called the woman, following Rhy as he scrambled up the stairs. "There can be only one—"

An arrow took her in the chest, loosed by a guard above. The young woman staggered a step before wrapping those same delicate fingers around the arrow's shaft and ripping it free. Blood spilled down her front, more black than red, but she dragged herself after him another few steps before her heart failed, her limbs folded, her body died.

Rhy reached the landing and spun back to see his city.

The first wave of the assault had reached the base of the palace steps. He recognized one of the men at the front—thought, for a terrifying second, that it was Alucard, before Rhy realized it was the captain's older brother. Lord Berras.

And when Berras saw the prince—and he *did* see him now—those curse-dark eyes narrowed and a feral, joyless smile spread across his face. Flame danced around one hand.

"Tear it down," he boomed in a voice lower and harder than his brother's. "Tear it *all* down."

It was more than a rally—it was a general's command, and Rhy stared in shock and horror as the mass surged up the stairs. He drew his sword as something blazed in the sky above, a comet of fire launched by another, unseen foe. A pair of guards hauled him backward into the palace a breath before the blast struck the wards and shattered in a blaze of light, blinding but futile.

The guards slammed the doors, the nightmarish view beyond the palace replaced suddenly by dark wood and the muted resonance of strong magic, and then, sickeningly, by the sound of bodies striking stone, wood, glass.

Rhy staggered back from the doors and hurried to the nearest bay of windows.

Until that day, Rhy had never seen what happened when a forbidden body threw itself against an active ward. At first, it was simply repelled, but as it tried again and again and again, the effect was roughly that of steel against thick ice, one chipping away at the other while also ruining itself. The wards on the palace shuddered and cracked, but so did the cursed. Blood ran from their noses and ears as they threw element and spell and fist against the walls, clawed at the foundation, threw themselves against the doors.

"What is going on?" demanded Isra, storming into the foyer. When the head of the royal guard saw the prince, she recoiled a step and bowed. "Your Highness."

"Find the king," said Rhy as the palace shook around him. "We are under attack."

❦

At this rate, the wards wouldn't hold. Rhy didn't need a gift for magic to see that. The palace gallery shook with the force of the bodies throwing themselves against the wood and stone. They were on the banks. They were on the steps. They were on the river.

And they were killing themselves.

The *shadow king* was killing them.

All around priests scrambled to draw fresh concentration rings on the gallery floor. Spells to focus magic. To bolster the wards.

Where was Kell?

Light flared against the glass with every blow, the spellwork straining to hold under the strength of the attack.

The royal palace was a shell. And it was cracking.

The walls trembled, and several people screamed. Nobles huddled together in corners. Magicians barred the doors, braced for the palace to break. Prince Col stood before his sister like a human shield while Lord Sol-in-Ar instructed his entourage in a rapid stream of Faroan.

Another blast, and the wards fractured, light webbing across the windows. Rhy lifted his hand to the glass, expecting it to shatter.

"Get back," ordered his mother.

"Every magician stand within a circle," ordered his father. Maxim had appeared in the first moments of the attack looking drawn but determined. Blood flecked his cuff, and Rhy wondered, dazedly, if his father had been fighting. Tieren was at his side. "I thought you said the wards would hold," snapped the king.

"Against Osaron's spell," replied the priest, drawing another circle on the floor. "Not against the brute force of three hundred souls."

"We have to stop them," said Rhy. He hadn't worked so hard and saved so few only to watch the rest of his people break themselves against these walls.

"Emira," ordered the king, "get everyone else into the Jewel."

The Jewel was the ballroom at the very center of the palace, the farthest from the outer walls. The queen hesitated, eyes wide and lost as she looked from Rhy to the windows.

"Emira, *now*."

At that moment, a strange transformation happened in his mother. She seemed to wake from a trance; she drew herself up and began to speak in crisp, clear Arnesian. "Brost, Losen, with me. You can hold up a circle, yes? Good. Ister," she said, addressing one of the female priests, "come and set the wards."

The walls shook, a deep, dangerous rattle.

"They will not hold," said the Veskan prince, drawing a blade as if the foe were flesh and blood, a thing that could be cut down.

"We need a plan," said Sol-in-Ar. "Before this sanctuary becomes a cage."

Maxim spun on Tieren. "The sleeping spell. Is it ready?"

The old priest swallowed. "Yes, but—"

"Then, for saint's sake," cut in the king, "*do it now*."

Tieren stepped in, lowering his voice. "Magic of this size and scale requires an anchor."

"What do you mean?" asked Rhy.

"A magician to hold the spell in place."

"One of the priests, then—" started Maxim.

Tieren shook his head. "The demands of such a spell are too steep. The wrong mind will break. . . ."

Understanding hit Rhy.

"No," he said, "not you—" even as his father's order came down:

"See it done."

The *Aven Essen* nodded. "Your Majesty," said Tieren, adding, "once it's started, I won't be able to help you with—"

"It's all right," interrupted the king. "I can finish it myself. Go."

"Stubborn as ever," said the old man, shaking his head. But he didn't argue, didn't linger. Tieren turned on his heel, robes fluttering, and called to three of his priests, who fell into his wake. Rhy hurried after them.

"Tieren!" he called. The old man slowed but didn't stop. "What is my father talking about?"

"The king's business is his own."

Rhy stepped in front of him. "As the royal prince, I demand to know what he is doing."

The *Aven Essen* narrowed his eyes, then flicked his fingers, and Rhy felt himself forced physically out of the way as Tieren and his three priests filed past in a flurry of white robes. He brought a hand to his chest, stunned.

"Don't stand there, Prince Rhy," called Tieren, "when you could help to save us all."

Rhy pushed off the wall and hurried after them.

Tieren led the way to the guards' hall, and into the sparring room.

The priests had stripped the space bare, all of the armor and weapons and equipment cleared save for a single wooden table on which sat scrolls and ink, empty vials lying on their sides, the dustlike contents glittering in a shallow bowl.

Even now, with the walls trembling, a pair of priests were hard at work, steady hands scrawling symbols he couldn't read across the stone floor.

"It's time," said Tieren, stripping off his outer robe.

"*Aven Essen,*" said one of the priests, looking up. "The final seals aren't—"

"It will have to do." He undid the collars and cuffs of his white tunic. "I will anchor the spell," he said, addressing Rhy. "If I stir or die, it will break. Do not let that happen, so long as Osaron's own curse holds."

It was all happening too fast. Rhy reeled. "Tieren, please—"

But he stilled as the old man turned and brought his weathered hands to Rhy's face. Despite everything, a sense of calm washed through him.

"If the palace falls, get out of the city."

Rhy frowned, focusing through the sudden peace. "I will *not* run."

A tired smile spread across the old man's face. "That is the right answer, *mas vares.*"

With that, his hands were gone, and the wave of calm vanished. Fear and panic surged, raging anew through Rhy's blood, and when Tieren crossed into the circle of the spell, the prince fought the urge to pull him back.

"Remind your father," said the *Aven Essen,* "that even kings are made of flesh and bone."

Tieren sank to his knees in the center of the circle and Rhy was forced to retreat as the five priests began their work, moving with smooth, confident motions, as if the palace weren't threatening to collapse around them.

One took up a bowl of spelled sand and poured the grainy contents around the traced white line of the circle. Three others took up their places as the last held a burning taper out to Rhy and explained what to do.

He cradled the small flame as if it were a life while the five priests joined hands, heads bowed, and began to recite a spell in a language Rhy himself couldn't speak. Tieren closed his eyes, lips moving in time with the spell, which began to echo against the stone walls, filling the room like smoke.

Beyond the palace, another voice whispered through the cracks in the wards. *"Let me in."*

Rhy knelt, as he'd been told to do, and touched the taper to the sand line that traced the circle.

"Let me in."

The others continued the spell, but as the sand's end lit like a fuse, Tieren's lips stopped moving. He drew a deep breath, and then the old priest began to exhale slowly, emptying his lungs as the flameless fire burned its way around the circle, leaving a charred black line in its wake.

"Let me in," snarled the voice, echoing in the room as the final inches of sand burned away and the last of the air left the priest's lungs.

Rhy waited for Tieren to breathe again.

He didn't.

The *Aven Essen*'s kneeling form slumped sideways, and the other priests were there to catch him before he hit the floor. They lowered his body to the stone, laying him out within the circle as if he were a corpse, cushioning his head, lacing his fingers. One took the taper from Rhy's hands and nested it in the old man's.

The flickering flame went suddenly steady.

The whole room held its breath as the palace shuddered a final time, and then went still.

Beyond the walls, the whispers and the shouts and the pounding of fists and bodies all . . . stopped, a heavy silence falling like a sheet over the city.

The spell was done.

VII

"Give me the ring," said Holland.

Lila raised a brow. It wasn't a question or a plea. It was a *demand*. And considering that the speaker had spent most of the trip chained in the hold, it struck her as a fairly audacious one.

Alucard, who was still cradling the silver band, started to refuse him, but Holland rolled his eyes and flicked his fingers, and the ring shot out of the captain's hand. Lila lunged for it, but Kell caught her arm and the ring landed in Holland's waiting palm.

He turned the band between his hands.

"Why should we let him have it?" she snarled, pulling free.

"Why?" echoed Holland as a sliver of silver came flying toward her. She plucked the second ring out of the air. A moment later, Kell caught the third. "Because I'm the strongest."

Kell rolled his eyes.

"Want to prove it?" growled Lila.

Holland was considering his ring. "There is a difference, Miss Bard, between power and strength. Do you know what that difference is?" His eyes flicked up. "Control."

Indignation flared like a match, not just because she hated Holland, hated what he was insinuating, but because she knew he was right. For all her raw power, it was just that, raw. Unformed. Wild.

She *knew* he was right, but her fingers still itched for a knife.

Holland sighed. "Your distrust is all the more reason to let me do it."

Lila frowned. "How do you figure?"

"The original ring is the anchor." He slipped it onto his thumb. "As such, it is bound to its copies, not the other way around."

Lila didn't follow. It wasn't a feeling she relished. The only thing she relished *less* was the look in Holland's eyes, the smug look of someone who *knew* she was lost.

"The rings will bind our power," he said slowly. "But *you* can break the connection whenever you want, whereas *I* will be tethered to the spell."

A cruel smile cut across Lila's face. She clicked her tongue. "Can't go a day without chaining yourself to someone, can y—"

He was on her in an instant, his fingers wrapped around her throat and her knife against his. Kell threw up his hands in exasperation, Jasta called out a warning about getting blood on her ship, and a second blade came to rest below Holland's jaw.

"Now, now," said Alucard casually, "I know, I've thought of killing you *both,* but in the interest of the greater good, let's try to keep this civil."

Lila lowered her knife. Holland let go of her throat.

They each took a single step back. Annoyance burned through Lila, but so did something else. It took her a second to recognize it. *Shame.* It sat, a cold weight, steaming in her stomach. Holland stood there, features carefully set as if the blow hadn't landed, but it clearly had.

She swallowed, cleared her throat. "You were saying . . . ?"

Holland held her gaze.

"I'm willing to be the anchor of our spell," he said carefully. "As long as we three are bound, my power will be yours."

"And until we choose to break that bond," she countered, "*our* power will be *yours.*"

"It is the only way," pressed Holland. "One *Antari*'s magic wasn't enough to entice Osaron, but together . . ."

"We can lure him in," finished Kell. He looked down at the ring in his hand, then slid it on. Lila saw the moment their powers met. The shudder that passed like a chill between them, the air humming with their combined power.

Lila looked down at her own silver band. She remembered the

power, yes, but also the terrifying sense of being exposed, and yet trapped, laid bare and subject to someone else's will.

She wanted to help, but the idea of binding herself to another—

A shadow crossed her vision as Holland stepped toward her. She didn't look up, didn't want to see his expression, filled with disdain, or worse, whatever was now visible through the crack she'd made.

"It's not easy, is it? To chain yourself to someone else?" A chill ran through her as he threw the words back in her face. She clenched her fist around the ring. "Even when it's for a higher cause," he went on, never raising his voice. "Even when it could save a city, heal a world, change the lives of everyone you know . . ." Her eyes flicked to Kell. "It's a hard choice to make."

Lila met Holland's gaze, expecting—maybe even hoping—to find that cold, implacable calm, perhaps tinged with disgust. Instead, she found shades of sadness, loss. And somehow, strength. The strength to go on. To try again. To trust.

She put on the ring.

ELEVEN

DEATH
AT
SEA

I

To the Nameless Saints who soothe the winds and still the restless sea . . .

Lenos turned his grandmother's talisman between his hands as he prayed.

I beg protection for this vessel—

A sound shuddered through the ship, followed by a swell of cursing. Lenos looked up as Lila got to her feet, steam rising from her hands.

—and those who sail aboard it. I beg kind waters and clear skies as we make our way—

"If you break my ship, I will kill you all," shouted Jasta.

His fingers tightened around the pendant.

—our way into danger and darkness.

"Damned *Antari*," muttered Alucard, storming up the steps to the landing where Lenos stood, elbows on the rail.

The captain slumped down against a crate and produced a flask. "This is why I drink."

Lenos pressed on.

I beg this as a humble servant, with faith in the vast world, in all its power.

He straightened, tucking the necklace back under his collar.

"Did I interrupt?" asked Alucard.

Lenos looked from the singe marks on the deck to Jasta bellowing from the wheel as the ship tipped suddenly sideways under the force of whatever magic the three *Antari* were working, and at last to the man who sat drinking on the floor.

"Not really," said Lenos, folding his long limbs in beside him.

Alucard offered Lenos the flask, but he declined. He'd never been much of a drinker. Never thought the during was much worth the after.

"How do you know they're listening?" asked Alucard, taking another sip. "These saints you pray to?"

The captain wasn't a spiritual man, as far as Lenos could tell, and that was fine. Magic was a river carving its course, picking who to flow through and who to bend around, and for those it bent around, well, there was a reason for that, too. For one thing, they tended to have a better view of the water from the bank. Lenos shrugged, searching for the words. "It's not . . . really . . . a conversation."

Alucard raised a brow, his sapphire glittering in the dying light. "What then?"

Lenos fidgeted. "More like . . . an offering."

The captain made a sound that might have been understanding. Or he might have simply been clearing his throat.

"Always were an odd one," mused Alucard. "How did you even end up on my ship?"

Lenos looked down at the talisman still cradled in one palm. "Life," he said, since he didn't believe in luck—it was the absence of design, and if Lenos believed one thing, it was that everything had an order, a reason. Sometimes you were too close to see it, sometimes too far away, but it was there.

He thought about that, then added, "And Stross."

After all, it had been the *Spire*'s gruff first mate who ran into Lenos in Tanek when he was fresh off the boat from Hanas, who'd taken a shine to him, for one reason or another, and marched him up onto the deck of a new ship, its hull shining, its sails a midnight blue. There an odd lot had gathered, but oddest to Lenos was the man perched atop the wheel.

"Taking in strays, are we?" the man had asked when he caught sight of Lenos. He had an easy way about him, the kind of smile that made you want to smile too. Lenos stared—the sailors in his village had all been sun scorched and scraggly. Even the captains looked like they'd been left out for a summer and a winter and a spring. But this man was young and strong and striking, dressed in crisp black with silver trim.

"The name's Alucard Emery," he'd said, and a murmur had gone through the gathered men, but Lenos didn't have a clue what an Emery was, or why he was supposed to care. "This here's the *Night Spire,* and you're here because she needs a crew. But you're not my crew. Not yet."

He nodded at the nearest man, a towering figure, muscles wound like coarse ropes around his frame. "What can you do?"

A chuckle went through the group.

"Well," said the broad man. "I'm decent at lifting."

"Can read any map," offered another.

"A thief," said a third. "The best you'll find."

Each and every man aboard was more than a sailor. They each had a skill—some had several. And then Alucard Emery had looked at Lenos with that storm-dark gaze.

"And you?" he'd said. "What can *you* do?"

Lenos had looked down at his too-thin form, ribs protruding with every breath, his hands roughened only by a childhood playing on rocky banks. The truth was, Lenos had never been very good at anything. Not natural magic or pretty women, feats of strength or turns of phrase. He wasn't even terribly skilled at sailing (though he could tie a knot and wasn't afraid of drowning).

The only thing Lenos had a knack for was sensing danger—not reading it in a darkened dish, or spotting it in lines of light, but simply *feeling* it, the way one might a tremor underfoot, a coming storm. Sensing it, and steering to avoid it.

"Well?" prompted Alucard.

Lenos swallowed. "I can tell you when there's trouble."

Alucard had raised a brow (there was no sapphire winking from it, then, not until their first outing in Faro).

"Captain," Lenos had added hastily, misreading the man's surprise for insult.

Alucard Emery had flashed another kind of smile. "Well, then," he'd said, "I'll hold you to it."

That was another night, another time, another ship.

But Lenos had always kept his word.

"I've got a bad feeling," he whispered now, looking out to sea. The water was calm, the skies were clear, but there was a weight in his chest like a breath held too long.

"Lenos." Alucard chuckled thinly and got to his feet. "A piece of magic is parading as a god, a poisoned fog is destroying London, and three *Antari* are sparring aboard our ship," said the captain. "I'd be worried if you *didn't*."

II

Bloody hell, thought Lila, as she doubled over on the deck.

After hours of practice, she was dizzy and Kell's skin was slick with sweat, but Holland barely looked winded. She fought the urge to hit him in the stomach before Hano called out from the crow's nest. The ship needed a breeze.

She slumped back onto a crate as the others went to help. She felt like she'd gone three rounds in the *Essen Tasch,* and lost every single one. Every inch of her body—flesh down to bone—ached from using the rings. How the other two *Antari* had the energy left to put wind in the sails, she had no idea.

But the training seemed to be working.

As the ship sailed through the first fingers of dusk, they'd reached a kind of equilibrium. They were now able to balance and amplify their magic without over-drawing from each other. It was such a strange sensation, to be stronger and weaker at the same time, so much power but so hard to wield, like an off-weighted gun.

Even still, the world blazed with magic, the threads of it tracing the air like light, lingering every time Lila blinked. She felt as if she could reach out and pluck one and make the world sing.

She held her hand before her eyes, squinting at the silver ring still wrapped around her middle finger.

It was control. It was balance. It was everything she wasn't, and even now Lila was tempted to chuck it in the sea.

She'd never been one for moderation. Not when she was just a street rat with a quick temper and a quicker knife, and certainly not now that she'd struck flint against the magic in her veins. She knew this about herself, she *liked* it, was convinced it had kept her alive. Alive, but also alone—hard to keep an eye on others when you were keeping both out for yourself.

Lila shivered, the sweat long cold along her scalp.

When had the stars come out?

She dragged herself upright, hopped down from the crate, and was halfway to the hold when she heard the singing. Her body ached, and she wanted a drink, but her feet followed the sound, and soon she found its source. Hastra sat cross-legged with his back against the rail, something cupped in his hands.

Even in the low light, Hastra's brown curls were threaded with gold. He looked young, even younger than she was, and when he saw her standing there, he didn't shy away like Lenos. Instead, Hastra grinned. "Miss Bard," he said warmly. "I like your new eye."

"So do I," she said, sliding to the floor. "What's in your hands?"

Hastra uncurled his fingers to reveal a small blue egg. "I found it on the docks in Rosenal," he said. "You're supposed to sing to eggs, did you know that?"

"To make them hatch?"

Hastra shook his head. "No, they'll do that anyway. You sing to them so they hatch happy."

Lila raised a brow. They were roughly the same age, but there was something *boyish* about Hastra—he was young in a way she'd never been. And yet, the air was always warm around him, the same way it was with Tieren, calm sliding through her mind like silk, like snow. "Kell tells me you should have been a priest."

Hastra's smile saddened. "I know I didn't make a very good guard."

"I don't think he meant it as an insult."

He ran his thumb over the brittle shell. "Are you as famous in your world as Kell is here?"

Lila thought of the wanted posters lining *her* London. "Not for the same reasons."

"But you've decided to stay."

"I think so."

His smile warmed. "I'm glad."

Lila blew out a breath, ruffling her hair. "I wouldn't be," she said. "I tend to make a mess of things."

Hastra looked down at the little blue egg. "Life is chaos. Time is order."

Lila drew her knees up to her chest. "What's that supposed to mean?"

He blushed. "I'm not certain. But Master Tieren said it, so it sounded wise."

Lila started to laugh, then cut off as her body crackled with pain. She really needed that drink, so she left Hastra to his egg and his songs and made her way down into the hold.

The galley wasn't empty.

Jasta sat at the narrow table, a glass in one hand and a deck of cards in the other. Lila's stomach growled, but the room smelled like Ilo had tried (and failed) to make a stew, so she went for the shelf instead, pouring herself a cup of whatever Jasta was already having. Something strong and dark.

She could feel the captain's gaze on her.

"This new eye," mused Jasta, "it suits you."

Lila tipped the cup her way. "Cheers."

Jasta set down her glass and shuffled the deck between both hands. "Sit with me. Play a hand."

Lila scanned the table, which was covered in the remains of a game, empty glasses piled to one side and cards to the other.

"What happened to your last opponent?"

Jasta shrugged. "He lost."

Lila smiled thinly. "I think I'll pass."

Jasta gave a soft grunt. "You won't play because you know you will lose."

"You can't goad me into playing."

"*Tac,* maybe you are not a pirate after all, Bard. Maybe you are just pretending, like Alucard, playing dress-up in clothes that do not fit. Maybe you belong in London, not out here, on the sea."

Lila's smile sharpened. "I belong wherever I choose."

"I think you are a thief, not a pirate."

"A thief steals on land, a pirate at sea. The last time I checked, I was both."

"That is not the true difference," said Jasta. "The true difference is *tarnal*." Lila didn't know the word. The woman must have seen, because she searched for several long seconds and then said, in English, "Fearless."

Lila's eyes narrowed. She didn't realize Jasta spoke anything but Arnesian. Then again, sailors had a way of snatching words up like coins, pocketing them for later.

"You see," continued Jasta, cutting the deck, "a thief plays the game only when they think they'll win. A pirate plays the game even when they think they'll lose."

Lila downed her drink and swung a leg over the bench, her limbs leaden. She rapped her knuckles on the table, her new ring glinting in the lantern light. "All right, Jasta. Deal me in."

The game was Sanct.

"You lose, you drink," said Jasta, dealing the cards. They hissed across the tabletop, face down. Their backs were black and gold. Lila took up her cards and scanned them absently. She knew the rules well enough to know it was less about knowing how to play and more about knowing how to cheat.

"Now tell me," continued the captain, stacking her own hand, "what do you want?"

"That's a broad question."

"And an easy one. If you don't know the answer, you don't know yourself."

Lila paused, thinking. She threw down two cards. A specter and a queen. "Freedom," she said. "And you?"

"What do I want?" mused Jasta. "To win."

She threw down a pair of saints.

Lila swore.

Jasta smiled crookedly. "Drink."

"*How do you know when the Sarows is coming?*" hummed Lila as she made her way down the ship's narrow hall, fingertips skimming either wall for balance.

Right about then, Alucard's warning about Jasta was coming back in full force.

"*Never challenge that one to a drinking contest. Or a sword fight. Or anything else you might lose. Because you will.*"

The boat rocked beneath her feet. Or maybe she was the one rocking. Hell. Lila was slight, but not short of practice, and even so, she'd never had so much trouble holding her liquor.

When she got to her room, she found Kell hunched over the Inheritor, examining the markings on its side.

"Hello, handsome," she said, bracing herself in the doorway.

Kell looked up, a smile halfway to his lips before it fell away. "You're drunk," he said, giving her a long, appraising look. "And you're not wearing any shoes."

"Your powers of observation are astonishing." Lila looked down at her bare feet. "I lost them."

"How do you lose shoes?"

Lila crinkled her brow. "I bet them. I lost."

Kell rose. "To who?"

A tiny hiccup. "Jasta."

Kell sighed. "Stay here." He slipped past her into the hall, a hand alighting on her waist and then, too soon, the touch was gone. Lila made her way to the bed and collapsed onto it, scooping up the discarded Inheritor and holding it up to the light. The spindle at the cylinder's base was sharp enough to cut, and she turned the device carefully between her fingers, squinting to make out the words wrapped around it.

Rosin, read one side.

Cason, read the other.

Lila frowned, mouthing the words as Kell reappeared in the doorway. "*Give—and Take,*" he translated, tossing her the boots.

She sat up too fast, winced. "How did you manage that?"

"I simply explained that she couldn't have them—they wouldn't have fit—and then I gave her mine."

Lila looked down at Kell's bare feet, and burst into laughter. Kell was leaning over her then, pressing a hand over her mouth—*You'll wake the boat*—a ghost of whisper, a caress of air—and she fell back onto the cot, taking him down with her.

"Dammit, Lila." He caught himself just before he slammed his head against the wall. The bed really wasn't big enough for two. "How much did you have to drink?"

Lila's laughter died away. "Never used to drink in company," she mused aloud. Odd to feel herself speaking even though she didn't think to do it. The words just spilled out. "Didn't want to get caught unawares."

"And now?"

That flickering grin. "I think I could take you."

He lowered himself until his hair brushed Lila's temple. "Is that so?" But then something caught his eye through the port window. "There's a ship out there."

Lila's head spun. "How can you see it in the dark?"

Kell frowned. "Because it's burning."

Lila was up in an instant, the world tipping beneath her bare feet. She dug her nails deep into her palms, hoping the pain would clear her head. Danger would have to do the rest.

"What does it mean?" Kell was asking, but she was already sprinting up the stairs.

"Alucard!" she called as she reached the deck.

For a brief, terrible second, the *Ghost* stretched quiet around her, the deck empty, and Lila thought she was too late, but there were no corpses, and a second later the captain was there, Hastra, too, still cradling his egg. Lenos appeared, rubbing the sleep from his eyes, shoulders tensed like he'd woken from bad dreams. Kell caught up, barefoot as he tugged on his coat.

In the distance, the ship burned, a flare of red and gold against the night.

Alucard came to a halt beside her.

"*Sanct,*" he swore, the flames reflected in his eyes.

"*Mas aven . . .*" started Lenos.

And then he made a strange sound, like a hiccup caught in his throat, and Lila turned in time to see the barbed blade protruding from his chest before he was wrenched back over the side, and the Sea Serpents boarded the *Ghost*.

III

For months, Kell had trained alone beneath the royal palace, leaving his sweat and blood to stain the Basin floors. There he'd faced a hundred enemies and fought a hundred forms, sharpened his mind and his magic, learned to use anything and everything at hand, all of it preparing—not for the tournament, which he'd never thought of entering—but for this very moment. So that when death came for him again, he would be ready.

He had trained for a fight in the palace.

Trained for a fight in the streets.

Trained for a fight in daylight and in darkness.

But Kell hadn't thought to train for a fight at sea.

Without Alucard's power filling the sails, the canvases collapsed, twisting the *Ghost* so the water struck sidelong, rocking the ship as the mercenaries spilled onto the deck.

All that was left of Lenos, after the short and fleeting splash, were the drops of blood dappling the wood. A square of calm in a night turned wild—water and wind in Kell's ears, wood and steel beneath his feet, all of it pitching and rolling as if caught in a storm. It was so much louder and sharper than those imagined battles in the Basin, so much more terrifying than those games in the *Essen Tasch,* that for an instant—*only an instant*—Kell froze.

But then the first shout cut the air, and a flash of water surged into ice as Alucard drew a blade from the dark sea, and there was no time to think, no time to plan, no time to do anything but *fight.*

Kell lost sight of Lila within moments, relying on the threads of her magic—the persistent hum of her power in his veins—to tell him she remained alive as the *Ghost* plunged into chaos.

Hastra was grappling with a shadow, his back to the mast, and Kell flicked his wrist, freeing the slivers of steel he kept sheathed within his cuff as the first two killers came for him. His steel nails flew as they had in the Basin so many times, but now they pierced hearts instead of dummies, and for every shadow he killed, another came.

Steel whispered behind him, and Kell turned in time to dodge an assassin's knife. It still found flesh, but sliced his cheek instead of his throat. Pain registered as a distant thing, sharpened only by sea air as his fingers brushed the cut and then caught the assassin's wrist. Ice blossomed up his arm, and Kell let go just as another shadow caught him around the waist and slammed him sideways into the ship's rail.

The wood broke beneath the force, and the two went crashing down into the sea. The surface was a frozen wall, knocking the air from Kell's lungs, icy water flooding in as he grappled with the killer, the churning darkness broken only by the light of the burning ship somewhere above. Kell tried to will the water calm, or at least clear it from his eyes, but the ocean was too big, and even if he'd drawn on Holland and Lila both it wouldn't have been enough. He was running out of air, and he couldn't stomach the thought of Rhy, a London away, gasping for breath again. He had no choice. The next time the killer slashed with a curved knife, Kell let the blow land.

A gasp escaped in a stream of air as the blade sliced his coat sleeve and bit deep into his arm. Instantly the water began to cloud with blood.

"*As Steno,*" he said, the words muffled by the water, his last expelled breath, but still audible and brimming with intent. The mercenary went rigid as his body turned from human flesh to stone and plummeted down toward the sea floor. Kell surged urgently upward in reflected movement and broke through the surface of the waves. From where he was, he could see the attackers' shallow rafts, handholds spelled from wood and steel leading up from the water to the *Ghost*'s deck.

Kell climbed, his arm throbbing and his waterlogged clothes weighing him down with every upward step, but he made it, hauling himself over the side.

"Sir, look out!"

Kell spun as the killer came at him, but the man was drawn up short by Hastra's sword slashing through his back. The assassin folded, and Kell found himself staring into the young guard's terrified eyes. Blood splattered Hastra's face and hands and curls. He looked unsteady on his feet.

"Are you hurt?" asked Kell urgently.

Hastra shook his head. "No, sir," he said, his voice trembling.

"Good," said Kell, retrieving the assassin's knife. "Then let's take back this ship."

IV

Holland was sitting on his cot, studying the band of silver on his thumb, when he heard Lila storming up the stairs, heard the splash of something heavy breaking water, the tread of too many feet.

He rose, and was halfway to the door when the floor tilted and his vision plunged into black, all of his power bottoming out for a sudden, lurching moment.

He scrambled for strength, felt his knees hit the floor, his body a thing severed from his power as someone else pulled on his magic as if it were a rope.

For a terrifying instant, there was nothing, and then, just as suddenly, the room was back, resolving just as it had been before, only now there were shouts overhead, and a burning ship beyond the window, and someone was coming down the steps.

Holland forced himself up, his head still spinning from the shortness of magic.

He tore the abandoned chains from the wall, wrapped them around his hands, and staggered out into the corridor.

Two strangers were coming toward him.

"*Kers la?*" said one as he let himself stumble, fall.

"A prisoner," said a second, seeing the glint of metal and assuming—wrongly—that Holland was still bound.

He heard the hiss of blades sliding free from sheaths as he drew his borrowed power back in like a breath.

Holland's blood sang, magic flooding his veins anew as the

intruder's hand tangled in his hair, wrenching his head back to expose his throat. For a single beat, he let them think they'd won, let them think it would be so easy, and could almost feel their guard lower, their tension ebb.

And then he sprang, twisting up and free in a smooth, almost careless motion and wrapping the chains around his foe's throat before turning the vise from iron to stone. He let go and the man toppled forward, clawing uselessly at his neck as Holland drew the blade from his hip and sliced the second man's throat.

Or tried to.

The killer was fast, dodging back one step, two, dancing around the blade the way Ojka used to, but Ojka never stumbled, and the killer did, erring just long enough for Holland to knock him over and drive the sword down through his back, skewering the man to the floor.

Holland stepped over the writhing bodies and toward the steps.

The scythe came out of nowhere, singing in its special way.

If Athos and Astrid hadn't favored the vicious curls of steel, if Holland hadn't dreamed of using the curved blades to cut their throats—he would have never recognized the tone, would not have known how and when to duck.

He dropped to a knee as the scythe embedded in the wall above his head, and turned just in time to catch a second blade with his bare hands. The steel cut quick and deep, even as he fought to cushion the blow, willing metal and air and bone. The killer leaned into the blade, and Holland's blood dripped thickly to the floor, triumph turning to fear on the man's face as he realized what he'd done.

"*As Isera,*" said Holland, and ice surged out from his ruined palms, swallowing blade and skin in the space of a breath.

The scythe slipped from frozen fingers, Holland's own hands singing with pain. The cuts were deep, but before he could bind them, before he could do anything, a cord wrapped around his throat. His hands went for his neck, but two more cords came out of nowhere, cinching each wrist and forcing his arms wide.

"Hold him," ordered an assassin, stepping over and around the few bodies littering the corridor. In one hand she held a hook. "They want the eye intact."

Holland didn't lash out. He went still, taking stock of their weapons and counting the lives he'd add to his list.

As the killer stalked toward him, his hands began to prickle with unfamiliar heat. The echo of someone else's magic.

Lila.

Holland smiled, wrapped his fingers around the ropes, and pulled—not on the cords themselves, but on the other *Antari*'s spell.

Fire erupted down the ropes.

The twisted threads snapped like bones, and Holland was free. With a slash of his hand, the lanterns shattered, the corridor went dark, and he was on them.

V

The Sea Serpents were good.

Frighteningly good.

Certainly better than the Copper Thieves, better than all the pirates Lila had come across in those months at sea.

The Serpents fought like it mattered.

Fought like their lives were on the line.

But so did she.

Lila ducked as a curved blade embedded itself in the mast behind her, spun away from a sword as it cut the air. Someone tried to loop a cord around her throat, but she caught it, twisted free, and slid her knife between a stranger's ribs.

Magic thudded through her veins, drawing the ship in lines of life. The Serpents moved like shadows, but to Lila, they shone with light. Her blades slipped under guards, found flesh, freed blood.

A fist caught her jaw, a knife grazed her thigh, but she didn't stop, didn't slow. She was humming with power, some of it hers and some of it borrowed and all of it blazing.

Blood ran into Lila's good eye, but she didn't care because every time she took a life, she saw Lenos.

Lenos, who'd feared her.

Lenos, who'd been kind despite that.

Lenos, who'd called her a portent, a sign of change.

Lenos, who'd seen her, before she knew to recognize herself.

Lenos, who'd died with a barb in his chest and the same sad confusion she'd felt in the alley at Rosenal, the same horrible understanding scrawled across his face,

She could feel Kell and Holland fighting too, on opposite sides of the ship, feel the flex and pull of their magic in her veins, their pain a phantom limb.

If the Serpents had magic, they weren't using it. Perhaps they were just trying to avoid damaging the *Ghost,* since they'd already sunk their own ship, but Lila would be damned if she went down trying to spare this shitty little craft. Fire flared in her hands. The floorboards groaned as she pulled on them. The ship tipped violently beneath her.

She would sink the whole fucking boat if she had to.

But she didn't get the chance. A hand shot out and grabbed her by the collar, hauling her behind a crate. She freed the knife from her hidden arm sheath, but the attacker's other hand—so much larger than her own—caught her wrist and pinned it back against the wood beside her head.

It was Jasta, towering over her, and for a moment Lila thought the captain was trying to help, trying for some reason to pull her out of harm's way, to spare her from the fight. Then she saw the body slumped on the deck.

Hano.

The girl's eyes shone in the dark, open, empty, a clean cut across her throat.

Anger rolled through Lila as understanding struck. Jasta's insistence on steering the *Ghost,* on going with them to the floating market. The sudden danger on the docks at Rosenal. The drinking game, earlier this evening, with its too-strong drink.

"You're with them."

Jasta didn't deny it. Only flashed a ruthless smile.

Lila's will ground against the turncoat captain's, and the other woman was forced back, away. "Why?"

The woman shrugged. "Out here, coin is king."

Lila lunged, but Jasta was twice as fast as she looked, and just as strong, and a second later Lila was being slammed back into the side of the ship, the rail catching her in the ribs hard enough to knock the air from her lungs.

Jasta stood exactly where she'd been before, looking almost bored.

"My orders are to kill the Arnesian princeling," she said, freeing a blade from her hip. "No one ever told me what to do with you."

Cold hatred surged through Lila's veins, overtaking even the heat of power. "If you wanted to kill me, you should have done it already."

"But I do not *have* to kill you," said Jasta as the ship continued to swarm with menacing shadows. "You are a thief and I am a pirate, but we are both knives. I see it in you. You know you don't belong. Not here, with them."

"You're wrong."

"You can pretend all you like," sneered Jasta. "Change your clothes. Change your language. Change your face. But you will always be a knife, and knives are good for one thing and one thing only: cutting."

Lila let her hands fall back to her side, as if considering the traitor's words. Blood dripped from her fingers, and her lips moved slowly, almost imperceptibly, the words—*As Athera*—lost beneath Jasta's preening and the clash of metal to every side.

Lila raised her voice. "Maybe you're right."

Jasta's smile widened. "I know how to spot a knife, always have. And I can teach you—"

Lila clenched her fist, pulling on the wood, and the crates behind Jasta slammed forward. The woman spun, tried to dodge, but Lila's whispered magic had worked—*As Athera, to grow*—and the ship boards had branched up over Jasta's boots while she was gloating. She went crashing to the deck beneath the heavy boxes.

Jasta let out a strangled curse in a language Lila didn't speak, her leg pinned beneath the weight, the snap of bone hanging on the air.

Lila squatted in front of her.

"Maybe you're right," she said again, lifting her blade to Jasta's throat. "And maybe you're wrong. We don't choose what we are, but we choose what we do." The knife was poised to bite in.

"Make sure you cut deep," goaded Jasta as blood welled around the tip, spilling in thin lines down her throat.

"No," said Lila, withdrawing.

"You won't kill me?" she sneered.

"Oh, I will," said Lila. "But not until you tell me everything."

VI

The ship was blood and steel and death.

And then it wasn't.

There was no in between.

The last body crumpled to the deck at Kell's feet, and it was over. He could tell by the silence, and the sudden stilling of the threads that ran between him and Holland and Lila.

Kell swayed from exhaustion as Holland strode up the stairs, stepping over a shining pool of wetness, his hands a mess of torn flesh. In the same moment, Alucard appeared, cradling one arm against his chest. Someone had torn the sapphire from his brow, and blood ran into his eye, turning the storm grey a violent blue.

Nearby, Hastra sagged onto a crate, still shaking and pale. Kell touched the young guard's shoulder.

"Was this the first time you took a life?"

Hastra swallowed, nodded. "I always knew that life was fragile," he said hoarsely. "Keeping something alive is hard enough. But ending it . . ." He trailed off, and then, quite abruptly, turned and retched onto the deck.

"It's all right," said Kell, kneeling over him, his own body screaming from a dozen minor wounds as well as the hollowness that always followed a fight.

After a few seconds Hastra straightened, wiping his mouth on his sleeve. "I think I'm ready to be a priest. Do you think Tieren will take me back?"

Kell squeezed the boy's shoulder. "We can talk to him," he said, "when we get home."

Hastra managed to smile. "I'd like that."

"Where's Bard?" cut in Alucard.

Lila appeared a moment later, hauling the massive, hobbled form of the *Ghost*'s captain behind her.

Kell stared in shock as Lila forced Jasta to her knees on the deck. The woman's face was swollen and streaked with blood, her hands bound with coarse rope, one leg clearly broken.

"Lila, what are you—"

"Why don't you tell them?" said Lila, nudging Jasta with her boot. When the woman only snarled, Lila said, "It was her."

Alucard made a disgusted sound. "*Tac,* Jasta. The Sea Serpents?"

It was the woman's turn to sneer. "We can't all be crown pets."

Kell's tired mind turned. It was one thing to be attacked by pirates. It was another to be made bounty. "Who hired you?"

"I found these on her," said Lila, producing a pouch of blue gems. Not just any kind, but the small oval chips used to adorn a Faroan's face.

"Sol-in-Ar," muttered Kell. "What was your task?"

When Jasta answered by spitting on the deck, Lila drove her boot down into the woman's wounded leg. A snarl escaped her throat.

"Killing the traitor would have been a perk," she growled. "I was hired to slaughter the black-eyed prince." Her gaze drifted up to meet Kell's. "And a Serpent doesn't stop until the job is done."

The knife came out of nowhere.

One moment Jasta's hands were empty, and the next, her last, hidden piece of steel was free and flying toward Kell's heart. His mind caught up before his limbs, and his hands rose, too slow, too late.

He would wonder for weeks, months, years, if he could have stopped it.

If he could have summoned the strength to will the steel away.

But in that moment, he had nothing left to give.

The blade struck home, embedding to the hilt.

Kell staggered back, braced for a pain that never came.

Hastra's curls floated up before his eyes, touched with gold even in the dark. The boy had moved like light, lunging between Kell and the knife, his arms not up to block the blade, but out, as if to catch it.

It took him in the heart.

An animal sound tore from Kell's throat as Hastra—Hastra, who made things grow, who would have been a priest, who could have been anything he wanted and chose to be a guard, *Kell's* guard—staggered, and fell.

"No!" he cried, catching the young man's body before it hit the deck. He was already so quiet, so still, already gone, but Kell had to say something, had to do something. What was the use of so much power if people still kept dying?

"*As Hasari,*" he pleaded, pressing his palm to Hastra's chest, even as the last rhythms of a pulse faded beneath Kell's hands.

It was too late.

He had been too late.

Even magic had its limits.

And Hastra was already gone.

Curls tumbled back from eyes that had once—*just*—been lit with life, that now sat dark, still, open.

Kell lowered Hastra's body, dragging the knife free of his guard's chest as he rose. His chest was heaving, ragged breaths tearing free. He wanted to scream. He wanted to sob.

Instead he crossed the deck, and cut Jasta's throat.

VII

Rhy groaned in pain.

It wasn't a sudden, lancing blow, but the deep ache of muscles pushed too far, of energy drained. His head pounded and his heart raced as he sat up, trying to ground himself in the silk sheets, the warmth of the fire still smoldering in the hearth.

You are here, he told himself, trying to disentangle his mind from the nightmare.

In the dream, he had been drowning.

Not the way he'd almost drowned on the balcony, just hours—days?—ago when Kell had followed Holland into the river. No, this was slower. Rhy's dream-self had been sinking, deeper and deeper into a wave-wracked grave, the pressure of the water crushing the air from his lungs.

But the pain Rhy felt now hadn't followed him out of the dream.

It didn't belong to him at all.

It belonged to Kell.

Rhy reached for the royal pin on the table, wishing he could see what was happening to his brother instead of only feeling the effects. Sometimes he thought he did, in glimpses and dreams, but nothing stuck, nothing ever stayed.

Rhy curled his fingers around the spelled circlet of gold, waiting to feel the heat of Kell's summons, and only then did he realize how helpless he truly was. How useless to Kell. He could summon his brother, but Kell wouldn't—or couldn't—ever summon him.

Rhy slumped back against the pillows, clutching the pin to his chest.

The pain was already fading, an echo of an echo, a tide receding, leaving only dull discomfort and fear in its wake.

He'd never get back to sleep.

The decanters on the sideboard glinted in the low firelight, calling, and he rose to pour himself a drink, adding a single drop of Tieren's tonic to the amber liquid. Rhy raised the glass to his lips, but didn't swallow. Something else had caught his eye. His armor. It lay stretched like a sleeping body on his sofa, gauntleted arms folded on its chest. There was no need of it now, not with the city fast asleep, but it still called to him, louder than the tonic, louder even than the darkness— always worst before dawn.

Rhy set the glass aside, and took up the golden helm.

VIII

Myths do not happen all at once.

They do not spring forth whole into the world. They form slowly, rolled between the hands of time until their edges smooth, until the saying of the story gives enough weight to the words—to the memories—to keep them rolling on their own.

But all stories start somewhere, and that night, as Rhy Maresh walked through the streets of London, a new myth was taking shape.

This was the story of a prince who watched over his city as it slept. Who went on foot, for fear of trampling one of the fallen, who wove his way between the bodies of his people.

Some would say he moved in silence, with only the gentle clang of his golden-armored steps echoing like distant bells through the silent street.

Some would say he spoke, that even in the far-off darkness, the sleeping heard him whisper, over and over, "You are not alone."

Some would say it never happened at all.

Indeed, there was no one there to see.

But Rhy *did* walk among them, because he was their prince, and because he could not sleep, and because he knew what it was like to be held by a spell, to be dragged into darkness, to be bound to something and yet feel utterly alone.

A sheen of frost was settling over his people, making them look more like statues than men and women and children. The prince had seen fallen trees slowly swallowed by moss, pieces of the world slowly reclaimed, and as he moved through the crowd of fallen, he wondered what would happen if London stayed under this spell a month, a season, a year.

Would the world climb up over the sleeping bodies?

Would it claim them, inch by inch?

It began to snow in earnest (strange, close as they were to spring, but not the strangest thing befalling London, then), and so Rhy brushed the ice from still cheeks, tore canvas down from the ghostly bones of the night market, and took blankets from homes now haunted only with the memories of breath. And patiently, the prince covered each and every person he found, though they did not seem to feel the cold beneath their shrouded safety of spellwork and sleep.

The chill ate at the prince's fingers. It seeped through armor and into aching skin, but Rhy did not turn back, did not break his vigil until the first light of day broke the shell of darkness and the dawn thinned the frost. Only then did the prince return to the palace, and fall into bed, and sleep.

TWELVE

BETRAYAL

I

Dawn broke in silence over the *Ghost*.

They'd dumped the bodies overboard—Hano, with her throat cut, and Ilo, whom they'd found dead below, Jasta, who'd betrayed them all, and every last one of the Serpents.

Hastra alone had been wrapped in a blanket. Kell fastened the fabric carefully around the boy's legs, waist, shoulders, sparing his face—the shy smile gone, the glossy curls now lank—as long as possible.

Sailors went into the sea, but Hastra wasn't a sailor. He was a royal guard.

If they'd had flowers on the ship, Kell would have laid one on the rent over Hastra's heart—that was the custom, in Arnes, to mark a mortal wound.

He thought of the blossom waiting back in the Basin, the one Hastra had made for Kell that day, coaxing life from a clod of dirt, a drop of water, a seed, the sum more than its parts, a sliver of light in a darkening world. Would it still be there, when they returned home? Or had it already withered?

If Lenos were there, he could have said something, sent a prayer to the nameless saints, but Lenos was gone too, lost to the tide, and Kell didn't have any flowers, didn't have any prayers, didn't have anything but the hollow anger swimming in his heart.

"*Anoshe*," he murmured as the body went over the side.

They should have cleaned the deck, but there seemed no point. The *Ghost*—what was left of it—would reach Tanek within the day.

His body swayed with fatigue.

He hadn't slept. None of them had.

Holland was focused on keeping wind in the sails while Alucard stood numbly at the wheel—power was precious, but Lila had insisted on healing the captain's wounds. Kell supposed he couldn't fault her. Alucard Emery had done his share to keep the ship afloat.

Lila herself stood nearby, tipping the Faroan gems from hand to hand, staring down at the blue chips, her brow furrowed in thought.

"What is it?" he asked.

"I killed a Faroan once," she mused, tipping the gems back into her first hand. "During the tournament."

"You *what*?" started Kell, hoping he'd misheard, that he wouldn't feel compelled to mention this to Rhy—or worse, Maxim—once they docked. "When would you have—"

"That's not the point of the story," she chided, letting the gems tumble between her fingers. "Have you ever seen a Faroan part with these? Ever seen one trade in anything but coin?"

Kell frowned a little. "No."

"That's because the gems are set into their skin. Couldn't pluck one off if you wanted to, not without a knife."

"I hadn't noticed."

Lila shrugged, holding her hand out over a crate. "It's the kind of thing you think about, when you're a thief."

She tipped her hand, and the gems clattered onto the wooden top. "And when I killed that Faroan, the gems in his face came free. Fell away, like whatever was holding them in place was gone."

Kell's eyes widened. "You don't think these came from a Faroan."

"Oh, I'm sure they did," said Lila, taking up a single gem. "But I doubt they had a choice."

II

Maxim finished his spell sometime after dawn.

He slumped back against the table and admired his work, the faceless men standing in formation, their armored chests locked over steel hearts. Twelve deep cuts ran along the inside of the king's arm, some healing and others fresh. Twelve pieces of steel-clad spellwork bound together before him, forged and welded and made whole.

The strain of binding the magic was grueling, a constant pull on his power, amplifying with every added shell. His body trembled faintly with the weight, but it would not take long, once the task was started. Maxim would manage.

He straightened—the room spun dangerously for several seconds before it settled—and went downstairs to share a last meal with his wife, his son. A farewell without the words. Emira would understand, and Rhy, he hoped, would forgive him. The book would help.

As Maxim walked, he imagined sitting with them in the grand salon, the table covered in pots of tea and fresh-baked bread. Emira's hand on his. Rhy's laughter spilling over. And Kell, where he had always been, sitting at his brother's side.

Maxim let his tired mind live within this dream, this memory, let it carry him forward.

Just one last meal.

One last time.

"Your Majesty!"

Maxim sighed, turning. His last dream died at the sight of the royal guards holding a man between them. The captive wore the purple-and-white wraps of the Faroan entourage, silver veins running like molten metal between the gems on his dark skin. Sol-in-Ar stormed down the hall after the men, closing the distance with every stride.

"Unhand him," ordered the Faroan lord.

"What is the meaning of this?" asked Maxim, fatigue wearing down every muscle, every bone.

One of the guards held out a letter. "We stopped him, Your Majesty, trying to slip out of the palace."

"A messenger?" demanded Maxim, rounding on Sol-in-Ar.

"Are we not permitted to send letters?" challenged the Faroan lord. "I did not realize we were prisoners here."

Maxim moved to tear the letter open, but Sol-in-Ar caught his wrist.

"Do not make an enemy of allies," he warned in his sibilant way. "You have enough of the former already."

Maxim drew his wrist free and sliced open the letter in a single, fluid gesture, eyes flitting over the Faroan script. "You called for reinforcements."

"We are in *need* of them," said Sol-in-Ar.

"No." Maxim's head pounded. "You will only draw more lives into the fray—"

"Perhaps if you had *told* us about your priests' spell—"

"—more lives for Osaron to claim and use against us *all*."

The Veskan prince had arrived by now, and Maxim turned his ire on him, too. "And you? Have the Veskans sent word beyond the city, too?"

Col paled. "And risk their lives as well? Of course not."

Sol-in-Ar glared at the Veskan prince. "You are lying."

Maxim didn't have the energy for this. He didn't have the time.

"Confine Lord Sol-in-Ar and his entourage to their rooms."

The Faroan stared at him, aghast. "King Maresh—"

"You have two choices," cut in Maxim, "your rooms, or the royal prison. And for your sake, and ours, I hope you only sent one man."

When Maxim's men led Sol-in-Ar away, he didn't protest, didn't fight. He said only one thing, the words soft, strained.

"You're making a mistake."

🐉

The Maresh family wasn't sitting in the grand salon. The chairs stood empty. The table hadn't been set—it wouldn't be for hours, he realized. The sun wasn't even up.

Maxim's body was beginning to shake.

He didn't have the strength to keep searching, so he returned to the royal chambers, hoping vainly that Emira would be there, waiting for him. His heart sank when he found the room empty, even as some small part of him exhaled, relieved at being spared the drawn-out pain of parting.

With trembling hands, he began setting his affairs in order. He finished dressing, cleared his desk, set the text he'd written for his son in the center.

The spell was pulling on Maxim with every breath, every heartbeat, threads of magic drawn taut through walls and down stairs, leaching energy with every unused moment.

Soon, the king promised the spell. Soon.

He penned three letters, one to Rhy, one to Kell, and the last to Emira, all too long and far too short. Maxim had always been a man of action, not words. And time was running out.

He was just blowing on the ink when he heard the door open.

His heart quickened, hope rising as he turned, expecting to find his wife.

"My dearest . . ." He trailed off at the sight of the girl, fair and blond and dressed in green, a crown of silver in her hair and crimson splashed like paint across her front.

The Veskan princess smiled. She had four polished blades between her fingers, thin as needles and each dripping blood, and when she spoke, her voice was easy, bright, as if she weren't trespassing in the royal chamber, as if there were no bodies in the hall behind her, no blood smeared on her brow.

"Your Majesty! I was hoping you'd be here."

Maxim held his ground. "Princess, what are you—"

Before he could finish, the first blade came sailing through the air, and by the time the king had his hand up, magic rising to turn the blow, a second knife was driving down through his boot, pinning his foot to the floor.

A growl of pain escaped as Maxim attempted to pivot, even so, to avoid a third blade, only to take a fourth through the arm. This one hadn't flown—it was still in his attacker's hand as she drove the steel in deep above his elbow, pinning his arm back against the wall.

It had taken less than a full breath.

The Veskan princess was standing on tiptoes as if she meant to kiss him. She was so young, to seem so old.

"You don't look well," she said.

Maxim's head pounded. He'd given too much of himself to the spell. Had too little strength left to summon magic for a fight. But there was still the blade sheathed at his hip. Another on his calf. His fingers twitched, but before he could grab either, one of Cora's discarded blades sailed back into her fingers.

She brought it to rest against his throat.

Maxim's arm and foot were going numb—not from pain alone, but something else.

"Poison," he growled.

Her head bobbed. "It won't kill you," she said cheerfully. "That's my job. But you've been a lovely host."

"What have you done? You foolish girl."

Her smile sharpened into a sneer. "This foolish girl will bring glory to her name. This foolish girl will take your palace and hand your kingdom to her own."

She leaned in close, voice slipping from sweet to sensual. "But first, this foolish girl will cut your throat."

Through the open door, Maxim saw the fallen bodies of his guards littering the hall, their armored arms and legs sprawled motionless across the carpet.

And then he saw the streak of dark skin, the shine of gems like tears catching the light.

"You are out of your depth, Princess," he said as the numbness spread through his limbs and the Faroans slipped silently forward, Sol-in-Ar in the lead. "Killing a king grants you only one thing."

"And what is that?" she whispered.

Maxim met her eyes. "A slow death."

Cora's blade bit in as the Faroans flooded the room.

In a flash, Sol-in-Ar had the murderous girl back against him, one arm around her throat.

She spun the needlelike knife in her hand, moved to drive the point into the Faroan's leg, but the others were on her fast, holding her arms, forcing her to her knees before Maxim.

The king tried to speak, and found his tongue heavy in his mouth, his body fighting too many foes between the poison and the cost of spent magic.

"Find the Arnesian guards!" ordered Sol-in-Ar.

Cora fought then, viciously, violently, all the girlish humor stripped away as they divested her of blades.

Maxim finally wrenched the knife free of his arm with half-numbed fingers and unpinned his foot, blood squelching in his boot as he moved with uneven steps to the sideboard.

He found the tonics Tieren kept mixed for him, those for pain and those for sleep, and one, just one, for poison, and poured himself a glass of the rosy liquid, as if he were simply thirsty and not fighting back death.

His fingers shook but he drank deeply, and set the empty glass aside as the feeling returned in a flush of heat, bringing pain with it. A new wave of guards appeared in the doorway, all of them breathless and armed, Isra at the front.

"Your Majesty," she said, scanning the room and paling at the sight of the slight Veskan princess pinned to the floor, the Faroan lord giving orders instead of bound to his palace wing, the discarded knives and bloody trail of steps.

V. E. SCHWAB

Maxim forced himself to straighten. "See to your guards," he ordered.

"Your wounds," started Isra, but the king cut her off.

"I am not so easily dispatched." He turned to Sol-in-Ar. It had been a near thing, and they both knew it, but the Faroan lord said nothing.

"I am in your debt," said Maxim. "And I will repay it." Fearing he might fall over if he lingered long, Maxim turned his attention to the Veskan girl kneeling on his floor. "You failed, little princess, and it will cost you."

Cora's blue eyes were bright. "Not as much as you," she said, her mouth splitting into a cold smile. "Unlike me, my brother Col has *never* missed his marks."

Maxim's blood ran cold as he spun on Isra and the other guards. "Where is the queen?"

III

Rhy hadn't gone looking for his mother.

He found her entirely by accident.

Before the nightmares, he had always slept late. He'd lie in bed all morning, marveling at the way his pillows felt softest after sleep, or the way light moved against the canopied ceiling. For the first twenty years of his life, Rhy's bed had been his favorite place in the palace.

Now he couldn't wait to be rid of it.

Every time his body sank into the cushions, he felt the darkness reaching up, folding its arm around him. Every time his mind slid toward sleep, the shadows were there to meet him.

These days Rhy rose early, desperate for the light.

It didn't matter that he'd spent the better part of the night holding vigil in the streets, didn't matter that his head was cloudy, his limbs stiff and sore and aching with the echo of someone else's fight. The lack of sleep worried him less than what he found in his dreams.

The sun was just cresting the river as Rhy woke, the rest of the palace still likely folded in their troubled sleep. He could have called a servant—there were always two or three awake—but instead he dressed himself, not in the princely armor or in the formal red-and-golds, but in the soft black cut he sometimes wore within the interior rooms of the palace.

It was almost an afterthought, the sword, the weapon at odds with the rest of his attire. Maybe it was Kell's absence. Maybe it was Tieren's sleep. Maybe it was the way his father grew paler by the day, or maybe he'd simply grown used to wearing it. Whatever the reason, Rhy took up his royal short sword, fastened the belt around his hips.

He made his way absently to the salon, his sleep-starved mind half expecting to find the king and queen taking breakfast, but of course it was empty. From there he wandered toward the gallery, but turned back at the first sounds of voices, low and worried and wondering questions to which he didn't have the answers.

Rhy retreated, first to the training rooms, filled with the exhausted remains of the royal guard, and then to the map room, in search of his father, who wasn't there. Rhy went to ballroom after ballroom, looking for peace, for quiet, for a shred of normalcy, and finding silvers, nobles, priests, magicians, questions.

By the time he wandered into the Jewel, he just wanted to be alone.

Instead, Rhy Maresh found the queen.

She was standing at the center of the massive glass chamber, her head bowed as if in prayer.

"What are you doing, Mother?" The words were said softly, but his voice echoed through the hollow room.

Emira raised her head. "Listening."

Rhy looked around, as if there might be something—or someone—he hadn't noticed. But they were alone in the vast chamber. Beneath his feet, the floor was marked with half-finished circles, the beginnings of spells made when the palace was under attack and abandoned once Tieren's spell had taken hold, and the ceiling rose high overhead, blossoms winding around thin crystal columns.

His mother reached out and ran her fingers along the nearest one.

"Do you remember," she said, her voice carrying, "when you thought the spring blossoms were all edible?"

His steps sounded on the glass floor, causing the room to sing faintly as he moved toward her. "It was Kell's fault. He's the one who insisted they were."

"And you believed him. You made yourself so sick."

"I got him back, though, remember? When I challenged him to see who could eat the most summer cakes. He didn't realize until the first bite the cooks had made them all with lime." A soft laugh escaped at the memory of Kell resisting the urge to spit it out, and getting ill into a marble planter. "We got into a fair amount of mischief."

"You say that as though you ever stopped." Emira's hand fell away from the column. "When I first came to the palace, I hated this room." She said it absently, but Rhy knew his mother—knew that nothing she said or did was ever without meaning.

"Did you?" he prompted.

"What could be worse, I thought, than a ballroom made of glass? It was only a matter of time before it broke. And then one day, oh, I was so angry at your father—I don't remember why—but I wanted to break something, so I came in here, to this fragile room, and pounded on the walls, the floor, the columns. I beat my hands on the crystal and the glass until my knuckles were raw. But no matter what I did, the Jewel would not break."

"Even glass can be strong," said Rhy, "if it is thick enough."

A flickering smile, there and then gone, and there again, the first one real, the second set. "I raised a smart son."

Rhy ran a hand through his hair. "You raised *me*, too."

She frowned at that, the way she had at his quips so many times before. Frowned in a way that reminded him of Kell, not that he would ever say so.

"Rhy," she said. "I never meant—"

Behind them, a man cleared his throat. Rhy turned to find Prince Col standing in the doorway, his clothing wrinkled and his hair mussed, as though he'd never been to bed.

"I hope I am not interrupting?" said the Veskan, a subtle tension in his voice that set the prince on edge.

"No," answered the queen coolly at the same time Rhy said, "Yes."

Col's blue eyes flicked between them, clearly registering their discomfort, but he didn't withdraw. Instead he stepped forward into the Jewel, letting the doors swing shut behind him.

"I was looking for my sister."

Rhy remembered the bruises around Cora's wrist. "She isn't here."

The Veskan prince gave the room a sweeping look. "So I see," he said, ambling toward them. "Your palace really is magnificent." He moved at a casual pace, as if admiring the room, but his eyes kept flicking back toward Rhy, toward the queen. "Every time I think I've seen it all, I find another room."

A sword hung at his hip, a jeweled hilt marking the blade for show, but Rhy's hackles still rose at the sight of it, at the prince's carriage, his very presence. And then Emira's attention flicked suddenly upward, as if she'd heard something Rhy couldn't.

"Maxim."

His father's name was a strangled whisper on the queen's lips, and she started toward the doors, only to come up short as Col drew his weapon free.

In that one gesture, everything about the Veskan changed. His youthful arrogance evaporated, the casual air replaced by something grim, determined. Col may have been a prince, but he held his sword with the calm control of a soldier.

"What are you doing?" demanded Rhy.

"Isn't it obvious?" Col's grip tightened on the blade. "I'm winning a war before it starts."

"Lower your blade," ordered the queen.

"Apologies, Your Highness, but I can't."

Rhy searched the prince's eyes, hoping to see the shadow of corruption, to find a will twisted by the curse beyond the palace walls, and shuddered when he found them green and clear.

Whatever Col was doing, he was doing it by choice.

Somewhere beyond the doors, a shout went up, the words smothered, lost.

"For what it's worth," said the Veskan prince, raising his blade. "I really only came for the queen."

His mother spread her arms, the air around her fingers shimmering with frost. "Rhy," she said, her voice a plume of mist. "*Run.*"

Before the word was fully out, Col was surging forward.

The Veskan was fast, but Rhy was faster, or so it seemed as the queen's magic weighted Col's limbs. The icy air wasn't enough to stop the attack, but it slowed Col long enough for Rhy to throw himself in front of his mother, the blade meant for her driving instead into *his* chest.

Rhy gasped at the savage pain of steel piercing skin, and for an instant he was back in his rooms, a dagger thrust between his ribs and blood pouring between his hands, the horrible sear of torn flesh quickly giving way to numbing cold. But this pain was real, was hot, was giving way to nothing.

He could feel every terrible inch of metal from the entry wound just beneath his sternum to the exit wound below his shoulder. He coughed, spitting blood onto the glass floor, and his legs threatened to fold beneath him, but he managed to stay on his feet.

His body screamed, his mind screamed, but his heart kept beating stubbornly, *defiantly,* around the other prince's blade.

Rhy drew in a ragged breath, and raised his head.

"How . . . dare you," he growled, mouth filling with the copper taste of blood.

The victory on Col's face turned to shock. "Not possible," he stammered, and then, in horror, "*What are you?*"

"I am—Rhy Maresh," he answered. "Son to Maxim and Emira—brother to Kell—heir to this city—and the future king of Arnes."

Col's hands fell from the weapon. "But you should be *dead.*"

"I know," said Rhy, dragging his own blade from its sheath and driving the steel into Col's chest.

It was a mirror wound, but there was no spell to shield the Veskan prince. No magic to save him. No life to bind his own. The blade sank in. Rhy expected to feel guilt—or anger, or even triumph—as the blond boy collapsed, lifeless, but all he felt was relief.

Rhy dragged in another breath and wrapped his hands around the hilt of the sword still embedded in his chest. It came free, its length stained red.

He let it fall to the floor.

Only then did he hear the small gasp—a soundless cry—and feel his mother's cold fingers tightening on his arm. He turned toward her. Saw the red stain spreading across the front of her dress where the sword had driven in. Through him. Through her. There, just above her heart. The too-small hole of a too-great wound. His mother's eyes met his.

"Rhy," she said, a small, disconcerted crease between her brows, the same face she'd made a hundred times whenever he and Kell got into trouble, whenever he shouted or bit his nails or did anything that wasn't princely.

The furrow deepened, even as her eyes went glassy, one hand drifting toward the wound, and then she was falling. He caught her, stumbled as the sudden weight tore against his open, ruined chest.

"No, no, no," he said, sinking with her to the prismed floor. No, it wasn't fair. For once, he'd been fast enough. For once, he'd been strong enough. For once—

"Rhy," she said again, so gently—too gently.

"No."

Her bloody hands reached for his face, tried to cup his cheek, and missed, streaking red along his jaw.

"Rhy . . ."

His tears spilled over her fingers.

"*No.*"

Her hand fell away, and her body slumped against him, still, and in that sudden stillness, Rhy's world narrowed to the spreading stain, the lingering furrow between his mother's eyes.

Only then did the pain come, folding over him with such sudden force, such horrible weight, that he clutched his chest and began to scream.

IV

Alucard stood at the ship's wheel, attention flicking between the three magicians on deck and the line of the sea. The *Ghost* felt wrong under his hands, too light, too long, a shoe made for someone else's foot. What he wouldn't have given for the steady bulk of the *Spire*. For Stross, and Tav, and Lenos—each name a shard of wood under his skin. And for Rhy—that name an even deeper wound.

Alucard had never longed so much for London.

The *Ghost* was making good time, but even with the cool, clear day and three recovering *Antari* keeping wind in the sails, someone still had to chart a course, and for all his posturing, Kell Maresh didn't know the first thing about steering ships, Holland could barely keep his food down, and Bard was a quick study but would always be a better thief than a sailor—not that he'd ever say so to her face. Thus the task of getting the *Ghost* to Tanek and the crew—what few were left—to London fell to him.

"What does it mean?" Bard's voice drifted up from the lower deck. She was standing close to the *Antari* prince while the latter held the Inheritor up to the sun.

Alucard winced, remembering what he'd gone through to get the blasted thing. The tip-off in Sasenroche. The boat to the cliffs at Hanas. The unmarked grave and the empty coffin and that was just the beginning, but it all made for a good story, and for Maris that was half the price.

And everyone paid. First timers most of all. If Maris didn't know you, she didn't trust you, and a modest prize was like to earn you a swift departure with no invitation to return, so Alucard had paid. Dug up that Inheritor and taken it all the way to Maris, and now here they were, and here it was, with him again.

Rhy's brother (Alucard discovered that he hated Kell a little less when he thought of him that way) was turning the device gingerly between his fingers while Bard leaned over him.

Holland was watching the others in silence, and so Alucard watched him. The third *Antari* didn't often speak, and when he did, his words were dry, disdainful. He had all the airs of someone who knew his own strength, and knew it went unequaled, at least in present company. Alucard might have liked him if he were a little less of an asshole. Or maybe a little more. He might have liked him, anyway, if he weren't a traitor. If he hadn't summoned the monster that now raged like a fire through London. The same monster that had killed Anisa.

"*Give* and *Take,*" said Kell, squinting.

"Right," pressed Bard. "But how does it *work*?"

"I imagine you pierce your hand against the point," he explained.

"Give it here."

"This isn't a toy, Lila."

"And I'm not a child, Kell."

Holland cleared his throat. "We should all be familiar with it."

Kell rolled his eyes and took a last studying look before offering up the Inheritor.

Holland reached to take it when Kell gasped suddenly and let go. The cylinder tumbled from his fingers as he doubled over, a low groan escaping his throat.

Holland caught the Inheritor and Bard caught Kell. He'd gone white as a sail, one hand clutching his chest.

Alucard was on his feet, racing toward them, one word pounding through his head, his heart.

Rhy.

Rhy.

Rhy.

Magic flared in his vision as he reached Kell's side, scanning the silvery lines that coiled around the *Antari*. The knot at Kell's heart was still there, but the threads were glowing with a fiery light, pulsing faintly at some invisible strain.

Kell fought back a cry, the sound whistling through his clenched teeth.

"What is it?" demanded Alucard, barely able to hear his own words over that panicked echo in his blood. "What's happening?"

"The prince," Kell managed, his breath ragged.

I know that, he wanted to scream. "Is he alive?" Alucard realized the answer even before Kell scowled at him.

"Of course he's alive," snapped the *Antari,* fingers digging into his front. "But—he's been attacked."

"By who?"

"I don't know," growled Kell. "I'm not psychic."

"My money's on Vesk," offered Bard.

Kell let out a small hiccup of pain as the threads flared, singeing the air before dimming back to their usual silver glow.

Holland pocketed the Inheritor. "If he can't die, then there's no reason to worry."

"Of course there's a *reason,*" Kell shot back, forcing himself up. "Someone just tried to *murder* the prince of Arnes." He drew a royal pin from the pocket of his coat. "We have to go. Lila. Holland."

Alucard stared. "What about *me?*" His pulse was steadying, but his whole body still hummed with the animal panic, the need to act.

Kell pressed his thumb to the pin's tip, drawing blood. "You can stay with the ship."

"Not a chance," snarled Alucard, casting his gaze at the meager crew left on board.

Holland was just standing there, watching, but when Lila made as if to go to Kell's side, his pale fingers caught her arm. She glared at him, but he didn't let go, and Kell didn't look back, didn't wait to see if they were following as he brought the token to the wall.

Holland shook his head. "That won't work."

Kell wasn't listening. *"As Tascen—"*

The rest of the spell was cut off by a crack splitting the air, accompanied by the sudden pitch of the ship and Kell's stunned yelp as his body was forcefully hurled backward across the deck.

To Alucard's eyes, it looked like a Saint's Day firework had gone off in the middle of the *Ghost*.

A crackle of light, a sputter of energy, the silver of Kell's magic crashing against the blues and greens and reds of the natural world. Rhy's brother tried to stand up, holding his head, clearly surprised to find himself still on the ship.

"What in the ever-loving hell was that?" asked Bard.

Holland took a slow step forward, casting a shadow over Kell. "As I was saying, you cannot make a door on a moving craft. It defies the rules of transitional magic."

"Why didn't you tell me sooner?"

The other *Antari* raised a brow. "Obviously, I assumed you knew."

The color was coming back into Kell's face, the pained furrows fading, replaced by a hot flush.

"Until we reach land," continued Holland, "we're no better than ordinary magicians."

The disdain in his voice raked on Alucard's nerves. No wonder Bard was always trying to kill him.

Lila made a sound then, and Alucard turned in time to see Kell on his feet, hands lifted in the direction of the mast. The current of magic filled his vision, power tipping toward Kell like water in a glass. A second later the gust of wind hit the ship so hard its sails snapped and the whole thing made a low wooden groan.

"Careful!" shouted Alucard, sprinting toward the wheel as the ship banked hard beneath the sudden gale.

He got the *Ghost* back on course as Kell drove it on with a degree of focus—of concentrated force—he'd never seen the *Antari* use. A level of strength reserved not for London, or the king and queen, not for Rosenal, or Osaron himself.

But for Rhy, thought Alucard.

The same force of love that had broken the laws of the world and brought a brother back to life.

Threads of magic drew taut and bright as Kell forced his strength into the sails, Holland and Lila bracing themselves as he drew past the limits of his power and leaned on theirs.

Hold on, Rhy, thought Alucard, as the ship skated forward, rising until it skimmed the surface of the water, sea spray misting the air around them as the *Ghost* surged anew for London.

V

Rhy descended the prison stairs.

His steps were slow, bracing. It hurt to breathe, a pain that had nothing to do with the wound to his chest, and everything to do with the fact that his mother was dead.

Bandages wove around his ribs and over his shoulder, too tight, the skin beneath already closed. *Healed*—if that was the word for it. But it wasn't, because Rhy Maresh hadn't *healed* in months.

Healing was natural, healing took *time*—time for muscle to fuse, for bones to set, for skin to mend, time for scars to form, for the slow recession of pain followed by the return of strength.

In all fairness, Rhy had never known the long suffering of convalescence. Whenever he'd been injured as a child, Kell had always been there to mend him. Nothing worse than a cut or bruise ever lasted more than the time it took to find his brother.

But even that had been different.

A choice.

Rhy remembered falling from the courtyard wall when he was twelve and spraining his wrist. Remembered Kell's quickness to draw blood, Rhy's quickness to stop him, because he could bear the pain more than he could bear Kell's face when the blade sank in, the knowledge that he'd feel dizzy and ill the rest of the day from the magic's strain. And because, secretly, Rhy wanted to know he had a choice.

To heal.

But when Astrid Dane had driven the blade between his ribs, when the darkness had swallowed him, and then receded like a tide, there'd been no choice, no chance to say no. The wound was already closed. The spell already done.

He'd stayed in bed for three days in a mimicry of convalescence. He'd felt weak and ill, but it had less to do with his mending body than the new hollowness inside it. The voice in his head that whispered *wrong, wrong,* with every pulse.

Now he did not heal. A wound was a wound and then it wasn't.

A shudder went through him as he reached the bottom step.

Rhy did not want to do this.

Did not want to face her.

But someone had to handle the living, as much as someone had to handle the dead, and the king had already laid claim to the latter. His father, who was dealing with his grief as though it were an enemy, something to defeat, subdue. Who had ordered every Veskan in the palace rounded up, put under armed guard, and confined to the southern wing. His father, who had laid out his dead wife on the stone grieving block with such peculiar care, as if she were fragile. As if anything could touch her now.

In the gloom of the prison, a pair of guards stood watch.

Cora was sitting cross-legged on the bench at the back of her cell. She wasn't chained to the wall, as Holland had been, but her delicate wrists were bound in iron so heavy her hands had to rest on the bench before her knees, making her look as though she were leaning forward to whisper a secret.

Blood dappled her face like freckles, but when she saw Rhy, she actually smiled. Not the rictus grin of the mad, or the rueful smirk of the guilty. It was the same smile she'd given him as they perched in the royal baths telling stories: cheerful, innocent.

"Rhy," she said brightly.

"Was it your idea, or Col's?"

She pursed her lips, sulking at the lack of preamble. But then her eyes went to the bandage that peeked through Rhy's stiffened collar. It should have been a killing blow. It had been.

"My brother is one of the best swordsmen in Vesk," said Cora. "Col has never missed his mark."

"He didn't," said Rhy simply.

Cora's brow crinkled, then smoothed. Expressions flitted across her face like pages flipping in a breeze, too fast to catch.

"There are rumors, in my city," she said. "Rumors about Kell, and rumors about you. They say you di—"

"Was it your idea, or his?" demanded Rhy, fighting to keep his voice even, to hold his grief at bay, the way his father did, sadness kept behind a dam.

Cora rose to her feet despite the weight of the manacles. "My brother has a gift for swords, not strategies." She curled her fingers around the bars, metal sounding against metal like a bell. The cuff slipped down, and again Rhy saw the bruised skin circling her wrist. There was something unnatural about those marks, he realized now, something inhuman.

"That wasn't your brother, was it?"

She caught him looking, chuckled. "Hawk," she admitted. "Beautiful birds. Easy to forget that they have claws."

He could see it now, the curve of talons he'd mistaken for fingers, the prick of the creature's nails.

"I'm sorry about your mother," said Cora, and what he hated most was that she sounded sincere. He thought of the night they'd spent together, the way she'd made him feel less alone. The ease of her presence, the realization that she was just a child, a girl pretending, playing at games she didn't fully understand. Now, he wondered about that innocence, if it had all been an illusion. If he should have been able to tell. If it would have changed anything. If, if, if.

"*Why* did you do it?" he asked, his resolve threatening to break. She cocked her head, perplexed, like a hooded bird of prey.

"I'm the sixth of seven children. What future is there for me? In what world would I ever rule?"

"You could have killed your *own* family instead of mine."

Cora leaned in, that cherubic face pressed against the cell bars. "I thought about it. I suppose one day I might."

"No, you won't." Rhy turned to go. "You'll never see the outside of this cell."

"I'm like you," she said softly.

"No." He shoved her words away.

"I have hardly any magic," she pressed on. "But we both know there are other kinds of power." Rhy's steps slowed. "There's charm, cunning, seduction, strategy."

"Murder," he said, rounding on her.

"We use what we have. We make what we don't. We're truly not so different," said Cora, gripping the bars. "We both want the same thing. To be seen as strong. The only difference between you and me is the number of siblings standing in our way to the throne."

"That's not the only difference, Cora."

"Does it drive you mad, to be the weaker one?"

He wrapped his hand around hers, pinning them to the bars of the cell. "I am alive because my brother is strong," he said coldly. "You are alive only because yours is dead."

VI

Osaron sat on his throne and waited.

Waited for the impostor's palace to fall.

Waited for his subjects to return.

Waited for word of his victory.

For any word at all.

Thousands of voices had whispered in his head—determined, weeping, crowing, pleading, triumphant—and then, in a single moment, they were gone, the world suddenly still.

He reached out again and plucked the threads, but no one answered.

No one came.

They couldn't all have perished throwing themselves against the palace wards. Couldn't all have vanished so easily from his power, from his will.

He waited, wondering if the silence itself was some kind of trick, a ruse, but when it stretched, his own thoughts loud and echoing in the hollow space, Osaron rose.

The shadow king walked toward his palace doors, the smooth dark wood dissolving to smoke before him and taking shape again in his wake, parting as the world should for a god.

Against the sky, the impostor's palace of stone stood, its wards cracked but not broken.

And there, littering the steps, the banks, the city, Osaron saw the bodies of his puppets, their strings cut.

Everywhere he looked, he saw them. Thousands. Dead.

No, not dead.

But not entirely *alive.*

Despite the cold, each had the essential glow of life, the faint, steady rhythm of a heart still beating, the sound so soft it couldn't crack the silence.

That silence, that horrible, deafening silence, so like the world— his world—when the last life had ebbed and all that was left was a shred of power, a withered sliver of the magic that had once been Osaron. He'd paced for days through the dead remains of his city, every inch gone black, until even he had stilled, too weak to move, too weak to do anything but exist, to beat stubbornly on like these sleeping hearts.

"*Get up,*" he ordered his subjects now.

No one answered.

"*Get up,*" he screamed into their minds, into their very cores, pulling on every string, reaching into memory, into dream, into bone.

Still, no one rose.

A servant lay curled at the god's feet, and Osaron knelt, reached into the man's chest, and wrapped his fingers around his heart.

"*Get up,*" he ordered. The man did not move. Osaron tightened his grip, pouring more and more of himself into the shell, until the form simply—fell apart. Useless. Useless. All of them, useless.

The shadow king straightened, ash blowing in the wind as he turned his gaze on that *other* palace, that seat of *redundant* royalty, the threads of spellwork spooling from its spires. So they had done this, they had stolen his servants, silenced his voice.

It did not matter.

They could not stop him.

Osaron would conquer this city, this world.

And first, he would tear the palace down himself.

VII

People spoke of love as if it were an arrow. A thing that flew quick, and always found its mark. They spoke of it as if it were a pleasant thing, but Maxim had taken an arrow once, and knew it for what it was: excruciating.

He had never wanted to fall in love, never wanted to welcome that pain, would have happily faked an arrow's bite.

And then he met Emira.

And for a long time, he thought the arrow had played its cruelest trick, had struck him and missed *her*. He thought she'd stepped around the point, the way she stepped around so many things she did not like.

He'd spent a year trying to free the barb from his own chest before he realized he didn't want to. Or maybe, he couldn't. Another year before he realized she was injured, too.

It had been a slow pursuit, like melting ice. A kinship of hot and cold, of strong forces equally opposed, of those who did not know how to soften, how to soothe, and found the answer in each other.

That arrow's barb had so long healed. He'd forgotten the pain entirely.

But now.

Now he felt the wound, a shaft driven through his ribs. Scraping bone and lung with every ragged breath, and loss the hand twisting the arrow, trying to rend it free before it killed and doing so much damage in the process.

Maxim wanted to be with her. Not the body laid out in the Rose Hall, but the woman he loved. He wanted to be with her, and instead he stood in the map room across from Sol-in-Ar, forced to bind up a mortal wound, to fight through the pain, because the battle wasn't yet won.

His spell was beating against the inside of his skull, and he tasted blood with every swallow, and as he lifted the crystal cut glass to his lips, his hand shook.

Sol-in-Ar stood on the other side of the map, the two of them divided by the wide expanse of the Arnesian empire on the table, the city of London rising at its center. Isra waited by the door, head bowed.

"I am sorry for your loss," said the Faroan lord, because it was a thing that had to be said. Both men knew the words fell short, would always fall short.

The part of Maxim that was king knew it wasn't right to mourn a single life more than a city, but the part of Maxim that had set the rose on his wife's heart was still breaking inside.

When was the last time he'd seen her? What was the last thing he'd said? He didn't know, couldn't recall. The arrow twisted. The wound ached. He fought to remember, remember, remember.

Emira, with her dark eyes that saw so much, and her lips that guarded smiles as if they were secrets. With her beauty, and her strength, her hard shell around her fragile heart.

Emira, who'd taken down her walls long enough to let him in, who'd built them twice as high when Rhy was born, so nothing could get in. Whose trust he'd fought for, whose trust he'd failed when he promised over and over and over again that he would keep them safe.

Emira, gone.

Those who thought death looked like sleep had never seen it.

When Emira slept, her lashes danced, her lips parted, her fingers twitched, every part of her alive within her dreams. The body in the Rose Hall was not his wife, not his queen, not the mother of his heir, not anyone at all. It was empty, the intangible presence of life and magic and personhood gutted like a candle, leaving only cooling wax behind.

"You knew it was the Veskans," said Maxim, dragging his mind back to the map room.

Sol-in-Ar's features were grim, set, the white gold accents on the lord's face strangely steady in the light. "I suspected."

"How?"

"I do not have magic, Your Majesty," Sol-in-Ar answered in slow but even Arnesian, the edges smoothing with his accent, "but I do have sense. The treatise between Faro and Vesk has become strained in recent months." He gestured at the map. "Arnes sits squarely between our empires. An obstacle. A wall. I have been watching the prince and princess since my arrival, and when Col answered you that he had not sent word to Vesk, I knew that he was lying. I knew this because you housed their gift in the chamber below mine."

"The hawk," said Maxim, recalling the Veskans' offering—a large grey predator—before the *Essen Tasch*.

Sol-in-Ar nodded. "I was surprised by their gift. A bird like that does not enjoy a cage. The Veskans use them to send missives across the harsh expanses of their territory, and when they are confined, they caw in a low and constant way. The one beneath my room fell silent two days ago."

"*Sanct,*" muttered Maxim. "You should have said something."

Sol-in-Ar raised a single dark brow. "Would you have listened, Your Majesty?"

"I apologize," said the king, "for distrusting an ally."

Sol-in-Ar's gaze was steady, his pale beads pricks of light. "We are both men of war, Maxim Maresh. Trust does not come easily."

Maxim shook his head and refilled his glass, hoping the liquid would quelch the lingering taste of blood and steady his hands. He hadn't meant to hold his spell aloft for this long, had only meant to—to see Emira, to say good-bye. . . .

"It has been a long time," he said, forcing his thoughts back, "since I was at war. Before I was king, I led command at the Blood Coast. That was the nickname my soldiers and I had for the open waters that ran between the empires. That gap of terrain where pirates and rebels and anyone who refused to recognize the peace went to make a little war."

"*Anastamar,*" said Sol-in-Ar. "That was our name for it. It means *the Killing Strait.*"

"Fitting," mused Maxim, taking a long sip. "The peace was new enough to be fragile, then—though I suppose peace is always fragile—and I had only a thousand men to hold the entire coast. Though I had another title. Not one given by court, or my father, but by my soldiers."

"The Steel Prince," said Sol-in-Ar, and then, reading Maxim's expression: "It surprises you, that the tales of your exploits reach beyond your own borders?" The Faroan's fingers grazed the edge of the map. "The Steel Prince, who tore the heart from the rebel army. The Steel Prince, who survived the night of knives. The Steel Prince, who slayed the pirate queen."

Maxim finished his drink and set the glass aside. "I suppose we never know the scale of our life's stories. Which parts will survive, and which will die with us, but—"

He was cut off by a sudden tremor, not in his limbs, but in the room itself. The palace gave a violent shudder around them, the walls trembling, the stone figures on the map threatening to tip. Maxim and Sol-in-Ar both braced themselves as the tremor passed.

"Isra," ordered Maxim, but the guard was already moving down the hall. He and Sol-in-Ar followed.

The wards were still weak in the aftermath of the attack, but it shouldn't have mattered, because everyone beyond the palace doors was asleep.

Everyone—but Osaron.

Now the creature's voice rumbled through the city, not the smooth, seductive whisper in Maxim's mind, but an audible, thunderous thing.

"This palace is mine."

"This city is mine."

"These people are mine."

Osaron knew about the spell, must have known too that it was coming from within the walls. If Tieren woke, the enchantment would shatter. The fallen would revive.

It was time, then.

Maxim forced himself toward the front of the palace, carrying the weight of his spell with every step, even as his heart called for Rhy. If only his son were there. If only Maxim could see him one last time.

As if summoned by the thought, the prince appeared in the doorway, and suddenly Maxim wished he hadn't been so selfish. Grief and fear were painted across Rhy's features, making him look young. He *was* young.

"What's going on?" asked the prince.

"Rhy," he said, the short word leaving him breathless. Maxim didn't know how to do this. If he stopped moving, he would never start again.

"Where are you going?" demanded his son as Osaron's voice shook the world.

"Face me, false king."

Maxim tugged on the threads of his power and felt his spell pull tight, cinching like armor around him as steel hearts came to life within steel breasts.

"Father," said Rhy.

"Surrender, and I will spare those within."

The king summoned his steel men, felt them marching through the halls.

"Refuse, and I will tear this place apart."

He kept walking.

"Stop!" demanded Rhy. "If you go out there, you will die."

"There is no shame in death," said the king.

"You are no god."

"You can't do this," said Rhy, barring his path as they reached the front hall. "You're walking right into his trap."

Maxim stopped, the weight of the spell and his son's stricken face threatening to drag him down. "Stand aside, Rhy," he ordered gently.

His son shook his head furiously. "Please." Tears were brimming on his dark lashes, threatening to spill. Maxim's heart ached. The palace trembled. The steel guard was coming. They reached the front hall, a dozen suits of armor spelled into motion with blood and will and magic. Royal short swords hung at their waists, and through their helmets, the soft light of their spelled hearts burned like coal. They were ready. He was ready.

"Rhy Maresh," said Maxim steadily, "I will ask you as your father, but if I must, I will command you as your king."

"*No,*" said Rhy, grabbing him by the shoulders. "I won't let you do this."

The arrow in his chest drove deep.

"Sol-in-Ar," Maxim said, and, "Isra."

And they understood. The two came forward and seized Rhy's arms, pulling him away. Rhy fought viciously against them, but at a nod from the king, Isra drove her gauntleted fist into the prince's ribs and Rhy doubled, gasping, "*No, no . . .* "

"*Sosora nastima,*" said Sol-in-Ar. *"Listen to your king."*

"Watch, my prince," added Isra. "Watch with pride."

"Open the doors," ordered Maxim.

Tears spilled down Rhy's face. "Father—"

The heavy wood parted. The doors swung back. At the base of the palace stairs stood the shadow, a demon masquerading as a king.

Osaron lifted his chin.

"Face me."

"Let me go!" cried Rhy.

Maxim strode through the doors. He didn't look back, not at the steel guard marching in his wake, not at his son's face, the eyes so like Emira's, now red with anguish.

"*Please,*" begged Rhy. "Please, let me go. . . ."

They were the last words Maxim heard before the palace doors fell shut.

VIII

The first time Rhy saw his father's map room, he was eight years old.

He hadn't been allowed past the golden doors, had only glimpsed the stone figures arrayed across the sprawling table, the scenes moving with the same slow enchantment of the pictures on the city's scrying boards.

He'd tried to sneak back in, of course, but Kell wouldn't help him, and there were other places in the palace to explore. But Rhy couldn't forget the strange magic of that room, and that winter, when the weather turned and the sun never seemed to come out, he built his own map, crafting the palace from a golden three-tiered cake stand, the river from a stretch of gossamer, a hundred tiny figures from whatever he could get his hands on. He made *vestra* and *ostra,* priests and royal guards.

"This one's you," he told Kell, holding up a fire-starter with a red top, a dab of black paint for an eye. Kell wasn't impressed.

"This one's you," he told his mother, brandishing the queen he'd fashioned from a glass tonic vial.

"This one's you," he told Tieren, proudly showing him the bit of white stone he'd dug out of the courtyard.

He'd been working on the set for more than a year when his father came to see. He'd never found the stuff to make the king. Kell—who didn't usually want to play—had offered up a rock with a dozen little grooves that *almost* made a ghoulish face, if the light was right, but Rhy thought it looked more like the royal cook, Lor.

Rhy was crouched over the board before bed one night when Maxim entered. He was a towering man draped in red and gold, his dark beard and brows swallowing his face. No wonder Rhy couldn't find the piece to play him. Nothing felt *large* enough.

"What's this?" asked his father, sinking to one knee beside the makeshift palace.

"It's a game," said Rhy proudly, "just like yours."

That was when Maxim took him by the hand, and led him down the stairs and through the palace, bare feet sinking into the plush carpet. When they reached the golden doors, Rhy's heart leapt, half in dread, half in excitement, as his father unlocked the doors.

Memory often bends a thing, makes it even more marvelous. But Rhy's own memory of the map room paled in comparison to the truth. Rhy had grown two inches that year, but instead of seeming smaller, the map was just as grand, just as sweeping, just as magical.

"This," said his father sternly, "is not a game. Every ship, every soldier, every bit of stone and glass—the lives of this kingdom hang in the balance of this board."

Rhy stared in wonder at the map, made all the more magical for his father's warning. Maxim stood, arms crossed, while Rhy circled the table, examining every facet before turning his attention to the palace.

It was no kettle, no cake tray. This palace shone, a perfect miniature—sculpted in glass and gold—of Rhy's home.

Rhy stood on his toes, peering into the windows.

"What are you searching for?" asked his father.

Rhy looked up, eyes wide. "You."

At last, a smile broke through that trimmed beard. Maxim pointed to a slight rise in the cityscape, a plaza two bridges down from the palace where a huddle of stone guards sat on horseback. And at their center, no larger than the rest, was a figure set apart only by the gold band of a crown.

"A king," said his father, "belongs with his people."

Rhy reached a hand into the pocket of his bedclothes and pulled out a small figure, a boy prince spun from pure sugar and stolen from his last birthday cake. Now, carefully, Rhy set the figure on the map beside his father.

"And the prince," he said proudly, "belongs with his king."

Rhy screamed, and thrashed, and fought against their grip.

A king belongs with his people.

He begged, and pleaded, and tried to tear free.

A prince belong with his king.

The doors were closed. His father had vanished, swallowed up by wood and stone.

"Your Highness, please."

Rhy threw a punch, catching Isra hard across the jaw. She let go, and he made it a single step before Sol-in-Ar locked him in a viciously efficient hold, one arm twisted up behind his back.

"Your Highness, no."

Pain flared through him when he tried to fight, but pain was nothing to Rhy now and he wrenched free, tearing something in his shoulder as he threw his elbow back into the Faroan's face.

More guards were arriving now, blocking the door as Isra shouted orders through bloodstained teeth.

"Stand aside," he demanded, voice breaking.

"Your Highness—"

"Stand aside."

Slowly, reluctantly, the guards stepped away from the doors, and Rhy surged forward, grasping for the handle just before Isra pinned his hand to the wood.

"Your Highness," she snarled, "don't you *dare*."

A king belongs with his people.

"Isra," he pleaded. "A prince belongs with his king."

"Then be with him," said the guard. "By honoring his last request."

The weight of Isra's hand retreated, and Rhy was left alone before the broad wood doors. Somewhere on the other side, so close and yet so far . . .

He felt something tear inside him, not flesh but something so much deeper. He splayed his hands across the wood. Rhy squeezed his eyes shut, pressed his forehead to the door, his whole body shaking with the urge to throw them open, to run after his father.

He didn't.

His legs gave way, body sinking to the floor, and if the world had chosen that moment to swallow him whole, Rhy would have welcomed it.

THIRTEEN

A
KING'S
PLACE

I

Maxim Maresh had forgotten about the fog.

The moment he stepped through the palace wards, he felt Osaron's poison lacing the air. It was too late to hold his breath. It forced its way in, filling his lungs as the curse whispered through his head.

Kneel before the shadow king.

Maxim resisted the fog's hypnotic pull, nerves crackling as he forced its hold away, focused instead on the sound of the steel guard marching in his wake and the rippling figure waiting at the base of the palace stairs.

Without a body, the shadow king looked like less like a man and more like smoke trapped within a darkened glass, the presence shifting within its false shell like a trick of the light. Only its eyes seemed solid, the glossy black of polished stone.

Like Kell's, thought Maxim, and then he revoked the thought. *No, not like Kell's at all.*

Kell's gaze had the warmth of a flame, while Osaron's eyes were sharp and cold and utterly inhuman.

At the sight of Maxim descending the stairs, the shadow king's face flickered, mouth twisting into a smile.

"False king."

Maxim forced his body down step after step as his vision blurred and his skin pricked with the beginnings of fever. When his boots struck the stone of the plaza floor, the twelve men of his final guard fanned out, taking up their places around the two kings like points on a clock. Each drew a steel short sword, its blade spelled to sever magic.

Osaron barely seemed to notice the figures in their steel trappings, the way they moved together like fingers on a hand, the way the shadows bent and swirled around their armor and their blades, never touching.

"Have you come to kneel?" asked the shadow king, the words echoing through Maxim's skull, ringing against his bones. *"Have you come to beg?"*

Maxim lifted his head. He wore no armor, no helm, nothing but a single sword at his hip and the gold crown resting in his hair. Still, he looked straight into those onyx eyes and said, "I've come to destroy you."

The darkness chuckled, a sound like low thunder.

"You've come to die."

Maxim's balance almost faltered, not from fear, but from fever. Delirium. The night danced before his eyes, memories transposing themselves on top of truth. Emira's body. Rhy's screams. Pain lanced jaggedly through Maxim's chest as he resisted the shadow king's magic. Sickness quickened his heart, Osaron's curse straining his mind as his own spell strained his body.

"Shall I make your own men kill you?"

Osaron's hand twitched, but the steel guard circling them did not move. No sword hands lifted to attack. No boots shifted obediently forward.

A frown crossed the shadow king's face like a passing cloud as he realized the guards weren't real, only puppets on clumsy strings, the armor nothing but a hollow enchantment, a last effort to spare Maxim's own men from this grim task.

"What a waste."

Maxim straightened, sweat sliding down the nape of his neck. "You'll have to face me yourself."

With that, the Arnesian king drew his sword, spelled like the others to break the threads of magic, and slashed at the shadowy mass before him. Osaron did not duck or dodge or strike. He did not move at all. He simply *parted* around Maxim's blade and re-formed a few feet to the left.

Again, Maxim attacked.

Again, Osaron dissolved.

With every lunge, every swing, Maxim's fatigue and fever rose, a tide threatening to overtake him.

And then, on the fifth or the sixth or the tenth attack, Osaron finally fought back. This time, when he took shape again, it was inside Maxim's guard.

"Enough," said the monster with a flickering grin.

He reached out an insubstantial hand, fingers splayed, and Maxim felt his body stall mid-stride, felt the bones beneath his skin groan and grind, pain lighting up his nerves as he was pinned like a doll against the night.

"So fragile," chided Osaron.

A twitch of that hand—more fog than fingers—and Maxim's wrist shattered. His short sword clattered to the ground, the metallic scrape of metal on stone drowning out his pained gasp.

"Beg," said the shadow king.

Maxim swallowed. "No, I—"

His collarbone snapped with the vicious crack of a stick over a knee. A strangled scream broke through his clenched teeth.

"Beg."

Maxim shuddered, his ribs shaking beneath the force of Osaron's will as it tap-tap-tapped like fingers over his bones.

"No."

The shadow king was teasing, toying, drawing it out. And Maxim let him, hoping all the while that Rhy was safe inside the palace, far from the windows, far from the door, far from this. His steel guards trembled in their places, gauntlets gripping swords. Not yet. Not yet. Not yet.

"I am the king . . . of this empire—"

Something cracked in his chest, and Maxim spasmed, blood rising in his throat.

"This is what passes for a king in this world?"

514 ·   V. E. SCHWAB

"My people will never—"

At that, Osaron's hand—not flesh and bone or smoke at all, but something dense and cold and *wrong*—wrapped around Maxim's jaw. *"The insolence of mortal kings."*

Maxim looked into the swirling darkness of the creature's gaze. "The . . . insolence of . . . fallen . . . gods."

Osaron's face broke into a terrible smile. *"I will wear your body through the streets until it burns."*

In those black eyes, Maxim saw the warped reflection of the palace, the *soner rast,* the beating heart of his city.

His home.

He pulled the final strings, and the guards finally stepped forward. Twelve faceless men drew their swords.

"I am the head . . . of the House Maresh," said Maxim, ". . . seventh king of that name . . . and you are not fit . . . to wear my skin."

Osaron cocked his head. *"We shall see."*

The darkness forced its way in.

It was not a wave, but an ocean, and Maxim felt his will give way beneath the weight of Osaron's power. There was no air. No light. No surface.

Emira. Rhy. Kell.

The arrows drove deep, the pain an anchor, but Maxim's mind was already breaking apart, and his body tore further as he pulled with the last of his strength on his steel guards. Gauntlets tightened and a dozen short swords rose into the air, points turning toward the center of their circle as Osaron poured himself like molten metal into the body of Maxim Maresh.

And the king began to *burn*.

His mind guttered, his life failed, but not before a dozen steel points sang through the air, driving toward the source of their spell.

Toward Maxim's body.

His heart.

He stopped fighting. It was like setting down a heavy weight, the dazzling relief of letting go. Osaron's voice laughed through his head, but he was already falling, already gone, when the blades found home.

II

Across the city of London, the darkness began to thin.

The deep gloom drew back, and the shining black pane of the river cracked, giving way, here and there, to violent ribbons of red as Osaron's hold faltered, slipped.

Maxim Maresh's body knelt in the street, a dozen swords driven in to the hilt. Blood pooled beneath him in a rich red slick, and for a few long moments, the body did not move. The only sound came from the drip-drip-drip of the dead king's blood hitting stone, the whistle of wind through the sleeping streets.

And then, after a long moment, Maxim's corpse rose.

It shuddered, like a curtain in a breeze, and then a sword drew itself free of the ruined chest and clattered to the ground. And then another, and another, one by one until all twelve blades were out, lengths of crimson steel lying in the street. Smoke began to leak in thin tendrils from every wound before drawing together into a cloud, then a shadow, and then, at last, something like a man. It took several tries, the darkness collapsing back into smoke again and again before finally managing to hold its shape, its edges wavering unsteadily as its chest rose and fell in smoldering breaths.

"*I am king,*" snarled the shadow as the whorls of red in the river vanished, and the mist thickened.

But the nightmare's hold was not quite as strong as it had been.

Osaron let out a growl of anger as his limbs dissolved, reformed. The spellwork etched into those swords still ran like ice through the veins of his power, stamping out heat and smothering flame. Such a stupid little spell, driven in so deep.

Osaron scowled down at the king's corpse, finally kneeling before him.

"All men bow."

Shadowy fingers flicked, once, and the body toppled, lifeless, to the ground.

Insolent mortal, thought the shadow king as he turned and stormed back across the sleeping city and up the bridge and into his palace, fuming as he struggled with every step to hold his shape. When his hand grazed a column, it went straight through as if he were *nothing.*

But the false king was dead, and Osaron lived on. It would take more than spelled metal, more than one man's magic, to kill a god.

The shadow king climbed the stairs to his throne and sat, smoking hands curled around the arms of his seat.

These mortals thought they were strong, thought they were clever, but they were nothing but children in this world—Osaron's world—and he had lived long enough to take their measure.

They had *no idea* what he was capable of.

The shadow king closed his eyes and opened his mind, reaching past the palace, past the city, past the world, to the very edges of his power.

Just as a tree might know itself, from deepest root to topmost leaf, Osaron knew every inch of his magic. And so he reached, and reached, and reached, grasping in the dark until he felt her there. Or rather, felt what was left of him inside her.

"Ojka."

Osaron knew, of course, that she was dead. Gone, blown away as all things were in time. He had felt the moment when it happened, even that small death rippling his psyche, the sudden sense of loss pale but palpable.

And yet—Osaron still ran through her. He was in her blood. That blood might no longer *flow,* but he still lived in it, his will a filament, a thread of wire woven through her straw body. Her consciousness was gone, her own will forfeit, but her form was still a form. A vessel.

And so Osaron filled the silence of her mind, and wrapped his will around her limbs.

"*Ojka,*" he said again. "*Get up.*"

III

White London

Nasi always knew when something was wrong.

It was a gut knowing, come from years of watching faces, hands, reading all the little tells a person made before they did a bad thing.

It wasn't a person going wrong now.

It was a world.

A chill was back in the air, the castle windows frosting at the corners. The king was gone, still gone, and without him, London was getting bad again, getting *worse*. The world felt like it was unraveling around her, all the color and life bleeding out the way it must have done the first time, all those years ago. Only according to the stories that was slow, and this was quick, like a snake shedding a skin.

And Nasi knew she wasn't the only one who felt it.

All of London seemed to sense the wrongness.

A few members of the king's Iron Guard, those still loyal to his cause, were doing their best to keep things from getting out of hand. The castle was under constant watch. Nasi hadn't been able to sneak out again, so she didn't have fresh flowers—not that many had survived the sudden chill—to lay near Ojka's body.

But she came anyway, in part because of the quiet, and in part because the rest of the world was getting scary, and if something happened, Nasi wanted to be near the king's knight, even if she was dead.

It was early morning—that time before the world woke up all the way, and she was standing beside the woman's head, saying a prayer, for power, for strength (they were the only prayers she knew). She was running out of words when, on the table, Ojka's fingers *twitched.*

Nasi startled, but even as her eyes widened and her heart skipped, she was talking herself down, the way she had done when she was little, and every little shadow had a way of becoming a monster. It could have been a trick of the light, probably was, so she reached out and tentatively touched the knight's wrist, feeling for a pulse.

Sure enough, Ojka was still cold. Still dead.

And then, abruptly, the woman sat up.

Nasi staggered back as the black cloth tumbled away from Ojka's face.

She didn't blink, didn't turn her head, or even seem to notice Nasi or the death table or the candlelit room. Her eyes were wide and flat and empty, and Nasi remembered the soldiers who used to guard Astrid and Athos Dane, hollowed out and spelled into submission.

Ojka looked like them.

She was real, and yet not real, alive and still very, very dead.

The wound at her neck was there and deep as ever, but now Ojka worked her jaw. When she tried to speak, a low hiss came from her ruined throat. The knight pursed her lips, and swallowed, and Nasi watched as tendrils of shadow and smoke wove over and around her neck, almost like a fresh bandage.

She leapt down from the table, upsetting the vines and bowls that Nasi had laid so carefully around her corpse. They fell to the floor with a clang and a crash.

Ojka had always been so graceful, but now her steps had the stilted quality of a colt, or a puppet, and Nasi backed up until her shoulder hit the pillar. The knight looked straight at the girl, shadows swimming through her pale eye. Ojka didn't speak, only stared, the drip of spilled water tapping on the stones behind her. Her hand had begun to drift toward Nasi's cheek when the doors swung open and two members of the Iron Guard stormed in, drawn by the crash.

They saw the dead knight standing upright and froze.

Ojka's hand fell away from Nasi as she spun toward them with returning grace. The air around her shimmered with magic, something from the table—a dagger—sailing into Ojka's hand.

The guards were shouting now, and Nasi should have run, should have done something, but she was frozen against the pillar, pinned by something as heavy as the strongest magic.

She didn't want to see what happened next, didn't want to see the king's knight die a second time, didn't want to see the last of Holland's guard fall to a ghost, so she crouched, squeezed her eyes shut, and pressed her hands over her ears. The way she used to when things got bad in the castle. When Athos Dane played with people until they broke.

But even through her hands, she heard the voice that came from Ojka's throat—not Ojka's at all, but someone else's, hollow and echoing and rich—and the guards must have been afraid of ghosts and monsters too, because when Nasi finally opened her eyes, there was no sign of Ojka or the men.

The room was empty.

She was all alone.

IV

The *Ghost* was almost back to Tanek when Lila felt the vessel drag to a sudden stop.

Not the smooth coasting of a ship losing current, but a jarring halt, unnatural at sea.

She and Kell were in their cabin when it happened, packing up their few belongings, Lila's hand drifting repeatedly to her pocket—the absence of her watch its own strange weight—while Kell's kept going to his chest.

"Does it still hurt?" she'd asked, and Kell had started to answer when the ship stuttered harshly, the groan of wood and sail cut off by Alucard calling them up. His voice had the peculiar lightness it took on when he was either drunk or nervous, and she was pretty sure he hadn't been drinking at the ship's wheel (though it wouldn't surprise her if he had).

It was a grey day above, mist clouding the world beyond the boat. Holland was already on deck, staring out into the fog.

"Why have you stopped?" demanded Kell, a crease between his brows.

"Because we have a problem," said Alucard, nodding ahead.

Lila scanned the horizon. The fog was heavier than it should have been given the hour, sitting like a second skin above the water. "I can't see anything."

"That's the idea," said Alucard. His hands splayed, his lips moved, and the mist he'd conjured thinned a little before them.

Lila squinted, and at first she saw nothing but sea, and then—

She went still.

It wasn't land ahead.

It was a line of ships.

Ten hulking vessels with pale wood bodies and emerald flags that cut the fog like knives.

A Veskan fleet.

"Well," said Lila slowly. "I guess that answers the question of who paid Jasta to kill us."

"And Rhy," added Kell.

"How far to land?" asked Holland.

Alucard shook his head. "Not far, but they're standing directly between us and Tanek. The nearest coast is an hour's sail to either side."

"Then we go around."

Alucard shot Kell a look. "Not in this," he said, gesturing at the *Ghost,* and Lila understood. The captain had maneuvered the ship so that its narrow prow faced the fleet's spine. As long as the fog lingered, as long as the *Ghost* held still, it *might* go unnoticed, but the moment it moved closer, it would be a target. The *Ghost* wasn't flying flags, but neither were the three small vessels bobbing like buoys beside the fleet, each running the white banner of a captured boat. The Veskans were clearly holding the pass.

"Should we attack?" asked Lila.

That drew looks from Kell, Alucard, *and* Holland.

"What?" she said.

Alucard shook his head, dismayed. "There are probably *hundreds* aboard those ships, Bard."

"And we're *Antari.*"

"*Antari,* not immortal," said Kell.

"We don't have time to battle a fleet," said Holland. "We need to get to land."

Alucard's gaze shifted back to the line of ships. "Oh, you can make it to the coast," he said, "but you'll have to *row.*"

Lila thought Alucard must be joking.

He wasn't.

V

Rhy Maresh kept his eyes on the light.

He stood at the edge of the spell circle where Tieren lay, and focused on the candle cradled in the priest's hands with its steady, unwavering flame.

He wanted to wake the *Aven Essen* from his trance, wanted to bury his head in the old man's shoulder and sob. Wanted to feel the calm of his magic.

In the last few months, he had become intimately acquainted with pain, and with death, but grief was new. Pain was bright, and death was dark, but grief was grey. A slab of stone resting on his chest. A toxic cloud stripping him of breath.

I can't do this alone, he thought.

I can't do this—

I can't—

Whatever his father had been trying to achieve, it hadn't worked.

Rhy had seen the river lighten, the shadows begin to withdraw, had glimpsed his city of red and gold like a specter through the fog.

But it hadn't lasted.

Within minutes, the darkness had returned.

He'd lost his father for what?

A moment?

A breath?

They'd recovered the king's body from the base of the palace steps.

His father, lying in a pool of cooling blood.

His father, now laid out beside his mother, a pair of sculptures, shells, their eyes closed, their bodies suddenly aged by death. When had his mother's cheeks grown hollow? When had his father's temples gone grey? They were impostors, gross imitations of the people they'd been in life. The people Rhy had loved. The sight of them—what was left of them—made him ill, and so he'd fled to the only place he could. The only person.

To Tieren.

Tieren, who slept with a stillness that might have passed for death if Rhy hadn't just seen it, hadn't pressed hands to his father's unmoving ribs, hadn't clutched his mother's stiffened shoulder.

Come back—

Come back—

Come back—

He did not say the words aloud, for fear of rousing the priest, some deep feeling that no matter how softly he might speak, the sadness would still be loud. The other priests knelt, their heads bowed, as if themselves in a trance, brows furrowed in concentration while Tieren's face bore the same smooth pallor of the men and women sleeping in the streets. Rhy would have given anything to hear the *Aven Essen*'s voice, to feel the weight of arms around his shoulders, to see the understanding in his eyes.

He was so close.

He was so far.

Tears burned Rhy's eyes, threatened to spill over, and when they did, they hit the floor an inch from the ashen edge of the binding circle. His fingers ached from where he'd struck Isra, shoulder throbbing where he'd twisted free of Sol-in-Ar's grip. But these pains were little more than memory, shallow wounds compared to the tearing in his chest, the absence where two people had been carved out, torn away.

His arms hung heavy at his sides.

In one hand, his own crown, the circle of gold he'd worn since he was a boy, and in the other, the royal pin capable of reaching Kell.

He had thought of summoning his brother, of course. Gripped the pin until the emblem of the chalice and sun had cut into his palm, even though Kell said blood wasn't necessary. Kell was wrong. Blood was always necessary.

One word, and his brother would come.

One word, and he wouldn't be alone.

One word—but Rhy Maresh couldn't bring himself to do it.

He had failed himself so many times. He wouldn't fail Kell, too.

Someone cleared their throat behind him. "Your Majesty."

Rhy let out a shuddering breath and stepped back from the edge of Tieren's spell. Turning, he found the captain of his father's city guard, a bruise blossoming along Isra's jaw, her own eyes lidded with grief.

He followed her out of the silent chamber and into the hall where a messenger stood waiting, breathless, his clothing slick with sweat and mud, as if he'd ridden hard. This was one of his father's scouts, sent to monitor the spread of Osaron's magic beyond the city, and for an instant, Rhy's tired mind couldn't process why the messenger had come to *him*. Then he remembered: there was no one else—and there it was again, worse than a knife, the sudden assault of memory, a raw wound reopened.

"What is it?" asked Rhy, his voice hoarse.

"I bring word from Tanek," said the messenger.

Rhy felt ill. "The fog has reached that far?"

The messenger shook his head. "No, sir, not yet, but I met a rider on the road. He spotted a fleet at the mouth of the Isle. Ten ships. They fly the silver-and-green banners of Vesk."

Isra swore beneath her breath.

Rhy closed his eyes. What was it his father said, that politics was a dance? Vesk was trying to set the tempo. It was time for Rhy to take the lead. To show that he was king.

"Your Majesty?" prompted the messenger.

Rhy opened his eyes.

"Bring me two of their magicians."

He met them in the map room.

Rhy would have preferred the Rose Hall, with its vaulted stone ceilings, its dais, its throne. But the king and queen were laid out there, so this would have to do.

He stood in his father's place behind the table, hands braced on the lip of the wood, and it must have been a trick of the senses, but Rhy thought he could feel the grooves where Maxim Maresh's fingers had pressed into the table's edge, the wood still lingering with warmth.

Lord Sol-in-Ar stood against the wall to his left, flanked on either side by a member of his retinue.

Isra and two members of the guard lined the wall to his right.

The Veskan magicians came, Otto and Rul, massive men led in by a pair of armored guards. On Rhy's orders, their manacles had been removed. He wanted them to realize that they weren't being punished for the actions of their crown.

Not yet.

In the tournament ring, Rul "the Wolf" had howled before every match.

Otto "the Bear" had beaten his chest.

Now, the two stood silent as pillars. He could tell by their faces that they knew of their rulers' treason, of the queen's murder, the king's sacrifice.

"We are sorry for your loss," said Rul.

"Are you?" asked Rhy, masking his sorrow with disdain.

While Kell had spent his childhood studying magic, Rhy had studied people, learned everything he could about his kingdom, from *vestra* and *ostra* down to commoner and criminal, and then he'd moved on to Faro and Vesk. And while he knew that a world couldn't truly be learned from a book, it would have to be a start.

After all, knowledge was a kind of power, a breed of strength. And Veskans, he'd been taught, respected anger and joy, even envy, but not grief.

Rhy gestured at the map. "What do you see?"

"A city, sir," answered Otto.

Rhy nodded at the line of figurines he'd placed at the mouth of Arnes. Small stone ships stained emerald green and flying grey banners. "And there?"

Rul frowned at the row. "A fleet?"

"A *Veskan* fleet," clarified Rhy. "Before your prince and princess attacked my king and queen, they sent word to Vesk and summoned a fleet of ten warships." He looked to Otto, who had stiffened at the news—not in guilt, he thought, but shock. "Has your kingdom grown so tired of our peace? Does it wish for war?"

"I . . . I am only a magician," said Otto. "I do not know my queen's heart."

"But you know your empire. Are you not a part of it? What does *your* heart say?"

The Veskans, Rhy knew, were a proud and stubborn people, but they were not fools. They savored a good fight, but did not go looking for war.

"We do not—"

"Arnes may be the battlefield," cut in Sol-in-Ar, "but if Vesk covets war, they will find it with Faro, too. Say the word, Your Majesty, and I will bring a hundred thousand soldiers to meet your own."

Rul had gone red as embers, Otto white as chalk.

"We did not *do* this," growled Rul.

"We knew nothing of this deceit," added Otto tightly. "We do not want—"

"*Want?*" snarled Rhy. "What does want have to do with it? Do I want my people to suffer? Do I want to see my kingdom plunged into war? The masses pay for the choices of a few, and if your royals had come to you and asked for your aid, can you say you would not have given it?"

"But they did not," said Otto coldly. "With respect, Your Majesty, a ruler does not follow her people, but a people must follow her rule. You are right, many pay for the choices of a few. But *royals* are the ones who choose, and we are the ones who pay for it."

Rhy fought the urge to cringe in the face of the words. Fought the urge to look to Isra or Sol-in-Ar.

"But you ask my heart," continued Otto, "and my heart has a family. My heart has a life and a home. My heart enjoys the fields of play, not war."

Rhy swallowed and took up one of the ships.

"You will write two letters," he said, weighing the marker in his palm. "One to the fleet, and one to the crown. You will tell them of the prince and princess's cold-blooded treason. You will tell them that they can withdraw now and we will take the actions of two royals to be their own. They can withdraw, and spare their country a war. But if they advance even a measure toward this city, they do so knowing they face a king who is very much alive, and an empire allied against them. If they advance, they will have signed the deaths of thousands."

His voice slipped lower as he spoke, the way his father's always had, the words humming like fresh-drawn steel.

"Kings need not raise their voices to be heard."

One of Maxim's many lessons.

"And what about this shadow king?" asked Rul icily. "Shall we write of him as well?"

Rhy's fingers tightened around the small stone ship. "My city's weakness will become yours if those ships cross into London. My people will sleep, but yours will die. For their sakes, I suggest you be as persuasive as possible." He set the marker back on the table. "Do you understand?" he said, the words more order than question.

Otto nodded. So did Rul.

As the doors closed behind them, the strength went out of Rhy's shoulders. He slumped back against the map room wall.

"How was that?" he asked.

Isra bowed her head. "Handled like a king."

There was no time to relish it.

The Sanctuary bells had gone silent with the rest of the city, but here in the palace, a clock began to chime. No one else stirred, because no one else had been counting time, but Rhy straightened.

Kell had been gone four days.

"Four days, Rhy. We'll make it back in that. And then you can get yourself into trouble. . . ."

But trouble had come and gone and come again without any sign of his brother. He had promised Kell he would wait, but Rhy had waited long enough. It was only a matter of time before Osaron recovered his strength. Only a matter of time before he turned his sights back on the palace. The city's last defense. It sheltered every waking body, every silver, every priest, guarded Tieren and the spell that kept the rest asleep. And if it fell, there would be nothing.

He'd made Kell a promise, but his brother was late, and Rhy could not stay here, entombed with the bodies of his parents.

He would not hide from the shadows when the shadows could not touch him.

He had a choice. And he would make it.

He would face the shadow king himself.

Once again, the captain of the guard barred his path.

Isra was his father's age, but where Maxim was—had been—broad, she was lean, wiry. And yet she was the most imposing woman he'd ever met, straight backed and severe, one hand always resting on the hilt of her sword.

"Stand aside," instructed Rhy, fastening the red-and-gold cape around his shoulders.

"Your Majesty," said the guard. "I was always honest with your father, and I will always be honest with you, so forgive me when I speak freely. How much blood must we feed this monster?"

"I will feed him every drop I have," said Rhy, "if it will sate him. Now, stand aside. That is an order from your king." The words scorched his throat as he said them, but Isra obeyed, stepping out of the way.

Rhy's hand was on the door when the woman spoke again, her voice low, insistent. "When these people wake," she said, "they will need their king. Who will lead them if you die?"

Rhy held the woman's gaze. "Haven't you heard?" he said, pushing open the door. "I am already dead."

VI

The *Ghost* had exactly one dinghy, a shallow little thing roped against the ship's side. It had one seat and two oars, meant to carry a single person between vessels, or perhaps between the vessel and the coast, if it either couldn't dock, or didn't want to.

The dinghy didn't look like it would hold four, let alone get them all to shore without sinking, but they didn't have much choice.

They lowered it to the water, and Holland went down first, steadying the little craft against the side of the *Ghost*. Kell had one leg over, but when Lila moved to follow, she saw Alucard still in the middle of the deck, attention trained on the distant fleet.

"Come on, Captain."

Alucard shook his head. "I'll stay."

"Now's not the time for grand acts," said Lila. "This isn't even your ship."

But for once Alucard's gaze was hard, unyielding. "I am the victor of the *Essen Tasch,* Bard, and one of the strongest magicians in the three empires. I cannot stop a fleet of ships, but if they decide to move, I'll do what I can to slow them down."

"And they'll kill you," said Kell, swinging his leg back onto deck.

The captain offered only a dry smile. "I've always wanted to die in glory."

"Alucard—" started Lila.

"The mist is my doing," he said, looking between them. "It should give you cover."

Kell nodded, and then after a moment, offered his hand. Alucard looked at it as if it were a hot iron, but he took it.

"*Anoshe,*" said Kell.

Lila's chest tightened at the word. It was what Arnesians said when they parted. Lila said nothing, because good-byes in any language felt like surrenders, and she wasn't willing to do that.

Even when Alucard wrapped his arms around her shoulders.

Even when he pressed a kiss to her forehead.

"You're my best thief," he whispered, and her eyes burned.

"I should have killed you," she muttered, hating the waver in her voice.

"Probably," he said, and then, so soft his words were lost to everyone but her, "Keep him safe."

And then his arms were gone, and Kell was pulling her toward the boat, and the last thing she saw of Alucard Emery was the line of his broad shoulders, his head held high as he stood alone on the deck, facing the fleet.

Lila's boots hit the dinghy floor, rocking it in a way that made Holland grip the side.

The last time she'd been in a boat this small, she'd been sitting in the middle of the sea with her hands tied and a barrel of drugged ale between her knees. That had been a bet. This was a gamble.

The dinghy pushed away, and within moments Alucard's mist was swallowing the *Ghost* from view.

"Sit down," said Kell, taking up an oar.

She did, reaching numbly for the second pole. Holland sat at the back of the little boat, casually rolling up his cuff.

"A little help?" said Lila, and his green eye narrowed at her as he produced a small blade and pressed it to his palm.

Holland brought his bleeding hand to the boat's side and said a phrase she'd never heard before—*As Narahi*—and the small craft lurched forward in the water, nearly throwing Kell and Lila from their bench.

Mist sprayed up into her eyes, salty and cold, the wind whipping around her face, but as her vision cleared she realized the dinghy was racing forward, skimming the surface of the water as if propelled by a dozen unseen oars.

Lila looked to Kell. "You didn't teach me this one."

His jaw was slack. "I . . . I didn't know it."

Holland gave them both a bland look. "Amazing," he said dryly. "There are still things you haven't learned."

VII

The streets were filled with bodies, but Rhy felt entirely alone.

Alone, he left his home.

Alone, he moved through the streets.

Alone, he climbed the icy bridge that led to Osaron's palace.

The doors swung open at his touch, and Rhy stilled—he'd half expected to find a grim replica of his own palace, but found instead a specter, a skeletal body hollowed out and filled in again with something less substantial. There were no grand hallways, no staircases leading up to other floors, no ballrooms or balconies.

Only a cavernous space, the bones of the arenas still visible here and there beneath the veneer of shadow and magic.

Pillars grew up from the floor like trees, branching toward a ceiling that gave way here and there to open sky, an effect that made the palace seem at once a masterpiece and a ruin.

Most of the light came from that broken roof, the rest from within, a glow that suffused every surface like fire trapped behind thick glass. Even that thin light was being swallowed up, blotted out by the same black slick he'd seen spreading through the city, magic voiding nature.

Rhy's boots echoed as he willed himself forward through the vast hall, toward the magnificent throne waiting at its center, as natural and unnatural as the palace around it. Ethereal, and empty.

The shadow king stood several paces to the side, examining a corpse.

The corpse itself was on its feet, held up by ribbons of darkness that ran like puppet strings from head and arms up toward the ceiling.

Threads that not only propped the body up, but seemed to be stitching it back together.

It was a woman, he could tell that much, and when Osaron twitched his fingers, the threads pulled tight, lifting her face toward the watery light. Her red hair—redder even than Kell's—hung lank against her hollow cheeks, and below one closed eye, black spilled down her face as if she'd been weeping ink.

Without a shell, Osaron himself looked as spectral as his palace, a half-formed image of a man, the light shining through him every time he moved. His cloak billowed, caught by some imaginary wind, and his whole form rippled and shuddered, as if it couldn't quite hold itself together.

"What are you?" said the shadow king, and though he faced the corpse, Rhy knew the words were meant for *him*.

Alucard had warned Rhy of Osaron's voice, the way it echoed through a person's head, snaked through their thoughts. But when he spoke, Rhy heard nothing but the words themselves ringing against stone.

"I am Rhy Maresh," he answered, "and I am king."

Osaron's shadowy fingers slipped back to his sides. The woman slumped a little on her strings.

"Kings are like weeds in this world." He turned, and Rhy saw a face made of layered shadow. It flickered with emotions, there and gone and there and gone, annoyance and amusement, anger and disdain. *"Has this one come to beg, or kneel, or fight?"*

"I've come to see you for myself," said Rhy. "To show you the face of this city. To let you know that I am not afraid." It was a lie—he was indeed afraid, but his fear paled against the grief, the anger, the need to act.

The creature gave him a long, searching look. *"You are the empty one."*

Rhy shivered. "I am not empty."

"The hollow one."

He swallowed. "I am not hollow."

"The dead one."

"I am not dead."

The shadow king was coming toward him now, and Rhy fought the urge to retreat. *"Your life is not your life."*

Osaron reached out a hand, and Rhy stepped back, then, or tried to, only to find his boots bound to the floor by a magic he couldn't see. The shadow king brought his hand to Rhy's chest, and the buttons on his tunic crumbled, the fabric parting to reveal the concentric circles of the seal scarred over his heart. Slivers of cold pierced the air between shadow and skin.

"My magic." Osaron made a gesture, as if to tear the seal away, but nothing happened. *"And not my magic."*

Rhy let out a shaky breath. "You have no hold on me."

A smile danced across Osaron's lips, and the darkness tightened around Rhy's boots. Fear grew louder then, but Rhy fought hard to smother it. He was not a prisoner. He was here by choice. Drawing Osaron's attention, his wrath.

Forgive me, Kell, he thought, leveling his gaze on the shadow king.

"Someone took my body from me once," he said. "They took my will. Never again. I am not a puppet, and there is *nothing* you can make me do."

"You are wrong." Osaron's eyes lit up like a cat's in the dark. *"I can make you suffer."*

Cold knifed up Rhy's shins as the bindings around his ankles turned to ice. He caught his breath as it began to spread, not up his limbs, but around his entire body, a curtain, a column, devouring first his vision of the shadow king and his dead puppet, and then the throne, and finally the entire chamber, until he was trapped inside a shell of ice. Its surface was so smooth, he could see his own reflection, distorted by the warp of the ice as it thickened. Could see the shadow of the creature on the other side. He imagined Osaron grinning.

"Where is the Antari *now?"* A ghostly hand came to rest against the ice. *"Shall we send him a message?"*

The column of ice shivered, and then, to Rhy's horror, it began to grow spikes. He tried to retreat, but there was nowhere to go.

Rhy bit back a scream as the first point pierced his calf.

Pain flared through him, hot and bright, but fleeting.

I am not empty, he told himself as a second spike cut into his side. A muffled cry as another shard drove through his shoulder, sliding in and out of his collar with terrible ease.

I am not hollow.

The air caught in his chest as ice pierced a lung, his back, his hip, his wrist.

I am not dead.

He had seen his mother run through, his father killed by a dozen steel blades. And he could not save them. Their bodies were their own. Their lives, their own.

But Rhy's was not. It was not a weakness, he realized now, but a strength. He could suffer, but it could not break him.

I am Rhy Maresh, he told himself as blood slicked the floor.

I am the king of Arnes.

And I am unbreakable.

VIII

They were nearly to the coast when Kell started to shiver.

It was a cold day, but the chill had come on from somewhere else, and just as he realized it for what it was—an echo—the pain caught up. Not a glancing blow, but sudden and violent and sharp as knives.

Not again.

It lanced through his leg, his shoulder, his ribs, opening into a full-blown assault against his nerves.

He gasped, bracing himself against the side of the boat.

"Kell?"

Lila's voice was distant, drowned out by the pulse raging in his ears.

He *knew* his brother couldn't die, but it didn't douse the fear, didn't stop the simple, animal panic that pounded in his blood, crying out for help. He waited for the pain to pass, the way it always had before, fading with every heartbeat like a rock thrown into a pond, the crash giving way to smaller ripples before finally smoothing.

But the pain didn't pass.

Every breath brought a new rock, a new crash.

Lila's hands hovered in the air. "Can I heal you?"

"No," said Kell, breath jagged. "It's not . . . his body isn't . . ." His mind spun.

"Alive?" offered Holland.

Kell scowled. "Of course it's *alive.*"

"But that life is not his," countered Holland calmly. "He's just a shell. A vessel for your power."

"Stop."

"You've cut strings from your magic and made a puppet."

The water surged around the small boat with Kell's temper.

"Stop." This time the word was coming from Lila. "Before he sinks us."

But Kell heard the question in her voice, the same one he'd asked himself for months.

Was something truly alive if it couldn't be killed?

A week after Kell had bound his brother's life to his, he'd woken with a sudden pain searing across his palm, white hot, as if the skin were burning. He'd stared down at the offending hand, certain the flesh would be blistered, charred, but it wasn't. Instead, he'd found his brother sitting in his rooms before a low table with a candle on it, eyes distant as he held his hand over the flame. Kell had snatched Rhy's fingers away, pressing a damp rag to the red and peeling skin as his brother slowly came back his senses.

"I'm sorry," Rhy had said, a now tiring refrain. "I just needed . . . to know."

"Know what?" he'd snapped, and his brother's eyes had gone lost.

"If I'm real."

Now Kell shuddered on the floor of the small boat, the echo of his brother's pain fierce, unyielding. This didn't feel like a self-inflicted wound, no candle flame or word scrawled on skin. This pain was deep and piercing, like the blade to the chest but worse, because it was coming from everywhere.

Bile filled Kell's mouth. He thought he'd already been sick.

He tried to remember that pain was only terrifying because of what it signaled—danger, death—that without those things, it was nothing . . .

His vision blurred.

. . . just another sense . . .

His muscles screamed.

. . . a tether . . .

Kell shivered violently, and registered Lila's arms circling him, thin but strong, the warmth of her narrow body like a candle against the cold. She was saying something, but he couldn't make out the words.

Holland's voice came in and out, reduced to short bursts of incoherent sound.

The pain was smoothing—not easing, exactly, just evening into something horrible but steady. He dragged his thoughts together, focused his vision, and saw the coast approaching. Not the port at Tanek, but a stretch of rocky beach. It didn't matter. Land was land.

"Hurry," he murmured thickly, and Holland shot him a dark look.

"If this boat goes any faster, it will catch fire before we have a chance to crash upon those rocks." But he saw the magician's fingertips go white with force, felt the world part around his power.

One moment the jagged shore was rising in the distance, and the next, it was nearly upon them.

Holland rose to his feet, and Kell managed to uncoil his aching body, his mind clearing enough to think.

He had his token in hand—the swatch of fabric the queen had given him, *KM* stitched on the silk—and fresh blood streaked the cloth as the dinghy drew precariously close to the rocky shore. Their coats were soaked with icy water by the time they drew near enough to disembark.

Holland stepped off first, steadying himself atop sea-slicked rocks.

Kell started to follow, and slipped. He would have crashed down into the surf, had Holland not been there to catch his wrist and haul him up onto the shore. Kell turned back for Lila, but she was already beside him, her hand in his and Holland's on his shoulder as Kell pressed the swatch of cloth to the rock wall and said the words to take them home.

The freezing mist and the jagged coast instantly vanished, replaced by the smooth marble of the Rose Hall, with its vaulted ceiling, its empty thrones.

There was no sign of Rhy, no sign of the king and queen, until he turned and saw the wide stone table in the middle of the hall.

Kell stilled, and somewhere behind him, Lila drew in a short, shocked breath.

It took him a moment to process the shapes that lay on top, to understand that they were bodies.

Two bodies, side by side atop the stone, each draped with crimson cloth, the crowns still shining in their hair.

Emira Maresh, with a white rose, edged in gold, laid over her heart.

Maxim Maresh, the petals of another rose scattered across his chest.

The cold settled in Kell's bones.

The king and queen were dead.

IX

Alucard Emery had imagined his death a hundred times.

It was a morbid habit, but three years at sea had given him too much time to think, and drink, and dream. Most of the time his dreams started with Rhy, but as the nights lengthened and the glasses emptied, they invariably turned darker. His wrists would ache and his thoughts would fog, and he'd wonder. When. How.

Sometimes it was glamorous and sometimes it was gruesome. A battle. A stray blade. An execution. A ransom gone wrong. Choking on his own blood, or swallowing the sea. The possibilities were endless.

But he never imagined death would look like this.

Never imagined that he would face it alone. Without a crew. Without a friend. Without a family. Without even an enemy, save the faceless masses that filled the waiting ships.

Fool, Jasta would have said. *We all face death alone.*

He didn't want to think of Jasta. Or Lenos. Or Bard.

Or *Rhy.*

The sea air scratched at the scars on Alucard's wrists, and he rubbed at them as the ship—it wasn't even *his* ship—rocked silently in the surf.

The Veskans' green and silver were drawn in, the ships floating grimly, resolutely, a mountainous line along the horizon.

What were they waiting for?

Orders from Vesk?

Or from within the city?

Did they know about the shadow king? The cursed fog? Was that what held them at bay? Or were they simply waiting for the cover of night to strike?

Sanct, what good was it to speculate?

They hadn't moved.

Any minute they *could* move.

The sun was sinking, turning the sky a bloody red, and his head was pounding from the strain of holding the mist for as long as he had. It was beginning to thin, and there was nothing he could do but wait, wait, and try to summon the strength to—

To do what? challenged a voice in his head. *Move the sea?*

It wasn't possible. That wasn't just a line he'd fed Bard to keep her from doing herself in. Everything had limits. His mind raced, the way it had been racing for the last hour, stubbornly, doggedly, as if it might finally round a corner and find an idea—not a mad notion parading as a plan, but an *actual* idea—waiting for him.

The sea. The ships. The sails.

Now he was just listing things.

No. Wait. The *sails.* Perhaps he could find a way to—

No.

Not from this distance.

He would have to move the *Ghost,* sail her right up to the ass end of the Veskan fleet and then—what?

Alucard rubbed his eyes.

If he was going to die, he could at least think of a way to make it count.

If he was going to die—

But that was the problem.

Alucard didn't *want* to die.

Standing there on the prow of the *Ghost,* he realized with startling clarity that death and glory didn't interest him nearly as much as living long enough to go home. To make sure Bard was alive, to try to find any remaining members of the *Night Spire.* To see Rhy's amber eyes, press his lips to the place where his collar curved into his throat. To kneel before his prince, and offer him the only thing Alucard had ever held back: the truth.

The mirror from the floating market sat in its shroud on a nearby crate.

Four years for a gift that would never be given.

Movement in the distance caught his eye.

A shadow gliding across the twilit sky—now a bruised blue instead of bloody red. His heart lurched. It was a bird.

It plunged down onto one of the Veskan ships, swallowed up by the line of mast and net and folded sail, and Alucard held his breath until his chest ached, until his vision spotted. This was it. The order to move. He didn't have much time.

The sails . . .

If he could damage the sails . . .

Alucard began to gather every piece of loose steel aboard the ship, ransacked the crates and the galley and the hold for blades and pots and silverware, anything he could fashion into something capable of cutting. Magic thrummed in his fingers as he willed the surfaces sharp, molded serrated edges into the sides.

He lined them up like soldiers on the deck, three dozen makeshift weapons that could rend and tear. He tried to ignore the fact that the sails were down, tried to smother the knowledge that even *he* didn't have the ability control this many things at once, not with any delicacy.

But brute force was better than nothing.

All he had to do was bring the *Ghost* in range to strike. He was lifting his attention to his own sails when he saw the Veskan sails draw taut.

It happened in a wave, green and silver blossoming out from the masts at the center ship, and then the ones to either side, on and on until the whole fleet was ready to sail.

It was a gift, thought Alucard, readying his weapons, pulling on the air with the remains of his strength as the first ship began to move.

Followed by a second.

And a third.

Alucard's jaw went slack. The last of his strength faltered, died.

The wind dissolved, and he stood there, staring, a makeshift blade tumbling from his fingers, because the Veskan ships weren't sailing toward Tanek and the Isle and the city of London.

They were sailing *away*.

The fleet's formation dissolved as they pivoted back toward open sea.

One of the ships passed close enough for him to see the men aboard, and a Veskan soldier looked his way, broad face unreadable beneath his helm. Alucard lifted a hand in greeting. The man didn't wave back. The ship continued on.

Alucard watched them go.

He waited for the waters to still, for the last colors to fade from the sky.

And then he folded to his knees on the deck.

X

Kell stared, numbly, at the bodies on the table.

His king and queen. His father and his mother . . .

He heard Holland say his name, felt Lila's fingers curl around his arm. "We have to find Rhy."

"He's not here," said a new voice.

It was Isra, the head of the city guard. Kell had taken the woman for a statue with her full armor and bowed head, had forgotten the rules of mourning—the dead were never left alone.

"Where?" he managed. "Where is he?"

"The palace, sir."

Kell started for the doors that led back into the royal palace, when Isra stopped him.

"Not that one," said the woman wearily. She pointed to the massive front doors of the Rose Hall, the ones that led out to the city street. "The *other* one. On the river."

Kell's pulse pounded madly in his chest.

The *shadow* palace.

His head spun.

How long had they been gone?

Three days?

No, four.

Four days, Rhy.

Then you can get yourself into trouble.

Four days, and the king and queen were dead, and Rhy hadn't waited any longer.

"You just let him go?" snapped Lila, accosting the guard.

Isra bristled. "I had no choice." She met Kell's eyes. "As of today, Rhy Maresh is the king."

The reality landed like a blow.

Rhy Maresh, young royal, flirtatious rake, resurrected prince.

The boy always looking for places to hide, who moved through his own life as if it were a piece of theatre.

His brother, who had once accepted a cursed amulet because it promised strength.

His brother, who now carved apologies into his skin and held his hands over candle flames to feel alive.

His brother was king.

And his first act?

To march straight into Osaron's palace.

Kell wanted to wring his Rhy's neck, but then he recalled the pain he'd felt, wave after wave rocking him in the boat, crashing through him even now, a current of suffering. *Rhy.* Kell's feet carried him past Isra, past row after row of large stone basins to the doors of the Rose Hall and out into the thin London light.

He heard their steps behind him, Lila's thief-soft and quick, Holland's sure, but he didn't look back, didn't look down at the sea of spelled bodies lying in the street, kept his eyes trained on the river, and the impossible shadow stretching up against the sky.

Kell had always thought of the royal palace like a second sun caught in perpetual rise over the city. If that was true, Osaron's palace was an eclipse, a piece of perfect darkness, only its edges rimmed with reflected light.

Somewhere behind him, Holland drew a weapon from a fallen man's sheath, and Lila swore softly as she wove through the bodies, but neither strayed far from his side.

Together, the three *Antari* climbed the onyx incline of the palace bridge.

Together, they reached the polished black glass of the palace doors.

The handle gave under Kell's touch, but Lila caught his wrist and held it firm.

"Is this really the best plan?" she asked.

"It's the only one we have," said Kell as Holland drew the Inheritor over his head and slipped the device into his pocket. He must have sensed Kell staring, because he looked up, met his gaze. One eye green and one black, and both as steady as a mask.

"One way or another," said Holland, "this ends."

Kell nodded. "It ends."

They looked to Lila. She sighed, freeing Kell's fingers.

Three silver rings caught the dying light—Lila's and Kell's the narrower echoes of Holland's band—all of them singing with shared power as the door swung open, and the three *Antari* stepped through into the dark.

FOURTEEN

ANTARI

I

As Kell's boot crossed the threshold, the pain flared in his chest. It was as if the walls of Osaron's palace had muted the connection, and now, without the boundaries, the cord drew tight, and every step brought Kell closer to Rhy's suffering.

Lila had two knives already out, but the palace was empty around them, the hall clear. Tieren's magic had worked, stripped the monster of his many puppets, but Kell still felt Lila's nervous tension in his own limbs, saw that same unease reflected again in Holland's inscrutable face.

There was a wrongness to this place, as if they'd stepped out of London, out of time, out of life entirely, and into somewhere that didn't quite exist. It was magic without balance, power without rule, and it was dying, every surface slowly taking on the glossy black pall of nature burned to nothing.

But in the center of the vast chamber, Kell felt it.

A pulse of life.

A beating heart.

And then, as Kell's eyes adjusted to the low light, he saw Rhy.

His brother hung several feet off the floor, suspended within a web of ice, held up by a dozen sharpened points that drove in and through the prince's body, their frosted surfaces slick with red.

Rhy was alive, but only because he could not die.

His chest stuttered and heaved, tears frozen on his cheeks. His lips moved, but his words were lost, his blood a broad dark pool beneath him.

Is this yours? Rhy had asked when they were young, and Kell had cut his wrists to heal him. *Is all this yours?*

Now Rhy's blood splashed under Kell's boots, the air metallic in his mouth as he raced forward.

"Wait!" called Lila.

"Kell," warned Holland.

But if it was a trap, they'd already been caught. Caught the moment they entered the palace.

"Hold on, Rhy."

Rhy's lashes fluttered at the sound of Kell's voice. He tried to raise his head, but couldn't.

Kell's hand was already wet with his own blood when he reached his brother's side. He would have melted the ice with a single touch, a word, if he'd had the chance.

Instead his fingers stopped an inch above the ice, barred by someone else's will. Kell fought against the magic's hold as a voice spilled from the shadows behind the throne.

"That is mine."

The voice came from nowhere. Everywhere. And yet, it was contained. No longer a hollow construction of shadow and magic, but bounded by lips and teeth and lungs.

She walked into the light, red hair rising into the air around her face as if caught up in some imaginary wind.

Ojka.

Kell had *followed* her.

Listened to her lies in the palace courtyard—the words mixing with doubt and anger into something poisonous—and let her lead him through a door in the world and into a trap.

And when he saw Ojka now, he shivered.

Lila had *killed* her.

Faced her in the hall with Kell screaming beyond the door and Rhy dying a world away and no choice but to fight, losing a glass eye before she cut the woman's throat.

And when she saw Ojka now, she smiled.

Holland had *made* her.

Plucked her from the streets of the Kosik, the alleys that had shaped his own past so many years before, and given her the chance Vortalis had given him, the chance to do more, to be more.

And when he saw Ojka now, he stilled.

II

Ojka, the assassin—

Ojka, the messenger—

Ojka, the *Antari*—

—wasn't Ojka anymore.

"*My king,*" she'd called Holland so many times, but her voice had always been low, sultry, and now it resonated through the hall and in his head, familiar and strange, just as this place was familiar and strange. Holland had faced Osaron in an echo of this palace when the shadow king was nothing but glass and smoke and the dying ember of magic.

And now he faced him again, in his newest shell.

Ojka once had yellow eyes, but now they both shone black. A crown perched in her hair, a dark and weightless ring that thrust up spikes like icicles into the air above her head. Her throat was wrapped in black ribbon, her skin at once luminous with power and unmistakably dead. She never drew breath, and her dark veins stood out on her skin, parched, empty.

The only signs of life, impossibly, came from those black eyes—*Osaron's* eyes—which danced with light and swirled with shadows.

"*Holland,*" said the shadow king, and anger burned in him to hear the monster form the word with Ojka's lips.

"I killed you," mused Lila, crouched at Holland's left side, her knives at the ready.

Ojka's face contorted with amusement.

"*Magic does not die.*"

"Let my brother go," demanded Kell, stepping in front of the other two *Antari,* his voice imperious, even now.

"Why should I?"

"He has no power," said Kell. "Nothing for you to use, nothing for you to *take.*"

"And yet he lives," mused the corpse. *"How curious. All life has strings. So where are his?"*

Ojka's chin tipped up, and the ice spearing Rhy's body splayed like fingers, drawing from the prince a stifled cry. The color drained from Kell's face as he fought back a mirrored scream, pain and defiance warring in his throat. The ring sang on Holland's fingers as their shared power hummed between them, trying to tip toward Kell in his distress.

Holland held it steady.

Ojka's hands, delicate but strong, rose, palms up. *"Have you finally come to beg,* Antari? *To kneel?"* Those swimming black eyes went to Holland. *"To let me in?"*

"Never again," said Holland, and it was true, though the Inheritor hung heavy in his pocket. Osaron had a talent for sliding through one's mind, turning over its thoughts, but Holland had more practice than most at hiding his. He forced his mind away from the device.

"We've come to stop you," said Lila.

Ojka's hands fell back to her sides. *"Stop me?"* said Osaron. *"You cannot stop time. You cannot stop change. And you cannot stop me. I am inevitable."*

"You," said Lila, "are nothing but a demon masquerading as a god."

"And you," said Osaron smoothly, *"will die slowly."*

"I killed that body once," she countered. "I think I can do it again."

Holland was still staring at Ojka's corpse. The bruises on her skin. The cloth wrapped tight around her throat. As if Osaron felt the weight of that gaze, he turned his stolen face toward Holland. *"Are you not happy to see your knight?"*

Holland's anger had never burned hot. It was forged cold and sharp, and the words were a whetstone along its edge. Ojka had been loyal, not to Osaron, but to *him.* She had served him. Trusted him. Looked at him and seen not a god, but a king. And she was dead—like Alox, like Talya, like Vortalis.

"She did not let you in."

A tip of the head. A rictus grin. *"In death, none can refuse."*

Holland drew a blade—a scythe, taken from a body in the square. "I will cut you from that body," he said. "Even if I have to do it one piece at a time."

Fire sparked across Lila's knives.

Blood dripped from Kell's fingers.

They had shifted slowly around the shadow king, circling, caging. Just as they'd planned.

"No one offers," instructed Kell. "No matter what Osaron says or does, no matter what he promises or threatens, *no one* lets him in."

They were sitting in the *Ghost*'s galley, the Inheritor between them.

"So we're just supposed to play coy?" said Lila, spinning a dagger point-down on the wooden table.

Holland started to speak, but the ship gave a sudden sway and he had to stop, swallow. "Osaron covets what he does not have," he said when the wave of illness had passed. "The goal is not to *give* him a body, but to force him into needing one."

"Splendid," said Lila dryly. "So all we have to do is defeat an incarnation of magic strong enough to ruin worlds."

Kell shot her a look. "Since when do you shy from a fight?"

"I'm not shying," she snapped. "I just want to be sure we can *win*."

"We win by being stronger," said Kell. "And with the rings, we just might be."

"*Might* be," echoed Lila.

"Every vessel can be emptied," said Holland, twisting the silver binding ring around his thumb. "Magic can't be killed, but it can be weakened, and Osaron's power might be vast, but it is by no means infinite. When I found him in Black London, he was reduced to a statue, too weak to hold a moving form."

"Until *you* gave him one," muttered Lila.

"Exactly," said Holland, ignoring the jab.

"Osaron has been feeding on my city and its people," added Kell. "But if Tieren's spell has worked, he should be running out of sources."

Lila dislodged her dagger from the table.

"Which means he should be good and ready for a fight."

Holland nodded. "All we have to do is give him one. Make him weak. Make him desperate."

"And then what?" demanded Lila.

"*Then,*" said Kell, "and only then, do we give him a host." Kell nodded at Holland when he said it, the Inheritor hanging around the *Antari*'s neck.

"And what if he doesn't pick *you*?" she snarled. "It's well and good to offer, but if he gives *me* a shot, I'm going to take it."

"Lila," started Kell, but she cut him off.

"So will you. Don't pretend you won't."

Silence settled over them.

"You're right," said Kell at last, and to Holland's surprise— though it shouldn't have surprised him anymore—Lila Bard cracked a smile. It was hard and humorless.

"It's a race, then," she said. "May the best *Antari* win."

Osaron moved with a fraction of Ojka's grace, but twice as much speed. Twin swords blossomed from her hands in plumes of smoke and became real, their surfaces shining as they sliced the air where Lila had been a moment before.

But Lila was already airborne, pushing off the nearest pillar as Holland willed a gust of wind through the hall with blinding force, and Kell's steel shards flew on the gust like heavy rain.

Ojka's hands came up, stilling the wind and the steel within as Lila plummeted down toward Ojka's body, carving a path down her back.

But Osaron was too quick, and Lila's knife barely grazed the shoulder of his host. Shadow poured from the wound like steam before stitching the dead skin closed.

"*Not fast enough, little* Antari," he said, backhanding her across the face.

Lila fell sideways, knife tumbling from her grip even as she rolled up into a fighting crouch. She flicked her fingers and the fallen blade sang through the air, burying itself in Ojka's leg.

Osaron growled as more smoke spilled out of the wound, and Lila flashed a cold smile. "I learned that one from her," she said, a fresh blade appearing in her fingers. "Right before I cut her throat."

Ojka's mouth was a snarl. "*I will make you—*"

But Holland was already moving, electricity dancing along his scythe as it cut the air. Osaron turned and blocked the blow with one sword, driving the other up toward Holland's chest. He spun out of the way, the blade grazing his ribs as Kell attacked from the other side, ice curled around his fist.

It shattered against Ojka's cheek, slicing through to bone. Before the wound could heal, Lila was there, blade glowing red with heat.

They moved like pieces of the same weapon. Danced like Ojka's knives—back when *she* had wielded them—every push and pull conveyed through the tether between them. When Lila moved, Holland felt her path. When Holland feinted, Kell knew where to strike.

They were blurs of motion, shards of light dancing around a coil of darkness.

And they were winning.

III

Lila was running out of knives.

Osaron had turned three of them to ash, two to sand, and a sixth—the one she'd won from Lenos—had vanished entirely. She had only one left—the knife she'd nicked from Fletcher's shop her first day in Red London—and she wasn't keen on losing it.

Blood ran into her good eye, but she didn't care. Smoke was seeping from Ojka's body in a dozen places as Kell and Holland and the demon clashed. They'd made their mark.

But it wasn't enough.

Osaron was still on his feet.

Lila swiped a thumb along her bloody cheek and knelt, pressing her hand against the stone, but when she tried to summon it, the rock resisted. The surface hummed with magic, yet rang hollow.

Because, of course, it wasn't *real*.

A dream thing, dead inside, just like—

The floor began to soften, and she leapt back an instant before it turned to tar. Another one of Osaron's traps.

She was sick of playing by the shadow king's rules.

Surrounded by a palace only he could will.

Lila's gaze swept the chamber, and then went up—up past the walls to the place where the sky shone through. She had an idea.

Lila reached out with all her strength—and part of Holland's, part of Kell's—and *pulled,* not on the air, but on the Isle.

"You cannot will the ocean," Alucard had told her once.

But he never said anything about a river.

✝ Blood trickled down Lila's throat as she pressed the kerchief to her nose.

Alucard was sitting across from her, chin in one hand. "I'm honestly not sure how you've lived this long."

Lila shrugged, her voice muffled by the cloth. "I'm hard to kill."

The captain shoved to his feet. "Stubborn's not the same thing as infallible," he said, pouring himself a drink, "and I've told you three times you cannot move the fucking ocean, no matter how hard you try."

"Maybe *you're* not trying hard *enough,*" she muttered.

Alucard shook his head. "Everything has a scale, Bard. You cannot will the sky, you cannot move the sea, you cannot shift the whole continent beneath your feet. Currents of wind, basins of water, patches of earth, that is the breadth of a magician's reach. That is the circumference of their power."

And then, without warning, he lobbed the wine bottle at her head.

She was quick enough to catch it, but just barely, fumbling the cloth from her bloody nose. "What the hell, Emery?" she snapped.

"Can you fit your hand around it?"

She looked down at the bottle, her fingers wrapped around the glass, their tips a breath away from touching.

"Your hand is your hand," said Alucard simply. "It has limits. So does your power. It can only hold so much, and no matter how hard you stretch your fingers around that glass, they will never touch."

She shrugged, spun the bottle in her hand, and shattered it against the table.

"And now?" she said.

Alucard Emery groaned. He pinched the bridge of his nose the way he did when she was being particularly maddening. She'd taken to counting the number of times a day she could make him do it.

Her current record was seven.

Lila sat forward in her seat. Her nose had stopped bleeding, though she could still taste the copper on her tongue. She willed the broken shards up into the air between them, where they formed a cloud in the vague shape of a bottle.

"You're a brilliant magician," she said, "but there's something you just don't get."

He slumped back into his chair. "What's that?"

Lila smiled. "The trick to winning a fight isn't strength, but strategy."

Alucard raised his brows. "Who said anything about fighting?"

She ignored him. "And *strategy* is just a fancy word for a special kind of common sense, the ability to see options, to make them where there were none. It's not about knowing the rules."

Her hand fell away, and the bottle crumbled again, falling in a rain of glass.

"It's about knowing how to break them."

IV

It wasn't enough, thought Holland.

For every blow they landed, Osaron avoided three, and for every one they dodged, Osaron landed three in turn. Blood began to dot the floor.

It spilled down Kell's cheek. Dripped from Lila's fingers. Slicked the cloth at Holland's side.

His head spun as the other two *Antari* drew on his power.

Kell was busy summoning a force of wind while Lila had gone very still, her head tipped back toward the place where the bones of the ceiling met the sky.

Osaron saw the opening and moved toward her, but Kell's wind whipped through the throne room, trapping the shadow king within a tunnel of air.

"We have to do something," he called over the wind as Osaron slashed at the column. Holland knew it wouldn't hold, and sure enough, moments later, the cyclone shattered, slamming Kell and Holland both backward in the blast. Lila staggered, but stayed on her feet, a trickle of red running from her nose as the pressure in the palace rose and darkness blacked the windows to either side.

Kell was just finding his feet when Osaron sprang toward her again, too fast for Kell to catch. Holland touched the gash across his ribs.

"*As Narahi,*" he said, the words thundering through him.

Quicken.

It was a hard piece of magic under the best circumstances, and a grueling one now, but it was worth it as the world around him *slowed.*

To his right, Lila still looked up. To his left, Kell was drawing his hands apart against the massive force of time, a fire sparking in slow motion between his palms. Only Osaron still moved with any semblance of speed, black eyes shifting his way as Holland spun the scythe and lunged.

They clashed together, apart, together again.

"I will make you bend."

Weapon against weapon.

"I will make you break."

Will against will.

"You were mine, Holland."

His back hit a pillar.

"And you will be mine again."

The blade raked his arm.

"Once I hear you beg."

"Never," Holland snarled, slashing the scythe. It should have met Osaron's swords, but at the last instant the weapons disappeared and he caught Holland's blade with Ojka's bare hands, letting the steel cut deep. Blood—dead, black, but still *Antari*—leaked around the blade, and Osaron's stolen face split into a grim, triumphant smile.

"As Ste—"

Holland gasped, letting go of the scythe before the spell was out.

It was a mistake. The weapon turned to ash in Osaron's grip, and before Holland could dodge, the demon wrapped one bloody hand around his face and pinned him back against the pillar.

Overhead, a shadow was blotting out the sky. Holland's hands wrapped around Osaron's wrists, trying to pry them loose, and for an instant the two were locked in a strange embrace, before the shadow king leaned in and whispered in his ear.

"As Osaro."

Darken.

The words echoed through his head and became shadow, became night, became a black cloth cinching over Holland's sight, blotting out Osaron, and the palace, and the wave of water cresting overhead, and plunging Holland's world into black.

❧

Blood was dripping from Lila's nose as the wave of black water curled over the palace—

Too big—

Far too big—

And then it *fell.*

Lila let go of the river, head spinning as it came crashing down onto the palace hall. She threw her hands up to block the crushing weight, but her magic was slow—too slow—in the conjuring's wake.

The pillar shielded Holland from the worst of the blow, but the water slammed Ojka's body down into the floor with an audible crack. Lila dove for cover but found none, and only Kell's quick reflexes spared them both the same fate. She felt her power dip as Kell pulled it close to his and cast it back in a shield above her head. The river fell like heavy rain, spilling in curtains around her.

Through the veil she saw Ojka's body twitch and flex, broken pieces already knitting back together as Osaron forced the puppet up.

Nearby, Holland was on his hands and knees, fingers splayed on the flooded floor as if searching for something he'd dropped.

"Get up!" shouted Lila, but when Holland's head swiveled toward her, she recoiled. His eyes were wrong. Not black, but shuttered, blind.

There was no time.

Osaron was up and Holland wasn't and she and Kell were both racing forward, boots splashing in the shallow water as it spun up around them into weapons.

A sword spilled from nothing into Osaron's hand as Holland struggled, empty-eyed. His fingers wrapped around the shadow king's ankle, but before he could issue a spell he was being sent backward with a vicious kick, skidding across the flooded ground.

Kell and Lila ran, but they were too slow.

Holland was on his knees in front of the shadow king with his raised sword.

"I told you I would make you kneel."

Osaron brought the blade down, and Kell slowed the weapon in a cloud of frost as Lila dove for Holland, tackling him out of the way the instant before the metal struck stone.

Lila spun up, throwing off water into shards of ice that sang through the air. Osaron flung up a hand, but he wasn't fast enough, wasn't *strong* enough, and several slivers of ice found flesh before he could will them away.

There was no time to relish the victory.

With a single sweep of his arm, every drop of river water she'd summoned came together and swirled up into a column before turning to dark stone. Just another pillar in his palace.

Osaron pointed at Lila. *"You will—"*

She sprang at him, shocked when the now-dry floor splashed beneath her feet. The stone pooled around her ankles, one moment liquid and the next solid again, pinning her the way the floor had pinned Kisimyr on the palace roof.

No.

She was trapped, and she had the last knife out and in her hand, fire starting in the other as she braced herself for an attack that never came.

Because Osaron had turned.

And he was heading for *Kell.*

Kell had only a stolen moment as Lila fought Osaron, but he sprinted for the prison of ice.

Hold on, Rhy, he pleaded, slashing his blade at the frozen cage, only to be rebuffed by the shadow king's will.

He tried again and again, a frustrated sob clawing up his throat.

Stop.

He didn't know if he heard Rhy's voice, or only felt it as he tried to reach him. His brother's head was bowed, blood running into his amber eyes and turning them gold.

Kell—

"Kell!" shouted Lila, and he looked up, catching Ojka's reflection in the column of ice as it surged toward him. He spun, drawing the crimson-stained water at his feet up into a spear, and lifting the weapon an instant before the shadow king struck.

Osaron's twin blades came singing down, shattering the spear in Kell's hands before lodging in the walls of Rhy's prison. The ice cracked, but didn't break. And in that moment, when Osaron's weapons were trapped, his stolen shell caught between attack and retreat, Kell drove the broken shard of ice into Ojka's chest.

The shadow king looked down at the wound, as if amused by the feeble attempt, but Kell's hand was a mess from gripping the shattered spear, blood slicking hand and ice alike, and when he spoke, the spell rang through the air.

"As Steno."

Break.

The magic tore through Ojka's body, warring with Osaron's will as her bones broke and mended, shattered and set, a puppet being torn apart in one breath, patched together in the next. Fighting—and failing—to hold its shape, the shadow king's stolen shell began to look grotesque, pieces peeling, the whole thing knit together more by magic than sinew.

"That body will not hold," snarled Kell as broken hands forced him up against his brother's cage.

Osaron smiled a ruined grin. *"You are right,"* he said, as an icy spike drove through Kell's back.

V

Someone screamed.

A single, agonized note.

But it wasn't Kell.

He *wanted* to scream, but Ojka's ruined hand was wrapped around his jaw, forcing his mouth closed. The frozen blade had pierced above his hip and come out his side, its tip coated with vivid red blood.

Beyond Osaron, Lila was trying to tear herself free, and Holland was on his hands and knees, searching the ground for something lost.

A groan escaped Kell's throat as the shadow king prodded the tear in his side.

"This is not a mortal wound," said Osaron. *"Not yet."*

He felt the monster's voice sliding through his mind, weighing him down.

"Let me in," it whispered.

No, thought Kell viscerally, violently.

That darkness—the same darkness that had caught him when he fell into White London so recently—wrapped around his wounded body, warm, soft, welcoming.

"Let me in."

No.

The column of ice burned cold against his spine.

Rhy.

Osaron echoed in his mind. Said, *"I can be merciful."*

Kell felt the shards of ice slide free—not from his own body but his brother's—pain withdrawing limb by limb. He heard the short gasp, the soft, wet sound of Rhy collapsing to the blood-slicked floor, and relief surged through him even as the cold took root again, branched, flowered.

"*Let me in.*"

In the corner of Kell's vision, something flashed on the floor. A shard of metal, near Holland's searching hand.

The Inheritor.

Kell's mind was slipping with the pain as he called it toward him, but as the cylinder rose into the air, his power failed, suddenly, completely. As if severed, stolen.

Snatched away by a thief.

Lila couldn't move.

The floor gripped her legs in a stone embrace, bones threatening to break with every motion. Across the chamber Kell was trapped and bleeding, and she couldn't reach him, not with her hands, couldn't force Osaron away. But she could draw him to her. She pulled on the tether between them, stealing Kell's magic, and Osaron's attention with it. Power flared like light before Lila's eyes, and the demon spun toward her, a moth drawn to a flame.

Look at me, she wanted to say as Osaron abandoned Kell. *Come to me.*

But as soon as those black eyes leveled on her, she would have given everything to get loose. To be free.

Kell was horribly pale, his fingers slipping over the blade of ice driven through his side. Holland clutched at a pillar and struggled to his feet. The Inheritor sat on the ground nearby, but before Lila could summon it, Osaron was there, one mangled hand knotted in her hair and a blade against her throat.

"*Let go,*" he whispered, and whether he meant her knife or her will, she didn't know. But at least she had his attention now. She let the weapon fall with a clatter to the floor.

He forced her face toward his, her gaze toward his, felt him sliding through her mind, probing thoughts, memories.

"So much potential."

She tried to pull away, but she was pinned, the floor gripping her ankles and Osaron her scalp and the blade still at her throat.

"I am what you saw in the mirror at Sasenroche," said the shadow king. *"I am what you dream of being. I can make you unstoppable. I can set you free."*

Across the throne room, Kell had finally summoned the strength to break free. The ice shattered around him and he collapsed to the floor. Osaron didn't turn. His attention was on her, eyes dancing hungrily in the light of her power.

"Free," she said softly, as if pondering the word.

"Yes," whispered the shadow king.

In the black of his eyes, she saw it, that version of herself.

Unbeatable.

Unbreakable.

"Let me in, Delilah Bard."

It was tempting, even now. Her hand drifted up to Ojka's arm. A dancer's embrace. Bloody fingers digging into ruined flesh.

Lila smiled. *"As Illumae."*

Osaron wrenched back, but he was too late.

Ojka's body began to burn.

The blade slashed blindly at Lila's throat but she dodged, and then it was gone, tumbling from Ojka's hand as the corpse went up in flames.

Smoke poured from the thrashing body, first the acrid stuff of burning flesh, and then the dark fog of Osaron's power as it was finally forced to flee its shell.

The palace shuddered with the sudden loss of his power, his control. The floor loosened around her boots and Lila stumbled forward, free, as Osaron struggled to find form.

The shadows swirled, fell apart, swirled again.

The Osaron that took shape was a ghost of himself.

A brittle facade, transparent and flat. His edges bled and blurred, and through his spectral center she could see Kell clutching the wound across his front. Rhy, struggling to rise.

This was it.

570 ·   V. E. SCHWAB

Her chance.

Their chance.

She flexed her fingers, reaching for the Inheritor. It trembled on the ground and rose toward her.

And then it fell, tumbled back to the floor as her strength vanished. It was like being swallowed by a wave in reverse. All the power flooding suddenly, violently, away. Lila gasped as the world tilted beneath her, legs buckling, her vision dim.

Magic was such a new thing that the absence of it shouldn't have hurt so much, but Lila felt gutted as every last ounce of power was wrenched away. She cast about for Kell, certain that he had stolen her strength, but Kell was still on the ground, still bleeding.

The shadow king loomed over her, hands splayed, and the air began to coil around Lila's throat, tightening until she couldn't speak, couldn't breathe.

And there, behind him, in a halo of silver light, stood Holland.

Holland couldn't see.

The darkness was everywhere, raging around him like a storm, swallowing the world. But he could hear. And so he heard Kell being stabbed, heard Ojka burn, heard the Inheritor as Lila called it from the ground, and knew it was his chance. And when he drew on the binding ring, and pulled the magic of the other two *Antari* to him, he found a kind of sight. The world took shape not in light and dark, but in ribbons of power.

The strands glowed, flowing around and through Lila's kneeling form, and Kell's, and Rhy's, all of it drawn in silver light.

And there, right in front of him, the absence.

A man in the shape of a void.

A void in the shape of a man.

No longer a puppet. Just a piece of rotten magic, smooth and black and empty.

And when the shadow king spoke, it was his own voice, liquid, susurrant.

"*I know your mind, Holland,*" said the darkness. "*I lived inside it.*"

The shadow king came toward him, and Holland took a single, final step back, his shoulders meeting the pillar as his fingers tightened on the metal cylinder.

He could feel Osaron's hunger.

His need.

"*Do you want to see your world? How it crumbles without you in it?*"

A cold hand, not flesh and blood but shadow and ice, came to rest against Holland's heart.

I am tired, he thought, knowing Osaron would hear. *Tired of fighting. Of losing. But I will never let you in.*

He felt the darkness smile, sickly and triumphant.

"*Have you forgotten?*" whispered the shadow king. "*You never cast me out.*"

Holland exhaled. A shuddering breath.

To Osaron, it might have sounded like fear.

To Holland, it was simply relief.

It ends, he thought as the darkness wrapped itself around him, and sank in.

VI

Lila was on her knees when it happened.

Osaron returned to Holland, like steam into a pot, and his body went rigid. His back arched. His mouth opened in a silent scream, and for an awful moment, Lila thought it was too late, thought he'd been too slow, hadn't had the time, or the strength, or the will to hold on—

And then Holland slammed the Inheritor's point into his palm and said a word through gritted teeth.

"Rosin."

Give.

An instant later, the shadow palace exploded into light.

Lila gasped as something began to tear inside her and she remembered the binding ring. She closed her hand into a fist and smashed the band against the stone floor, severing the connection before the Inheritor could pull her in as well.

But Kell wasn't fast enough.

A scream escaped his throat and Lila scrambled up, stumbling toward him as he curled in, clawing at the ring with blood-slicked fingers.

Rhy reached him first.

The prince was shuddering, his body slipping between life and death, whole and unmade and whole again as he knelt over Kell, his ghostly fingers wrapped around his brother's hand. The ring came free. It skated across the floor, bouncing once before dissolving into smoke.

Kell collapsed against Rhy, ashen and still, and Lila fell to her knees beside them, smearing blood on Kell's cheek as she felt his face, ran a hand through his hair, the copper parted by a streak of silver.

He was alive, he had to be alive, because Rhy was still there, leaning over him, eyes empty and full at the same time, soaked in blood, but breathing.

In the center of the room, Holland was a sphere of light, a million silver threads laced with black, all of it visible, all of it unraveling into the air around him in silence that wasn't silent at all but ringing in her ears.

And then, suddenly, the light was gone.

And Holland's body folded to the floor.

VII

Kell opened his eyes and saw the world falling apart.

No, not the world.

The palace.

It was crumbling, not like a building made of steel and stone, but like embers burning, rising up instead of down. That was the way the shadow palace fell. It simply broke apart, the imagined dissolving, leaving only the real behind, bit by bit, stone by stone, until he was lying on the floor not of a palace, but in the ruined remains of the centered arena, the seats empty, the silver-and-blue banners still drifting in the breeze.

Kell tried to sit up, and gasped, forgetting he'd been stabbed.

"Easy," said Rhy with a wince. His brother was kneeling beside him, covered in blood, his clothing torn in a dozen places where the ice had run him through. But he was alive, the skin beneath the cloth already knitting, though the ghost of pain lingered in his eyes.

Holland's words came back to Kell.

"You've cut strings from your magic and made a puppet."

Holland. He dragged himself slowly upright, and found Lila crouching over the other *Antari*.

Holland was lying on his side, curled up as if he'd simply gone to sleep. But the only time Kell had seen him sleep, everything about him had been tense, wracked by nightmares, and now his features were smooth, his sleep dreamless.

Only three things broke the image of peace.

His charcoal hair, which had turned a shocking white.

His hands, which still clutched the Inheritor, its point driven through his palm.

And the device itself, which had taken on an eerie but familiar darkness. An absence of light. A void in the world.

Holland had done it.

He had trapped the shadow king.

VIII

In myths, the hero survives.

The evil is vanquished.

The world is set right.

Sometimes there are celebrations, and sometimes there are funerals.

The dead are buried. The living move on.

Nothing changes.

Everything changes.

This is a myth.

This is not a myth.

The people of London still lay in the streets, wrapped tight within the cloth of sleep. Had they woken at that very moment, they would have seen the light flare within the spectral palace, like a dying star, banishing the shadows.

They would have seen the illusion crumble, the palace collapsing back into the bones of the three arenas, banners still waving overhead.

If they had gotten to their feet, they would have seen the oily darkness on the river crack like ice, giving way to red, the mist thinning the way it does in the morning, before the market opens.

If they had looked long enough, they would have seen the figures picking their way out of the rubble—the prince (now their king) staggering down the crumbling bridge with his arm around his brother, and they might have wondered who was leaning on whom.

They would have seen the girl standing where the palace doors had been, not the collapsed entrance to the stadium. Would have seen her cross her arms against the cold and wait until the royal guards came.

Would have seen them carrying the body out, with its hair the same white as that dying star.

But the people in the street didn't wake. Not just yet.

They didn't see what happened.

And so they never knew.

And none who had been within the shadow palace—which was not a palace anymore but the bones of something dead, something ruined, something broken—said anything of that night, save that it was over.

A myth without a voice is like a dandelion without a breath of wind.

No way to spread the seeds.

FIFTEEN

ANOSHE

I

The king of England did not like to be kept waiting.

A goblet of wine hung from his fingers, sloshing precariously as he paced the room, prevented from spilling over only by his constant sips. George IV had left the party—a party in *his* honor (as were most of those he bothered to attend)—to make this monthly meeting.

And Kell was late.

He had been late before—his arrangement, after all, had been with George's father, and as the old man failed in health, Kell had made a point of being late to spite him, George was sure—but the messenger had never been *this* late.

The agreement was clear.

The trade of letters scheduled for the fifteenth of every month.

By six in the evening, and no later than seven.

But as the clock against the wall struck *nine,* George was forced to refill his own glass because he'd dismissed everyone else. All to please his guest. A guest who was absent now.

A letter bulged on the table. Not only a missive—the time for idle correspondence was passed—but a set of demands. Instructions, really. One artifact of magic per month in exchange for England's best technology. It was more than fair. The seeds of magic for the seeds of might. Power for power.

The clock chimed again.

Half past nine.

The king sank onto the sofa, buttons straining against his not inconsiderable form. His father had only been in the ground six weeks, and already Kell was proving a problem. Their relationship would have to be corrected. The rules defined. He was not a daft old man, and he would not stand for the messenger's temper, magic or no.

"Henry," called George.

He did not shout the name—kings need not need raise their voices to be heard—but a moment later the door opened and a man came through.

"Your Majesty," he said with a bow.

Henry Tavish was an inch or two taller than George himself—a detail that irked the king—with a heavy mustache and dark, trim hair. A handsome fellow with the rather unhandsome job of conducting business the crown wouldn't—couldn't—do itself.

"He's late," said the king.

Henry knew of his visitor's name and station.

George had been careful, of course, hadn't gone about spreading the word of this other London, much as he'd have liked to. He knew what would happen if word got out too soon. Some might see eye to eye, but woven in with the wonder, there would be a poisonous thread of skepticism.

"Such tales," they'd say. "Perhaps troubled minds run in the family."

Revolutionaries were too easily mistaken for madmen.

And George would not have that. No, when he revealed magic to this world—*if* he revealed it—it would not be a whisper, a rumor, but a demonstrable, undeniable threat.

But Henry Tavish was different.

He was essential.

He was a *Scotsman,* and every good Englishman knew that a Scotsman had few qualms about getting his hands dirty.

"No sign of him as yet," said the man in his gruff but lilting way.

"You checked the Stone's Throw?"

King George was no fool. He'd been having the foreign "ambassador" followed since before he was crowned, had his fair share of men reporting that they'd lost sight of the strange man in the stranger coat, that he had simply disappeared—*apologies, Your Majesty, so sorry, Your*

Majesty—but Kell never left London without a visit to the Stone's Throw.

"It's called the Five Points now, sir," said Henry. "Run by a rather squirrelly fellow named Tuttle after the death of its old owner. Gruesome thing, according to authorities, but—"

"I don't need a history lesson," cut in the king, "only a straight answer. Did you check the tavern?"

"Aye," said Henry, "I went by, but the place was closed up. Strange thing, though, as I could hear someone in there, scurrying around, and when I told Tuttle to open up, he said he couldn't. Not wouldn't, mind, couldn't. Struck me as suspicious. You're either in or you're out, and he sounded even more wound up than normal, like something had him spooked."

"You think he was hiding something."

"I think he was *hiding*," amended Henry. "It's a known thing that that pub caters to occultists, and Tuttle's a self-proclaimed magician. Always thought it was a scam, even with your telling me about this Kell—I went inside once, nothing but some curtains and crystal balls— but maybe there's a reason your traveler frequented that place. If he's up to something, perhaps this Tuttle knows what. And if your traveler's got a mind to stand you up, well, maybe he'll still show there."

"The insolence of it," muttered George. He set his cup on the table and hauled himself to his feet, snatching up the letter from the table.

It appeared there were still some things a king must do himself.

It was getting worse.

Much worse.

Ned had tried banishing spells in three different languages, one of which he didn't even *speak*. He'd burned all the sage he had stockpiled, and then half the other herbs he kept in the kitchen, but the voice was getting louder. Now his breath fogged no matter how high the hearth was stoked, and that black spot on the floor had grown first to the size of a book, then a chair, and it was now larger than the table he'd hurriedly pushed against the doors.

He had no choice.

He had to summon Master Kell.

Ned had never successfully summoned anyone, unless you counted his great-aunt when he was fourteen, and he still wasn't entirely sure it was her, since the kettle had been overfilled, and the cat quick to spook. But desperate times.

There was, of course, the problem of Kell's being in another world. But then, so was this creature, it seemed, and *it* was reaching through, so perhaps Ned could whisper back. Perhaps the walls were thinner here. Perhaps there was a draft.

Ned lit five candles around the element kit and the coin Kell had gifted him on his last visit, a makeshift altar in the center of the tavern's most auspicious table. The pale smoke, which was spreading even in the absence of the sage, seemed to bend around the offering, which Ned took as a very good sign.

"All right, then," he said to no one and to Kell and the darkness in between. He sat, elbows on the table and palms up, as if waiting for someone to reach out and take his hands.

Let me in, whispered that ever-present voice.

"I summon Kell—" Ned paused, realizing he didn't know the other man's full name, and began again. "I summon the traveler known as Kell, from London far away."

Worship me.

"I summon a light against the dark."

I am your new king.

"I summon a friend against an enemy I do not know."

Goose bumps broke out along Ned's arm—another good sign, at least, he hoped. He pressed on.

"I summon the stranger with the many mantles."

Let me in.

"I summon the man with eternity in his eye, and magic in his blood." The candles shivered.

"I summon *Kell.*"

Ned closed his hands into fists, and the quivering flames went out.

He held his breath as five tendrils of thin white smoke trailed into the air, forming five faces with five yawning mouths.

"Kell?" he ventured, voice trembling.

Nothing.

Ned sank back into his chair.

Any other night, he would have been over the moon to extinguish the candles, but it wasn't enough.

The traveler hadn't come.

Ned reached out and took up the foreign coin with the star at its center and the lingering scent of roses. He turned it over in his fingers.

"Some magician," he muttered to himself.

Beyond the bolted door, he heard the heavy clomp of a coach and four drawing up, and a moment later, a fist pounded on the wood.

"Open up!" bellowed a deep voice.

Ned sat up straight, pocketing the coin. "We're closed!"

"Open this door!" ordered the man again, "by orders of His Majesty the King!"

Ned held his breath as if he could starve the moment out with lack of air, but the man kept knocking and the voice kept saying *Let me in* and he didn't know what to do.

"Break it down," ordered a second voice, this one smooth, pompous.

"Wait!" called Ned, who really couldn't afford to lose the front door, not when that slab of wood was one of the only things keeping the darkness from spilling out.

He slid the bolt, opened the door a crack, just enough to see a man with a sleek handlebar mustache filling the step.

"I'm afraid there's been a leak, sir, not fit for—"

The mustached man shoved the door inward with a single push, and Ned stumbled backward as George the Fourth strode into his pub.

The man wasn't dressed as the king, of course, but a king was a king whether they wore silk and velvet or burlap. It was in his bearing, his haughty look, and, of course, the fact that his face was on the newly minted coin in Ned's pocket.

But even a king would still be in danger.

"I beg of you," said Ned. "Leave this place at once."

The king's man snorted, while George himself sneered. "Did you just issue an order to the king of England?"

"No, no, of course not, but, Your Majesty—" His gaze darted nervously around the room. "It isn't safe."

The king crinkled his nose. "The only thing poised to cause me ill is the state of this place. Now where is Kell?"

Ned's eyes widened. "Your Majesty?"

"The traveler known as Kell. The one who's frequented this pub once a month without fail for the last seven years."

The shadows were beginning to draw together behind the king. Ned swore to himself, half curse, half prayer.

"What was that?"

"Nothing, Your Majesty," stammered Ned. "I haven't seen Master Kell this month, I swear it, but I could send word—" The shadows had faces now. The whispers were growing. "—Send word if he comes around. I know your address." A nervous laugh. The shadows leered. "Unless you'd rather I make it out to—"

"What the devil are you looking at?" demanded the king, glancing back over his shoulder.

Ned couldn't see His Majesty's face, so he couldn't gauge the expression that crossed it when the king saw the ghosts with their gaping mouths and their scornful eyes, their silent commands to *kneel,* to *beg,* to *worship.*

Could they hear the voices, too? wondered Ned. But he never got the chance to ask.

The king's man crossed himself, turned on his heel, and left the Five Points without a backward glance.

The king himself went very still, jaw working up and down without making any sound.

"Your Majesty?" prompted Ned as the ghosts yawned and collapsed into smoke, into mist, into nothing.

"Yes . . ." said George slowly, smoothing his coat. "Well, then . . ."

And without another word, the king of England drew himself up very straight, and walked very briskly out.

II

It was raining when the hawk returned.

Rhy was standing on an upper balcony, under the shelter of the eaves, watching as freights hauled the remains of the tournament arenas from the river. Isra waited just inside the doorway. Once the captain of his father's city guard, now the captain of *his* royal one. She was a statue dressed in armor, while Rhy himself wore red, as was the custom for those in mourning.

Veskans, he'd read, streaked their faces with black ash, while Faroans painted their gems white for three days and three nights, but Arnesian families celebrated loss by celebrating life, and that they did by wearing red: the color of blood, of sunrise, of the Isle.

He felt the priest come through the door behind him, but did not turn, did not greet him. He knew that Tieren was grieving, too, but he couldn't bear the sadness in the old man's eyes, couldn't bear the calm, cold blue. The way he'd listened to the news of Emira, of Maxim, his features still, as if he'd known, before the spell was done, that he would wake to find the world changed.

And so they stood in silence beneath the curtain of rain, alone with their thoughts.

The royal crown sat heavy in Rhy's hair, much larger than the golden band he'd worn for most of his life. That band had grown with him, the metal drawn out every year to fit his changing stature. It should have lasted him another twenty years.

Instead, it had been stripped away, stored for a future prince.

Rhy's new crown was too great a weight. A constant reminder of his loss. A wound that wouldn't close.

The rest of his wounds *did* heal—far too fast. Like a pin driven into clay, the damage absorbed as soon as the weapon was gone. He could still summon the feelings, like a memory, but they were distant, fading, leaving that horrible question in their wake.

Was it real?

Am I real?

Real enough to ache with grief. Real enough to reach out a hand and savor the spring rain as it dripped coolly on his skin. To step out of the palace's shelter and let it soak him to the bone.

And real enough to feel his heart quicken when the streak of darkness slid past against the pale sky.

He recognized the bird at once, knew it came from Vesk.

The foreign fleet had retreated from the mouth of the Isle, but the crown had yet to answer for its crimes. Col was dead, but Cora sat in the royal prisons, waiting to learn her fate. And here it was, strapped to the ankle of a hawk.

Word of Col and Cora's treason had spread with the waking of the city, and London was already calling for Rhy to take the empire to war. The Faroans had pledged their aid—a little too quickly for his tastes—and Sol-in-Ar had returned to Faro in the name of diplomacy, which Rhy feared meant readying his soldiers.

Sixty-five years of peace, he thought grimly, ruined by a pair of bored, ambitious children.

Rhy turned and made his way downstairs, Isra and Tieren falling into step beside him. Otto was waiting in the foyer.

The Veskan magician shook the rain from his coarse blond hair, a scroll—its seal already broken—clutched in his hand.

"Your Majesty. I bring news from my crown."

"What news?" asked Rhy.

"My queen does not court war."

It was a hollow phrase. "But her children do."

"She wishes to make amends."

Another empty promise. "How?"

"If it pleases the Arnesian king, she will send a year's worth of winter wine, seven priests, and her youngest son, Hok, whose gift for stone magic is unsurpassed in all of Vesk."

My mother is dead, Rhy wanted to scream, *and you would give me drink and danger.* Instead he said only, "And what of the princess? What will the queen give me for her?"

Otto's expression hardened. "My queen wants nothing of her."

Rhy frowned. "She is her blood."

Otto shook his head. "The only thing we despise more than a traitor is a failure. The princess went against her queen's command for peace. She set her own mission, and then she failed to see it through. My queen grants Your Majesty leave to do with Cora as he will."

Rhy rubbed his eyes. Veskans did not look at mercy and see strength, and he knew the only solution the queen sought, the only one she would *respect,* was Cora's death.

Rhy resisted the urge to pace, to chew his nails, to do a dozen different things that were not *kingly.* What would his father say? What would his father *do*? He resisted the urge to look at Isra, or Tieren, to defer, to escape.

"How do I know the queen won't use her daughter's execution against me? She could claim I broke the final strands of peace, slaughtered Cora in the name of revenge."

Otto said nothing for a long moment and then, "I do not know my queen's mind, only her words."

It could all be a trap, and Rhy knew it. But he could see no other choice.

His father had told him so many things about peace and war, had compared it to a dance, a game, a strong wind, but the words that rose in Rhy's mind now were some of the first.

War against an empire, Maxim had said, was like a knife against a well-armored man. It may take three strikes or thirty, but if the hand was determined, the blade would eventually find its way in.

"Like your queen," he said at last, "I do not covet war. Our peace has been made fragile, and a public execution could either quell my city's anger or inflame it."

"Something need not be a demonstration to be an act," said Otto. "So long as the right eyes see it done."

Rhy's hand drifted to the hilt of the gold short sword at his hip. It was meant to be decorative, another piece of his elaborate mourning garb, but it had been sharp enough to cut down Col. It would do the same for Cora.

At the sight of the gesture, Isra stepped forward, speaking for the first time.

"I will do it," she offered, and Rhy wanted to let her, wanted to shed the business of killing. There had been enough blood.

But he shook his head, forced himself toward the prison cell.

"The death is mine," he said, trying to infuse the words with an anger he didn't feel—wished he felt, for it would have burned hot where grief ran cold.

Tieren did not follow—priests were made for life, not death—but Otto and Isra fell in step behind him.

Rhy wondered if Kell could feel his racing heart, if he would come running—the king wondered, but didn't wish it. His brother had his own chapters to close.

As soon as Rhy's boots hit the stairs, he knew something was wrong.

Instead of being met by Cora's lilting voice, he was met by silence and the metal tang of blood on his tongue. He plunged down the last few steps into the prison, taking in the scene.

There were no guards.

The princess's cell was still locked.

And Cora lay inside, stretched out on the stone bench, her fingers trailing limply along the floor, nails swallowed by the shining slick of blood.

Rhy rocked back.

Someone must have slipped her a blade. Had it been a mercy or a taunt? Either way, she'd slashed her arms from elbow to wrist and written a single Veskan word on the wall above the bench.

Tan'och.

Honor.

Otto stared in silence, but Rhy rushed forward to open the cell, to what end, he didn't know. Cora of Vesk was dead. And even though he'd come to kill her, the sight of her lifeless body, her empty gaze, still made him sick. And then—shamefully—relieved. Because he hadn't known if he could do it. Hadn't wanted to find out.

Rhy unlocked the cell and stepped inside.

"Your Majesty—" started Isra as blood stained his boots, splashed up onto his clothes, but Rhy didn't care.

He knelt, brushing the limp blond hair from Cora's face before he forced himself upright, forced his voice steady. Otto's gaze was trained not on the body but the bloody word painted on the wall, and Rhy sensed the danger in it, the call to action.

When the Veskan's blue eyes swung back to Rhy's, they were flat, steady.

"A death is a death," said Otto. "I will tell my queen it's done."

III

Ned was drooping with fatigue. He hadn't slept more than a handful of hours in the past three days, and then not at all since the king's visit. The shadows had stopped sometime before dawn, but Ned didn't trust the silence any more than he had the sound, so he kept the windows boarded and the door locked, and stationed himself at a table in the center of the room with a glass in one hand and his ceremonial dagger in the other.

His head was beginning to loll when he heard the voices coming from the front step. He stumbled to his feet, nearly overturning the chair as the locks on the tavern door began to *move*. He watched in abject horror as the three bolts slid free one by one—drawn back by some invisible hand—and then the handle shuddered, the door groaning as it opened inward.

Ned took up the nearly empty bottle in his free hand, wielding it like a bat, oblivious to the last few drops that spilled into his hair and down his collar as two shadows crossed the threshold, their edges rimmed with mist.

He moved to strike, only to find the bottle stripped from his fingers. A second later it struck the wall and shattered.

"*Lila,*" said a familiar—and exasperated—voice.

Ned squinted, eyes adjusting to the sudden light. "Master Kell?"

The door swung shut again, plunging the room back into a lidded dark as the magician came forward. "Hello, Ned."

He had his black coat on, the collar turned up against the cold. His eyes shone in their magnetic way, one blue, the other black, but a streak

of silver now marred the copper of his hair, and there was a new gaunt-
ness to his face, as though he'd been long ill.

Beside him, the woman—Lila—cocked her head. She was rakishly
thin, with dark hair that brushed her jaw and trailed across her
eyes—one brown, the other black.

Ned stared at her with open awe. "You're like him."

"No," said Kell dryly, striding past him. "She's one of a kind."

Lila winked at that. She was holding a small chest between her
hands, but when Ned offered to take it from her, she pulled back,
setting it instead on the table, one hand resting protectively on its lid.

Master Kell was making a circle of the room, as if looking for in-
truders, and Ned started, remembering his manners.

"What can I do for you?" he asked. "Have you come for a drink? I
mean, of course you haven't just come for a drink, unless you have,
and then I'm truly flattered, but . . ."

Lila made a decidedly unladylike noise, and Kell shot her a look before offering Ned a tired smile. "No, we haven't come for a drink, but
perhaps you'd better pour one."

Ned nodded, ducking behind the bar to fetch a bottle.

"Bit gloomy, isn't it?" mused Lila, taking a slow turn.

Kell took in the shuttered windows, the spell book and the ash-
strewn floor. "What's happened here?"

Ned needed no further encouragement. He launched into the story
of the nightmares and the shadows and the voices in his head, and to
his surprise, the two magicians listened, their drinks untouched, his
own glass emptying twice before the tale was done.

"I know it sounds like lunacy," he finished, "but—"

"But it doesn't," said Kell.

Ned's eyes widened. "Did you see the shadows too, sir? What were
they? Some kind of echo? It was dark magic, I'll tell you that. I did
everything I could here, blockaded the pub, burned every bit of sage
and tried a dozen different ways to clear the air, but they just kept coming. Until they stopped, quick as you like. But what if they come
again, Master Kell? What am I to do?"

"They won't come again," said Kell. "Not if I have your help."

Ned started, certain he'd misheard. He'd dreamed a hundred times of this moment, of being wanted, being needed. But it was a dream. He always woke up. Beneath the counter's edge, he pinched himself hard, and didn't wake.

Ned swallowed. "*My* help?"

And Kell nodded. "The thing is, Ned," he said, eyes trailing to the chest on the table. "I've come to ask a favor."

Lila, for one, thought it was a bad idea.

Admittedly, she thought anything involving the Inheritor was a bad idea. As far as she was concerned, the thing should be sealed in stone and locked inside a chest and dropped down a hole to the center of the earth. Instead, it was sealed in stone and locked inside a chest and brought here, to a tavern in the middle of a city without magic.

Entrusted to a man, *this* man, who looked a bit like a pigeon, with his large eyes and his flitting movements. The strange thing was, he reminded her a little of Lenos—the nervous air, the fawning looks, even if they were geared at Kell instead of her. He seemed to teeter on the line between wonder and fear. She watched as Kell explained the chest's contents, not entirely, but enough—which was probably too much. Watched as this Ned fellow nodded so fast his head looked hinged, eyes round as a child's. Watched as the two carried the chest down into the cellar.

They would bury it there.

She left them to it, drifting through the tavern, feeling the familiar creak of boards under her feet. She scuffed her boot on a small, smooth patch of black, the same suspicious slick that lingered in the streets of Red London, places where magic had rotted through. Even with Osaron gone, the damage stayed done. Not everything, it seemed, could be fixed with a spell.

In the hall, she found the narrow stairs that led up to a landing, then up again to the small green door. Her feet moved without her, climbing the worn steps one by one until she reached Barron's room. The door stood ajar, giving way to a space that was no longer his. She averted her gaze, unsure if she would ever be ready to see it, and continued up, Kell's voice fading by the time she reached the top. Beyond the small green door, her room sat untouched. Part of the floor was dark, but not smooth, the faintest trace of fingers in the ruddy stain where Barron had died.

She crouched, brought her hand to the marks. A drop of water hit the floor, like the first sign of a London rainfall. Lila wiped her cheek brusquely and stood up.

Scattered across the floor, like tarnished stars, were beads of shot from Barron's gun. Her fingers twitched, the magic humming in her blood, and the metal rose into the air, drawing together like a blast rewound until the beads gathered, fused, formed a single sphere of steel that fell into her outstretched palm. Lila slipped the ball into her pocket, savoring the weight as she went downstairs.

They were back in the tavern, Ned and Kell, Ned chattering and Kell listening indulgently, though she could see the strain in his eyes, the fatigue. He hadn't been well, not since the battle and the ring, and he was a fool if he thought she hadn't noticed. But she didn't say anything, and when their eyes met, the strain faded, replaced by something gentle, warm.

Lila drew her fingertips along a wooden tabletop, the surface branded with a five-point star. "Why did you change the name?"

Ned's head swiveled toward her, and she realized it was the first time she'd spoken to him.

"It was just a thought," he said, "but you know, I've had the worst luck since I did it, so I'm thinking it's a sign I should change it back."

Lila shrugged. "It doesn't matter what you call it."

Ned was squinting at her now, as if she were out of focus.

"Have we met?" he asked, and she shook her head, even though she'd seen him in this place a dozen times, back when it was called the Stone's Throw, back when Barron had been the one behind the bar, serving watered-down drinks to men seeking a taste of magic, back when she came and went like a ghost.

"If your king comes around again," Kell was saying, "you give him this letter. *My* king would like him to know that it will be the last. . . ."

Lila slipped out the front door and into the grey day. She looked up at the sign over the entrance, the dark clouds beyond, threatening rain.

The city always looked drab this time of year, but it looked even bleaker now that she had come to know Red London and the world that surrounded it.

Lila tipped her head back against the cool bricks, and heard Barron as if he were standing there beside her, a cigar between his lips.

"Always looking for trouble."

"What's life without a little trouble?" she said softly.

"Gonna keep looking till you find it."

"I'm sorry it found you."

"Do you miss me?" His gravelly tone seemed to linger in the air.

"Like an itch," she murmured.

She felt Kell come up beside her, felt him trying to decide if he should touch her arm or give her space. In the end, he hovered there, half a step behind.

"Are you sure about him?" she asked.

"I am," he said, his voice so steady she wanted to lean against it. "Ned's a good man."

"He'd cut off a hand to make you happy."

"He believes in magic."

"And you don't think he'll try to use it?"

"He'll never get the box open, and even if he did, no. I don't think he will."

"Why's that?"

"Because I asked him not to."

Lila snorted. Even after all they'd seen and done, Kell still had faith in people. She hoped, for all their sakes, he was right. Just this once.

All around them, carriages clattered and people jogged and strolled and stumbled by. She'd forgotten the simple solidity of this city, this world.

"We could stay awhile, if you want?" offered Kell.

She took a long breath, the air on her tongue stale and full of soot instead of magic. There was nothing for her here, not anymore.

"No." She shook her head, reaching for his hand. "Let's go home."

IV

The sky was a crisp blue sheet, drawn tight behind the sun. It stretched, cloudless and bare, save for a single black-and-white bird that soared overhead. As it crossed into the sphere of light, the bird became a flock, shattering like a prism when it meets the sun.

Holland craned his neck, mesmerized by the display, but every time he tried to count their number, his vision slid out of focus, strained by the dappled light.

He didn't know where he was.

How he'd gotten here.

He was standing in a courtyard, the high walls covered in vines that threw off blossoms of lush purple—such an impossible hue, but their petals solid, soft. The air felt like the cusp of summer, a hint of warmth, the sweet scent of blossoms and tilled earth—which told him where he *wasn't,* where he couldn't be.

And yet—

"Holland?" called a voice he hadn't heard in years. Lifetimes. He turned, searching for the source, and found a gap in the courtyard wall, a doorway without a door.

He stepped through, and the courtyard vanished, the wall solid behind him and the narrow road ahead crowded with people, their clothes white but their faces full of color. He *knew* this place—it was in the Kosik, the worst part of the city.

And yet—

A pair of muddy green eyes cut his way, glinting from a shadow at the end of the lane.

"Alox?" he called, starting after his brother, when a scream made him reel around.

A small girl raced past, only to be swept up into the arms of a man. She let out another squeal as the man spun her around. Not a scream at all.

A short, delighted laugh.

An old man tugged on Holland's sleeve and said, "The king is coming," and Holland wanted to ask what he meant, but Alox was slipping away, and so Holland hurried after him, down the road, around the corner, and—

His brother was gone.

As was the narrow lane.

All at once, Holland was in the middle of a busy market, stalls overflowing with brightly colored fruits and fresh-baked bread.

He knew this place. It was the Grand Square, where so many had been cut down over the years, their blood given back to the angry earth.

And yet—

"Hol!"

He spun again, searching for the voice, and saw the edge of a honey-colored braid vanish through the crowd. The twirl of a skirt.

"Talya?"

There were three of them dancing at the edge of the square. The other two dancers were dressed in white, while Talya was a blossom of red.

He pushed through the market toward her, but when he broke the edge of the crowd, the dancers were no longer there.

Talya's voice whispered in his ear.

"The king is coming."

But when he spun toward her, she was gone again. So was the market, and the city.

All of it had vanished, taking the bustle and noise with it, the world plunged back into a quiet broken only by the rustle of leaves, the distant caw of birds.

Holland was standing in the middle of the Silver Wood.

The trunks and branches still glinted with their metallic sheen, but the ground beneath his boots was rich and dark, the leaves overhead a dazzling green.

The stream snaked through the grove, the water thawed, and a man crouched at the edge to run his fingers through, a crown sitting in the grass beside him.

"Vortalis," said Holland.

The man rose to his feet, turned toward Holland, and smiled. He started to speak, but his words were swallowed by a strong and sudden wind.

It cut through the woods, rustling the branches and stripping the leaves. They began to fall like rain, showering the world with green. Through the downpour, Holland saw Alox's clenched fists, Talya's parted lips, Vortalis's dancing eyes. There and gone, there and gone, and every time he took a step toward one, the leaves would swallow them up, leaving only their voices to echo through the woods around him.

"The king is coming," called his brother.

"The king is coming," sang his lover.

"The king is coming," said his friend.

Vortalis reappeared, striding through the rain of leaves. He held out his hand, palm up.

Holland was still reaching for it when he woke up.

Holland could tell where he was by the plushness of the room, red and gold splashed like paint on every surface.

The Maresh royal palace.

A world away.

It was late, the curtains drawn, the lamp beside the bed unlit.

Holland reached absently for his magic before remembering it wasn't there. The knowledge hit like loss, leaving him breathless. He stared at his hands, plumbing the depths of his power—the place where his power had always been, where it should be—and finding nothing. No hum. No heat.

A shuddering exhale, the only outward sign of grief.

He felt hollow. He *was* hollow.

Bodies moved beyond the door.

The shuffle of weight, the subtle clang of armor shifting, settling.

Haltingly, Holland drew himself upright, unearthing his body from the bed's thick blankets, its cloudlike mass of pillows. Annoyance flickered through him—who could possibly sleep in such a state?

It was kinder, perhaps, than a prison cell.

Not as kind as a quick death.

The act of rising took too much, or perhaps there was simply too little left to give; he was out of breath by the time his feet met the floor.

Holland leaned back against the bed, gaze traveling over the darkened room, finding a sofa, a table, a mirror. He caught his reflection there, and stilled.

His hair, once charcoal—then briefly, vibrantly black—was now a shock of white. An icy shroud, sudden as snowfall. Paired with his pale skin, it rendered him nearly colorless.

Except for his eyes.

His eyes, which had so long marked his power, defined his life. His eyes, which had made him a target, a challenge, a king.

His eyes, *both* of which were now a vivid, almost *leafy* green.

V

"Are you sure about this?" asked Kell, looking out at the city.

He thought—no, he *knew*—it was a terrible idea, but he also knew the choice wasn't his.

A single deep crease cut Holland's brow. "Stop asking."

They were on a rise overlooking the city, Kell on his feet and Holland on a stone bench, recovering his breath. It had clearly taken all of his strength to make the climb, but he had insisted on doing it, and now that they were here, he was insisting on this as well.

"You could stay here," offered Kell.

"I don't want to stay here," Holland answered flatly. "I want to go home."

Kell hesitated. "Your home isn't exactly kind to those without power."

Holland held his gaze. Against his pale complexion and shock of newly white hair, his eyes were an even more vivid shade of green, and all the more startling now that they both were. And yet, Kell still felt like he was looking at a mask. A smooth surface behind which Holland—the *real* Holland—was hiding even now. Would always hide.

"It's still my home," he said. "I was born in that world. . . ."

He didn't finish. Didn't need to. Kell knew what he would say.

And I will die there.

In the wake of his sacrifice, Holland didn't look *old,* only tired. But it was an exhaustion that ran deep, a place once filled with power now hollowed out, leaving the empty shell behind. Magic and life were intertwined in everyone and everything, but in *Antari* most of all. Without it, Holland clearly wasn't whole.

"I'm not certain this will work," said Kell, "now that you're—" Holland cut him off. "*You've* nothing to lose by trying."

But that wasn't strictly true.

Kell hadn't told Holland—hadn't told anyone but Rhy, and only then out of necessity—the true extent of the damage. That when the binding ring had lodged on his finger and Holland had poured his magic—and Osaron's, and nearly Kell's—into the Inheritor, something had torn inside of him. Something vital. That now, every time he summoned fire, or willed water, or conjured anything from blood, it pained him.

Every single time, it hurt, a wound at the very center of his being. But unlike a wound, it refused to heal.

Magic had always been a part of Kell, as natural as breathing. Now, he couldn't catch his breath. The simplest acts took not only strength, but will. The will to suffer. To be hurt.

Pain reminds us that we're alive.

That's what Rhy had said to him, when he first woke to find their lives tethered. When Kell caught him with his hand over the flame. When he learned of the binding ring, the cost of its magic.

Pain reminds us.

Kell dreaded the pain, which seemed to worsen every time, felt ill at the thought of it, but he would not deny Holland this last request. Kell owed him that much, and so he said nothing.

Instead, he looked around at the rise, the city beneath them. "Where are we now, in your world? Where will we be, once we step through?"

A flicker of relief crossed Holland's face, quick as light on water.

"The Silver Wood," he said. "Some say it was the place where magic died." After a moment he added, "Others think it's nothing, has never been anything but an old grove of trees."

Kell waited for the man to say more, but he just rose slowly to his feet, leaning ever so slightly on a cane, only his tense white knuckles betraying how much it took for him to stand.

Holland put his other hand on Kell's arm, signaling his readiness, and so Kell drew his knife and cut his free hand, the discomfort so simple compared to the pain that waited. He pulled the White London token from around his neck, staining the coin red, and reached out to rest his hand on the bench.

"*As Travars,*" he said, Holland's voice echoing softly beneath his as they both stepped through.

Pain reminds us . . .

Kell clenched his teeth against the spasm, reaching out to brace himself against the nearest thing, which was not a bench or a wall but the trunk of a tree, its bark smooth as metal. He leaned against the cool surface, waiting for the wave to pass, and when it did, he dragged his head up to see a small grove, and Holland, a few feet away, alive, intact. A stream cut into the ground before him, little more than a ribbon of water, and beyond the grove, White London rose in stony spires.

In Holland's absence—and Osaron's—the color had begun to leach back out of the world. The sky and river were a pale grey once more, the ground bare. This was the White London Kell had always known. That other version—the one he'd glimpsed in the castle yard, in the moments before Ojka closed the collar around his throat—was like something from a dream. And yet Kell's heart ached to see it lost, and to see Holland bear that loss, the smooth planes of his mask finally cracking, the sadness showing through.

"Thank you, Kell," he said, and Kell knew the words for what they were: a dismissal.

Yet he felt rooted to the spot.

Magic made everything feel so impermanent, it was easy to forget that some things, once changed, could never be undone. That not everything was either changeable or infinite. Some roads kept going, and others had an end.

For a long moment the two men stood in silence, Holland unable to move forward, Kell unable to step back.

At last, the earth released its hold.

"You're welcome, Holland," said Kell, dragging himself free.

He reached the edge of the grove before he turned back, looking at Holland for a last time, the other *Antari* standing there at the center of the Silver Wood, his head tipped back, his green eyes closed. The winter breeze tousled white hair, ruffled ash-black clothes.

Kell lingered, digging in the pockets of his many-sided coat, and when at last he turned to go, he set a single red *lin* on a tree stump. A reminder, an invitation, a parting gift, for a man Kell would never see again.

VI

Alucard Emery paced outside the Rose Hall, dressed in a blue so dark it registered as black until it caught the light just so. It was the color of the sails on his ship. The color of the sea at midnight. No hat, no sash, no rings, but his brown hair was washed and pinned back with silver. His cuffs and buttons shone as well, polished to beads of light.

He was a summer sky at night, speckled with stars.

And he had spent the better part of an hour assembling the outfit. He couldn't decide between Alucard, the captain, and Emery, the noble. In the end, he had chosen neither. Today he was Alucard Emery, the man courting a king.

He'd lost the sapphire above his eye and gained a new scar in its place. It didn't wink in the sun, but it suited him anyway. The silver threads that traced over his skin, relics of the shadow king's poison, shone with their own faint light.

I rather like the silver, Rhy had said.

Alucard rather liked it, too.

His fingers felt bare without his rings, but the only absence that mattered was the silver feather he'd worn wrapped around his thumb. The mark of House Emery.

Berras had survived the fog unscathed—which was to say he'd fallen to it—and woken in the street with the rest, claiming he had no memory of what he'd said or done under the shadow king's spell. Alucard didn't believe a word of it, had kept his brother's company only long enough to tell him of the estate's destruction and Anisa's death.

After a long silence, Berras had said only, "To think, the line comes down to us."

Alucard had shaken his head, disgusted. "You can have it," he'd said, and walked away. He didn't throw the ring at his brother, as good as that would have felt. Instead he simply dropped it in the bushes on his way out. The moment it was gone, he felt lighter.

Now, as the doors to the Rose Hall swung open, he felt *dizzy*.

"The king will see you," said the royal guard, and Alucard forced himself forward, the velvet bag hanging from his fingers.

The hall wasn't full, but it wasn't empty, either, and Alucard suddenly wished he'd requested a private meeting with the prince—the *king*.

Vestra and *ostra* were gathered, some waiting for an audience, others simply waiting for the world to return to normal. The Veskan entourage was still confined to its quarters, while the Faroan assembly had divided, half sailing home with Lord Sol-in-Ar, the others lingering in the palace. Councilors, once loyal aides to Maxim, stood ready to advise, while members of the royal guard lined the hall and flanked the dais.

King Rhy Maresh sat on his father's throne, his mother's empty seat beside him. Kell stood at his side, head bowed over his brother in quiet conversation. Master Tieren was at Rhy's other side, looking older than ever, but his pale blue eyes were sharp among the hollows and wrinkles of his face. He rested a hand on Rhy's shoulder as he spoke, the gesture simple, warm.

Rhy's own head was tipped down as he listened, the crown a heavy band of gold in his hair. There was sadness in his shoulders, but then Kell's lips moved, and Rhy managed a fleeting smile, like light through clouds.

Alucard's heart lifted.

He scanned the room quickly and saw Bard leaning against one of the stone planters, cocking her head the way she always did when she was eavesdropping. He wondered if she'd picked any pockets yet this morning, or if those days were over.

Kell cleared his throat, and Alucard was startled to realize that his feet had carried him all the way to the dais. He met the king's amber eyes, and saw them soften briefly with, what—happiness? concern?—before Rhy spoke.

"Captain Emery," he said, his voice the same, and yet different, distant. "You requested an audience."

"As you promised I might, Your Majesty, if I returned"—Alucard's gaze flicked to Kell, the shadow at the king's shoulder—"without killing your brother."

A murmur of amusement went through the hall. Kell scowled, and Alucard immediately felt better. Rhy's eyes widened a fraction—he'd realized where this was going, and he had obviously assumed Alucard would request a *private* meeting.

But what they'd had—it was more than stolen kisses between silk sheets, more than secrets shared only by starlight, more than a youthful dalliance, a summer fling.

And Alucard was here to prove it. To lay his heart bare before Rhy, and the Rose Hall, and the rest of London.

"Nearly four years ago," he began, "I left your . . . court, without explanation or apology. In doing so, I fear I wounded the crown and its estimation of me. I have come to make amends with my king."

"What is in your hand?" asked Rhy.

"A debt."

A guard stepped forward to retrieve the parcel, but Alucard pulled away, looking back to the king. "If I may?"

After a moment, Rhy nodded, rising as Alucard approached the dais. The young king descended the steps and met him there before the throne.

"What are you doing?" asked Rhy softly, and Alucard's whole body sang to hear *this* voice, the one that belonged not to the king of Arnes, but to the prince he'd known, the one he'd fallen in love with, the one he'd lost.

"What I promised," whispered Alucard, gripping the mirror in both hands and tipping its surface toward the king.

It was a *liran*.

Most scrying dishes could share the contents of one's mind, ideas and memories projected on the surface, but a mind was a fickle thing—it could lie, forget, rewrite.

A *liran* showed only the truth.

Not as it had been remembered, not as one *wanted* to remember it, but as it had happened.

It was no simple magic, to sift truth from memory.

Alucard Emery had traded four years of his future for the chance to relive the worst night of his past.

In his hands, the mirror's surface went dark, swallowing Rhy's reflection and the hall behind him as another night, another room, took shape in the glass.

Rhy stiffened at the sight of his chamber, of *them,* tangled limbs and silent laughter in his bed, his fingers trailing over Alucard's bare skin. Rhy's cheeks colored as he reached out and touched the mirror's edge. As he did, the scene flared to life. Mercifully, the sound of their pleasure didn't echo through the throne room. It stayed, caught between them, as the scene unspooled.

Alucard, rising from Rhy's bed, trying to dress while the prince playfully undid every clasp he fastened, unlaced every knot. Their final parting kiss and Alucard's departure through the maze of hidden halls and out into the night.

What Rhy couldn't see—then or now—in the mirror's surface was Alucard's happiness as he made his way across the copper bridge to the northern bank, his racing heart as he climbed the front steps to the Emery estate. Couldn't feel the sudden horrible stutter of that heart when Berras stood waiting in the hall.

Berras, who had followed him to the palace.

Berras, who *knew.*

Alucard had tried to play it off, feigning drunkenness, letting himself tip casually back against the wall as he rattled off the taverns he'd been to, the fun he'd had, the trouble he'd gotten himself into over the course of that long night.

It didn't work.

Berras's disgust had hardened into stone. So had his fists.

Alucard didn't want to fight his brother, had even dodged the first blow, and the second, only to be caught upside the head by something sharp and silver.

He went down, world ringing. Blood dripped into his eyes.

His father was standing over him, his cane glinting in his grip.

Back in the Rose Hall, Alucard closed his eyes, but the images played on in his mind, scorched into memory. His fingers tightened on the mirror, but he didn't let go, not when his brother called him a disgrace, a fool, a whore. Not when he heard the snap of bone, his own muffled scream, silence, and then the sickening slosh of a ship.

Alucard would have let the memory play on, let it run through those first horrific nights at sea, and his escape, all the way to the prison and the iron cuffs and the heated rod, his forced return to London and the warning in his brother's eyes, the hurt in the prince's, the hatred in Kell's.

He would have let it play on as long as Rhy wanted, but something weighed suddenly against the mirror's surface, and he opened his eyes to see the young king standing very close, one hand splayed across the glass as if to block out the images, the sounds, the memories.

Rhy's amber eyes were bright, his brow knitted with anger and sadness.

"Enough," he said, voice trembling.

Alucard *wanted* to speak, tried to find the words, but Rhy was already letting go—too soon—turning away—too soon—and retaking his throne.

"I have seen enough."

Alucard let the mirror fall back to his side, the world around him dragging into focus. The room around him had gone still.

The young king gripped the edges of his throne and spoke in hushed tones with his brother, whose expression flickered between surprise and annoyance before finally settling into something more resigned. Kell nodded, and when Rhy turned toward the room and spoke again, his voice was even.

"Alucard Emery," he said, his tone soft, but stern. "The crown appreciates your honesty. *I* appreciate it." He looked to Kell one last time before continuing. "As of right now, you have been stripped of your title as privateer."

Alucard nearly folded under the sentence. "Rhy . . ." The name was out before he realized his error. The impropriety. "Your Majesty . . ."

"You will no longer sail for the crown on the *Night Spire,* or any vessel."

"I do not—"

The king's hand came up in a single silencing gesture.

"My brother wishes to travel, and I have granted him permission." Kell's expression soured at the word, but did not interrupt. "As such," continued Rhy, "I require an ally. A proven friend. A powerful magician. I require you here in London, Master Emery. With me."

Alucard stiffened. The words were a blow, sudden, but not hard. They teased the line between pleasure and pain, fear that he'd misheard and hope that he hadn't.

"That is the first reason," continued Rhy evenly. "The second is more personal. I have lost my mother, and my father. I have lost friends, and strangers who might one day have been friends. I have lost too many of my people to count. And I will not suffer losing you."

Alucard's gaze cut to Kell. The *Antari* met his eyes, and he found a warning in them, but nothing more.

"Will you obey the will of the crown?" asked Rhy.

It took Alucard several stunned seconds to summon his faculties enough to bow, enough to form the three simple words.

"Yes, Your Majesty."

The king came to Alucard's room that night.

It was an elegant chamber in the western wing of the palace, fit for a noble. A royal. There were no hidden doors to be found. Only the broad entrance with its inlaid wood, its golden trim.

Alucard was perched on the edge of the sofa, rolling a glass between his hands, when the knock came. He had hoped, and he had not dared to hope.

Rhy Maresh entered the room alone. His collar was unbuttoned, his crown hanging from his fingers. He looked tired and sad and lovely and lost, but at the sight of Alucard, something in him brightened. Not a light Alucard could see in the molten threads that coiled around him, but a light behind his eyes. It was the strangest thing, but Rhy seemed to become *real* then, solid in a way he hadn't been before.

"*Avan*," said the prince who was no longer a prince.

"*Avan*," said the captain who was no longer a captain.

Rhy looked around the room.

"Does it suit?" he asked, drawing his hand absently along a curtain, long fingers tangling in red and gold.

Alucard's smile tilted. "I suppose it will do."

Rhy let the crown fall to the sofa as he came forward, and his fingers, now freed from their burden, traced Alucard's jaw, as if assuring himself that Alucard was here, was real.

Alucard's own heart was racing, even now threatening to run away. But there was no need. Nowhere to go. No place he'd rather be.

He had dreamed of this, every time the storms raged at sea. Every time a sword was drawn against him. Every time life showed its frailty, its fickleness. He had dreamed of this, as he stood on the bow of the *Ghost,* facing death in a line of ships.

Now he reached to draw Rhy in against him, only to be rebuffed.

"It is not right for you to do that," he reprimanded softly, "now that I am king."

Alucard withdrew, trying to keep hurt and confusion from his face. But then Rhy's dark lashes sank over his eyes, and his lips slid into a coy smile. "A king should be allowed to *lead*."

Relief flooded through him, followed by a wave of heat as Rhy's hand tangled in his hair, mussing the silver clasps. Lips brushed his throat, warmth grazed his jaw.

"Don't you agree?" breathed the king, nipping at Alucard's collarbone in a way that stole the air from his chest.

"Yes, Your Majesty," he managed, and then Rhy was kissing him, long and slow and savoring. The room moved beneath his tripping feet, the buttons of his shirt coming undone. By the time Rhy drew back, Alucard was against the bedpost, his shirt open. He let out a small, dazed laugh, resisting the urge to drag Rhy toward him, to press him down into the sheets.

The longing left him breathless.

"Is this how it's to be now?" he asked. "Am I to be your bedmate as well as your guard?"

Rhy's lips split into a dazzling smile. "So you admit it, then," he said, closing the last of the distance to whisper in Alucard's ear, "that you are mine."

And with that, the king dragged him down onto the bed.

VII

Arnesians had a dozen ways to say *hello,* but no word for *good-bye.*

When it came to parting ways, they sometimes said *vas ir,* which meant *in peace,* but more often they chose to say *anoshe—until another day.*

Anoshe was a word for strangers in the street, and lovers between meetings, for parents and children, friends and family. It softened the blow of leaving. Eased the strain of parting. A careful nod to the certainty of today, the mystery of tomorrow. When a friend left, with little chance of seeing home, they said *anoshe.* When a loved one was dying, they said *anoshe.* When corpses were burned, bodies given back to the earth and souls to the stream, those left grieving said *anoshe.*

Anoshe brought solace. And hope. And the strength to let go.

When Kell Maresh and Lila Bard had first parted ways, he'd whispered the word in her wake, beneath his breath, full of the certainty— the hope—they'd meet again. He'd known it wasn't an end. And this wasn't an end, either, or if it was, then simply the end of a chapter, an interlude between two meetings, the beginning of something new.

And so Kell made his way up to his brother's chambers—not the rooms he'd kept beside Kell's own (though he still insisted on sleeping there), but the ones that had belonged to his mother and father.

Without Maxim and Emira, there were so few people for Kell to say good-bye *to.* Not the *vestra* or the *ostra,* not the servants or the guards who remained. He would have said farewell to Hastra, but Hastra, too, was dead.

Kell had already gone to the Basin that morning, and come across the flower the young guard had coaxed to life that day, withering in its pot. He'd carried it up to the orchard, where Tieren stood between the rows of winter and spring.

"Can you fix it?" asked Kell.

The priest's eyes went to the shriveled little flower. "No," he said gently, but when Kell started to protest, Tieren held up a gnarled hand. "There's nothing to fix. That is an acina. They aren't meant to last. They bloom a single time, and then they're gone."

Kell looked down helplessly at the withered white blossom. "What do I do?" he asked, the question so much bigger than the words.

Tieren smiled a soft, inward smile and shrugged in his usual way. "Leave it be. The blossom will crumble, the stem and leaves, too. That's what they're *for*. Acina strengthen the soil, so that other things can grow."

Kell reached the top of the stairs, and slowed his step.

Royal guards lined the hall to the king's chamber, and Alucard stood outside the doors, leaning back against the wood and flipping through the pages of a book.

"This is your idea of guarding him?" said Kell.

The man pointedly turned a page. "Don't tell me how to do my job."

Kell took a steadying breath. "Get out of my way, Emery."

Alucard's storm-dark eyes flicked up from the book. "And what is your business with the king?"

"Personal."

Alucard held up a hand. "Perhaps I should have you searched for weapo—"

"Touch me and I'll break your fingers."

"Who says I have to touch you?" His hand twitched, and Kell felt the knife on his sleeve shudder before he shoved the man back against the wood.

"Alucard!" called Rhy through the door. "Let my brother in before I have to find *another* guard."

Alucard smirked, and gave a sweeping bow, and stepped aside.

"Ass," muttered Kell as he shoved past him.

"Bastard," called the magician in his wake.

Rhy waited on the balcony, leaning his elbows on the rail.

The air still held a chill, but the sun was warm on his skin, rich with the promise of spring. Kell came storming through the room.

"You two are getting along well, then?" asked Rhy.

"Splendidly," muttered his brother, stepping through the doors and slumping forward over the rail beside him. A reflection of his own pose.

They stood like that for some time, taking in the day, and Rhy almost forgot that Kell had come to say good-bye, that he was leaving, and then a breeze cut through, sudden and biting, and the darkness whispered from the back of his mind, the sorrow of loss and the guilt of survival and the fear that he would keep outliving those he loved. That this borrowed life would be too long or too short, and there forever was the inevitable cusp, blessing or curse, blessing or curse, and the feeling of leaning forward into a gust of wind as it tried with every step to force him back.

Rhy's fingers tightened on the rail.

And Kell, whose two-toned eyes had always seen right through him, said, "Do you wish I hadn't done it?"

He opened his mouth to say *Of course not,* or *Saints no,* or any of the other things he should have said, *had* said a dozen times, with the mindless repetition of someone being asked how he is that day, and answering *Fine, thank you,* regardless of his true temperament. He opened his mouth, but nothing came out. There were so many things Rhy hadn't said since his return—wouldn't *let* himself say—as if giving the words voice meant giving them weight, enough to tip the scale and crush him. But so many things had tried, and here he was, still standing.

"Rhy," said Kell, his gaze heavy as stone. "Do you wish I hadn't brought you back?"

He took a breath. "I don't know," he said. "Ask me in the morning, after I've spent hours weighed down by nightmares, drugged beyond reason just to hold back the memories of dying, which was not so bad as coming back, and I'd say yes. I wish you'd let me die."

Kell looked ill. "I—"

"But ask me in the afternoon," cut in Rhy, "when I've felt the sun cutting through the cold, or the warmth of Alucard's smile, or the steady weight of your arm around my shoulders, and I would tell you it was worth it. It *is* worth it."

Rhy turned his face to the sun. He closed his eyes, relishing the way the light still reached him. "Besides," he added, managing a smile, "who doesn't love a man with shadows? Who doesn't want a king with scars?"

"Oh, yes," said Kell dryly. "That's really the reason I did it. To make you more appealing."

Rhy felt his smile slip. "How long will you be gone?"

"I don't know."

"Where are you going?"

"I don't know."

"What will you do?"

"I don't know."

Rhy bowed his head, suddenly tired. "I wish I could go with you."

"So do I," said Kell, "but the empire needs its king."

Softly, Rhy said, "The king needs his brother."

Kell looked stricken, and Rhy knew he could make him stay, and he knew he couldn't bear to do it. He let out a long, shuddering sigh and straightened. "It's about time you did something selfish, Kell. You make the rest of us look bad. Try to shrug that saint's complex while you're away."

Across the river, the city bells began to ring the hour.

"Go on," said Rhy. "The ship is waiting." Kell took a single step back, hovering in the doorway. "But do us a favor, Kell."

"What's that?" asked his brother.

"Don't get yourself killed."

"I'll do my best," said Kell, and then he was going.

"And come back," added Rhy.

Kell paused. "Don't worry," he said. "I will. Once I've seen it."

"Seen what?" asked Rhy.

Kell smiled. "Everything."

VIII

Delilah Bard made her way toward the docks, a small bag slung over one shoulder. All she had in the world that wasn't already on the ship. The palace rose behind her, stone and gold and ruddy pink light.

She didn't look back. Didn't even slow.

Lila had always been good at disappearing.

Slipping like light between boards.

Cutting ties as easily as a purse.

She never said good-bye. Never saw the point. Saying good-bye was like strangling slowly, every word tightening the rope. It was easier to just slip away in the night. Easier.

But she told herself he would have caught her.

So in the end, she'd gone to him.

"Bard."

"Captain."

And then she'd stalled. Hadn't known what to say. This was why she hated good-byes. She looked around the palace chamber, taking in the inlaid floor, the gossamer ceiling, the balcony doors, before she ran out of places to look and had to look at Alucard Emery.

Alucard, who'd given her a place on his ship, who'd taught her the first things about magic, who'd—her throat tightened.

Bloody good-byes. Such useless things.

She picked up her pace, heading for the line of ships.

Alucard had leaned back against the bedpost. "Silver for your thoughts?"

And Lila had cocked her head. "I was just thinking," she'd said, "I should have killed you when I had the chance."

He'd raised a brow. "And I should have tossed you in the sea."

An easy silence had settled, and she knew she'd miss it, felt herself shrink from the idea of missing before heaving out a breath and letting it fall, settle. There were worse things, she supposed.

Her boots sounded on the wooden dock.

"You take care of that ship," he'd said, and Lila had left with only a wink, just like the ones Alucard had always thrown her way. He'd had a sapphire to catch the light, and all she had was a black glass eye, but she could feel his smile like sun on her back as she strode out and let the door swing shut behind her.

It wasn't a good-bye, not really.

What was the word for parting?

Anoshe.

That was it.

Until another day.

Delilah Bard knew she'd be back.

The dock was full of ships, but only one caught her eye. A stunning rig with a polished dark hull and midnight-blue sails. She climbed the ramp to the deck, where the crew were waiting, some old, some new.

"Welcome to the *Night Spire,*" she said, flashing a smile like a knife. "You can call me Captain Bard."

IX

Holland stood alone in the Silver Wood.

He had listened to the sounds of Kell's departure, those few short strides giving way to silence. He tipped his head back and took a deep breath, squinting into the sun.

A spot of black streaked through the clouds overhead—a bird, just like in his dream—and his tired heart quickened, but there was only one, and there was no Alox, no Talya, no Vortalis. Voices long silent. Lives long lost.

With Kell gone, and no one left to see, Holland sagged back against the nearest tree, the icy surface of its side like cold steel against his spine. He let himself sink, lowering his tired body to the dead earth.

A gentle breeze blew through the barren grove, and Holland closed his eyes and imagined he could almost hear the rustle of leaves, could almost feel the feathery weight of them falling one by one onto his skin. He didn't open his eyes, didn't want to lose the image. He just let the leaves fall. Let the wind blow. Let the woods whisper, shapeless sounds that threaded into words.

The king is coming, it seemed to say.

The tree was beginning to warm against his back, and Holland knew, in a distant way, that he was never getting up.

It ends, he thought—no fear, only relief, and sadness.

He had tried. Had given everything he could. But he was so tired.

The rustle of leaves in his ears was getting louder, and he felt himself sinking against the tree, into the embrace of something softer than metal, darker than night.

His heart slowed, winding down like a music box, a season at its end.

The last air left Holland's lungs.

And then, at last, the world breathed in.

X

Kell wore a coat that billowed in the wind.

It was neither royal red, nor messenger black, nor tournament silver. This coat was a simple, woolen grey. He wasn't quite sure if it was new or old or something in between, only that he'd never seen it before. Not until that morning when, turning his coat past black and red, he'd come across a side he didn't recognize.

This new coat had a high collar, and deep pockets, and sturdy black buttons that ran down the front. It was a coat for storms, and strong tides, and saints knew what else.

He planned to find out, now that he was free.

Freedom itself was a dizzying thing. With every step, Kell felt unmoored, as if he might drift away. But no, there was the rope, invisible but strong as steel, running between his heart and Rhy's.

It would stretch.

It would reach.

Kell made his way down the docks, passing ferries and frigates, local vessels, the Veskan impounds, and Faroan skiffs, ships of every size and shape as he searched for the *Night Spire*.

He should have known she'd choose that one, with its dark hull and its blue sails.

He made it all the way to the boat's ramp without looking back, but there at last he faltered, and turned, taking in the palace one last time. Glass and stone, gold and light. The beating heart of London. The rising sun of Arnes.

"Having second thoughts?"

Kell craned his neck to see Lila leaning on the ship's rail, spring wind tousling her short dark hair.

"Not at all," he said. "Just enjoying the view."

"Well, come on, before I decide to sail without you." She spun away, shouting orders at the ship's crew like a true captain, and the men aboard all listened and obeyed. They leapt to action with a smile, threw off ropes and drew up anchor as if they couldn't wait to set sail. He couldn't blame them. Lila Bard was a force to be reckoned with. Whether her hands were filled with knives or fire, her voice low and coaxing or lined with steel, she seemed to hold the world in her hands. Maybe she did.

After all, she'd already taken two Londons as her own.

She was a thief, a runaway, a pirate, a magician.

She was fierce, and powerful, and terrifying.

She was still a mystery.

And he loved her.

A knife struck the docks between Kell's feet, and he jumped.

"Lila!" he shouted.

"Leaving!" she called from the deck. "And bring me back that knife," she added. "It's my favorite one."

Kell shook his head, and freed the blade from where it had lodged in the wood. "They're *all* your favorite."

When he climbed aboard, the crew didn't stop, didn't bow, didn't treat him as anything but another pair of hands, and soon the *Spire* pushed away from the docks, sails catching the morning breeze. His heart was thudding in his chest, and when he closed his eyes, he could feel a twin pulse, echoing his own.

Lila came to stand beside him, and he handed back her knife. She said nothing, slipping the blade into some hidden sheath, and leaning her shoulder into his. Magic ran between them like a current, a cord, and he wondered who she would have been if she'd stayed in Grey London. If she'd never picked his pocket, never held the contents ransom for adventure.

Maybe she would never have discovered magic.

Or maybe she would have simply changed her world instead of his.

Kell's eyes went to the palace one last time, and he thought he could almost make out the shape of a man standing alone on a high balcony. At this distance, he was little more than a shadow, but Kell could see the band of gold glinting in his hair as a second figure came to stand beside the king.

Rhy raised his hand, and so did Kell, a single unspoken word between them.

Anoshe.